THE NORWEGIAN ASSASSIN

A RESISTANCE GIRL NOVEL #4

HANNAH BYRON

A Resistance Girl Novel
Book #4

ISBN eBook: 978-90-832156-3-1
ISBN Paperback: 978-90-832156-2-4
Book Cover Design by Ebooklaunch
Editor: Three Point Author Services
Website: Hannah Byron

"Your task is not to seek love, but to seek and find all the barriers within yourself that you have built against it."

~ Rumi ~

NOTE FOR HISTORIANS & NORWEGIANS

For the sake of the story line, I deviated — in certain places — from the historical facts as happened in Norway during WWII.

My Author's Note explains where and why I took liberties with history and why I shed an extra light on women during the war.

1

THE ENGAGEMENT PARTY

Obertauern, Austria, February 1938

Abrittle sun rose over the snow-capped Radstädter Tauern Pass, scintillating the white slopes with sparkles of diamonds and splinters of ice. The sky above the rugged mountaintops was steeped in azure blue — cold, wintry, and breathtakingly beautiful. Vast and sheltered at the same time, the landscape lay as if folded by a giant hand into a crisp, white sheet of tops, slopes and gorges. *Gottes Land.*

High up in the firmament hovered a lone black eagle, wings expanded, its watchful eye on an early solo skier zigzagging down the Pass. The air was still, the scenery was still, the earth was holding its breath but for the small brown figure racing down at breakneck speed.

Sheltered from the cold by a double-glass window and a roaring fire in the corner of the Himmlhof Inn's breakfast room, Esther Weiss's gaze was also fixed on the graceful movements of the skier coming toward her. A Rosenthal cup and saucer with her morning tea in one hand, she never took her sea-green eyes from the emerging figure until he forced the tips of his skis together and came to a screeching halt right outside her window. She recognized him as one of the giant blond Vikings of the Norse national skiing team who were also staying at the inn.

Though some part of Esther's mind registered the scene, longing with every fiber in her body to race downhill herself on this glorious morning, the larger part of her thoughts was focused on the day ahead. Sipping her tea, she once again meticulously went through all the upcoming events, checking she'd not forgotten anything. At this important moment in time, she couldn't let her elders down, even if...

She gave a last glance at the robust, healthy Norseman, breathing white plumes of cold air as he took off his red woolen hat to show a shock of tangled hair the color of ripe corn. He smiled roguishly at her with eyes as blue as the sky above him. A promise of freedom, of a life lived in deep embrace with nature.

But no. She frowned angrily at the liberty of his gaze. What was he thinking? Had she invited this? Esther put her cup hastily on its gold-rimmed saucer, pulling her cashmere cardigan tighter around her shoulders.

Focus!

Today was the day. *Her* day had finally come.

At that moment the door to the breakfast room opened, and Esther turned to see her mother and grandmother enter together. Her mother wore a flowery morning dress, already fully adorned with her most precious gold, the dark curls foamed luxuriously and the lovely chestnut eyes full of pride. She strode in as straight as a stick, and yet something was wrong.

Mutti looks tired, Esther thought, as her lips curled into a smile. *She must have been sleeping badly again.*

Esther knew how much her mother suffered from the trampling of the Jewish race by the Nazis, how she feared for her children's future.

Oma, tall, blonde and regal — a rare trait in the Austrian Jewish community which Esther had inherited — had a demure look on her statuesque face. But her eyes twinkled at seeing her beloved granddaughter.

"Shouldn't you be getting dressed, *Bärchen?*"

"I should," Esther answered promptly, basking in the use of her pet name 'little bear.' "I just couldn't break free from the lovely scenery. It's so good to be at peace here in the mountains, isn't it?"

Seeing her mother's shoulders slump, Esther bit her tongue. Wrong move. No mentioning of the strained atmosphere at home in Vienna, where the Germans were stamping their ugly black boots at Austria's northern borders, threatening to invade any minute.

The boycott of Jewish businesses, Jewish scientists and judges losing their jobs, the burning of books by Jewish writers, German Jews being stripped of their citizenship. All that was happening at their borders and many Austrians worshipped Hitler. Wanted those same rules. Mutti constantly worried.

Thankfully, neither the Weiss properties nor the Bernstein's shops had been an anti-Jew target. Not yet.

"Come and have breakfast with us, dear," her mother urged. "Carl Bernstein Sr. phoned Papi an hour ago to confirm that your betrothed is on the early train and is expected to arrive in Radstädter at noon."

Her mother and grandmother had already seated themselves at the round breakfast table. Slipping the ivory rings from the damask napkins, unfolding the white squares and spreading them over their thighs, every movement the Weiss ladies made had the precise grace of good breeding and long practice. Esther followed suit. It had taken some time — in fact, over a decade — to master all the etiquette rules necessary for a bride-to-be, but Oma's short nod of approval from across the table showed she was well-prepared.

While they waited for the maid to serve breakfast, her mother repeated the extensive list of makeup and gown as a preparation for her grand entrée before her betrothal. Esther already knew the drill by heart. She sighed behind her napkin, knowing her mother meant well and truly believed repetition was the only road to proper behavior.

"I've instructed Helga to dress you and how to do your hair. Let her do it, Esther. Don't be obstinate."

Helga Müller was her mother's and grandmother's personal maid, who'd accompanied them from Vienna. It was supposed to be a great honor she'd be Esther's maid for today, so Esther swallowed her longing to dress herself and not end up like some stiff doll, in which she wouldn't recognize herself.

"I don't know if I can get anything inside of me," Esther observed, as two maids pushed in a trolley stacked with Semmeln, steaming Melange coffee, cut veal sausages, Schinkenspeck, boiled eggs, Danish buns and apricot jam. Though the smell was delicious, her stomach protested. But her mother would hear nothing of the sort.

"An empty stomach breeds weak nerves."

Another motto Naomi Weiss-Aronson lived by. It didn't take Oma long to chime in with her daughter-in-law.

"You know you're going to have a prolonged engagement, Bärchen, so you'd better grow nerves of steel. You and Carl insisted on getting engaged now when you knew you'd still have your finishing school year in Switzerland. Better grow some patience with a proper breakfast."

Esther sighed. Of course, they were right, she thought as she tentatively put her white teeth in a Danish bun. If it had to be anything, then something sweet. The scent of the sausages and Speck made her nauseous. But she suppressed what her mother would call "her weak nerves." It wasn't weakness. It was a weird premonition that all wasn't well, and that was hard to shake off. If only she knew from whence it came.

She knew how the women in her family rejoiced in her engagement and her impeccable choice in Carl Bernstein. Within eighteen months she would be stepping into the shoes of her illustrious Oma and Mutti, who had reigned as supreme hostesses of Viennese society for decades. Even Papi had made peace with her choice for the son of his biggest rival and now dreamed about an eventual merger of *Weiss Goldschmied* with *Bernstein & Son Juweliers*.

Carl Bernstein was to be her husband. Esther still had to pinch herself every day to believe it was true.

"At least the weather is finally behaving itself," Oma observed, as if it was a living thing. Naomi nodded, deftly cutting a slice of sausage in small cubes and popping them in her mouth.

"Franz was complaining this morning that he preferred a day of skiing to being packed indoors again. Men!" She shook her well-coiffed head in disbelief.

The first week the Weiss family had taken up residence in the Himmlhof Inn for their annual skiing holidays, the weather had been cold and forbidding with incessant snowfall, even blizzards, but today was as bright and crisp as a dewy rose. At more than 6,000 feet above sea level, no open roads led to the guest house, and everything had to be transported by horse-drawn sledges from Radstädter village in the valley.

Trapped but snugly together, the family had passed the time playing chess and card solitaire, going for walks when there was a lull in the snow. But it had been a disappointment, especially to the youngest member of the family, ten-year-old Adam, who got increasingly bored and listless being cooped up inside.

Like her brother and father, Esther was itching to stand on her skis and go. They were the real skiers of the family, with her sister Rebecca and mother and grandmother more recreational skiers.

"Hopefully the weather will hold, and we can all go skiing tomorrow." Esther spoke her longing out aloud, though it made her slightly ill at ease. It had been *her* wish to get engaged in the exact same place where her father had gone down on one knee to ask her mother in marriage in the winter of 1920. Of course, she hadn't been there herself but Opa Weiss, then still well and alive, had recorded the event with his Ur-Leica and Oma had lovingly pasted the snapshots in one of her many snow holiday albums. The tiny, square black and whites were faded and well-thumbed by now but had never lost their romantic appeal to Esther.

This was the location she'd dreamed of since childhood. And now it was finally here.

"We'll see about doing any skiing tomorrow," her mother replied with a bleak smile. "Carl may not be in favor of such an expedition. He might prefer going for a walk. Does he ski at all? I've never known the Bernsteins to be into winter sports."

Esther's face fell. It was true. Carl didn't ski. She saw her chances of even getting a good go downhill diminish. He would vacation with them for a week and when he left for Vienna again, they'd only have a few days left themselves.

"Don't sulk, Esther. It doesn't befit a young lady. Maybe Carl will agree to taking some lessons and you can go down the children's slope with him together. Now go and get dressed."

"Yes, Mutti."

Being engaged suddenly seemed a little more complicated than she had anticipated.

~

CHIN UP AS TRAINED, but inwardly quivering, Esther stood inspecting herself in the full-length mirror that Helga had propped up in the corner of the guesthouse bedroom.

"I'll let you have a minute to yourself, Fräulein Esther," the German maid said, leaving on soft, slippered feet and closing the door behind her.

Esther's chest heaved as her fingers curled into her palms and her jawbones clamped shut like the shells of an oyster. A sudden terror struck her, an almost physical attack that made her shrink backwards, away from the mirror. She had no idea where the invisible attack came from; it swished at her like the explosive lash of a whip. She kept staring at her waxlike face, not recognizing herself.

Did she or didn't she want to get engaged? What was this sudden folly? This weakness of mind?

But the truth was, it all seemed too much, too soon. What if Hitler did what he'd been threatening for months and annexed her country? It was silly, immature even, to assume she was heading toward a bright and happy future on the arm of dashing Carl Bernstein. The Kristallnacht meant just that: all their crystal, diamonds, and gold would be taken from them. Their balls, their music nights...their dignity.

And yet. At the edge of the precipice, Esther did what she knew she could do. Be her mother's daughter and face the fear head on. Good breeding would never go to waste. Not even in the face of the worst brutality.

Esther forced her breath to slow down and deepen, in and out, as she tucked a blonde escapee under one of the many hairpins Helga had stuck into her lush blonde curls. She adjusted the gemstoned earrings her parents had given her for her sixteenth birthday, dabbed some powder over the tiny sweat beads on her nose bridge and finally rearranged the matching gem brooch on her chest.

"Relax!" she ordered herself, inoculating her bloodstream with her mother's potent etiquette lessons. "You know you want this, Esther Weiss. You've wanted to get married for as long as you can remember. Carl Bernstein is going to be an excellent husband and father. So stop this nonsense."

She saw the fear dissipate from her emerald eyes, and proud Esther Weiss reappeared from behind the frightened mouse that had stared at her the minute before. A Weiss woman could do this. A Weiss woman could do anything to make the men in her life happy.

"Now go!" she told her mirrored image, smoothing her ice-blue dress once more over her slender hips. One last nod. As good as perfect.

～

WHEN ESTHER ENTERED the Inn's dining hall, she stepped into a thick wall of voices and cigarette smoke. The cacophony mingled with the blue haze triggered her already frail nerves. She blinked, looked around her in the crowded, low-ceilinged room and was glad to spot her family in their finest standing in the bay window. Another deep breath and she purposefully strode across the room, the heels of her new shoes clicking on the red-tiled floor.

"Hey Missy, you look splendid!" It was the Norwegian skier again, greeting her with a flirty wink. Esther gave him a furious look. How dared he address her like that with her family in the room? But his friends laughed at his cockiness.

The Norsemen were sitting in a semicircle in front of the open fire, causing a great deal of noise and filling the room with the thick smoke of their pipes and cigarettes. Esther frowned more deeply. For sure, Papi had instructed Felix the innkeeper to make this a private family affair? She turned her slender, ice-blue back on them as she joined her parents, seeing with a pang of disappointment that Carl was not yet among them.

"Ah, my beautiful Essie!" Franz Weiss exclaimed, his round cheeks beaming from ear to ear. "Come and stand with your Papi. I want you close now while I still can." Instantly drawn into her father's jovial embrace, Esther felt the weight drop from her shoulders. She would always be Papi's little girl, no matter whether she was engaged or married. Kissing his cologne-dabbed cheeks, she leaned into him.

"Papi, the other people...?"

"Have no worries, my dear. They're just having a hot cocoa, and then they're out skiing again. Felix asked me if they could use the room just for half an hour and as he's lending us the dining room all afternoon, I could hardly refuse the good chap, now could I?"

Safely in her father's embrace, Esther peeked in the direction of the rowdy clan near the fire. Her eyes met the tall Norwegian's steady blue gaze. She instantly cast down hers. The fierce gaze — as if an open request — threatened to melt her already wavering resolve to pursue her engagement in these uncertain times. There was no other life for Esther. And this was what she wanted.

Turning resolutely to her siblings, still tight and close to her father, she complimented Adam for his new, grown-up suit. The boy looked clumsy and uncertain in his formal attire, throwing longing glances out of the window and up the Tauern Pass.

"Adam, you look like a little prince. I'm so proud of you." The face he pulled was even more precious.

"I'd rather be a rascal and fly outdoors," he sulked.

"Adam," his mother cooed to the unhappy boy, "there will be Biedermeier Torte later. That's your favorite, isn't it?"

His face lit up, revealing a coy smile. "Can I have two *Schnitte*?"

"We'll see about that."

"Do you like my dress?" Rebecca piped in, holding the hem of her soft pink skirt wide between thumb and finger and swirling around. At fourteen Rebecca, petite, slim and dark-haired, was the spitting image of their mother, but always looking up to her big sister and mimicking her every move.

"You're picture perfect." Esther smiled. "I'm so proud of you, Rebbie. And thank you, Papi and Mutti, for organizing this impromptu party for me."

"You're welcome, *Bärchen*." Her father gave her arm a little squeeze, turning his stout back in the pin-striped suit in such a way that he blocked his own ensemble from the rowdy Norsemen.

"Now, where's that fellow of yours hiding? He shouldn't be late to his own *vort*." Franz Weiss took his golden-chained watch from his waistcoat pocket and frowned. "Felix sent one of the wood chopper boys down with the horse sledge over an hour ago. I hope the snow hasn't caused trouble on the track and the train is delayed."

"I'm going to be seated for a while," Oma announced, folding her rough silk morning dress neatly under her as she perched on a chair, straight as an arrow, hands folded in her lap and feet crossed at the ankles. Rebecca immediately took up the same position on the opposite couch.

Another burst of laughter from the fireplace. All heads at the table turned towards the commotion. One of them had dropped his cigarette on his ski pants and burned a hole in it. He was pummeling his thigh in mock pain. Esther frowned. *What unbe-*

coming behavior. And how uncouth at her party. She wished Felix would come and intervene before it all got out of hand.

Her female examples at the table refrained from mentioning the disruption, but the thinning of their lips and the deliberate return of their attention to their own circle proved enough. Rebecca smiled at Esther, cocking her small head in a becoming way.

How good it was to have manners. And how awful it must be to go without.

All the Weiss' heads turned again but this time with broad grins, when Carl Bernstein, trilby in hand and carrying a small leather valise, entered the dining room. Tall, dark and handsome, he was far from an ordinary man. Carl exuded an imperial aura, proud and phlegmatic, the strong cheekbones set firmly and the dark eyes in command but not in an arrogant way. He surveyed the room, and when his eyes found Esther, he smiled, admiringly and pleased.

Esther smiled back and her heart made a little jump. He was here. He'd come. It wasn't an elusive fantasy that she had made up in her mind. She had to stop herself from running toward him and into his arms. He crossed the distance between them with measured, decisive steps, ignoring the noise and random spectators.

As a well-bred man, he shook hands in the sequence that was appropriate — his future father-in-law, then Oma, and then his mother-in-law. When he came to Esther, they stood for a second, both unsure what was expected of them. Carl took her ringless right hand in his firm grip and brushed it with his lips. Then he made a little bow for her with that radiant, self-assured smile.

Her lips formed the letters of his name, "Carl," but she had no idea what to say to him. Their former Vienna life, where they had frequented the same circles since they were children, seemed on quite another planet right now. Again, it gnawed on her that choosing this simple mountain inn for their engagement, far from all that bound them and was dear, had been wrong, fanned more by romantic notions than by the level-headed, practical decisions she was supposed to make as a future wife and mistress of the house.

But Carl tried to put her at ease immediately by chatting about his adventurous trip up the mountain.

"At some point, I had to put on my overshoes and help push the sledge. The horses' hooves couldn't get a grip on the slippery surface anymore. We were going downhill instead of up. Never have done anything like it in my life, but it was a new experience. I say, Herr Weiss, your daughter makes me travel to the end of the world for her sake. What more will be in store for me in the future?"

As he gave her a conspiring wink, Esther felt all the ice in and around her melt. She started glowing, believing again. Carl was a great socializer and sublime breaker of ice. All would be fine.

Everyone started chatting and laughing at once as they took their seats at the nicely adorned table in the middle of the room. Esther sat in between Carl and her mother, with Rebecca and Adam opposite them. Oma and Papi resided at the respective heads of the lunch table.

"Weren't your parents frightfully disappointed not to be able to attend our engagement?" Esther whispered to Carl, who was clipping his diamond-studded tie pin to his white shirt before covering himself with his serviette.

He turned his dark eyes to her, the eyebrows knit, a studious look on his handsome face.

"Somewhat," he acknowledged. "It took some explaining on my part that this place..." he made a rather circumspect movement with his arm, "holds a special place in your heart and that of your family. But I think they understood. Eventually."

"I'm sorry," she muttered. "We'll hold the wedding in Vienna, of course."

Felix, the giant innkeeper with hands like snow shovels, bent his grizzly head to enter under the door beam. He was followed on his heels by his two adult daughters who worked at Himmlhof as servers. Felix frowned, his gray eyes glaring under bristly white eyebrows when he saw the Norwegians still lounging around the fireplace, long stockinged legs stretched, talking loudly in their pitch-accent Viking language while smoke rose from their pipes.

"Time to leave, *meine Herren*," he roared in a rather unfriendly manner. "This is a private room now. Your lunch will presently be served in the breakfast room." He shooed the Norwegians away. They got up rather reluctantly and, still chatting with each other, made for the door.

The next thing happened so fast that no one understood the sequence of events. On his way to the door the blue-eyed Norseman tripped, made a sliding motion, and the last contents of his cocoa landed on Esther's bodice. The brown liquid splashed onto the pale blue silk and spread like a scandalous oil spill over her breast. She jumped up and shrieked as if being flayed alive.

"You oaf, you wretched Viking!"

"Esther, watch your language!" Her mother's voice was terse and sharp.

She backed off immediately, especially as she saw Carl's shocked reaction to her anger. Bowing her head meekly, she looked down at her bodice. Her dress was ruined. As was her day. The anger suppressed, all emotion drained from her. What was it with this stranger that he was so keen on thwarting her future happiness? Tears filled her eyes despite her steely anger. Tears of disbelief and frustration. Why couldn't she have something that was perfect? She tried so hard to live up to the promise.

Her mother and Oma raced toward her, shouting to the servers for "a clean cloth and some soap and water." The culprit got to his feet, still holding the mug. He tried to come toward her, an apologetic, almost sheepish look in his eyes. But before he could reach her, he was grabbed roughly by the collar by Carl and pushed out of the room. Carl closed the door behind the rowdy gang with a bang before hastening back to his distraught fiancée.

He sank on his knees before Esther, who sank down on a chair like a wooden statue, while her mother tried to get the worst stain out of the dress.

"It's no use, Naomi," Oma observed. "You'll have to take it off, *Bärchen,* and put on your second best. There, there now. It's not the end of the world. These accidents happen, and I'm sure that oaf is feeling as bad about this as you do."

The two servers, dressed in identical dirndl dresses, gaped open-eyed at the consternation, clearly uncertain what to do with the steaming soup terrines.

"Go and fetch Helga," Naomi instructed Rebecca, who quickly fled as fast as her patent leather shoes would carry her. Carl was still down in front of Esther, his hands affectionately on her knees while she blew her nose and felt some feeling of warmth return to her veins. The look of love in his eyes calmed her somewhat. Carl would be good in times of calamities. He would be there when anger overtook her. The tension seeped out of her like the air out of a tight balloon.

"Well, at least you've seen me in the dress I had chosen," she said with a wan smile. "Now you'll have to decide if you still want me in my ordinary day dress."

"You look lovely in everything, my dear Esther."

There had never before been so much passion in his voice. She was slightly ashamed to admit to herself that the incident seemed to have been needed to break down the last barrier of reserve between them.

"Thank you."

She got up again as he touched her cheek. Happy to be able to feel love again, instead of that suffocating anger. Carl rose to his full length, protective arms around her. This was what she'd chosen. This!

"Now I'd love to go and give that Nordic geezer a good slapping, but I suppose that's out of the question." Playing the heroic role was certainly grist to Carl's mill and made Esther feel proud of him.

~

THEY BROKE the white earthenware plate as was a good Jewish custom, kissed and ate Biedermeier Torte. In her off-white dress with a floral pattern of red roses and blue hydrangea, her curls loosened from their earlier tight bun and rosy cheeks brought on by the rich port wine, Esther felt freer than she'd been in months. She looked deep into Carl's brown eyes and saw nothing but providence. He kissed her warm cheek, shy in front of her family, but she smiled up at him.

"You may kiss me now. It's not a sin."

He smiled back and did just that. Her other cheek. He was such a gentleman.

Esther cheered inside. It was done. They were engaged. Now, Carl would take care of the rest. Of her, of their babies. Of everything. In due time. Her family would be so proud of her. The eldest daughter carrying on the Weiss tradition of sophistication and elegance.

Bliss, brilliance and benevolence settled on the happy couple as they danced to Glenn Miller's *"Doin' the Jive"* while the parents looked on and a silver slithered moon rose above the mountain top.

Esther shivered. She was sure she could never be happier in her life than she was right at that moment.

2

VIENNA TRAMPLED

Vienna, 12 March 1938

The windows of the Weiss apartment on the Prater Strasse rattled as an ongoing stream of military vehicles raced past, followed by the stamping of heavy boots and coarse German commands.

Esther startled awake, instinctively drawing the bedding over her head. The linen sheet smelled of the rose soap bars her mother put in all the storing cupboards and lime-scented starch. But it didn't drown out the noise.

She knew exactly what the commotion in the Prater Strasse meant. For months, it had been clear as the note of doom that the Germans would annex her country. The only question had been *when* the *Anschluss* would take place, not *if*. Clearly, Hitler had not wanted to wait for the outcome of Chancellor Schuschnigg's referendum. So here they were. Raising Cain.

Clapping and loud cheering sounded in the street below her window, where her father's shop opened straight onto the Prater Strasser. It spelled out that most *Österreicher* cared fiddlesticks about Austria's independence and instead applauded the arrival of the German troops. Being part of the Third Reich was like coming home for them. But for Esther, the vicious banging on the glass panels of her father's shop followed by *"Jüde rauss"* was a harrowing harbinger of her people's destiny.

Esther resolutely threw off the bedclothes, scolding herself for her weakness.

"You're a Weiss. Don't be a jellyfish. There is work to be done."

She quickly splashed her face with cold water from the wash-stand's basin. As she rubbed the soft towel over her cheeks, her eyes met the reflection of her sea-green eyes in the mirror. She squinted. Fear. Trepidation. Uncertainty. It was all there. But she straightened her back. *No. No surrender. Not to the Germans. Not to bullies of any sort.* Instinctively, her hand went to her slender throat. She swallowed hard.

No.

Straight as a candle, she approached the massive chestnut cupboard leaning against the bedroom's white plastered wall. Bare-foot, still in her silk nightie, she knelt and opened the bottom drawer, touching the soft fabrics of her trousseau. The diamond engagement ring on her left hand sparkled among the white towels with their golden C&E initials hand-embroidered in every corner. Crisp white sheets, all with the same elegant lettering. It felt so perfect, so true. Her life in stitches. She'd started the deft needle-work immediately after Carl had asked her to become his wife, at the tender age of seventeen. She was so lucky. A glorious life ahead of them.

Unless...

With her fingers still caressing the linen of her future house, Esther's mind drifted back to that memory now a year ago...

In floor-length dresses of white crêpe de Chine, Catholic Romy Gruber and Jewish Esther Weiss stood side by side inside the audi-torium of the State Opera House. Everyone was waiting for Presi-dent Miklas and his guests to step onto the imperial balcony. Esther was nervously picking at the fingertips of her white gloves.

Dark-haired and almost a head shorter than her school friend,

Romy stood stock-still, her amber gaze the only movement in her oval face as she scanned the crowds. Then Esther felt a nudge in her ribs, and Romy's clear voice rang over the shuffling and buzzing voices around them.

"Don't worry, Essie. I see Carl Bernstein's just arrived. You're not the only Jew here. Doesn't he look handsome?"

The well-meant but clumsy remark did little to steady Esther's nerves. She shouldn't be here. The Vienna Opera Ball was a Christian celebration ball. Why had she let Romy talk her into it? Well, of course, because *he* would be here. And now he was on the other side of the lavishly decorated auditorium. Tall, dark and handsome. At least a dozen white-clad debutantes turned their well-coiffed heads to eye the jeweler's son. The boldest among them picked up the hems of their dresses and tripped over in his direction.

Esther tried to shrink within her tall frame as best as she could, but Romy was sure to ruin all attempts at hiding herself. With her usual good-humored bluntness, her friend pulled her across the dance floor in the direction of the fluttering girls around young Mr. Bernstein.

"Come on, Es, let's say hello to your beau before he's kidnapped by one of these damsels. We have to rescue the poor fellow. He looks quite forlorn among the minor swans."

"Don't! And Carl's in no way my beau," Esther protested, her cheeks reddening at mentioning his name, her size-6 feet jogtrotting alongside Romy's dainty little steps. 'Don't' was as absent a part of decisive little Miss Gruber's vocabulary as tact was.

"Might be the last time they allow Jews to attend the Opera Ball, so you'd better let Carl know you're here and expect him to dance with you at your debutante ball."

They reached the slippered heels of the girls just as their chatter and fluttering eyelids pressed the trapped newcomer against the Art Deco wallpaper.

Romy's clear, authoritative voice brought their swooning classmates from the *Wasagasse Gymnasium* to a hush.

"Carl," she cried out indignantly, "have you no manners? I

would truly have expected you to pay your first respects to Esther Weiss. Didn't you tell me as much when I was in your shop last week?"

"What?" Esther's eyes flashed. Had Carl and Romy talked about her behind her back?

She saw Carl's dark eyes flinch and knew her friend was telling the truth. Why wouldn't she? Romy wasn't a person to mince her words. Esther was about to turn her back on the entire scene, feeling exposed in this glare of attention when she heard Carl's strong but kind voice.

"Don't leave, Esther. Please reserve the first waltz for me. I beg you."

At that moment, the master of ceremonies hit the parquet floor three times with his golden staff.

"*Meine Damen und Herren, Präsident Wilhelm Miklas und Frau Leopoldine Miklas.*"

The 1937 Vienna Ball had opened, and the orchestra struck the first chords of Johann Strauss's "Wiener Launen-Waltzer." Before she knew what was happening, Esther saw Carl come toward her, the deep dark eyes glittering in the reflecting light of a thousand crystal chandeliers.

"May I?"

He didn't even wait for the answer, grabbed her right hand firmly in his and his own right hand slid around her waist. Instinctively, she placed her hand on his shoulder and they were off. He'd chosen her over all others. She felt like the queen of the ball, as if a light bulb had been switched on in the dark.

Vaguely, Esther was aware of the staring gazes of some guests. Despite her feeling of bliss, it was impossible to ignore them. The Jewish couple of well-known Viennese Jews being the center of attention on the dance floor. Handsome but unwanted. Esther drew closer to Carl, trying to ignore the stares and the certain gossiping that went on behind false smiles. He tightened his grip, understanding her trepidation.

Of course, she knew all about Carl Bernstein. They frequented the same circles though their fathers were considered competitors, covering between the two families the best part of Vienna's jeweler's business. Besides, Carl had enjoyed quite a celebrity status at the *Wasagasse Gymnasium* before he'd graduated four years earlier. He had the central role in the school play, first violinist in the school orchestra, winning every dance contest. Carl Bernstein was rich, respected, unrivaled. And now *she* was in his arms. A position she and Romy had dreamed about so often...

"Esther! Are you awake?"

Papi was calling her. It was a rough awakening from her rousing reminiscence of the previous year's events. Esther closed the drawer with a bang.

"Coming!"

The noise outside had reached a crescendo. A cacophony of angry voices and frightened shrieks. There was a banging on the front door and she could hear the trampling of horses' hooves on the cobblestones.

"Esther! Come quickly!"

This time it was Rebecca, her voice the squeak of a frightened mouse. With a hastily thrown day dress over her bed wear and skidding into her house slippers, Esther raced down the mahogany stairs, almost tripping over her own feet.

"What's going on? Where are Mutti and Papi?"

Rebecca's big eyes were filling with tears. She held Adam securely scooted under her arm. The look on her little brother's face was one more of curiosity than fear.

"Papi's at...at the door."

At that moment Helga came spurting down the stairs, a silver brush in her hand as she'd been tending to Frau Weiss. The resolute lady's maid immediately took control.

"Away from the front windows, children. Go to the kitchen. Where's Cook Emilia?"

"She's out on errands," Rebecca piped.

"Right. Do as I tell you, while I go and check out what this infernal din is about."

Obeying the maid, Esther felt her heart slam against her rib cage in fear and indignation as she ushered her siblings to the back of the house.

"Are the Germans going to throw us out of our house?" Adam's eyes were round as marbles.

"No, silly," Esther tried to soothe him but — with the door ajar — all three of them watched closely how Helga with decisive steps went through the hall to the front door. The silver brush in her raised hand as a weapon of defense.

Then from the other side, a chinking rat-tat-tat sounded from the back of the house. The knocker on the garden gate. Esther spun around.

"Stay here!"

Feeling rather exposed in her half-dressed state, lacking half of Helga's courage, Esther went down the garden path, stopped in front of the closed wooden door, panting. She could hear her own blood sing in her ears.

Calm down!

"Who's there?"

"It's Frau Hoffmann."

Esther unlatched the door and let the slight Jewish woman, who'd been their neighbor for as long as she could remember, into the garden, locking it quickly behind her. Esther knew the harsh voices in the backstreet were German soldiers and not the Viennese traders and shopkeepers who used that part of Vienna to park their vehicles.

Adina Hoffmann looked hurried and flustered, her black felt hat askew on her head and the top buttons of her woolen coat buttoned up the wrong way. She was carrying a large square box with gilded letters in the black velvet lid. Jewelry. The daughter of a goldsmith knew these things. Esther was puzzled.

"Sorry for the interruption, Esther, when everyone's so upset with the Anschluss," the petite woman, who as usual was dressed entirely in black and wearing her wig, uttered. "I have a request to ask your father."

"Please come in. It's just... that my father is busy at the moment." Esther ushered the short-legged neighbor into the kitchen.

"I know your father is busy," Frau Hoffmann whispered, "these awful Nazis. Can I leave him a note?"

Cook Emilia's kitchen was in disarray. She'd been busy with the preparations for the family lunch, before dashing out to the week market. Esther hastened to shove aside a glass bowl with piecrust dough covered with a checked cloth, a bunch of fresh green spring onion and a half-prepared beetroot salad. Adina put the box on the counter.

"I'm sorry to be bothering you right now, but I hoped your father would store our family jewels in your safe. We're leaving for Holland and it's too dangerous to take all of them with us, especially as we'll be traveling through Germany. Samuel says we can't take the risk. We'll be back as soon as possible."

"You're leaving Austria?"

Frau Hoffmann nodded. Esther knew Samuel Hoffmann had a heart condition and that their only son, Asher, had always dreamed of continuing his ballet education abroad. But leave? Just like that?

Adina sank onto one of the kitchen chairs while, as an automaton, Esther poured her a cup of tea from the large pot that Emilia always prepared before she went out. The noise at the front door was slowly subsiding. Rebecca and Adam also slinked near and sat down at the table where they could sometimes have breakfast when Mutti didn't insist on a formal family get-together.

"I'm sure my father will put your heirlooms in the safe in the shop," Esther said pensively. She wasn't thinking of the diamonds and rubies. She was thinking of Ash leaving and what that would do to her fiancé. Carl and Ash were best friends, had been so since Kindergarten. Carl had always protected his artistic friend, who had faced years of ridicule from his peers. Until they'd seen him dance the role of The Prince in Tchaikovsky's *Swan Lake,* and even his bullies had been silenced.

As if guessing her thoughts, Adina Hoffmann carefully placed the Artzberg cup on its white saucer, and said, "Yes, we go as much for Asher as for my husband. He's sure he can dance more freely in Holland. And we have family there. We're leaving for Amsterdam next week."

"Next week?" Esther felt like a dumb parrot repeating her neighbor's words. She glanced sideways at her younger siblings and saw the question mark in their eyes, too. More and more Jews were leaving Vienna. Something she knew her parents would never do. Well, maybe Mutti and Oma would, but not Papi. Her father was afraid of no one. A proud Viennese business owner, rich and respected. Though the Jew-hate was starting to create a dent even in his difficult-to-put-down dignity.

A piercing shriek sounded through the kitchen that sent everyone's already rattled nerves over the edge. It was Rebecca, her face white, one trembling finger pointing to a gigantic spider that leisurely crawled up the kitchen wall.

"Oh no!"

Esther acted swifter than lightning, knowing her sister's disproportional anxiety of spiders. She grabbed one of Emilia's dish cloths and, as an accomplished markswoman, squashed the poor insect before any of the others had even batted their eyelashes.

"Sorry spider," she muttered apologetically as she studied the shriveled-up black dot on the floor, "we can't have any of that now."

At that moment Franz Weiss came into the family kitchen, looking slightly disheveled from his run-in with the Nazis. He quickly recovered himself by puffing out his cheeks in his customary way and checking his gold chain watch, as if to check whether a normal day was about to begin.

Esther rose to her feet, ready to take the lead, but her father turned his attention to Frau Hoffmann.

"Adina? You here?" He was clearly surprised at seeing his neighbor so early in the morning and not having come through the front door. Puzzlement wrinkled his broad forehead.

"Papi, were those Germans at the door?" Adam interrupted and not waiting for the answer added, "What did they want?"

"Nothing, son. Just a nuisance." He cleared his throat, agitated as if something troublesome was stuck there.

Knowing her father, Esther understood better than her younger siblings that he would not bring up the discussion with the SS officers in front of them. Instead, he wanted to redirect his attention to Adina. But just then the heavyset cook stormed in through the back door, carrying a loaded wicker basket. Her face was red and her kerchief askew on one ear. A string of not-so-nice curse words spat from her lips.

"That godforsaken German vermin! What are they thinking? Stealing our food and upsetting the whole town. No lamb to be gotten, anywhere, even potatoes on ration. *Rauss*, I'd say..." She stopped mid-sentence, aware of multiple sets of eyes on her flustered face.

"Excuse me, Sir." Emilia pulled her kerchief in place as she saw her employer standing wide-legged in the middle of her domain. Her light-blue eyes went tentatively from one to the other.

"Where's the Missus?" she implored, looking at Helga.

"She's still upstairs," Helga replied. "I'm going upstairs to help the ladies now, so Emilia, make sure breakfast is ready for them in half an hour."

The restored hierarchy among the Weiss staff seemed to calm the cook somewhat. She just nodded and turned her back on them all to give her attention to the stove. There was porridge to be made and sausages to be baked.

"Come on, children—to the living room, while I talk with Frau Hoffmann," their father ordered. "There's enough turmoil upsetting Cook already."

Emilia shot him a grateful nod over her shoulder.

"Breakfast will be served as soon as the ladies are downstairs."

After breakfast, Esther wandered aimlessly through the living room. Rebecca and Adam were doing their lessons in the back room. As Jewish children, they were no longer welcome at the Alte Donau Schule. So, Naomi Weiss had taken the teaching of her offspring upon herself.

"I was the private tutor to children of the richest Jewish families of all Austria," she'd argued. "How difficult can it be?" It wasn't the first time the proud mother of three would remind them of her glory days as Miss Naomi Aronson among the *Haute Juiverie* of Ringstrasse, the Rothschildts and the Sandgrubers. Now she returned to teaching like a fish in water.

Esther's lessons would follow in the afternoon. English literature, music theory, art history, and a stiff dose of housekeeping. Both mother's and daughter's favorite subject.

"I'll make sure you will never regret not having gotten your *Matura*," her mother would comfort her. To be honest, Esther didn't know whether or not it mattered to her. The final year at the *Wasagasse Gymnasium* had been far from fun for the Jewish students. Yet, not finishing what she'd started felt contradictory to her disciplined mind. She'd been so close. Only a couple more months to graduation, and now it was unlikely she would ever return to the gymnasium while chances of going to the finishing school in Switzerland became slimmer by the day.

As she paced from wall to wall, Esther thought of Carl. He too must have been informed of the departure of his best friend Ash. How was he feeling about it?

Samuel Hoffmann had been working for the government and been unemployed since early January. But neither the Bernsteins nor the Weiss family had much choice but to stay put in Austria. Their entire livelihood depended on their shops, their clients, their personnel. Esther sighed deeply. Why was everything so complicated, so chaotic when life itself was so simple, straightforward and seemly?

But was it?

Esther could no longer endure her own pacing. Her legs wanted to go out, to do more. She needed to see her fiancé's face and to let him know it pained her he'd lost his childhood friend to Holland.

But it was dangerous to go out into the streets swarming with SS officers. There was no way to know how they would treat a single Jewish girl. As always, Esther blessed the inheritance of her Oma's blonde hair and green eyes. She, unlike many of her people, could pass the enemy unnoticed.

Sneaking through the hall to the coatrack at the front door, Esther slipped into her maroon fur-trimmed coat. It seemed a little hot for mid-March, but the wolf trim would shade half her face and Austria was still at the tail-end of winter, chill winds waiting for the promise of spring.

Passing through the kitchen to leave through the back entrance, she said to Emilia who was plucking a chicken, her face still red and angry at the intruders to her country, "If anyone asks where I am, tell them I've popped over to the Bernstein shop."

"I don't think you should go out today, Missy! Them bastards are everywhere."

"I'll be careful, Emilia. Don't worry. And I won't be long."

"Don't say I didn't warn you!" Emilia ripped off a pluck of feathers with a grim pull.

Esther looked right and left on opening the gate, but life in the alley had returned to normal. Two neighbors were busy repairing the wheel of a cart that had come off and greeted her as if it was just another March morning. *No wonder*, Esther thought. She knew the Braun brothers, as everyone knew each other on this side of Prater Strasse. They thought the Anschluss was a good thing, Austria being united back with the Third Reich. Their Third Reich too now. What they thought of their many Jewish neighbors, they so far kept to themselves.

She stealthily made her way to the end of the alley that ran back into Prater Strasse. The Bernstein shop and living quarters were only half a mile to the east. Esther halted in her tracks. The street she'd known all her life seemed to have changed overnight. The predominant color had become the khaki of the German uniforms mixed with the sinister black of the SS. The normal bustle of shopping had been turned into a grim war scene. Soldiers everywhere, on motorcycles, in Jeeps, while black Mercedes cruised down the broad avenue filled with officers in high black caps and menacing looks.

Her city was no longer hers. The walk she'd taken almost every day in the past year to get to her fiancé's house now seemed like a course full of landmines. She must have stood still in the middle of the pavement because something prodded in her back.

A rough voice commanded, "Move on, woman, stop gaping."

She did as she was told, mechanically, befuddled, only to slow down again. Across the street she saw one of their neighbors, Herr Grauss, down on his knees cleaning the pavement with a brush and soap. Esther didn't know whether to look away or to study what was going on. More men were down on all fours. Two Germans, their long guns pointed at the men, urged them to go on with cleaning the stones. Esther was puzzled but also frightened. Herr Grauss was a Jew. Were they openly humiliating her people? What was going on?

With every step Esther felt her cheeks go redder with indignation, an inner fury she knew she had to quench. For herself and for her family. Tight fists in the pockets of her winter coat, she wanted to rebel against the humiliations as she reached the gilded façade of Bernstein & Son Juweliers.

She hesitated. *Go in? Or ring the bell next door to the Bernstein's apartment over the shop?* The shop door was closed. No movement inside, no expensive cars on the curb, no broad-smiling Carl to welcome the distinguished clientele. This was out of the ordinary. She'd never known the shop to be closed on a weekday. Only on Sabbath.

"Who's there?" She heard Carl's voice, frantic and almost unfriendly, from the top of the stairs.

"It's me. Esther. Can I come up?"

Everything was now different and questionable. Even a simple visit.

"Of course. Just make sure you close the door carefully behind you."

Seconds later. How good it was to feel Carl's strong arms around her. It was hard not to burst out in tears. But he would think her weak when the real reason for her wet eyes was her fury.

Look at the bleakness of their apartment now! Carl's father was coughing in a single bed under a pile of blankets in the corner of the living room. A small fire smoldered in the ornate fireplace, not even capable of warming the large space with the tall windows. His mother, gray and exhausted and wearing her mink coat indoors, sat at her husband's side, wringing her hands.

Once, Frau Bernstein had been famous for her elegant afternoon teas and musical soirées, her sterling silver tea set or Art Deco wine glasses twinkling in the hundred lights of her empire crystal basket chandelier. Here, Vienna's elite had once enjoyed the best music and the richest food.

Before those same clients, who'd drunk her best champagne and worn her husband's custom-made jewelry, had turned their back on them.

Carl, his arms still around her, stroked her back as she asked, "Will we be okay? Please tell me we will be okay."

"We will, my Essie, we will. Our love will conquer all, you'll see."

She couldn't help but notice the tremor in his voice, the hint of uncertainty, and she swallowed hard. It was unfair to think she could lean on him. He was an only child with elderly parents. How would they cope if worse came to worst? She was lucky. She had her family with two strong parents and two siblings.

"I hope we will. We must keep our faith, Carl. Together..."

Her heart was so heavy. Tears flowed despite her will. She couldn't stop them. Not anymore.

3

GOING TO SWITZERLAND

August 1938

It was a sunny summer day that the Weiss family with tears in their eyes waved goodbye to their loyal maid Helga, who'd lived with them since Esther's birth.

"I'll never forget your kindness, Ma'am, and all the things you taught me," Helga sobbed as she grabbed both Frau Weiss's gloved hands and squeezed them.

"I wish, too, Helga, that you could stay," Franz answered for his wife, who needed all her fortitude not to break down in front of her children. "But the Nazis leave us no options; we're not allowed staff. Who knows how long we'll be allowed to have a say over our own flesh and blood?" He looked grim and sunken.

Esther silently watched the brief scene, more upset for Helga and her parents than for herself. She would be out of here herself within days. Cook Emilia had left the month earlier, so it was just the family now, her mother and grandmother taking care of the household themselves as best as they could.

"I'll stay in Vienna, just in case the situation changes again and you can reemploy me." She heard the kind Helga sniffle. "I dislike those Nazis as much as you do, and I'm not going back to Münich. Not me!"

Two days later, the Weiss household for once found itself in their usual pre-Anschluss bustle. Despite many deliberations and doubts, her parents had decided that Esther would go to Lausanne in Switzerland to complete her education at the same finishing school her mother and Oma had also attended.

Esther was dressed in her prettiest mousseline white dress, gloved and with hat. She sat ready in the back room, her body trembling, chewing on her full lower lip. At times, a deep sigh escaped her.

"I shouldn't go. I shouldn't leave you all. We should save the money for more important things."

"Nonsense," her father's voice boomed through the living room, while he fished his golden watch from the waistcoat pocket over his growing stomach. "We've gone over this before, *Bärchen*, and this is how we will do it. You'll be safe in Switzerland. That's one worry less for your old Papi. This is no life for anyone, you know that as well as I, but certainly not for an engaged young woman. Hopefully it will all soon be over. Next time we meet, you'll be standing under your chuppah. Mark my words."

Esther sighed again. He was right, of course. Her Papi was always right, and in her heart of hearts she couldn't wait to be leaving the depressing city Vienna had become after German occupation. To be free of fear again, to breathe in the air of the mountains she adored. Perhaps there would even be skiing the Alps in winter, her most favorite of all pastimes. But more importantly, she would learn all she needed to become a worthy wife to Carl and mother of his children.

"What's taking that young man of yours so long?"

Her father was still inspecting the watch his own grandfather had given him on his eighteenth birthday. It was a rare silver and silver-plate, late-eighteenth century verge chain-driven, fuzee consular-cased pocket watch made by the famous John George Hirsh of Gratz.

"Papi, may I read the time on your watch?" Adam had slinked closer to his father. The ten-year-old was obsessed with the watch to such a degree that he even forgot his tears about his big sister's departure. One day it would be his, and young Adam Weiss lived for that day.

"Not now, son!"

At that moment Esther's mother and grandmother came in, composed and regal as ever, though the past months of constant harassment by the Germans had even eroded some of the formidable strength in the Viennese ladies.

"Have you got everything, my dear? Your hatbox, your two suitcases, your train ticket, passport?" Naomi Weiss went through her entire spiel, as she'd done more than Esther cared to remember in the past days.

"I have everything, Mother, really. I'm prepared. I'll be fine. Carl's going to escort me to Innsbruck, and then I'm already almost in Switzerland. He'll see me onto the train to Zürich. It's you I'm worried about."

Esther's green eyes filled with tears. No matter how hard she tried, everything was so emotional these days. Leaving her family for the first time in her life, being totally on her own, without their protection. But more than she herself, who would be safe from danger in Lausanne, she worried about her loved ones. Vienna was a cesspool of danger and crime these days, and her father's business hung on to a shoestring.

"Now, stop fussing," Oma interrupted her granddaughter's gloomy thoughts. "You think of your own future, Bärchen. We're all excited about your engagement, and forthcoming wedding."

"Don't forget to give my regards to Madame Paul," her mother added. "She was always so kind to me. Her father and mine fought together at the Hindenburg line. She was born in Austria, you knStar of Davidow."

There was a knock on the back door.

"Carl!" Adam ran from his seat to open the door to his future brother-in-law. Oma frowned. She was still not used to not having the servants let in visitors. Esther was pained by the fragile facial expression on her beloved grandparent, but her heart leaped at the arrival of her betrothed.

Carl entered, tall, distinguished and calm apart from the tired look on his handsome face, wringing his kid gloves in his hands. Esther knew why. Every walk through town was an ordeal one longed to escape from. And now there was even talk of Jews having to wear the Star of David on their breast to single them out further from other Austrians.

He went around the room in his usual order before kissing Esther on the cheek. She smelled his cologne — Caron's Pour Un Homme — which she loved to inhale with all her might, but today she could smell his disquiet through the musky amber and cedar. If even Carl was upset, something was truly amiss. She held her breath.

"Your parents well?"

Her father's chitchat broke through her somber thoughts. Carl had taken a seat on the straight chair next to her and had grabbed her hand.

"Father is worse," he said with a deep etch between his eyebrows. "He's been coughing all night."

"Should you be going with me then?" Esther looked up at him with doubt in her eyes.

"Of course! I phoned Chaim, my nephew. He will look after the shop. Not that there are many customers these days."

A stab in her heart, for him, for the Bernstein family. From a proud, distinguished jeweler's family, they'd turned into little more than paupers. She knew Carl went out to help in the launderette several days a week, delivering the crisp washed linen to the posh Metropole Hotel and Imperial Hotel with a cart behind his old bicycle, just to earn some pfennigs. No one was supposed to know. Certainly not his sick father.

"Are you ready?" He broke through her grim daydream with a smile.

"Sure." She tried to put a brave smile square on her face but knew she failed miserably. The hardest part was yet to come. Saying goodbye.

Esther first hugged her Oma, who had grown paler and older and thinner after the Anschluss and sometimes said incoherent things like "I'm having breakfast" when the family sat down for a meager dinner. Oma felt bony and fragile, like a scared little bird, nothing like the regal matron who in her maiden years had made all men's heads turn. In 1880, she'd even opened the Vienna State Opera Ball in Kaiser Wilhelm's arms.

"Let the Waltz begin!" the Kaiser had boomed — and off he went with blonde Esther Adler, daughter of Austria's Foreign Minister.

Esther could not hold back her tears. Oma had been part of her life since she could remember. Steady, strong, self-assured Oma who'd finally caved in to old age and defeat. In a wave of panic, she wondered if she'd ever see her again.

"Bye, Oma. I'll write."

"You do that, *Bärchen*, you do that."

Saying goodbye to Rebecca and Adam wasn't easy but slightly less burdensome than her parents. They were young; they would survive.

But would they?

Rebecca sobbed against Esther's chest until their mother said softly, "Let her go, Rebbie. You'll soil Essie's coat."

Typically Mother, but this was rightfully so. Esther was dressed in the best clothes they still owned.

"I'll be back, Rebbie. Don't worry. And I'm going to send you postcards from the Alps."

"Also for me!" Adam cried out as he joined in the sibling hug.

"Also for you, Addie!"

After her brother and sister finally let her go, Esther lifted her eyes to her mother. Naomi Weiss's gaze was strong, confident still. Her eyes commanded her daughter to keep her back straight, believe in herself, get the best education a well-to-do Jewish girl could get. Her gaze said, "Times will change, my dear, and you'll need this backbone to bring up a family in better times."

The hug her mother gave her was warm and scented but somewhat withdrawn. That was the only signal she gave off that this was difficult for her. Esther knew her absence would also mean one pair of hands less to do the unfamiliar household chores. And her support, something Frau Weiss had leaned on after her eldest became engaged. Her portion now rested on the women in her family, including fourteen-year-old Rebecca.

"You'll be fine, my dear! Now go." She firmly propelled her daughter toward the door.

Her father walked them to the back door carrying her suitcase, a brown-leather, bulky one that had been her loyal companion on their skiing trips. Now it held most of Esther's worldly possessions and would have to last her for a year. There was nothing to spare for pocket money. Most of the family cash had been spent on her train ticket.

"Now be a good girl," her father growled, checking the alley for unwanted visitors. There were none on this early Friday morning.

"Papi?" Esther turned to her solid father, fighting hard against her tears. Her throat felt thick, and she had to force the words out of her. He looked impatient. Franz Weiss never liked questions and certainly not the hard type of questions his daughter's expression alluded to.

"Yes?"

"Papi." She had to ask — there was no other way, though Carl was waiting to walk her to the station. He was checking his watch. "Papi, will you consider taking the family to Tante Isobel and Oncle Frerik in Oslo when... you know... now the Nazis closed the goldsmith's atelier?"

Esther had the eerie feeling she wasn't returning to Vienna after her year in Switzerland, but her father still didn't want to hear about it.

"Nonsense. There's plenty of other work to be gotten for a man like me. Don't fret, Bärchen, and don't worry about us. Now go." He gave her a quick, absent hug, and she realized he had lost weight. His suit jacket, tailor-made of an excellent gabardine, was sagging at his shoulders and the fabric was becoming thin and shiny at elbows that stuck out. The once fleshy, well-fed Franz Weiss might not want to give in to Hitler's tyranny over his people, but his body was telling another tale.

Side-by-side, Carl and Esther walked the short distance to Vienna's train station. Heads bent down, not making eye contact with anyone, as all Viennese Jews scurried down the pavements these days. Vienna had turned into a grim, mechanical city since the Germans swung their military scepter over the once so vibrant and noisy city. People only left the safety of their houses when they really had to, no longer to socialize or go out.

They didn't speak either. Esther wouldn't have been able to utter one syllable. Not only did her throat feel blocked, but her chest and stomach also hurt so badly, she thought she was breaking in half. At least a dozen times, she was about to retrace her steps and go back home. What was the use of an expensive education that seemed so terribly out of place these days?

When they turned toward the main entrance of Vienna railroad station, Esther broke the silence. "Are you sure about this, Carl? I'll be fine on my own." She didn't dare to mention her blonde hair that had been a blessing on innumerous times since the Anschluss. The Nazis invariably saw her as one of them. But Carl, with his dark hair and prominent nose, had the distinguished look of a professional Jew. He was much more the center of mockery and humiliation. She'd fretted over this so often, wanting to discuss it, but didn't dare to bring it up in front of him. Somehow it didn't seem right. Everything Jewish was hidden as best as it could be, outwardly but also inside.

"We've gone over this already, Esther, so let's please not repeat ourselves. I want to see you safely to the Swiss border." She gazed up at his face; it was stony, as it was so often these days, and she sighed. She shouldn't press him. But she had so many questions and they had so little time left. What was he really feeling about their future, about them? Sometimes Carl was so hard to read, and she felt like she was just a nuisance. If only he'd let her into his thoughts and feelings.

"Thank you." She briefly squeezed his free hand. "I'm looking forward to some time alone with you. We haven't had that for quite a while." She didn't mention the long hours Carl was now working at the Imperial Hospital, washing dishes while also guarding the family's shop like a hawk and looking after his parents.

She would always forgive him his taciturn behavior. He had every right.

There had been few minutes left for them, but Esther had understood and accepted. As she understood everything about this hardworking, dedicated man who never complained about his fate gone wrong and still gave her something every time they met — a pair of earrings, a bunch of flowers he'd brought from the restaurant, still half in bloom, a piece of velvet fabric from his mother's cupboard. She loved him for it.

Ignoring the suspicious looks they got, they boarded the train that would take them to Innsbruck. As ordinary travelers, they showed their tickets and thronged together with other passengers to find their seats. Most people were silent but for the rowdy and aggressive SS officers who pushed everyone inside as if they were cattle. There was loud talk, domineering commands, and the sneering humiliation of the Jews.

Sitting close together on the plush upholstery, her luggage safely stored above their heads, Esther relaxed against the backrest, taking Carl's hand. Her engagement ring firmly resting in his palm. She knew Carl wouldn't show much emotion now. She was the one who had enough emotions for both of them. He felt it was his task to stay steady, her rock, his family's rock. Yet, she had to know.

"Are you going to be fine, Carl? I mean, with Ash gone and now me?" A soundless sigh listed his chest, the beautiful eyes darker than usual.

"I hope so, Liebling. I'll do my best. I promise. All we can hope for is that this situation will be over soon, though I sometimes doubt it. There seems to be no end to Hitler's thirst." He whispered the last part, aware of the enemy's eyes and ears around them.

"I know. I secretly hope my parents will decide to go north to Tante Isobel and Oncle Frerik. I heard my parents talk about it the other night when they thought I wasn't listening."

Carl looked surprised.

"To Oslo? Really? I would never expect your father to leave his business behind. I know my father wouldn't."

Esther didn't know if his remark was a criticism of her father's lack of resilience, but she didn't care. What she cared about was whether she and Carl could marry in Vienna. Of course, her father loved Vienna. It was just idle talk, but the idea of being separated from Carl was why she'd brought it up.

Carl studied her, and she watched as his eyes narrowed, lighting with understanding.

"We'll get married as soon as you return from Switzerland, Liebling. If necessary, I'll travel to Lausanne myself and we'll get married there."

Relief flooded through her. They would get married; she would be Frau Bernstein in twelve months.

"Maybe I should let go of this whole idea of finishing school." Her doubt escaped her aloud. "Then we could get married this fall." She leaned in closer to him and he hugged her tightly, sheltering her in the crook of his arm. She could hear his heart thump under his breast pocket, beating for her, for them both. For a brief moment she felt safe, her future certain.

"We'll be just fine, Liebling. Don't fret. I know you've wanted this education since you were still in bloomers. Don't give up on *your* dream and I won't on mine. I know I may temporarily have to work in the restaurant or elsewhere, but it won't last forever. This Anschluss won't last forever. Mark my words. We'll even all emigrate to America, if push comes to shove. Both families. Start out in New York again. There are so many diamond merchants and cutters and jewelers and goldsmiths moving to the Bronx right now. We could always leave Vienna and learn to fit in in the New World."

"I'd like that idea better than living alone in Norway," Esther observed as she looked out of the window. The distant snowcapped mountains made her heart surge, thinking about skiing and fresh air and no Germans but it all seemed so far away, so elusive. Her nerves were wearing thin.

The closer they came to Innsbruck, the more Esther clung to Carl's embrace. Taking leave of him would be saying goodbye to the last tie with her former life. After that, she would be on her own, something she'd never been.

He drew her still tighter in his arms and she washed up against him, drowning in his scent, his strength, his steadiness. The tears came against her will.

"I can't! I can't! What if...?"

"Don't, Esther!" He kissed her tear-stained cheeks and when his mouth found hers, she tasted her own salty tears. She sobbed even as they kissed, even as she tried to drink him in with all her might.

Esther had no sense of time, of Germans or people watching them. Finally, finally they were really together and really alone, just when they had to part for a year.

"I've got a last present for you," he murmured, still kissing her. He loosened his hold on her and pulled a small, flat parcel from the inside pocket of his suit jacket. It was wrapped in Bernstein Juweliers's blue and gold striped paper, with a gold ribbon tied around it.

"What is it?" Esther dried her tears, for a heavenly moment forgetting her grief.

"Open it!"

With trembling fingers she tried to keep the paper intact but, in her haste, tore it anyway. What she stared down at was their engagement photo in a brand-new silver frame. Only six months. Only six months earlier that had been them, so carefree as they gazed into Papi's camera lens. Happy, carefree, nothing but in love.

She kissed the glass panel, then put it back in its wrapping paper and into her handbag.

"Thank you, Carl! How thoughtful."

"So you like it?" Why was there something so youthful about him, like a puppy, when he waited for the verdict of his newest gift? Oh, how she loved him. How!

"I'll cherish it till my dying day. As I will do you."

"Come here one final time, Liebling." His brown eyes brimmed with love and devotion. Esther knew it then. As sure as birth and death. If given the chance, they would be the happiest of couples.

They followed the other passengers to the exit and disembarked, finding themselves on a crowded platform, where people shouted *hello* and *goodbye* and bulky suitcases were hauled onto trolleys by sweating porters.

Everything happened both at high speed and in slow motion. Esther couldn't grasp all that went on around her. A last kiss, a last farewell, the squeeze of his arms around her, his scent, his strong face. Then she was roughly shoved aside, almost losing her balance.

"Let go of that fair girl, *dreckige Jude!*" A rough German voice yelled in her ear. Carl was pulled from her but held on tight. He didn't protest, just replied in his polite manner.

"She is my fiancée."

Light-blue haughty eyes scanned Esther from under a high black cap, the Nazi's expression slowly changing from superiority to disgust.

"Foul Jew lover," he repeated as he turned to walk away. Esther was stunned, then anger overtook her. How dare he! And how dare he spoil their last moment together.

But there was no more time. Carl let her go — too quick, too sudden. Through a mist of tears, she felt how control of time and place slipped away from her.

For good?

As she watched his navy jacket disappear in the crowds, she felt everything — love, anger, despair, hope. Mostly love.

"Carl!" she whispered, "Carl, come back to me!"

4

ON HER OWN

Esther was alone. She would have to board the train that would cross the border into Switzerland on her own. Following the porter who was carrying her luggage to the next platform, she craned her neck to see if she could get one more glimpse of Carl, but he'd been already swallowed by the throng of people heading for the Vienna train.

There was a long wait at the border. The SA, Hitler's paramilitary police, took their time barging through the train accompanied by gruff German shepherds. Esther held her breath as they finally disembarked on the Austrian side and the train rolled into St Gallen.

Switzerland!

She was safe. She could breathe again, though guilt crept into her conscience. Breathe freedom while her family was in danger? Her fiancé at this very moment most likely humiliated and ridiculed by the same Nazis that had just given her an appreciative nod. Why was only she granted this breath of fresh air?

"Stop it!" She scolded herself. "Look around you. Live life now."

A mother with two young children frolicking at her side moved across the platform, ready to embark. The girl, slightly younger than Rebecca, had lush brown curls and a sweet, oval face with the bluest eyes. She was wearing a frilly red dress, which clearly made her feel like a posh little madam. The boy, who was about Adam's age, was dressed in a sailor's uniform, cute white legs peeping from under his navy shorts. A freckled open face under a thick mop of tawny hair. The mother, elegant and tall, with a large, brimmed hat on hair the same color as her son, looked down on her children with a big smile on her red-painted lips while a heavy-set, sweating porter followed them, pushing a cart with their embossed leather suitcases piled high.

Through the open windows, Esther heard the mother's American accent. "Oh darlings, Daddy's coming back from Paris today."

"Heavenly!" The girl's voice was ecstatic. "Did Daddy meet with Uncle Edward and Aunt Wallis? I so hope Auntie Wallis sends me the Chanel cat brooch. The one she has too. She promised, you know!"

Esther's interest was fired up, so she listened closely over the bustling noise as the family came into her carriage. This must be Katherine Rogers, Wallis Simpson's close friend. They were talking about the abdicated British King Edward and his new American wife. How exciting!

From the time she'd been a little girl, she'd adored everything that had to do with the British royal family. Especially former King Edward, when he was still Prince of Wales, had been such a dashing and cosmopolitan young prince. The daring love affairs and scandals that followed him like a shadow had only made British royalty more interesting, especially after the Habsburg House had collapsed after the Great War and Karl I of Austria had abdicated. Esther loved royalty with every vein of her being.

The train had meanwhile set in motion again and the glamorous little family had moved on to the first-class compartment, clearly on their way to their summer house in Cannes. Esther sank back in the cushion of her second-class compartment and gave herself over to happy reminiscence about her childhood infatuation with royal families, especially the recent happenings in

England. Anything to keep her thoughts away from Carl's blue coat disappearing in the crowds.

A story gone wrong when it had all the potential for a fairy tale. Everyone blamed Wallis, but Esther in fairness didn't know if that was the whole truth. After Edward had abdicated in December 1936 and had "only" been the Duke of Windsor, he'd more or less fled to Esther's country and stayed at Schloss Enzesfeld with Baron Eugen and Baroness Kitty de Rothschild.

Esther had still been interested in their love story with Wallis tucked away with the Rogers in Cannes, but over time it had become rather sordid. Especially as there were rumors that the couple were friends with Hitler, going to tea with him in 1937. Photographs of Hitler kissing Wallis's hand and she giving him her most seductive smile.

Esther hadn't thought about them for a long time, but now it all came back with the endearing scene on the platform. Royalty, class, distinction. It had meant everything to her. These people had been her hallmark, her dot on the horizon, her climb on the social ladder of Viennese society, where she would be introduced to film stars and royalty alike. But everything seemed to be shifting these days, and she didn't know whom to trust and use as an example anymore.

"I hope Madame Paul will be that example to me," she thought to herself. "Mutti said she was good, the head mistress of Le Manoir, so I'll set my hopes on her. At least she'll teach me what manners are and manners are always good. No manners immediately shows and is frowned upon by moral society."

As the train rolled deeper into Switzerland, first Zürich, then Bern and ultimately toward Lausanne in the south, the landscape became more and more rugged, and Esther had to curb herself from pressing her nose to the window. Snow and summits were to her what diamonds and gold were to her father and fiancé. The pristine white slopes, the brisk cold of high altitudes where every breath counted, the rush of adrenaline when she beat every other skier on the race downhill. Oh, outdoor life, oh, risk of adventure. It all rushed through her veins as she squeezed her gloved hands together and sat as still and ladylike as she could in her lavender travel suit.

"I'm such a barrel of contradictions," she mused. "It's a good thing I'll learn to behave properly now. Wildness is not a trait for ladies."

But she kept glancing out of the window, now trying to admire the Swiss mountains as a tourist would do, not an insider. Their picture-perfect shapes and forms, taller than the Austrian Alps she'd known her whole life. For the first time in months Esther felt her hopes go up, her heart beat faster. She could do this, return home as they wanted her to be.

It was a relief to find out the Swiss didn't look down on Jews as the Austrians did. Many Austrian Jews had already sought asylum with their neighbors in the certainty that Hitler would not burn his fingers on the country that had a reputation of having been neutral since 1815, when Switzerland finally became independent from France and the European powers agreed to recognize Swiss neutrality.

After a stop for the night in Bern, Esther boarded the last train that would take her to her destination. The late August day was hot, the train crowded and stuffy. But the Swiss were quiet and polite. Esther distinguished a variety of languages, German, Italian and French. French she understood as she had learnt it at Wasagasse Gymnasium, but from the singsong Italian she could only make out certain words.

A young couple her own age sat down on the bench opposite her and started talking rapidly in Italian. Through her eyelashes Esther studied them with interest. They were both dark-haired with olive skin, slight in build with beautiful, dark-flashing eyes. Very alive. She tried to make out if they were boyfriend and girlfriend or brother and sister. As they were sitting so close together, she first thought them a couple but now she wasn't so sure. They were talking in an agitated way but in half whispers. Esther felt as if she'd landed in another world. A very welcome other world.

How she loved studying people. It had been at least a year since she'd sat in the shade of a parasol at restaurant Griechenbeisl on the Fleischmarkt, sipping a Wiener Eiskaffee and savoring little forkfuls of Sachertorte, her whole family ensembled around her. The bells of the Holy Trinity Greek Orthodox Church would chime at regular times, giving structure and order to their happy lives. Those days!

Those days were gone!

"But they will return," Esther told herself, "perhaps even better than before!"

Again, she was displeased with herself. It was high time not to turn into a whining, dissatisfied person when the entire purpose for her Swiss adventure was to become an accomplished, always-positive lady. Esther shifted uncomfortably in her seat.

The rapidness of that Italian, their exotic looks, the thrill of traveling in a strange country. There was a whole world out here that she knew nothing about but would like to explore. It was so hard at times to curb her longings to break free from the reins of proper behavior. But Esther knew that in the end, she would feel she'd fallen short if she gave in to that desire.

"I promised betterment and I will be better when I arrive at Le Manoir. The lessons will teach me all I need in *my* life, becoming more of a lady, worthy of Carl and a pride to my family."

So she turned her gaze from the fascinating youngsters and studied the cows in the Alpine meadows, not knowing why she felt a nagging sadness nibble at her.

Weary and tired but full of expectation, Esther felt the train glide to a stop at Lausanne railroad station. Suddenly she panicked. She didn't know how to get to Le Manoir and had forgotten to ask her mother what the plan was when she eventually was at her destination. How typical of her!

She rummaged in her bag to find her purse. She only had a few Swiss francs left; all the rest of her money were German Reichsmarks. The Germans had replaced the Austrian schillings after the Anschluss. For a moment she thought of the coins she'd grown up with, and a surge of melancholy swept through. Papi had been devastated. His whole business was in schillings. He was such a proud Austrian.

"The Weisses came to Vienna after the second Ottoman siege of Vienna in 1683," he'd told his children many times. Esther could repeat her father's actual phrasing word by word. "Our founding father was Samuel Wolf Oppenheimer who came from Heidelberg to Vienna. Our forefather was appointed Court Jew by Emperor Leopold I. So hold your heads high, my brethren. Important historical blood flows through your veins."

"Poor Papi," Esther thought angrily, as she gathered her belongings. What use was all that important blood now as they were hunted down by the Nazis. She would fight for her family if it came to that. Use her fiery, old blood for a good cause.

A porter entered the carriage, wearing a stiff white uniform and white cap. His blonde hair was damp with sweat, his youthful face pinched.

"Mademoiselle Weiss?"

"Yes," Esther reacted, glad her problem of transport to the finishing school seemed solved.

"The Manoir chauffeur is waiting for you at the front of the station, Mademoiselle. Please follow me." He spoke in a clipped French voice, seemingly with no intent of wasting any more time than needed in that sweltering train compartment.

Esther hesitated as the young man hoisted all her luggage into his arms. Should she help? But he'd already turned his back on her and strode through the gangway to the exit. It was strange to be served again. Esther was jolted back to her old life where she'd been a well-to-do young woman with servants and strict rules. She was glad that her hands, which in past months had washed and scrubbed, were hidden in white lace gloves. She'd done her best to polish and varnish her nails before her trip, but the skin of her hands was red and rough. What was she now? Upper class or working class? Somehow, she was falling short of every class label in picture-perfect Switzerland.

The platform was crowded, people rushing past her for connections to Milan and Nice. The young couple who had been with her in the compartment pressed past her, still engaged in their lively conversation. Her eyes sought the Rogers' family, and she was glad to take one last glance at them some yards ahead of her. The children were still skipping happily at the side of their all-American socialite mother.

Esther loved the ambiance at the station, all doom and gloom evaporating in the upbeat calling of porters, the swishing of ladies' dresses and the melting pot of languages. She couldn't wait for what lay ahead of her. Her letters home would surely perk everyone up.

A solemn, stocky and short chauffeur wearing a black suit despite the heat and donning a black driver's cap on his raven-black hair was already hoisting her luggage into a Renault with Le Manoir in golden lettering on the front doors.

"Bonjour, Mademoiselle Weiss. I'm Filippo, your driver." He addressed her in a strong Italian accent while his busy hands were placing her belongings in the trunk. "Did you have a good trip? Vienna, I believe?"

His kind words made her feel at ease. She gave him another glance. He spoke with differential earnestness, but there was something about Filippo that didn't really match this subordinate attitude. She sensed a strength in him he'd rather stayed hidden, as if — under the circumstances — the aura of polite driver suited him best.

"Thank you, yes I have. It's beautiful here!"

"Wait till you see Lake Geneva, Mademoiselle. It's *bellissimo!*" He shut the boot lid with one hand and kissed the tips of his thumb and forefinger with the other. The gesture made Esther chuckle.

"You'll love it here! Mark Filippo's words!" He shot her an intense look with his dark brown eyes while he smiled, turning his entire face into a wrinkled mass. Esther had the eerie feeling he knew she was Jewish and the dramatic circumstances she'd left behind. It made his kindness all the more welcome.

"Hop in, Mademoiselle Weiss. Time for your new adventure."
There it was again. Filippo was rather too informal for his position
as chauffeur, but there was something touching and humane about
him that she liked.

"Thank you."

He held the back door open for her and she gratefully sank into
the soft upholstery of the back seat. The crème-colored leather was
warm from the sun, but the luxurious touch of smooth leather was
heaven nonetheless. As Filippo pulled out of the parking place,
Esther had her first glimpse of Lausanne. It looked wealthy, clean,
organized. Everything her heart yearned for. How good life would
be if her entire family could live here.

5

LE MANOIR

The afternoon poured down on Esther like liquid honey as she stood a little shaky after the long trip on the gravel court that led up to a square, white four-story building with rows of red and green awnings above every window. Doors and shutters were closed to keep out the heat. It was still in the courtyard, no voices, only the buzzing of honeybees and the slow ticking of the black Renault as the motor cooled off.

Down the sloped lawn at one side of the school, she caught a glimpse of glittering Lake Geneva with tiny waves lapping in the soft breeze. Across the lake, the Savoy Alps rose up from the water surface like massive giants dressed in a purplish haze of simmering sunlight and skittish shadows.

For a blessed moment Esther felt no heat or exhaustion. It was as if she'd arrived in paradise. This place, this school would offer her all she'd ever yearned for. Instant love and gratitude flowed through her. Mutti and Oma had not exaggerated.

Inhaling the clean air with big gulps, letting the tangy scent of pine needles and sweet alpine flowers caress her nostrils, her beauty-loving soul was replenished. Her eyes feasted on the pure meridian of the lake, the sloping veridian grass, the charming, white-stuccoed school building.

"Beautiful!" she exclaimed. The stocky Italian was busying himself with her luggage again but kept her in his sight with one vigilant eye.

"Oh yes, Mademoiselle, Le Manoir is pretty enough. And it has its perks."

The way he said it — a suppressed tinge of sarcasm in his clipped voice — gave Esther a feeling he wasn't as taken with the whole scenery as she was. She bit her lip.

"If only you knew where I come from, you wouldn't judge me," she thought, assuming Filippo had had quite enough of all the hoity-toity little madams who did nothing but treat him as dirt. She forced a smile, the way she'd been taught to treat everyone with dignity and not to overlook even the smallest kindness a servant offered her. But she was different now, probably different from the other girls, who still basked in their upper-class lives and hadn't had to endure living among Jew-hating people. To them she'd been equal to this chauffeur, or perhaps even less.

At that moment the large oak doors of the school building swung open, and the woman Esther supposed was Madame Paul Vierret stood in the opening, inspecting the scene on the gravel through her bejeweled spectacles. Esther gazed at the school director with breathless admiration.

Here was what one considered female perfection, style, poise, genteel expression. Every movement purposeful, every word no doubt spoken with clarity and command. She automatically straightened her own spine, painting the welcome smile she'd seen her mother exude to guests on her road-weary face.

The grand dame sailed toward her as if not touching the marble steps, the folds of her navy taffeta dress, complete with white collar and cuffs, swishing elegantly while her fashionable shoes crunched the gravel with measured steps. Madame's smile was just a slight upturn of mauve lips at the corners. A waist so slender she looked like a young girl. Sparkly blue eyes the color of celestite fixed Esther. The shine in those eyes was hard and demanding.

Should she walk toward her or stay where she was? What was more polite? Before Esther could decide, the woman was opposite her, pushing the spectacles that were attached to two strings of pearls higher on her nose.

"Mademoiselle Esther Weiss, welcome to Le Manoir."

"Bonjour Madame Vierret." Esther stretched out her gloved hand when she realized her mistake. The headmistress made a short "uh-uh" sound and shook the tightly-coiffed hair that ended in a light-brown coil at the nape of her neck. She raised a tapered forefinger with soft-mauve nail varnish the color of her lipstick.

"Lesson one, Mademoiselle Esther. Wait until the older person extends his or her hand." She frowned lightly, bringing two penciled eyebrows closer together over the celestite-blue gaze. "I'd expected your mother or grandmother to have already instilled this rule in you."

Esther wanted to admit her mistake, opening her mouth but realizing it would be considered rude to speak unless given permission. She felt her cheeks color. She'd wanted to do right by this schoolmistress but had already started off on the wrong foot.

Her hand was shaken, firm, cool and dry, no emotion, no warmth.

"Well, Mademoiselle Esther, it is customary for my students to call me Madame Paul, not Madame Vierret. I take it your family is well?" A hard look followed, which gave Esther a queasy feeling. What was she to say? How much did the Swiss know about the situation in Austria after the Anschluss? That it had been uneventful for most Austrians, satisfactory to the pro-Germans and a disaster to the Jewish minority?

"Yes," she replied hesitantly, "my mother and my grandmother send you their regards."

"Fine! Filippo, room six!" The majestic schoolmistress turned on her high-heeled shoes to give the chauffeur a curt nod. "Follow me!" she said to Esther.

Grabbing her handbag and taking off her straw hat, Esther followed Madame Paul up the steps, taking a good look at how she moved, straight back, only legs moving but torso kept still, a slight but not provocative swaying of the slender hips. Esther imitated her gait as best as she could but found it was much harder to do on her flat-heeled shoes. Thank God, she'd packed her engagement heels. She would wear them from now on every day. Even if that meant that they were worn by the time she'd be heading home and there would be no money for her wedding shoes.

"Of course, there will be money for my wedding outfit, silly," she reprimanded herself before letting go of her own thoughts and striding up the stone steps and into the cool school hall.

It was an immense auditorium, decked with a black-and-white marble floor and a huge mahogany staircase parting in the middle where it led to the upper floors. But Esther saw no students. Apart from a row of Greek and Roman busts on pillars, the hall was empty.

As if guessing her confusion, Madame Paul turned her long neck toward her as they walked up the stairs after Filippo's black suit with the luggage.

"The girls are engaged in their afternoon lessons. Your lessons will start tomorrow. I'll show you to your room."

"Thank you."

"We have one other new arrival today, an American girl. Mademoiselle Océane Bell. She will be your roommate."

"An American," Esther thought, "how exotic." A fast learner when it came to etiquette, she said nothing in reply to Madame Paul's announcement but showed her approval with the kind of curt nod that had been bestowed on the chauffeur. There were, of course, plenty of burning questions racing through her. What other nationalities could she expect, how many students?

"You'll meet the other girls during afternoon tea. Due to the pleasant weather, tea is served on the lawn. You'll have thirty minutes to freshen up, and then I'll send a girl to your room to escort you down."

She had that eerie feeling again that Madame Paul could read her mind.

All this information was showered on Esther while they reached the landing of the second floor and Madame Paul, not a drop of sweat despite the heat and the high-heeled climb, gyrated down a long corridor with identical teak doors on either side. There was no sign of Filippo, but Madame Paul opened the door with the number 6 copperplate.

"Voilà! You and Mademoiselle Océane will share this room. She'll be arriving from Paris on the evening train. So, you can choose which bed you want. I'll see you at teatime."

"Thank you, Madame Paul," Esther murmured as the striking navy figure of the headmistress strode back down the hall. Esther stepped into what would be her room for the next twelve months and looked around her.

It wasn't a very wide room but spacious enough to have two single beds on either side, tucked against the whitewashed walls. An armoire on each side. A small writing table with two chairs pushed against the window. In the middle of the table on a crocheted flower doily stood a slim vase with fresh alpine flowers. Their sweet scent filled the room and caressed Esther's sense of beauty and style.

Her suitcase and hatbox stood against the left bed, and she decided it would do for her. Putting her hat and gloves on the bed, she opened a door in the wall and saw it held a white-tiled bathroom with a tub, two wash basins with oval mirrors above them and a toilet. Soft white towels with Le Manoir embroidered in gold hung over a towel rack. Everything was spick-and-span, functional, logical. To Esther it was a sublime example of good taste. The sight of it soothed her tired eyes and the months of chaos she'd lived through.

Knowing she would have to hurry, she could not resist the urge to push open the shutters and look at the view. She drew in a hard breath.

"*Wunderschön!* How magnificent!" She had to press a hand to her mouth not to shriek out loud. She'd never seen a lake like this. It was so big that it was more like a sea than a lake, stretching out left and right and at least ten kilometers to the shore at the other end. The water was unusually blue and transparent, and subject to amazing fluctuations; the whole fluid surface was swinging rhythmically from shore to shore. It spoke to Esther's musical and fluid soul. It was impossible not to fall in love with Lake Geneva.

"If only I could come here for my honeymoon!"

To share this view with Carl, feel his arms around her, her head against his chest, still lovesick from their first night together with her stomach demanding coffee and fresh bread. Oh, the luxury, the singsong lullaby of satisfied love in soul and body.

In total captivation, she drank in the moving mass of water and felt as if it was enveloping her whole body as she sank into its cool, fresh caress, her skin still burning of passionate kisses. Esther had to clench her hands around the window railing not to jump into her swimming costume, race down the stairs and dive headfirst into the lake that would quench her passion, revive her senses.

But finishing schoolgirls didn't rush into water half-naked. Le Manoir would teach her how to peg these immature passions.

She could still yearn, in a subdued and civilized way. Tearing her attention from the alluring water, she looked at the mountain ridge across the lake. The purple-blue mountains were now in full view, and again the wildfire in her belly made her weak with longing. The mountains called to her as strongly as the lake. To walk there, all day, her hand securely in Carl's, picking fragrant flowers along the way, picnicking on a red-white checkered cloth and kiss and kiss and laugh without end. Esther felt her body tingle.

That life.

That was why she was here.

To make that possible.

Resolutely, she turned from the window to unpack and wash when she heard high-pitched voices below her. Unable to restrain her curiosity, she turned to the window once again and, hanging over the railing, peered down. Two girls, one with a short dark bob and one with a long chestnut ponytail, were spreading out a white tablecloth over a table that was set on the lawn. Two livered men hastened toward them to open the parasols that would provide the necessary shade. The girls were giggling, talking in rapid French.

Now invisible to her eye, but still chatting under the parasols, Esther rejoiced in their merry tones. Cooped up in the Prater Strasse family home for months, Esther's heart yearned for peers. It reminded her of her carefree years at the Wasagasse Gymnasium, her future still simple and straightforward.

"Discipline, Fraulein Weiss! Remember why you're here!" she scolded herself.

She quickly continued her unpacking, then went to the bathroom for a hasty wash. Her reflection in the mirror came as a shock. Normally round-faced with a healthy complexion, she saw she'd lost weight and that her skin was *grau* despite the lovely weeks of summer they'd had in Vienna during July. Her hair, usually a lush, ashen blond with natural waves, looked damp and out of shape. But the expression in her eyes made her frown the most.

"Our *Bärchen* has eyes the color of green diamonds, as rare and beautiful as her soul!" She heard her father's voice and peered again at her irises. It was true, had been true. Her green eyes were her most beautiful asset. But now? The sun hadn't shone in them for a long time, dimming her bright spirit. Dabbing her face dry with the embroidered guest towel, she promised herself to regain her spirit. Carl wouldn't want to marry a gray mouse.

Strengthened by her own determination, Esther returned to the bedroom to take off her travel suit and put on her best Robert Piquet dress, soft cream with black polka dots and a calf-length pleated skirt. She tightened the thin black belt around her slim waist and slipped into her engagement heels.

Then she sat on the bed and waited.

"Oh, how could I forget!"

Jumping up again, she retrieved Carl's gift from her handbag. Unwrapping the paper, she gazed down at their engagement photo as she had done the day before. Only now Carl wasn't with her. She caressed the glass with the tips of her fingers, especially his figure, dressed in a beautiful dark-gray suit, his tie immaculate, his hair immaculate, his face loving and august.

"Carl," she whispered, "I love you so."

The photo would get a prized position on her nightstand, facing her bed. Last thing at night and first thing in the morning, his smile would be for her.

REMEMBERING HER ELDERS' lessons, Esther walked confidently behind the young woman who'd fetched her to afternoon tea. She introduced herself as Lady Sable Montgomery.

Apart from stating her titled name — clearly on purpose — and her slight Scottish accent, Esther couldn't make out the doll-like creature. Affected, maybe spoiled, certainly not interested in German-speaking students. That was the vibe this raven-black haired sphinx gave off, but Esther addressed her in a friendly manner nonetheless.

"How long have you been here, Sable?" she asked, as they descended the mahogany stairs and were joined by more girls thronging around the British girl, who didn't even care to answer Esther's question.

"Come," Sable said hastily, "I'll show you the way to the garden." It was clear she wanted to have her escort job over and done with and link up with her own friends. Esther felt disappointed. Not a good start but luckily a new girl was arriving that evening, hopefully also without friends. And they were to be roommates. Her pride swallowed, she followed Sable's swaying hips in a tight black dress into the garden. The sun hit her with an unexpected intensity. She'd forgotten her hat and could hear her mother's voice: "Lesson one, Esther, never go out without your hat!"

Sable meanwhile pointed to one of the wicker chairs that stood around the long, half-laid table.

"You sit there."

Turning her back on Esther, Sable was already engaged in conversation with a group of five girls that closed around her.

"Huffy miss!"

Esther was the first and only one to sit down at the table.

A girl, long and slender as a poplar, was setting the table. She smiled in Esther's direction. One kind face, at least, was in this strange paradise. So far, they'd been hard to come by at Le Manoir. The tall girl, who despite her length, looked graceful and athletic, was limping slightly.

"Where are you from?" Her accent was one Esther didn't recognize.

"Vienna."

"Vienna?" the willowy girl replied in surprise. "Does Hitler still allow you to travel abroad?"

"Yes, why wouldn't he? Besides, he's in München."

"Okay!"

Nothing more followed as she measured the distance between the plates with a measuring tape, movements Esther followed with interest and made a mental note of her actions.

"Where're you from?"

"I'm Edda Van der Falck. From Holland. I'm a dancer. What's your name?"

"Esther Weiss."

"Are you Jewish?"

Esther nodded, feeling uncomfortable with her last name. It made Edda stare hard at her. Dark eyes with long lashes looking incredulous, a white porcelain plate between her long fingers.

"You don't look..."

"Jewish at all. I know," Esther sighed, "and maybe that's a good thing these days." She relaxed a little. "And you...you certainly look like a ballerina, but why are you limping?"

"I broke my ankle. Complicated fracture and needs a lot of rest, so I decided to take a break and come here just for the change. Almost done now and time to return to my ballet lessons."

Edda seemed nice, normal and outgoing. She could become a

friend. At least an ally. This was her opportunity to ask. "How is it here at Le Manoir?"

"It's okay," Edda shrugged. "As long as you stay away from the London and Paris dames."

"You mean like Sable?" Esther nodded to the giggling group at the edge of the lawn.

"Yes, them. All five of them. Sable, Julie, Margarita, Bella and Blanche. But Sable in particular. That one is bad business. I call them the 'titled bunch' though my family is probably more aristocratic than most of them. But Dutch nobility isn't as well-known, of course." Edda wrinkled her perfect nose. "The rest of them are sort of okay."

"How many girls are there?"

"About twenty, but it varies," Edda answered. She'd meanwhile finished setting the table and came to sit with Esther.

"Oh, and make sure to watch the Sphinx." Edda pushed a dark curl from her forehead, while her eyes spied toward the veranda.

"Who's the Sphinx?"

"Who do you think?" Edda giggled.

"Madame Paul?"

"Of course." Another snicker. "She'll be all manners and friendliness in your face, but it's only a thin veneer." Edda wrinkled her nose again, and Esther understood she did that when she disapproved.

Esther felt the hope in her heart sink, then reminded herself that this might just be empty gossip from a girl who was spiteful for not being part of the popular group. She straightened her back. She would do her best to be accepted by everyone. Especially by Madame Paul.

The subject of her thoughts came parading down the wooden steps of the veranda, with a throng of girls at her heels carrying tea pots and plates of sandwiches and cakes covered by glass bell jars. Suddenly Esther was ravenous, realizing she hadn't eaten since the breakfast in the Bern hotel.

Madame Paul threw her a quick look, unclear to Esther if it was approving or disapproving. No inquiry if she'd settled in all right. Instead, the impassive face with the glittering blue eyes turned to the girls carrying the trays of food and tea. The headmistress put her full attention to the placements on the table. Addressing Edda, the penciled eyebrows almost reached the schoolmistress's hairline.

"What have we forgotten!"

It wasn't a question, and the 'we' didn't mean Madame Paul was part of the equation. It was obvious why the students called her the Sphinx. She was unreadable. What she conveyed on the outside was incongruous with what lay underneath. Probably only God knew what Madame Paul kept hidden.

"I don't know, Madame Paul." Edda hesitated. "I followed the instructions on the table card. This was my first..."

Madame Paul snapped her fingers and Sable slid to her side.

"The flower bouquets, three in total," the British girl smirked. Edda mumbled a muffled *pardonnez-moi,* then seemed to remember something.

"But they weren't on the card, Madame."

"You should've asked me," Sable's haughty voice broke in. "You always consult with the more experienced students when doing a new task."

"What a strange pecking order," Esther thought, discomfort replacing her hunger.

Madame Paul concluded the so-called misunderstanding by repeating Sable's instruction in her clipped, neutral voice. The girls settled around the long table, each at their assigned place. Two girls Esther hadn't met yet, both looking uncomfortable and uncertain, started serving them, interrupted many times by Madame Paul's dissatisfaction with their handling of this important assignment.

Esther was aware the finishing school entailed every housekeeping chore possible, so also cooking and cleaning and serving meals. Her mother and grandmother were both almost religious about the mistress of the house having to do all the tasks, especially those she would never actually carry out herself.

One of Mutti's golden sayings was, "Better be prepared than sorry!"

Then Oma would compare it to all her son had to know about his profession. "Franz must know the origin and history of the gold and the gemstones before he can create the shiny, precious jewelry that the customers enjoy. It's not enough to know just the finished project; you have to know all that went into it."

That was all well and good, Esther pondered as she sunk her white teeth into a tiny beef sandwich without crusts and sipped her Earl Gray tea, but a good instructor was helpful and supportive. Madame Paul had probably grown tired and sour over the years. Or she enjoyed finding fault in others. Some people just did.

Used to drawbacks by now, Esther decided to learn fast to get even faster into Madame Paul's good books. It was clear how she'd get there. Befriend Sable, who was clearly her favorite.

Once, before her people had become the focus of mockery and disdain, Esther had been a popular girl herself. Her pretty face, good manners and excellent family relations had helped her both on the Alte Donau Schule and the first years at Wasagasse Gymnasium. She'd never had to beg for friendships or favors, and she intended to become that girl once again. Whatever the costs.

Directly after tea, Esther made sure she stayed in Sable's orbit, choosing her as her mentor for the ironing class, which was the last assignment for the day. Firmly deciding to not give up, she asked as they took one embroidered pillowcase from the pile.

"Have you been here long, Sable?" She didn't expect an answer but because it was only the two of them in the ironing room, the British girl wouldn't be able to ignore her for a whole hour.

Sable glanced at her sideways, a mischievous look in the light-blue eyes, which in an uncanny way resembled those of Madame Paul.

"You know what, Esther, I'll give you instructions on ironing, although by the looks of it, a chipper German girl like you knows more about ironing than me."

"I'm not German, I'm Austrian."

"Whatever!" Sable made an impatient movement with her manicured hand and sat herself in the windowsill. From her cardigan pocket, she retrieved a packet of Craven A and a silver lighter, then brought a tapered finger to her red painted lips.

"Not a word! We're not allowed to smoke in and around Le Manoir. Only hellish part so far. You do the ironing, I smoke. If you keep your little mouth shut, you and I are on a good footing."

"Sure," Esther shrugged. She didn't get the infatuation young women had with smoking but was glad to keep her own hands busy with her ironing job. Carefully pushing the heavy cast-iron iron with its wooden handle around the fine embroidery so as not to flatten it, she gave it all her attention. Esther loved this job and could have stayed at the ironing board all day. Anything that brought order and neatness brought her pleasure.

"To answer your question." Sable let a long swirl of gray smoke escape from both nostrils. "I've been here way too long. At first it was doable, certainly because of all the argle-bargle at home, my parents getting a divorce and Mummy subsequently being caught in the arms of a married admiral by the scandal sheets. Not the kind of exposure that's wanted for a marriageable girl with blue blood in her veins. As if I care two fiddlesticks about marriage. Fun with men, yes — marriage, no thank you!" Sable gave a scornful laugh, extinguished her cigarette on the windowsill and threw the stub out of the window.

"I'm sorry," was all Esther could offer. She felt inwardly relieved that Sable seemed to open up to her. "So, what do you not like about Le Manoir?"

Sable started pacing the room, her hands fisted in her cardigan pockets. She looked like a caged lion. Stopping abruptly in front of Esther's ironing board, she fixed her with those blue eyes.

"Just what I told you. No men to have fun with. At least not until the skiing season and we get some instructors who aren't at least one hundred years old like Monsieur Petrov and Monsieur Georges. I love kidding around in the snow with good-looking skiing instructors. I arrived in January of this year, so that was fun. Since then, it's been downhill."

Esther had meanwhile finished ironing the pillowcases and looked around for another task. Just then the door to the laundry room opened, and a spindly woman of about forty dressed in a dark dress with white apron entered the room. Sable jumped into action, pulling the pillowcases out of Esther's hands and storing them in the cupboard.

"We're doing fine, Mademoiselle Brunner," she cried in a rather shrill voice. The sudden change to subservient action by the haughty Brit confused Esther. So far, Sable had seemed unimpressed by authority. Mademoiselle Brunner sniffed.

"Who's been smoking here?"

"No one," Sable lied. "I smelled it too. Must be one of the garden boys down behind the bushes."

Mademoiselle Brunner, thin, stiff and upright, shoved her round glasses higher on her nose and went to the window to gaze down. Behind her back, Sable made a movement to Esther as if saying, "don't betray me." Her blue eyes flashed, and Esther saw what this girl was capable of. Her mother would say "*Eine menge Ärger.*" A whole lot of trouble.

"Mademoiselle Sable, can you wait outside the door while I make Mademoiselle Esther's acquaintance?"

"Biensûr!" Sable slipped out of the door, clearly relieved.

The thin woman turned to Esther, who still stood next to the cooling iron behind the board.

"So you just arrived today?"

"Yes, Ma'am."

"Good, let me see your work. As you may have understood, I'm the household teacher. That includes subjects like laundry, ironing, cleaning, polishing. I think these are the most important subjects any self-respecting mistress of the house must master."

"I agree!" Esther's enthusiasm was raised. "These are the subjects I really enjoy. Contrary to most girls, I suppose. I just love it when the house is clean and smells nice. There's nothing like the scent of fresh laundry, is there?"

"Really?" Mademoiselle Brunner eyed her with acorn-brown eyes from behind her spectacles. An almost invisible smile hovered around her thin lips. "Well, let me see what you've done as I don't suppose our little Miss Misfit has put her weight behind this."

Esther felt torn, split in her loyalties. It wouldn't be good for her to side with a teacher and snitch on another girl. Especially not now that she'd become a little closer to Sable in the past hour.

"Mademoiselle Sable showed me how to do the ironing. She was very helpful." Esther raised her voice, hoping she'd be heard on the other side of the door. Mademoiselle Brunner gave her a sharp look, then shrugged.

"That girl will meet her fate on the appointed day." The contempt in the teacher's voice made Esther cringe. Le Manoir was so different from what she'd expected it to be: a place where understanding and compassion would reign. It was the opposite. So far.

During dinner, Esther tried to catch Sable's eye but failed. For once the loud British girl was subdued and stared mostly at her food. Esther wondered if she'd been scolded for her behavior in the laundry room after all.

"Well, it's none of my business," she decided. "I haven't given her away. so she can't blame me."

After dinner, the girls had some free time to go for a walk or play a board game in the sitting room. As the evening was sultry and humid, Esther walked out on the veranda to go down the sloping lawn and to the lake shore. She hoped she would run into Edda, her best bet on friendship so far. Though she was really looking for Sable. The raven minx had fire, something Esther had to admit she secretly admired.

"No!" she said in her stern mother's voice. "Romy Gruber was enough trouble, but at least she had a good heart and matched you up with the right boy. From now on you befriend the good girls, Esther Weiss, not the wild ones!"

As Edda was nowhere in sight, Esther sauntered down to the

waterside, taking deep breaths of the soft air and the slight breeze on her bare arms. She suppressed an aching longing for home, for Carl as she sat down on a flat stone almost in the water. Taking off her white socks and flat shoes — the engagement heels were impractical outside — she dipped her feet in but instantly withdrew them. The water was icy cold! But she tried again and slowly eased her feet in again until they got used to the chill. Crystal clear, she saw the pebbled bottom and the reflection of her feet in the lapping water. Peace settled on her, the anxiety of living in Nazi-occupied Vienna slowly washing off her in Lake Geneva.

An immense red sun was fast sinking behind the mountain ridge, creating a palette ranging from deep purple to burning red to an almost deathly yellow. The whole vault was alight; breathtaking, beautiful, and bone-chilling in its fierce power.

Götterdammerung.

She didn't know where the thought came from, but it was as if God was putting the sky on fire as a warning to humanity.

"Hey, what you're doing here on your own?"

She instantly recognized Sable's upper-class voice. Esther didn't turn. She held her gaze fixed on the blood-red sky, which seemed more interesting than the new squabbles Sable was no doubt involved in. But a slight thrill went through her that Sable had sought her out.

Sable sat her slim behind down on the stone next to her. Her breath and skin smelled of expensive perfume and cigarette smoke. For a moment they sat side by side, worlds apart.

"I got caught." Sable reached for one of her cigarettes, lit it, inhaled deeply. The contradiction was striking was all Esther could think with a wryness that was new to her.

"I'm sorry." Level voice.

"Oh, I don't blame you, not directly that is. But it is *good* girls like you who ruin it for the rest of us." The stress on 'good' was strange, mocking, challenging. Esther refrained from answering. Sable smoked her cigarette while playing with the sash on her belted dress.

"Gosh, I'm bored," she yawned. "You don't play an instrument, by any chance?"

Esther brightened up. Music was her big love.

"I do. I play the piano and I sing."

"Exactly what we need!" Sable got up and, with her cigarette dangling from her red lips, grabbed both Esther's hands and pulled her to her feet. "I'm in no way a musician but I love dancing. Can you play modern tunes? Not just boring Mozart?"

Esther had learned to put her heart and soul into loving Mozart but let it pass. The prospect of making music again was so exciting.

"Is there a piano here? I haven't seen one?"

"Of course, silly! There's a whole music room with even a theatre with stage. We're supposed to act and sing and dance like the hussies Madame Paul looks down on with a vengeance. Come now!"

Sable let out a strange, high-pitched laugh. Esther wasn't sure this was a good plan. Everything seemed so structured at Le Manoir. Were they allowed to just go into the music room and play as they liked? But she felt a shiver of delight.

"I'm not sure," she said hesitantly. "It's been a long day and maybe my roommate has arrived."

"Don't be a spoilsport, Weiss. Do you want to hang out with me and the girls, or do you rather prefer that cripple De Vries?

"I do," Esther wanted to say, feeling hurt by Sable's cruel words on behalf of the Dutch girl but said nothing in her defense.

"All right," she agreed, "one song and then I'm going to my room."

"Do you play Jazz? Benny Goodman? Sing, Sing, Sing?" Sable was already swinging her slender hips provocatively.

"Of course, I love it! I might need sheet music, though, as it wasn't what I generally practiced." She was still of two minds about this new prank.

"Come, quick, before Madame Paul sees us. I know a safe route." She grabbed her hand and didn't let go as they skittered to the school's back entrance.

"But you said..."

"Shh... never mind. The girls are all waiting. It's a surprise."

An unpleasant feeling rose in Esther's stomach. What was this girl up to? But then, angry with herself for her suspicion, she followed the dark-haired beauty through the back corridor until they came to a brown door with the words Music Room & Theatre on the copper plate.

After spying around her, Sable opened the door. She pushed Esther in front of her and quickly closed the door behind them. They found themselves in a large, dusky room. The velvet curtains were drawn and only a couple of small lamps along the walls were lit. A grand piano stood close to the elevated stage that was also closed with burgundy red curtains. Esther had the uncanny feeling they weren't supposed to be here at all, but Sable gave her no time to turn around. Waving to her friends who stood clustered in a small group near the front row of chairs, they came nearer. Soft giggles and much poking of each other's ribs.

"She's doing it!" Sable resolutely went up to the grand piano and opened the lid. Then she ruffled through the sheet music that lay in a neat pile on top of the piano. The pile was instantly trans-formed into a mess with several sheets floating to the floor. Esther bent to pick them up, but Sable hissed,

"Let them be. The music teacher Monsieur Grimaldi will see to that. Now sit. Here it is."

Sable placed the sheet on the stand and backed away from Esther, who sat herself on the plush seat of the rectangular piano stool. A Steinway. Her favorite. Behind her, the girls fell silent. Esther was unfamiliar with the music at first but quickly read through the first sheet. She saw she could play it.

Her slender fingers landed on the keys, and she was gone. She loved to play classical music but any music rippled through her soul. In fact, this was better than Bach or Chopin. This was modern and alive. Esther felt a wildness in her soul, her whole musical being coming alive. Unaware of anything that went on around her she played and played, euphoria mixing with a deep sense of contentment.

"What do you think you're doing!?"

The voice didn't yell, wasn't even raised, but the undertone was thunder as the lid came down on her fingers and Esther screamed in pain.

"Ouch!"

Madame Paul's blue eyes shot icicles of anger!

"What do you think you're doing?"

"Madame..." she stammered, "the girls..."

"What girls?"

Esther turned around but the front row of seats was empty. They had secretly left.

"There is no music after dinner, Mademoiselle Esther. I have no idea how you landed here and decided to play this awful racket, but it's strictly inappropriate. I will never want to see this kind of free-thinking behavior from you again. Do you understand?"

Esther stared down at her red fingers where the lid had hit her hard. Then to the strewn papers on the floor. She'd clearly been set up. Tears welled in her eyes, of frustration and anger.

How mean! What a low thing to do.

"I'm so sorry, Madame Paul. It will not happen again."

"It had better not, Mademoiselle! Now clear this mess and go to your room. I'll see you tomorrow at breakfast. Don't leave your room again."

"No, Madame Paul, I won't."

Through her tears, Esther collected the music sheets as best she could and put them back on the piano. Madame Paul was already at the door waiting to turn off the lights. Esther slipped past her, wondering how in this labyrinth she would find the way back to her room.

"Straight ahead, go through that door and you'll find the back-stairs to the floors." Madame Paul went the other way, leaving Esther to find her own way. As she opened the door and saw the stairs, she heard snickering from somewhere in another room. Her shoulders hunched. She felt so humiliated and so unprepared now to meet her roommate. What would the American girl think if she saw her like this, in tears, being reprimanded sternly when all she wanted was make a good impression on everyone.

Crying, she went up the stairs and stood in front of room 6. She didn't know if she should knock or just walk in. All the rules were muddled in her head now, and she wished she'd never left her beloved family in their fragile situation to come to this unfriendly school.

Esther had never felt more alone and more miserable in her whole life.

6

FRIENDS

Esther pressed down the door-handle and stepped inside the room. She tried hard to suppress her tears. Through them, she saw a slender dark-haired girl seated on the bed opposite hers. The look in her hazel eyes was one of surprise, then consternation. Before Esther could say anything, she'd leapt up from the bed, swift as a hind and stood before her, almost an inch shorter than Esther.

"What's going on? Sorry, I'm Océane Bell. Why are you crying?"

Esther was too distraught for words, though she picked up on the sincerity of the girl's concern. Retrieving a handkerchief from her sleeve, she attempted to stem the flow of tears that kept welling up. It was as if all her burdens were suddenly too heavy.

"I'm sorry," she sniffed, "I didn't want to upset you, but I had nowhere else to go. I'm Esther, by the way." Océane stretched out her slim hand with long fingers and shook hers. The crying somewhat subsided. Still holding her hand, the girl led Esther to the bed she'd been sitting on and sat down with her. Esther suddenly felt protected and safe with this stranger, who spoke French with a strong American accent, and seemed as lovely as the day herself.

Esther thanked God for this friendliness. As only God knew how much she needed it.

"Tell me what happened. I've got a minute before I'll have to go down to supper."

Esther's shoulders stopped shaking, and the tears dried up. She really didn't want to come across as a milksop to this new girl, who — though petite and looking tired — seemed to have a reservoir of power inside of her that Esther felt she totally lacked at the moment. And she also didn't want Océane to get the idea Le Manoir wasn't pleasant and instructive. Her bad luck didn't need to carry over to her new roommate.

While still doubting whether she would tell Océane the truth or make up a story of being suddenly homesick, Esther heard the girl next to her mutter.

"Well, I can always leave, can't I? It's not like they can keep me here against my will. I'll just get hold of a telephone somewhere and tell Maxipa to come and fetch me. No one in my family would want me to suffer here."

Esther stopped crying, tried to smile. Maxipa was probably her father. But weren't her parents in the States? Well, what did she know? To make contact and to assure Océane life wasn't as bad here as this, she sniffled and shared her story.

"I just arrived in Switzerland this afternoon. I'm also not sure whether I should have come. After the Anschluss in March, and with the Nazis all over Austria, my country hasn't been the same anymore. Life for us Jews is getting more and more complicated. I was worried about leaving Mutti and Papi and ... of course ... my fiancé Carl."

Esther's eyes went to her nightstand. A strange, squeaky sound escaped from her throat but before she could say anything, Océane jumped up to open the drawer of Esther's nightstand.

"Don't worry, Esther, it's here. Madame Paul said we can't have pictures of men standing around, but she will not take it away from you. Just keep it hidden in your drawer."

Esther took the photo frame from her and stared down at it.

Carl. He seemed so far away after only one day. Her whole Viennese life swallowed up, as if it was a different epoch. She stroked the glass. *Homesick.* Yes, she was homesick, even though Océane seemed nice and understanding. Sinking down on the bed, Esther mused she didn't recognize herself like this. Things were supposed to turn out for the better here, not worse.

They both remained silent until Océane asked in a soft but demanding voice, "What happened just then? What made you cry?"

Esther looked up from the photo, tearing herself away from the past. She saw compassion in the hazel eyes, and something very grown up that she, Esther, apparently lacked. But then, this girl had traveled half the world on her own. Of course, she was as mature as a grown-up. Putting the photo back in the place ordained by Madame Paul, she folded her hands in her lap.

"Madame Paul wasn't entirely friendly when I arrived. How was that for you?"

"Same here," Océane grumbled, "but she will not see me in tears. I swear that much."

"I usually am not a crybaby myself," Esther assured her. "But it wasn't Madame Paul who sent me over the edge. It was the other girls."

"What did they do to you?"

"I ... I don't know if they do it to all the newcomers, you know, make them do things that are forbidden just to make Madame Paul lash out at you. Well, at least you are warned by what they did to me." Esther sighed, fighting the brimming tears once again. "I so much wanted to come here. Both my mother and my grandmother did their year at Le Manoir before they married. It is like a tradition in my family. My mother was here before Madame Paul took over; it was during the First World War. Strange to think schools like this just continued, but Switzerland stays neutral in any war. My parents wanted me to come so I can be a good wife and proper hostess when I marry Carl. Viennese and international relations are important to us. So, I hoped I wouldn't make mistakes, and train for the same impeccable reputation my mother and grandmother have."

Hearing herself say these things, Esther hesitated, doubting whether this was really what she wanted, now that the first cracks had shown. And why was she telling it all to this stranger, who might not be waiting for a heart-to-heart?

Océane made an impatient movement with her hand. "Go on!"

"I never talk that much about myself. It's not appropriate. I'm sure I'm boring you and sound biased. Well, that's why I'm here, I guess."

"Oh, fiddlesticks," Océane exclaimed. "I like you already, but just quickly tell me what the girls did before I go down and they start grilling me, too."

"Well, after dinner one of the English girls, Sable is her name, asked me if I played an instrument, so I said yes, the piano, and then they asked me to play something for them. I thought it was an innocent request, and I wanted to be liked. So, I started playing a jazz piece by Benny Goodman and got really carried away but ... but suddenly Madame Paul stormed in and banged the lid shut on my hands, and looked at me with those queer eyes.

"She kept repeating, 'What do you think you're doing?'

"Well, how was I to know? The girls had quietly left while I was playing, so they were in the clear. Then she said in that slow, deliberate tone of hers, 'There-is-no-playing-on-the-piano-after-dinner.' I felt mortified, not so much by her reprimand but because Sable and her friends had clearly set me up. It was mean. They knew the rules, of course. They've been here much longer. Now my first impression on Madame Paul is not a positive one, when I thought I was doing something nice, you know, to entertain them."

Without a second thought, Océane fumed, "Bullies! They're just bullies. It's good that you've warned me. How mean. Well, I'm glad Madame Paul put us new girls together so we can have each other's back. Shall we enter a pact? I used to do that in college with my best friend Eliza, and it always worked. Two are stronger than one."

Bullies? Esther shifted easily on the bed. She'd not thought of

Sable and her friends as bullies, but the word left a bad taste in her mouth, and a vague remembrance of something, she didn't know what.

Esther felt a need to quickly change the subject. "You went to college? You mean like university? Heavens, you must be smart." She instantly disliked that addition. She could have, too, if she'd wanted and the Nazis hadn't thrown a spanner in the wheels. Océane shrugged off the compliment.

"It's not important right now; I'll tell you all about it later. So, do you want us to be friends and stick up for each other?" Esther wondered what the impatient look in the hazel eyes meant but she nodded, still wanting to know all about college in the United States. It sounded so exotic. It quite took her out of her own misery.

"So, what did you study? Now I take a closer look at you, I can see you look very learned indeed."

"Horsefeathers!" Océane frowned, waving a dismissive hand as Esther giggled at the quaint expression.

"Now tell me!"

"Okay." Océane sighed, clearly not comfortable with the conversation. "I prepared for medical school at Radcliffe in Boston, but I came here because I'm not sure I want to be a doctor anymore. I'd much rather paint. Now you know!" She looked relieved at the intervention of a rap on the door, and a female voice called, "Mademoiselle Océane!"

As Océane made for the door, Esther said, "Thank you. We'll be great friends. I know it."

Whatever it is she's preoccupied with, I'll help her, she mused.

As Océane prepared for going downstairs, putting on a white blouse and buttoning it up, she mimicked Madame Paul's self-aggrandizing voice. "By the way, dear girl, I much prefer you call me OC instead of Mademoiselle Océane."

A freeing giggle escaped from Esther's throat, the first time she could laugh that long first day at Le Manoir.

After Océane was gone, Esther lay down on her bed for a good thinking. Her heart was in turmoil, her thoughts jumpy as toads in a thunderstorm. The word bully buzzed unpleasantly in her head.

Breathe, Esther, breathe!

A flashback of sunlight, summer in Vienna, so much light!

Esther's breath quickened, not knowing where that flash of light came from. Her throat always contracted when she was afraid. And the truth *was* she was afraid. Of Madame Paul, of Sable and her gang, of her Jewish background.

"Fear is a bad advisor." One of her father's sayings. The thought of her brave father with his round cheeks and positive outlook on life galvanized her. She was a Weiss; she could do it. With this, Esther fell asleep.

The next morning, she woke to playful sunlight peeping through the lattice work of the shutters, making zebra-like, dancing marks on the walls. She heard the down-slurred, burry and nasal call of birds in flight, terns or gulls, she didn't know but it reminded her of the seaside trip to Heiligendamm on the Baltic Sea when she'd been eight. The white town on the sea had enchanted her. And now again she was at the waterside, although it was a lake, but a lake as large as a sea. Lucky girl! No *grau* and black Nazi uniforms, no barking orders, no fear.

Fear mixed with anger.

Esther rubbed her eyes and turned to face the other bed. Océane was still sleeping, one slender brown hand under her oval face. The dark lashes and eyebrows in perfect composure.

She looks more Jewish than I do, Esther thought. *Well, maybe she is. I will ask her.*

Before Hitler rose to power and started accusing the Jews of all things that went wrong in Germany and abroad, being Jewish had never been a big deal to Esther. Her family wasn't strictly religious. Naomi would've preferred more religious rituals in the Weiss house, but Papi was a 'liberal' as he called it. They observed the Sabbath, of course, and adhered to Kosher rules but that was about it. Her parents had occasionally worshipped at the Leopoldstädter

Tempel, but after it was destroyed in the Kristallnacht, they'd given up going to the synagogue.

Esther shook herself from her spiraling thoughts about home. Océane awoke, stretched and said in a long-drawn yawn, "Well, that was interesting at supper yesterday. You said you were sort of harassed by a girl called Sable?"

"Not really harassed, just bullied," Esther corrected as she slipped into her dressing gown to go to the bathroom.

"I overheard a conversation a British girl — I assume it was Sable — and another girl were having."

Esther turned, curious to hear what Océane had picked up.

"You may not be punished after all, Esther. Sable whispered that Madame Paul knew they'd set you up, and that they had to be more careful. Apparently, Sable's family donated a lot of money to Le Manoir, and Madame Paul wants to stay in the girl's parents' good book by educating their daughter properly. If ever that's going to be possible," Océane added with a sneer. "One look at the girl, and you know she's trouble with a capital T. Too good looking, too sure of herself, too spoiled."

"So what happened?" Esther urged.

"Not sure, but she'll probably be taken down a peg from now on."

"Good!"

Esther instantly felt better. Océane's support shored her confidence.

Getting ready for the first day of lessons was something Esther looked forward to. And she wasn't disappointed. It was an etiquette lesson by the Russian teacher Monsieur Petrov, a studious, serious professor in an immaculate three-piece suit, complete with stiff upturned collar, bowtie and lace pocket square. His enormous moustache and side whiskers in a narrow white face, short-cut hair and bulging blue eyes behind a pince-nez reminded Esther of the strict Hungarian grammar schoolteacher she'd had at Wasagassa Gymnasium, who'd apparently been a famous romantic poet in his spare time. Herr Benó.

But Monsieur Petrov's behavior was not at all like the Calvinist teacher with the romantic heart. Monsieur Petrov wore his heart on his sleeve, but in a cute, animated and amiable way. He clapped his petite hands enthusiastically and chirped in French that was heavily Russian accented.

"Demoiselles Esther and Océane, come forward please, and you, too, Mademoiselle Edda. I'm going to use you as guinea pigs, but don't worry — you'll be the cutest little pigs in the universe."

All the girls laughed except for Sable, who snorted something like, "Pigs for sure!"

Esther, with Océane at her side, stepped forward into the open space in the middle of the room. She looked toward the Dutch girl, who graciously came toward them, her limp almost invisible. Esther was glad she and Océane were in it together. Monsieur Petrov might seem nice enough, but her encounter the night before with Madame Paul in the music room still lingered in the back of her mind. And she felt Sable's catlike gaze on her.

She heard Monsieur Petrov say, "Okay, Mademoiselle Edda, you know the routine. Show it to the new girls."

"Sure, Monsieur Petrov, with pleasure." Edda made a slight bow toward the Russian teacher and, very straight-backed and with her elegant ballerina movements, went over to a stack of books that lay on the table while Monsieur Petrov put Bach's Adagios on the record player. Edda moved to one side of the room. She balanced the five books on top of her head, waited for the music to start and slowly, steadily walked across the room, straight as a lily on its stem and with a grace that made all the girls in the room hold their breath.

At the end of the room, she took the books from her head, made another bow for Monsieur Petrov and handed the books to Esther. Monsieur Petrov clapped his hands again.

"Bravo, bravo! That's how it's done. Remember, dear girls, grace *can* be learned and is a lady's greatest asset, especially..." He wagged his finger at them while his signet ring flashed in the electric light. "Especially in the face of danger! And that also holds good for men, but I'm not teaching men here. However, it was grace and good manners that helped me out of Russia when the Bolsheviks took over in 1918. Nothing else. I may have lost my estate, had all my belongings in one small suitcase, but I walked to the Moscow Kiyevskaya railway station to get on the train to Warsaw with my head held high and my manners intact. So, this is lesson one, new demoiselles. Walk straight, even when we increase the weight of gravity. Your turn, Mademoiselle Esther."

Esther felt all eyes on her as she took the books from Edda, who mouthed, "You'll do fine!"

She took her position at the end of the room and tried to place the books on her head, but they slipped to the floor immediately with a loud thud.

"Sorry," she murmured, and heard Sable and her friends snicker. With more anticipation, she picked up the heavy volumes and this time held onto them as she placed them on her head.

"That's right," Monsieur Petrov encouraged her, "hold onto them the first time. You'll get the hang of it. Don't worry."

Esther stepped forward gingerly at first, but then more boldly, and halfway across the room slowly let her arms sink. Bach gave her the confidence, the music and the top of her head the only concentration.

"A natural! Just practice, practice, practice!" Monsieur Petrov exclaimed in his peculiar French with the trilled R's and soft consonants, remnants of his Slavic background. Esther beamed. Such praise on her first assignment. She suddenly felt much lighter as she watched Océane struggle through the assignment with exasperation.

"I will help you with this assignment," she whispered to Océane, who stood panting next to her. But her friend seemed less assured as she hissed in Esther's direction, "I've never experienced a more nonsensical exercise in my life."

Esther adored the etiquette lesson and Monsieur Petrov. Shaking hands in the correct way, how to hold a wineglass, opening your napkin. It came all easily to her. Mutti and Oma had been Le

Manoir examples and taught her these simple, yet elegant gestures from the time she still wore pigtails. And yet to see them explained by the exotic epitome of etiquette was sheer delight. Ignoring the grumbling and snickering around her, she lapped it all up. They would be so proud of her back home.

After lunch, Edda came toward her in her ballet-like gait, feet slightly turned outwards, smooth and beautiful.

"You're all right?" Her singsong voice was kind. Esther nodded.

"I heard about the prank Sable and her sort played on you. Well, you learned your lesson, I guess. I had to learn it the hard way as well." Then Edda's face fell.

"I'm here to say goodbye. I'm leaving on the night train. Back to Amsterdam. Been given a unique opportunity to train with Martha Graham, who'll be in Holland this fall. Though I'm classically trained, as a modern dancer she's been my idol since I was in first grade."

Esther nodded again, swallowed. Edda would've been a good friend, but it was not to be. At least, she had Océane.

"Will you look out for yourself?" Edda asked, "I'm glad you and OC have become friends so quickly. She's a tough cookie, just like you. I hope you'll both give these bullies a taste of their own medicine one day. I never got the time to confront them, but you will!"

Esther smiled. Edda was fiery. But she was right. Sable's actions shouldn't continue to go on unanswered, but confronting her would be dangerous as she was Madame Paul's favorite.

"I'll miss you, Edda."

"Same here. I would've liked to get to know you better. Here." She took a small notebook from the pocket of her linen dress and ripped out a blank page. Esther saw it was strewn with well-drawn ballet poses. Edda apparently was a bit of an artist as well. She scribbled an address on the torn piece of paper and handed it to Esther.

"In case you're ever in Holland."

"Thank you. Let me give you mine, though I wouldn't advise

you to travel to Vienna right now." She wrote down her address on another torn sheet.

"God forbid, these Nazis stay in power for long," Edda agreed. "Anyway, do write to me about your adventures here."

"I will."

They stood. Unsure how to say goodbye. Then Edda opened her slender, elegant arms and Esther walked into her embrace. Though slim, almost bony as a hazel-twig, Esther felt the dancer's formidable strength and warmth, drinking it in gratefully. Friendship between women, so precious and unparalleled.

But Océane was still here. Esther would manage. Focus on the lessons.

7

DOWN THE SLOPE

St Moritz, January 1939

"I truly didn't know you were such a tremendous skier!" The admiration sparkled in Océane's hazel eyes. Esther beamed from head to toe from her friend's compliment.

"I think it is my absolute favorite pastime." They were seated next to each other on the wooden boardwalk, unlacing their ski boots. Their cheeks were red with exertion and cold. A low sun sunk down the ridge of the Piz Nair, quickly bringing the ice-cold of the evening. Lake Moritz lay like a large frozen plaque at the edge of the glaciated valley of the Upper Engadine.

The Manoir students had traveled to the ski resort for a week's lessons. But it was considered a vacation as there were no formal classes. Esther was the only one with Alpine experience and had been asked to show her skills by the instructors several times — two handsome young men with impressive, muscled bodies and a keen interest in the young females. It led to much giggling and flirting on both sides.

While Esther got out of her outdoor equipment, much faster than the others, she babbled on in a cheerful voice.

"I wanted to compete in the Alpine World Ski Championships in 1934, but unfortunately I was too young. I so wanted an Austrian skier to win, but it was only Germans and Swiss. Still, Christl Crantz won silver at that competition and has been dominating the skiing scene since. She's my absolute heroine. I don't think I'll be allowed to compete anymore though, — you know, as a Jew and because I'm getting married..."

Océane was staring at her frozen laces while her numb fingers struggled to untie them.

"Let me help you; I've done it hundreds of times." Esther sank on her knees in the snow and unlatched the laces in no time, while Océane blew on her blue-white fingers.

"I'm not sure I'm that keen on skiing," she admitted. "It's damn cold, and I think I've fallen at least half a dozen times. My body is black and blue."

"You'll learn. Give it some time."

Esther wanted Océane to love winter sports as much as she did. As long as she was the only girl adept at it, she had only the instructors to fly down the slope with. It was fun, but she'd much rather have Océane with her and let the instructors dally with Sable and her group. The attention she got from the handsome Swiss males only led to more scorn from the "titled bunch."

As they were about to clear their equipment and head to the warmth inside, a loud scream echoed between the mountains. At the same moment, a form flashed past them heading in the wrong direction, straight down the slope that was already disappearing in dusk. Esther quickly scanned the yard and saw the instructors had seen it as well, and put their skis back on in a hurry.

"Something is wrong."

Both she and OC said it at the same time. Esther was already lacing up her snowshoes again and slipped into her skis, clicking them in their slots. As she grabbed her ski poles, she realized she was even faster than the instructors.

"Someone went down; I think it's one of us!" she yelled over her shoulder, garnering speed.

Gerry, whose real name was Gerhard, came alongside her. He'd switched on the safety lamp on his forehead. So had Bernt, instructor number two, who stayed slightly behind them. Esther had no lamp.

"You sure you want to do this, Miss? Bernt and I can manage together," Gerry cried to her. Esther knew he knew the answer. Three people could do more in this treacherous territory, especially if the person down there was wounded, or worse.

"I can do it, don't worry."

The lamplight showed the reverence on his face. "All right. Bernt, are you okay with Miss Esther accompanying us?"

"I think Miss Esther's an even better skier than I am," Bernt answered, "so yes. We might need her help."

"Okay, then go first, Miss. That way, we'll shine the way for you."

She did as she was told, feeling the cold wind hit her face while she peered ahead in the glow of two weak yellow lamps. "What if she's hit an avalanche?" she cried back.

"Not a big chance of avalanches in Upper Engadine this time of year. She can't be that far."

They went down another mile, trying to see as much as they could in the enveloping darkness of the falling night.

Esther spotted her, a little black clump almost covered by snow. Before she even reached the girl, she knew it was Sable. For Heaven's sake, what had she been thinking? She could hardly stand on two skis, let alone go out on her own after the lessons were done.

Bringing her skis to a halt near the still figure, Esther called out to the men. It wasn't needed, as they were right behind her.

"Her head's crashed against a rock."

Quickly unclicking her skis in the narrow spot, Esther ran to her, slipping over the snow on her unpractical snowboots. "Sable," she cried, "are you okay?"

Of course, she wasn't!

The men had also stepped out of their skis, and all three went down on their knees around the unconscious girl. Esther gently shook Sable's shoulder.

"It's Miss Sable, isn't it?" Gerry's voice was emotional. He'd showed quite a liking for the raven-haired Brit in the past days. It was Sable who'd baptized him Gerry instead of Gerhard.

To everyone's relief, Sable opened her eyes and started wailing. Her helmet was askew on her head and blood was dripping on the snow. Not to scare her, Esther said as gently as she could, "Gerry and Bernt are here, and we'll get you back to the hotel. Don't worry."

Her real thoughts were, *how on earth are we going to lift her up this steep mountain when it's already completely dark?*

Gerry eased off her helmet, which made Sable shriek like a wounded pig. "I'm sorry, Miss, but we have to make sure we can still take it off before any swelling. Bernt, give me a light."

Esther felt in her pocket and found some soft mints. It wasn't much, but it might perk Sable up, just enough. Bernt retrieved a first-aid kit from his rucksack and fed her some water and aspirin, while Gerry made a quick inspection of the extent of her wounds.

"Probably concussion, Miss, and a cut above the eye. But nothing too serious, I'd say. You've been lucky we saw you disappear. A couple of hours in this cold, and it would be a totally different story."

"What were you thinking, Miss, going down the hill like this after the lessons? Putting us all in danger now?"

Bernt was clearly not as understanding as his colleague, and Esther couldn't help thinking he was right. She was not only putting herself in danger with this action, but all of them. The trek to the plateau where the hotel was located was steep, and it would take them a long time to get there under treacherous circumstances. Sable's teeth clattered, and at first she couldn't utter a word.

"I read... I read a novel where the heroine was saved by her skiing instructor. I never... never intended..." She looked helplessly at Esther. The young men both frowned. This was serious; it held nothing romantic or fictional. Esther felt them both tense, their professionalism put in jeopardy. She tried to soothe the foolish girl.

"You'll be okay, Sable. We'll start carrying you to safety now. Just never... ever..."

"...do something so stupid again!" Bernt roared, "You could have had us all killed! You still can!"

Sable began to sniffle, both from shock and reaction to the instructor's anger.

"I'm so... so... sorry."

Bernt barked instructions while Gerry loosened a dark lock of Sable's hair that had stuck in the bloody wound. There was gentleness in his touch, which seemed to soothe Sable as she stopped sniffling.

"We'll have to climb our way to the top, so we can't use our skis. I'll carry them. Gerry, you carry the Miss. Esther, you lead the way with my lantern. We'll change roles halfway."

Without further ado, they followed Bernt's instructions and Sable had her romantic moment after all as Gerry hoisted her in his arms. But she winced as her head rested against his chest. Esther took a deep breath. It was a steep trek, devious and dangerous. What had she gotten herself into, racing downhill like this?

But then she heard Bernt say softly behind her, "We mountain people are survivors, Miss Esther. Come. Pull *tout courage* together and make the climb of your life."

His words gave her heart. She went first, finding steady places on the perilous surface, glad it was not the usual skiing track so they could climb in soft new snow. At least her soles had a grip on the snow. They made slow progress. Nobody talked. High above them twinkled the electric lights of the ski resort and the lighted front of Badrutt Palace Hotel where they were staying. It seemed so far away still, with the four of them vulnerable and exposed to the cold Swiss night. An arduous trek ahead.

They trudged on and on, sometimes slipping back and losing their footing for a moment. Then what Esther feared happened. It started to snow. First, just thin flakes whirling around them, but soon an incessant white curtain came down from the black sky. She could hardly see a hand in front of her eyes.

"You're okay, Miss?" She heard one of the instructors call to her but hardly had breath to answer. She managed a squeaky, "Yes."

Yet, she was the one responsible for finding and keeping them on some sort of path with her light.

"Please keep running, dry cell battery," she prayed, as now and then the light flickered and fell away. Gazing upward for the hundredth time, fear tightened her chest as she could hardly see the lights of St Moritz through the heavy snowfall. With no idea how the men and Sable behind her were doing, Esther gritted her teeth and clambered on.

"Please let us make it!" Prayer seemed the only solace. And then something curious happened. A deadly calm settled on Esther. She became bold and strong-willed, remembering she was a Weiss. Not just from a long lineage of strong souls, but also a kid of the mountains. Of course, they would make it. She would see to it. This thought gave her new energy. Placing her feet higher and higher, listening intently if the men were following her but not looking backward so as not to lose her balance, she finally, finally saw the lights through the snow again only one hundred feet above them.

"Almost there," she cried triumphantly.

"Watch out!" Bernt behind her bellowed, and then she saw it. Other black figures came down the slope, creating a minor avalanche. She stepped aside just in time, directing the others with her.

"We're here to help!" voices cried out. "What happened?"

"Help!" Esther cried through frozen tears. "We're saved."

Ten minutes later, Sable was hauled onto a stretcher and Océane was by the wounded girl's side. Feeling her pulse as the doctor-in-training ran alongside the stretcher, she shouted, "Vital functions all right!"

"We'll take Miss Sable to Doctor Buch in the village and have her examined. Someone take care of Miss Esther. She did an amazing job but may suffer from shock and hypothermia." It was Bernt's stern voice, directing attention to the shivering Esther.

"I'm fine, don't fuss over me. Look after Miss Sable first." But she gladly took Océane's hand and let herself be led into the warm, brightly lit hall of the posh Swiss hotel. Her knees felt tired and weak, but her cheeks shone. She saved a human being. Well, had helped saving her. Sable Montgomery of all people.

Someone pushed a cup of hot cocoa in her hand, and someone else put a warm blanket around her shoulders. Océane never left her side, anxiously asking every few minutes, "Are you sure you're okay? Should we get you to a doctor, too?

Though her teeth chattered and her whole body was numb, Esther felt exhilarated by what she had accomplished, so she just nodded as she sipped the sweet, hot beverage and let someone take her heavy shoes off her frozen toes.

"You're so brave." Océane squeezed her hand. At that moment, Signora Peccine, their gymnastics teacher who had accompanied the girls to the ski resort, hastened into the hotel lobby.

"Dear girl!" She exclaimed rushing toward her. "I guess I should actually reprimand you for such a rash decision, but I can't! You saved the poor girl's life. I was just on the phone with Madame Paul. She asked me to tell you that she's impressed by your swift action. And so am I. I've been told by Doctor Buch that Mademoiselle Sable will be okay. Diagnosis is a concussion and a nasty cut. That's all. The reprisals for her brash behavior will follow, but I would not be surprised if she will be expelled from Le Manoir. It's not the first time Mademoiselle Sable has caused trouble, but it might well be the last time."

The avalanche of words that poured out of the small mouth of their Italian teacher never seemed to cease, and her disclosures were always too honest and out of line. But Esther didn't care, not what would happen to Sable and not what this flibbertigibbet signora prattled. All she wanted was a hot bath and sleep. And maybe a big plate of potatoes, Sauerkraut and Cervelat.

Esther slept like a rose, dreaming of white snow and swishing wind, her skis her best friends, and the slope her Elysée. Winter was made for Esther. She thrived in it.

Cold was her partner.

8

THE DREAM STOLEN

April 1939

I t was a bleak morning in April. A thick mist enveloped the Jura Mountains. Lake Geneva had turned to a black sheet of wet fog. A distant ship blew its horn, low and long. Invisible from the shore, it sounded like a foretoken of doom.

Le Manoir, a building constructed in the 1850s, had only recently had central heating installed on the ground floors where the schoolrooms and community spaces were situated. The dorms were still heated with electric fires that seemed inadequate all the time. Esther was used to the cold and wet climate but Océane suffered, invariably wearing two sweaters over her day dress.

It wasn't just that the school building was cold. A chill had crept into the hearts of many of the teachers as well and especially in Madame Paul's heart. No matter how much they proclaimed neutrality on the outside, the growing power of Hitler's Nazism in the north and Mussolini's hysteric fascism south of the border seemed to make the staff of the posh finishing school feel they had to take sides, too.

The Swiss were further cornered by the sitting one-year President of the Confederation, Philipp Etter, who took no firm stand against the jubilant warfare cries on either side of their borders. The population silently condoned the fact the big man behind the Conservative Catholic Party was anti-Semitic himself. Etter had found a staunch supporter in Madame Paul Vierret, whose late Zug husband had been a close friend and party member of the Conservative Catholic Party.

Esther could stand the harsh weather God bestowed on them, but had a much harder time coping with the covert references to her Jewishness. Both Madame Paul and the art teacher Monsieur George were skilled at rubbing salt in her wounds, both she and quiet Miss Anna Levi being easy targets.

"All that *Entartete Kunst*, degenerate Art" — she heard Monsieur George orate during paint class — "is created by Jews or men who aren't real men." *Snap,* said the thin wooden paintbrush between her fingers. Esther looked down at her trembling hands, disgust like acid in her throat. Not disgust at the paintbrush, but at the teacher's nasal voice. Before he had time to reprimand her, the door to the classroom swung open.

"Mademoiselle Esther?"

Madame Paul's gray-coiffed head peeked around the door. The penciled eyebrows slightly raised, which meant there was trouble in paradise. "Can you come with me?"

"What now?" Esther thought despairingly. What minor flaw had Madame spotted through her microscope this time? The praise upon their return from St. Moritz with the expulsion of Sable Montgomery was a distant moment of glory, long faded. It clearly had nothing to do with Esther's braveness.

While she tried to do everything right, she — even more than the other girls — was trained by the best example at home, and she was a fast learner.

"Yes, Madame Paul."

What else could she do? She heard OC's voice in her head. "That odious woman is just taking it out on you. What a sorry lot!"

For the first six months, it hadn't seemed to matter much who she was by birth. But now? She braced herself for the hollow Madame Paul phrases: 'for your own good', 'what is expected of you in the real world', 'no mistake is made when you thoroughly prepare.'

Esther stepped across the threshold of Madame Paul's office, the most opulent room in the whole school with an immense mahogany desk, the portraits of the four Le Manoir school directors on the walls, wide windows with sash curtains overlooking the schoolyard and the west lawn, impressive file cabinets and always a sickening-scented bouquet of white lilies. Madame Paul's favorites. They exuded a deathly scent.

The most impressive element in the whole grandiose office was the mistress herself. *How does she do it?* Esther thought. *Look so immaculate, so regal, so perfect while her soul is black like the inside of that marble chimney place over there?*

Madame Paul Vierret, who went by her late husband's name and who was whispered to have as her first name, Narcissa. Didn't that say it all? And yet. Esther still had to learn from her. She desperately clung to her idea of her grand Vienna house, an elegant hostess on her husband's arm, the nursery full of the happy cheers of their adorable children.

"Two letters have arrived for you." Madame Paul shoved the silver tray in Esther's direction. "One from your family. I hope it brings good tidings. The other letter surprised me, and that's why I called you in. You'll find it opened. It is from Sable Montgomery." Madame Paul spit out the name as if she'd accidentally put a piece of garbage in her mouth.

Esther sat still in the trained statuesque posture, raging inside. How dare she open a letter that was addressed to her? Manners, huh? But she saw the letter from home, and her heart melted. It had been months since the last sign of life in Vienna, just after Christmas. Also, Carl's letters arrived sporadically, no matter that she wrote to both him and her family every Friday night.

"Well?" Madame Paul remarked with a little sigh. "Are you going to take them?"

"Yes, Madame Paul. Thank you, Madame Paul." Esther slipped the two letters in the pocket of her housedress as she backed out of that odious office.

Finding a quiet spot in the school library, Esther took a moment to study the envelopes, one with the stamp of King George VI and one that read Norge and had a lion on it. Esther choked up, blinking hard. Her parents had gone, moved to Norway, but what about Carl? She started shivering all over, feeling positively unwell. It meant life had become too unendurable in Austria, the shop and the workshop gone. Fled! Her proud parents fled the only country they'd ever lived in and loved. Would the Bernsteins have gone too? But they had no relatives in Norway. Maybe they went to Holland?

So many questions, and the answers in this letter that she didn't dare to open. She kept staring at that strange stamp. Norge. It meant a language they didn't speak, and tall, blond people who had rowdy manners and probably ate raw fish. She recalled the loud skiers. One of them had thrown hot cocoa over her engagement dress, and Carl had jumped on him. That sort of people. Not their people. She'd never even seen Tante Isobel's husband, Oncle Frerik.

Breathe, Esther, stay calm.

A flash of bright light. She is bouncing up and down as her friends Lise and Charlotte turn the skipping rope for her. The backstreet of her Vienna house.

What is going on?

Blood singing in her ears, her body hot and flustered.

Esther shook herself. Another flashback, something deep inside her trying to come to the surface. But there was no time for this nonsense now; she had to concentrate on Norway.

Norway. It had never seemed a part of their reality, but now it was.

Sable's envelope was also opened, but for now Esther shoved her irritation aside. She dreaded the contents of her mother's letter. Esther pulled out the single sheet of lavender paper and read:

London, 10 February 1939

Dear Esther,

I never properly thanked you for saving my life in those bloody Alps, so that's why I'm writing you now. Especially after how I treated you, I didn't expect this from you. I'm trying to better my life, but it's difficult. I'm born trouble, my mother says, and she should know because after all, I'm her daughter. She's onto her fourth marriage next week, and the husbands get worse as time progresses.

Anyway. I'm sure you're not interested in my story, which is quite bleak and unhappy despite the title and the looks. You're much better off, my dear. Your soul is as Weiss as your name, mine as black as mine.

I'm not a writer, as you can tell from this letter. I just wanted to let you know I adored you from the first day you stood there on Le Manoir gravel, straw hat, and all that loveliness. Gosh, girl, make something of your life and marry that dashing fellow of yours and be happy ever after. I'll root for you!

This address is where my mother lives, but it's owned by my Scottish Dad (my real dad, not one of the stepdads). In case you'd like to stay in touch, you can use this address because my Mum isn't able to squander it in one of the Monte Carlo casinos. Yes, that's how bad it is, but as we say here in rainy London, "Chin up, old girl!"

Take care, Esther! You were my favorite.

Sable Montgomery (without the Lady stuff!)

"Lordy," Esther muttered, "I'd never expected that!" But she had to admit Sable's letter gave her a thrill. It reminded her of one of her father's favorite German expressions, *'was sich liebt das neckt sich.'* You loved most those that you fight tooth and nail. Suddenly being Sable's favorite was probably just one of her exaggerations. Still, it made Esther feel good, rewarded by the one person she wanted to be rewarded by.

Putting Sable's precious letter back in the envelope, she took a while to study her mother's handwriting before daring to take out the letter. The handwriting was not as neat and steady as usual as if her mother had written the letter in haste.

Esther quickly scanned the two pages. Her mother had written most of it; Papi and Oma having only closed off the letter with a few lines. Oma's handwriting almost slid off the page. No message from Rebecca or Adam.

Esther took a deep breath, bracing herself.

12 March 1939

Dearest Esther,

We hope you're doing fine and have already mastered a lot of the great teachings at Le Manoir. That is your father's, your Oma's and my deepest wish.

We are doing relatively fine. We are in good health, and Rebecca and Adam send their love and say they miss you terribly. Papi worked at the Glassfabrik until we really had to leave Vienna two months ago.

I know this will come as a huge shock to you that we left for Norway. I'm very sorry that we could not let you know earlier. Our departure was rather hasty and in the middle of the night. You knew, of course, that Oma and I were in favor of leaving even last year, but Papi thought the Germans would need the gold and diamond industry and the skilled Jewish workers. Well, they didn't. Days before we left, the Nazis plundered both the shop and the workshop and took everything, including the contents of the safe. They just blew out the lock with their guns. It broke your dear Papi, and he finally consented to going north.

I will save you the details of our arduous journey, but we eventually reached Holland and could board a freight ship from Rotterdam to Oslo. We arrived here on the 10th of March and got immediately welcomed by a snowstorm and -20 degrees Celsius. There had been no way to let Oncle Frerik and Tante Isobel know of our arrival, but they have been nothing but accommodating and nice to us. But the house is small, and they have Ole and David, so we need to find accommodation for ourselves as soon as possible. Papi will first have to find a job and maybe then we can rent a house. It's hard to start from nothing again.

I know your first thought will be what after I have finished Le Manoir? Go to Carl in Vienna and get married, or come to us here in Norway for as long as we need to stay here? Well, Carl has promised to come to Oslo as soon as he can, but you know, of course, he can't leave his parents. He also works in the Glassfabrik. We discussed it with him before we left, and he said it would be safest if you come to us in

September and we'll have the wedding in Oslo. He will write to you himself as soon as he can.

Dear Esther, don't worry about us. We are safe now! We will work out how you can travel from Lausanne to Oslo in September.

Papi and Oma will add a few words.

Much love from your adoring Mutti

Post Script: Your father here, Esther. Our life has changed a lot, and I don't know if it is for the better, but we'll set up temporary camp here with the Oslo family and pray for the day we can return to Vienna. Behave well, my dear girl, and see you in September. Your father!

Post Post Script: Dear Bärchen. I hope you're well! We are in a new, cold country. I miss you. When are you going to have your wedding? Will I be invited? Much love, Oma!

Esther's whole body froze. She couldn't move a muscle, not even if she'd wanted to. Her brain knew she had to get up and out of the library. Go to her room, find shelter, lie down. She was too unwell to get to her feet, though. A paralysis she'd never encountered before.

Luckily, there were only two other students in the library, right on the other side and not paying attention to her. Mademoiselle Rimbaud, the librarian, was reading under the table lamp, her gray cap of hair illumined by the soft light. Esther tried again to get up. Total weakness. Her head registered shock, her body having forgotten how it ought to function.

Breathe, Esther! Breathe!

She bounces up and down, while Lise and Charlotte are counting 49, 50, 51. Her skirt dances with her.

The flash is gone again.

Esther shuddered. Slowly, very slowly, she felt some force come back to her rigid body, and she rose on unstable legs, her fingers gripping the table edge for support. She shuffled out of the room without drawing attention to herself, her mother's letter burning in her pocket like a badge of shame and defeat. Eventually, she made it to her bedroom, holding on to the banister and taking shallow gulps of breath. Aching for that moment to recover herself with no one seeing her. The first impossible tears already spilled down her cheeks.

Through a blur of tears, she saw Océane sitting at the table by the window. She immediately abandoned her writing and came to Esther, a questioning look in the hazel eyes.

"What is it? Is it Carl?"

Esther shook her head, and then the words came and wouldn't stop.

"No, it's my own family. Mutti has persuaded Papi to move to Norway. They've left Austria. They mentioned it already when I was still at home, but — oh — now it is real. They left my... our... house. Just like that. To go to Oslo, of all places."

More tears came, her shoulders now shaking in the gray merino cardigan with its alpine flower embroidery. Océane put a firm arm around her trembling body.

"Tell me all!"

But all the words she had were spilled. Panic hit her. Life in Vienna gone, but with Carl still living there. What was her future going to be now? She tried to calm down but couldn't. Everything was being ripped from her. Now she'd probably never even see Carl again. And how was she ever going to travel to Norway alone? She was abandoned by the entire world.

Breaths came with difficulty. *Noooo!*

She felt Océane take her pulse, all professional and calm as ever. Big, begging eyes gazed up into the sweet, oval face of her friend. She wanted to scream 'help me,' but no sound left her lips.

As if spoken to through a tunnel, she heard Océane instruct her, "Lie down, sweetie, you'll become very dizzy in a moment. I'll just pop to the bathroom to get a cool flannel, but I'll be back in a sec. Try to breathe a little deeper, so you won't get a hyperventilation attack."

She was on the bed, the entire room turning upside-down. Once at the Alte Donau Schule, she'd had that same hyper-light feeling of rising up in the air, and falling back down with a thud while Frau Gerber tapped the map with a pointed stick — Wien, Salzburg, Graz, Innsbr...

Mumps...

The world turned black.

The reliable rhythmic rapping of her grandfather's clock on the wall. Excited, high-pitched voices outside. *Rebecca? Adam?* But the staccato ha-ha-ha-ha of the gulls soaring the winds made no sense. It wasn't Vienna! Where was home?

The world of sound and reality slowly dawned on dazed Esther.

She blinked, felt a hand on her tummy. OC's face was close, the smooth, slightly tanned skin, the lovely hazel eyes, that perfect cupid mouth.

Such fine-boned beauty, Esther thought. *I'd love to see her always. Seeing her makes me happy.*

Océane was smiling at her.

"You'll be okay, Es. You passed out because your body revolted at the extreme stress. Breathe as calmly as you can now. Do that for a while. Try to move your legs, waggle your fingers, whatever. And don't worry, I'm here and I'm not going anywhere."

Esther did what her friend instructed her to do, still admiring her natural beauty, and her strength as a kind but resolute healer. OC with her plans to become an artist. Fiddlesticks, she'd say herself! She was missing the point. If there ever was a doctor, it was this slip of a girl. Medical professionalism radiated from her whole soul. Esther believed in God's will for humans. With a sudden urgency, she had to speak up.

"Going to art school would be an absolute waste of your talent, OC. You're a natural-born doctor. Look at you, all that reassurance and confidence right now. You step onto a scene of emergency with a heart as calm as Lake Geneva."

As she concentrated on getting her plea across to Océane, Esther felt her own strength return to her. She wanted to be a people connector, the gentle but decisive female touch in people's lives. Focusing on OC's life, instead of her own, boosted her. At least, in this instance.

OC's eyes widened in surprise, then adopted a relieved look. A chord was struck. It was a surprise when Océane, in her turn, began to sniffle.

"You're right. I shouldn't fight what I'm supposed to be doing here on earth. It's just... after my debacle at Radcliffe, you know, cheating on the exam and being expelled, I thought that was the sign. But probably it wasn't. You, of all people, letting me see that — it's wonderful."

"You can still paint, OC. It's not like you can't have a hobby, or a second career."

Knowing her friend would make something important of her life, especially in the trying times they found themselves, invigorated Esther further. She sat up to hug her. Now Océane really burst out in tears, and it turned the tables.

"There, there, Doctor Océane Bell. I wish you could be my doctor all my life. I'm so glad to see how you can use your superior brain to help humanity. Not many people are cut out to be a doctor, but you're one of them."

Esther sensed Océane needed time to process this new insight. Giving up a deep love for a mission wasn't something one did overnight. Maybe she was on the brink of having to do that herself. But how? To hang on to it! No matter how elusive, how distant her own mission seemed to be. Frau Esther Bernstein. When? Ever?

"Are you feeling a little better now?" Océane brought her back to the here and now.

Her forehead still felt clammy, but her heart rate was back to normal, and her breath came easier. There was just this great sadness, this feeling as if someone had placed a sack of bricks on her chest that couldn't be taken away.

"You'll still be marrying Carl when you're done here?" Océane's voice was tentative, as if she knew how frail the dream was that Esther hung onto.

She wanted to agree but knew everything was up in the air now.

"I don't think so, unless there's a miracle. How is he to come to Oslo when he has to look after his parents in Vienna? I have to choose whether I'll go to Vienna and marry Carl, or go to my family in Oslo without him..." She hesitated, breathing as Océane had instructed to calm herself, her eyes big and worried.

"People can travel?"

"It's complicated and I'm still underage. I'd rather not marry without my family, and I've promised Carl that his parents will be present at our wedding. They already missed our engagement, but they're too old and frail to travel."

Océane was listening intently to her, soothing her forehead and blonde curls.

"Go on!"

"My mother tried to cheer me up in her letter, promising Carl will come to Oslo as soon as he can and bring his parents via Holland. That we'll all be together and get married in Norway. But I don't know what will happen with Hitler and the Jewish situation. We're no longer the rich and prosperous Jewish families we used to be. Most has been taken from us. So, so ..." She sighed, twisting her engagement ring around her finger. "I'm afraid things will only get worse, and it will take a long time before we can get married. What am I to do in Oslo? Unlike you, I don't have a profession. I haven't even got my Matura diploma. I wish I could go back to Vienna, but I'm torn. I want to be with Carl but also with my family."

"What does Carl say?" Océane was stroking her back now, trying to soothe some of her anguish. It helped, sort of.

"It's been so long since I've heard from Carl. I worry about him and his parents so much. And his best friend, Asher, moved to Holland last year, so he's all on his own with his parents. Working in the Glassfabrik. At least that was the last I heard from him, but it's been at least two months since his last letter. I don't think the postal services are working properly anymore, or they don't let Jews write to family and friends abroad. I don't know. His last letter was cautiously optimistic, but I can read between the lines. Vienna is clearly a horrible place to be right now. God knows how long it will last. There's no sign of Hitler slowing his occupational frenzy. He's recently seized Czechoslovakia."

"What will you do?"

Esther shook her shoulders. "I'll wait for Carl's letter to decide, though I already know what he will say. 'Go to Oslo and wait for me.' Do I have a choice?"

"I guess not. At least you'll be safe there. Hitler seems more interested in the middle of Europe than in the northern countries."

"Let's hope so."

It took a long time before Esther could sleep that night, and every time she fell into a fitful sleep, she woke with a shock. Her life was broken. She had no idea how she could glue the pieces together again. If ever.

9

UNBREAKABLE BONDS

July 1939

"Mademoiselle Esther, can you come into my office after lunch?"

That question alone sent shivers up Esther's spine. The cold celestite eyes of the school director on her. Open hostility these days. The veneer of politeness and manners had long since broken down. Though Esther never gave up doing all the assignments to utter perfection, they always fell short due to Madame Paul's contempt for her. Raw, uncivilized hate.

"Yes, Madame Paul."

What else could she say? The unthinkable had occurred. Esther no longer cared much for Le Manoir. The certificate, yes, but for her parents and Oma, not for herself.

She dragged herself through the days, hoping against hope for a letter from Carl. It never came. He couldn't write, or else he would have. So much was sure to her. Their bond was unbreakable, but the silence was deafening. Rumors of deportations of Jews from Germany and Austria had even reached the soft, rippling shores of Lake Geneva. How much of it was true?

Where are you? She screamed in the black of the night, but no answer came. The days were long, the nights longer. Loneliness and depression had permanently wormed its way into her system.

She entered the opulent office, inhaling Madame Paul's overbearing perfume and the sickening scent of the eternal lilies. She stared at the hard glint of the pearls against the navy-blue of the silk dress, never meeting the headmistress's eyes these days.

"Aha, Mademoiselle Esther, there you are."

The tone was friendlier than usual, which put Esther even more on her qui vive. Madame Paul wasn't friendly by any measure to anyone, but particularly not to her or to Anna Levi. Esther braced herself for what would come from behind this suspicious syrupy setup.

Suddenly, Esther's heart jolted in her chest. Was it Mutti or Papi? Was something wrong with them? Or, Heaven forbid, with Carl? Esther's cheeks flushed; her pupils dilated. *Don't faint!* Madame Paul cleared her throat.

"Mademoiselle Esther, how is the training for you these days?"

What? A sidetrack?

"Fine, thank you, Madame Paul. I'm still learning a lot."

A strange, squeaky sound escaped her. Nothing was fine these days, except OC's loyalty and the gorgeous, tranquil Swiss summer in the fields. And sometimes Debussy on the piano.

"I'm glad to hear it. You for sure have made good progress, and I'm convinced you'll graduate with distinction at the end of the course." Esther kept her eyes down. Hypocrisy hurt, especially when larded with cynicism. It was wrong. And Madame Paul was hinting at something, sly fox as she was.

"We, however, have an unfortunate situation. You know that part of the school building is under repairs? Much-needed repairs. So, I have very few dorm places but just received a request for an unexpected new student, who is from an English family that has come to Le Manoir for generations. It's — what shall I say? — a delicate matter as the girl has maneuvered herself into an impossible situation back home. The only girl I could think of to have a steadying effect on this little-Miss-Impulse is Mademoiselle Océane."

Madame Paul tapped her mauve-lacquered fingertips together. "Therefore," she continued, "I've arranged for you and Anna to be roommates, while Mademoiselle Lili is monitored by Océane while she settles in."

Esther's eyes shot up despite herself, meeting the cold blue stare. The nasty woman was taking her last bit of joy away from her. How cruel could a person be? Of course, she knew how much Esther valued being with and being protected by Océane.

"But...?"

Then her shoulders slumped, her lips pressed together. What was the use? It was all planned and decided already.

Esther rose from her chair opposite the impassive headmistress and walked out of the office without even bidding her goodbye. She was past being the polite future mistress of the house. Being thwarted at every step, her family in danger, her fiancé's whereabouts unknown.

Esther did what she'd done at the times she couldn't breathe. She made herself recalcitrantly untouchable, in a safe spot within herself.

Just breathe!

No flashback, fortunately.

THE TABLE SETTING that day was Esther's exam piece, and she would give it her all. If only for the memory of the splendor she's hoped to realize one day. A memory, not even a hope anymore. But she would play her trump card. Create splendor like nothing before.

The Le Manoir dining room was one of the most magnificent rooms in the school. Someone who would have walked into it unfamiliar with the purpose of the *salle a manger* would have thought she'd stepped into a grand house. It was Esther's favorite room next to the music room.

Instantly feeling better being in that gorgeous place on her own, she set out measuring the exact location of the plates, the cutlery and the glasses. The fresh flower arrangements, three in a row, were already in place on the long white damask tablecloth. Heavenly sweet roses, heady lilacs and the crisp tawny scent of green twigs. The room was an oasis of silence and scent.

Finally, order reigned in Esther's house, while her hands worked rapidly and the dark cloud evaporated from her mind. How she adored the fine porcelain plates, creamy white with just a touch of mimosa around the edges, the twinkle of the crystal glasses, the shiny silver forks and spoons.

For a brief span of time, Esther was at peace, forgetting her worries and her uncertain future. Graduate with distinction from *her* finishing school. Her dream materialized. One eternal moment of bliss.

Esther was so engrossed in her task that she hadn't heard Océane enter the room. She startled, brought back to reality.

"What do you think? I want it to be sublime, so I get no comments." She gestured to her table, spick-and-span in the sparkling light of the two chandeliers that hung over the table.

"Looks prize-winning to me!"

Océane clearly couldn't care less. Esther chewed her lip. No matter how much Esther loved her, she knew Océane would never share her passion for housekeeping. So, this was as good as the best compliment she'd ever get out of her doctor friend.

Océane came closer.

"Did you hear there's a new girl arriving from England today? I hope she and Anna will get on well, you know, as Brits among themselves." Now it was Esther's turn to chew her lip until it almost bled.

"So, have you heard, or not?"

"Heard what?" Océane took a seat at the set table, crossing her slim legs at the ankles. There was something in her face that wasn't as sincere as it normally was.

"For sure, Madame Paul told you that she's going to put the

unruly new girl under your wing, and I have to share a room with Anna?"

"Oh, Esther, what are we to do? I thought you probably didn't know. You seemed happy for a moment. That vile, vile woman!"

"Shush, OC, the walls have ears here!"

"Don't start about it!" Océane snarled while Esther doggedly continued to re-measure the distance between each plate and cup with a ruler.

"I've just had an entire lecture on guarding that new girl. She's kind of wild, according to the Sphinx. And I have to keep an eye on her? Me? I only want you as a roommate, Essie."

Esther shot her a sad look and sighed.

"I want that, too, but I don't think it will happen again. But you and I will always be best friends, OC. And if she's really horrible, there will be no other option but to tell her straight out. We can't have your last months here being wrecked by a spoiled brat. Don't worry, I'll help you."

At that moment, they heard the Renault come up the driveway. Unable to restrain their curiosity, they sneaked out of the dining room and up to the corner of the building from where they could watch the gravel parking place in front of the school. They were too far away to hear what Madame Paul was saying to the girl.

She stood rather forlornly on the spot, clearly uncomfortable with the sermon and heat. Red curls peeped from under her fashionable hat. She looked far from dangerous or haughty.

"If that's a fallen girl, I'm the devil myself," Océane whispered.

"Yes, she looks rather nice, and the way Madame Paul is talking to her, all airs and stiffness, is surely making her feel terrible," Esther added.

As if she had heard talk of the devil, Madame Paul looked in their direction. They quickly withdrew their heads, giggling in the ivy leaves that grew along the south wall.

"Let me help you with the last part of the table setting," Océane remarked. "Meanwhile, we'll wait for the new girl to come down to tea. So far, I see no reason not to be nice to her. Imagine arriving here when almost everyone has finished the course."

Esther agreed. "And with the threat of war everywhere, it must be awful being separated from your family." The reminder brought pain, but this time she shrugged it off. Nothing would come between OC and her. Nothing.

THE MAID HAD ALREADY MOVED ESTHER'S belongings out of room 6 and carried it up the stairs to the much smaller rooms on the third floor where the staff also boarded. Esther felt the degradation in her blood as she climbed the steep stairs to the ill-lit corridor.

She'd left her splendid table below for everyone to admire and hoped Madame Paul would remark on her special folded napkin. After much studying, she had decided on a classic fold with the silver ring holders, in which she had placed a small sprig of dried lavender. On the plates, she placed another fold within a glass in the form of a yellow rose matching the mimosa. It was daring, as Madame Paul wasn't overly fond of too much decoration, but Esther knew she had to stand out. The 'graduation with distinction' meant so much to her, especially now.

Let me do something right! Something at all!

She stopped a moment before the ill-painted door at the far corner of the third floor and took a deep breath. When she opened the door, she saw a cramped, square space ill-lighted by a small skylight that gave no view.

Anna was sitting on one of the two beds, looking as small and invisible as she usually was, an open book in her lap. Her dark hair hanging flatly around her face. Two brown eyes behind round spectacles too big for a narrow, pale face. Her mouth a thin white strip. Esther could see she'd recently been crying.

"Hi."

"Hi."

They knew each other, of course, but not well. Anna kept to

herself, didn't make friends, seemed out of place among the loud, well-fed and glamorous girls who sprawled over Le Manoir's lawns and hung relaxed in the armchairs in the sitting room, gossiping and dreaming of escape with a handsome dark stranger.

Anna was different. Bookish, deep, unknown. But now she was mostly sad, and Esther's heart went out to her. Though she was also the center of scorn and mockery, she'd always had OC whereas Anna, who'd been at Le Manoir since after Christmas, had no one.

"How are you doing?"

"Okay. And you?"

"Not so well!"

Anna gazed at her through the thick glasses, her mouth twisting, dried smears of tears on her cheeks.

"I know you and Océane are friends, and you never wanted to be with me in a room."

The truth hurt.

"It's not that," Esther hesitated, "it's us. What have they got against us?"

To her surprise, Anna sneered, "What they've always had against us, through the ages. They've only found a megaphone for it now in Hitler."

Esther sat down on the other bed, her hands folded in her lap. Pondering Anna's words. For her, this was new, something that had come into existence since Hitler's rise to power. She and her family had never felt discriminated against before, being Jewish never an issue. What did Anna mean?

"Maybe you're right," she said slowly. "Maybe it's been there all along, but what do we do about it?"

Anna closed her book, fixed the bespectacled eyes on her new roommate as if saying, "You are a fool, aren't you?" And that was just how Esther felt. This silent, withdrawn girl knew things, thought about things, unraveled things Esther had never considered. It put Anna Levi in a whole new light.

"I'm sure we'll get on just fine," she said eventually, biting her lip at how lost and insecure she felt.

HALF AN HOUR later as they sat down to Esther's splendid table display, which even Madame Paul was unable to find fault with, the new girl in an expensive navy-blue Elsa Schiaparelli suit came sauntering toward them. Esther sensed she was all shyness and freckles and exhaustion. There certainly was spirit in the flaming red hair, but no innate badness.

This was not a second minx like Sable Montgomery. Esther liked her and, sharing a glance with OC, saw her opinion reflected in the hazel eyes. This mix of diffidence and determined resolution was something they hadn't seen here yet in one of the other girls at Le Manoir. This could ultimately become a new friend.

They had a few minutes before the other girls came down to dinner. A wordless consent took place between Esther and Océane.

"Hi," all three of them said at the same time.

Océane was the first to extend a hand to the newcomer, who was taking them both in with intelligent aquamarine eyes. Esther thought she looked like a picture of a magazine, all lovely, with pale, translucent skin and soft red curls. Like Esther had always imagined the Celtic race.

Océane introduced herself, adding she was her new roommate. For a moment, Esther cringed at that mentioning but straightened her back. The bond with OC was unbreakable. No other girl could steal their friendship away.

"Lili Hamilton, enchanté."

She had a lovely, singsong voice. Esther shook her hand as well, looking into the beautiful eyes that smiled gratefully.

"Just sit at the table. This is what Esther created. Isn't it magnificent? Her beau is a lucky guy."

Océane waved a slender arm at the perfect display before them and added, "It'll give you an idea what's in store for you, Lili."

Lili's deep-blue eyes gazed up at them with disbelief, wrinkling her pretty nose. "Do we have to do the waitressing, too?"

"Oh yes," Esther chimed in, "if you want to be the mistress of a grand house, you have to know all the details of what that means. We cook, we clean, we polish, we set tables, and we do the waitressing."

"Heavens! Never done any of these things in my life."

She sounded genuinely perplexed. And Esther was happy with her role of explaining the details to Lili.

The ice melted. Not another hoity-toity damsel with whom she and Océane had nothing in common. Lili was real, albeit a little innocent and loose-lipped.

"We've been where you are right now," Esther assured her. "Don't worry. We'll help you in any way we can. Just stick with us."

Another brief glance between Esther and OC. A nod. *Yes, she's okay.*

Esther was happy to see Lili smile at their reassurance, but then the new girl added with a tinge of sadness, "But Madame Paul told me you'll both be leaving soon."

"Es and I will be here for another two months. We'll have time to help you settle in."

"Sure!"

Right then, Madame Paul came parading in as a mother hen, with the rest of the girls as her chicks trickling behind her. Immediately the atmosphere changed and Océane took the lead, whispering to Lili, "Sit with us. We'll help you."

Whatever lays ahead, friendship will endure, Esther thought as she heard Madame Paul say, "Splendid display, Mademoiselle Esther. Truly superb."

The praise hurt almost more than the scorn. Esther knew she'd done an outstanding job. But for what?

10

ANNA

3 September 1939

The war in Europe was finally a fact. It had been lingering over the continent for almost a decade, Hitler snatching land here and there, Austria, Czechoslovakia, Carpathia and now... Poland. A bridge too far for Britain and France. Esther sighed a breath of relief. Now things would change. Her country's death cry heard. Help was on its way.

But that was not the general atmosphere at the so-far peaceful finishing school in Lausanne. A steep panic broke out and the school more resembled a chicken coop where a fox had landed in their midst than the orderly, almost austere atmosphere Madame Paul always insisted on.

War broke through the fortress Madame Paul had built around her personality. She was running with everyone else, shouting orders to staff who didn't listen and clustering them all around the radio set in the library to listen to Churchill's announcement and then to Dadlier's French confirmation of war in the afternoon. Telephones rang; distressed parents ordered their children home. *De suite, de suite!*

Esther was the only pillar of strength in it all. She put smelling salts under the nose of fainting girls, helped pack suitcases, dried tears and smiled. At some point, she ran into Anna doing exactly the same. Calm, conviction, a chance at a new life.

"I think we're the only two welcoming this war," Esther confided to Anna as they settled in their small room under the slanted wall for the night.

"For us, it might mean liberation," Anna agreed. "For others, it's the beginning of slavery that we've already endured."

"For sure, it will be over soon!" Esther yawned, feeling better than she had in ages. Her course may be cut short by two weeks, as she was soon to travel to her new home country. Her finishing school diploma was drawn up, 'with distinction' written in curly red letters at the top.

In her confusion, Madame Paul had given it to her and now it was safely in Esther's suitcase under her bed. She finally owned a diploma, whatever its future use would be. She'd earned it with blood, sweat, and tears. It was hers. Now, perhaps sooner than later, her ticket to a lifetime of love with Carl. Just as had been in the cards for her since birth.

"I am afraid, though. We've got an arduous trip ahead of us. You to London and I to Oslo. It's not like the Germans are defeated yet."

"Don't worry, Esther. We'll travel together for the first part, and Hitler is too busy in Poland at the moment to pay much attention to us in the West."

"I hope you're right."

The next day was the beginning of the clearance at Le Manoir. Girls were picked up by parents or by chauffeurs. Some of them had to travel home alone by train. Esther still felt good about her departure. It was like a liberation.

The only thing that made her heart heavy was the dawning separation from Océane and Lili. They'd grown so close over the summer. Not even Madame Paul could tear them apart. But war had.

It was their last day together. None of them knew what lay

ahead. They'd been so secluded from things on the grand scheme in sleepy Switzerland.

Dipping their bare feet in the pleasantly cool water of Lake Geneva, something they would never have dared to do when Madame Paul's reign was supreme, while the sun sank further down the Jura mountains across the lake, it was as usual Océane who broke the silence.

"We must somehow stay in touch. It may be difficult if the mail's not working properly, but at least we must try."

Esther nodded, and Lili followed.

"And after the war — which will hopefully only last a couple of weeks — we must meet up again. What would be a good place, do you think?

"Paris!" they said in unison, which made them chuckle.

"Let's swear on it," Océane suggested.

Three pairs of slim hands, one light brown, one white, and one rosy, put on top of each other as they swore alliance to their friendship and to their reunion.

"How afraid are you of this war?" Esther asked, to her surprise hearing her voice catch in her throat.

"Hopefully it will be over soon," Océane observed, as always calm and sensible. Lili slipped her arm around Esther's waist and said through gritted teeth, "Stupid men. It's always men who want to fight and conquer other countries. It's never women wanting to own another piece of land and its people."

Esther, feeling strengthened by her two more feisty friends, agreed in a milder tone. "I don't get it either. All I want is peace and everything ordinary. Not these shock waves that terrify millions of people and turn their lives upside down."

With her usual vehemence, Lili retorted, "I believe that sometimes it's necessary to make your stand and fight back. If I were in Poland right now, I'd fight the Nazis with all my might."

"Of course," Océane agreed, "that's logical, but if Hitler invaded France — which, by God, I hope he won't — I'm not sure I'd fight. I'd do everything I could to help the wounded, but I don't think I would run up the barricades and shoot a bullet at the enemy. It's just not for me."

"Neither would I," Esther added, the golden glow of the sunset catching the silver-green in her eyes. "I would cook for the men fighting, and help them, but I would not do any fighting myself. That would just not be right for me."

"I would!" Lili declared with vigor. "I definitely would. I think we women are equal to men and we should be there, shoulder to shoulder with our men when the Nazis attack our country. But maybe it's easy for me to say because Hitler will never try to conquer Britain. That would be sheer suicide. But my French roots would fight at the barricades in Paris, so if Herr Hitler decides to turn westward, I might join any Resistance movement that rises up."

The other two girls looked at Lili with admiration, but also a trace of doubt. All bold and invigorated, the little Celt went a step further. "I'm a Communist, you know. Now I think I can say it out loud, as Madame Paul can't harm me anymore. I've secretly been getting information from the head of the Communist party in London, Leo Oppenheim."

Both girls stared at Lili open-mouthed. Then Esther put a hand over her mouth not to cry out while Océane studied Lili with a level-minded yet surprised look.

"Well, Lili, if you believe in that, you must do what you think best, but it's my feeling that the Communists will not be successful here in Western Europe. I know they're in power in Russia, since the people were really living under the yoke of repression there, but here, in the West? No way. But I understand your ideals, and if you're happy with it, by all means, go for it."

"Want a nice tidbit of news that would give Madame Paul a heart attack? Filippo Maltese is a Communist, too," Lili declared with triumph. "He's ready to take on Mussolini."

Oh, that's what it is, Esther mused, her thoughts on the free-thinking, stocky Italian who'd seemed so out of place as Le Manoir driver. *Typical of Lili to find that out! She will make an excellent reporter!*

Out loud she said with her best diplomacy, "Enough talk of strife and sides. I'll never understand politics and I don't want to. Let us talk about where and when we shall meet."

"How about the weekend of 28 October, in eight weeks' time. We can all stay at my grandfather's house in Neuilly-sur-Seine. Maybe I'll even have my own flat by then," Océane put forward.

"Deal!" Lili agreed.

Esther was more doubtful about the date. "What if the war isn't over at the end of October?" She didn't want to disclose she might not have the money for another travel so soon.

"Of course," Océane agreed. "Only if the war is over. We must remain positive. If it takes longer, we postpone."

"We need to exchange addresses," Lili suggested. Esther scribbled down her aunt's address on the Grønlandsleiret in Oslo and stared down at it. How odd, how unfamiliar. But there was no time for that now.

"Let's choose the oldest restaurant in Paris, À La Petit Chaise on the Rue de Montserrat in the 7th Arrondissement." Océane had reached a decision.

"Oh, yes," Lili cheered, "I know that one! It's just the place for us!"

Esther battled a wave of melancholy as she listened to the happy babbling of her two friends. Would she ever see them again? And under what circumstances? Contrary to Océane and Lili, she wasn't so sure the Nazis would be defeated in two months. She'd seen their strength, their deep-rooted anger at their neighbors, their hatred of all that wasn't Aryan. Not wanting to spoil their last hours together, she stayed silent.

"You know what!" Océane cried out. "Madame Paul is in no fit state to reprimand us. You're sleeping with us tonight, Esther! Just the three of us! Friends forever!"

A warm, fuzzy feeling rippled through her. Love. The love of friends. These girls were her life, their friendship soothing as a melodious song.

ESTHER AND ANNA were dropped off at Lausanne train station early the next morning by Filippo. The chauffeur's brow was grim and dark below his cap, and he'd been even more taciturn than other times. As he retrieved their valises from the boot, Esther wondered what would happen to him. For sure, he'd become a freedom fighter, an anti-fascist. Somehow, that idea seemed noble. At least Mr Maltese had a cause to fight for. She had no clue what was waiting for her in Norway. Forget the war, most likely, wait for Carl. If...

"Bye, Filippo," they said in chorus.

"Be good, girls, and au revoir!"

He heaved his short body behind the wheel. A farewell wave, and the last tie with Le Manoir was severed.

The station was already packed with ill-tempered travelers. Porters tried to get through the crowds, shouting in agitation. "*Laissez-moi passer! S'il vous plaît!*" Their get-out-of-the-way-please rang through the entire high-ceilinged station building and along the platforms.

The porters, in their black uniforms and high caps, weren't the only ones sweating and shouting. The throngs of people who followed them and their luggage were just as vocal.

In the first week of September 1939, cacophonies like ill-tuned orchestras rose from every Western-European station, where frightened people had but one thought: get home! The world might dissolve in flames any minute. Private hearth and family the top priorities.

Despite Switzerland's self-proclaimed neutrality, there was definitely an anti-Jew, superior-Swiss atmosphere in the air, yet also a certain restlessness about Mussolini's power just south of the

border with Italy. Squashed between two fascist countries, Switzerland played its role of haughty spectator as best as it could.

"Fascism clearly breeds on chaos," Esther observed as she and
Anna stood waiting for *le train blue*. Her observation surprised
herself. Since when was she watching political developments? They
were none of her business. Anna was clearly not interested in the
spread of threat and violence either.

Esther concentrated on boarding the train that would first take
them to Lyon in France, and from there via Paris to Le Havre. In the
French port town, the two last Le Manoir students would end their
mutual journey.

Though Esther still did not feel at ease with Anna as she had
done with Océane and Lili, she shared the hope for a better future
with the introverted London Jewess whose roots lay in Poland.
With her, Esther could be silent but not awkward. There would not
be a teary goodbye, a ripping each other from memories that would
forever be associated with youth, and the magical Lake Geneva, the
snowcapped mountains in a scenery so pure and aesthetic as if
given special attention by God. The laughter, the deep heart-
connecting bond, the certainty that — if possible — they would
meet again and continue where they had left off.

All this Esther pondered as she sat opposite Anna, staring
through the dusty, fly-splattered window as the train rushed toward
France, further and further away from what she once had called
home. Her Vienna, her people.

Anna, as always, sat with her nose in a book, paying no heed to
past or future it appeared, and even less to the bustle around her
and the magnificent last glimpse of pictorial Switzerland.

Just as well, Esther thought, *no ties, no heartache.*

She had to admit she understood where Anna came from. It
wasn't for everyone to lay their heart on the platter. She reached for
her pocket, suddenly remembering the letter that in all the commotion of the past days had been given to her by the jovial Swiss
postman whom everyone called Batty, a name that sent them all
into a fit of giggles. Esther smiled. Of course, it had been Sable who

misunderstood Batiste. Sable. Where would she be now? Doing what? That raven girl certainly was mysterious. She would write back to her once she arrived in Norway.

Esther stared at the envelope with a stamp showing a busty Queen Wilhelmina. Edda's letter. She'd completely forgotten about its arrival, but it was a welcome distraction now.

Arnhem, 3 August 1939

Dear Esther,

I hope this letter arrives in time before you go back to Vienna. I'm sorry it's taken me so long to write, but last week something happened that I absolutely must share with you, so that forced me to put pen to paper and finally get around to it.

I was fortunate to continue at the Amsterdam Conservatory for Dance shortly after my return home. My parents are still in Leiden but I'm glad to be back in my Amsterdam flat. With the talk of war getting louder, I'm not sure if my parents will request me to move back to Leiden. I don't hope so, as we all think Holland will remain neutral, and the Germans won't attack our country.

What I wanted to tell you is that I met someone at the Conservatory who you know!!!! Asher Hoffmann. Isn't that a coincidence? He told me a lot about his "Nachbarmädchen" as he calls you affectionately. And of course, about his best friend, your fiancé Carl, whom he misses greatly.

Asher sends you his greetings, and so do his parents. They're worried because they can't reach your parents. Ash says he hasn't heard from Carl in months, so if you have news, please write back to me and I can tell the Hoffmans.

To return to Asher, he's a fabulous dancer and I'm really lucky to be partnering with him. We will perform Swan Lake in the Amsterdam Schouwburg (theater) next week.

Anyway, I hope you're fine and that this letter reaches you before you leave Le Manoir. I pray the course brought you everything you wanted, as you were so adamant to excel at it. I'm just glad I'm no longer under the Sphinx's yoke, and I'm free to dance and not think of table setting or manners. But you're a class of your own, Esther Weiss!

Please write!

Best wishes,

Edda xxx

The letter moved Esther deeply. It took her a moment to recollect herself. Ash in Holland, the Hoffmanns safe. Her own family in Norway. Austrians scattered over all the countries of Europe with the Bernsteins still trapped at home.

She gazed up from the letter to Anna. Her nose deep inside her book, her travel companion was oblivious to all that went on around her. Esther retrieved her lace handkerchief from her purse and dabbed her eyes.

No matter how hard she tried, her thoughts remained gloomy as *le train bleu* rattled along its tracks through southern France, rapidly reaching Lyon. They passed recently harvested cornfields, flowing hills of sunflowers, their yellow-tipped faces devotedly toward the light. Larks rose into the azure blue sky, startled by the blue caterpillar crossing their path, while frozen falcons floated high above like gray sails. Not a soldier or army vehicle in sight.

War on 5 September 1939 was a beguiling, bizarre concept that no one could grasp. The French countryside basked in a glow of afternoon light, tranquil, free.

As they passed Lyon and were on their way to Paris, Esther felt herself relax a little. The swaying carriage was like a lullaby, a growing grain of joy she'd be with her family again, while it soothed the pain of not being with Carl.

Anna kept stubbornly reading her book, had actually finished Daphne du Maurier's *Rebecca* and with the same ease was now immersed in what seemed the latest hype, *The Grapes of Wrath*. Esther knew Anna to be a voracious reader, but she also felt the silent girl tried to make herself invisible in her books.

"Was *Rebecca* any good?" Esther yearned for Anna's attention, as she really could do with a chat.

Anna's dark eyes lit up. Her pinched face glowed, which made her gray countenance evaporate and her fine, natural beauty emerge. John Steinbeck's book dropped into her lap, like a secondhand choice.

"Oh Esther, *Rebecca* is *the* best book I've read in ages. It's superb. I so adore Gothic stories, but there has been nothing since the Brontë Sisters that could measure up to *Jane Eyre* or *Wuthering Heights*. Now there is, thanks to Daphne du Maurier, and that makes me so happy. I wish I could write suspenseful stories like hers, but I'm afraid I'll always fall short. Listen to this sentence. It's my absolute favorite, though there are many." Anna flipped through the book and read, "*Every moment was a precious thing, having in it the essence of finality.*"

For a moment Anna's face clouded, resuming its habitual still, withdrawn features. But remembering her delight and own passion, she continued, "What she does so cleverly is making you root for the new Mrs De Winter from the beginning. And that first line, just listen — '*Last night I dreamt I was at Manderley again...*' Such perfection. I hear myself whispering that sentence so often, just as an inspiration."

Esther had a hard time not gaping at the fiery Anna across from her. She'd never seen her former roommate like this, but this new Anna was OC's and Lili's fiery spirits combined and multiplied. She'd love for her to keep talking like this, be it about books she'd never read.

Esther's library choices were mainly Georgette Heyer's romance novels, though at the Wasa Gymnasium she'd had to plough through the great Austrian authors. It had put her off reading for a while, though she knew Carl had exquisite reading taste, stimulating her to pick up Kafka, Rilke and Werfel. Maybe she would try *Rebecca*?

"Does it have a happy ending?"

Anna smirked. "It has, though it's not always necessary for a book to have a happy ending. I always say a satisfactory ending is much more important. Would you like to try it?"

Esther nodded, unsure of herself. Whenever her lack of literature education surfaced, she became self-conscious. Such a different topic from music and composers, about whom she knew almost everything. It was so important as mistress of the house to be also well-read. Maybe she could try another book.

"Here!" Anna handed her the stout volume, and Esther stared down at a very romantic picture of a couple walking a sandy path to a beautiful castle, surrounded by greenery. An azure blue sea was shimmering in the distance. She gasped. It was so perfect, so romantic, and she knew that though the word Gothic appalled her, she would love this book, but she handed it back to Anna.

"I can't take this. You love it yourself. It's yours."

"Don't worry. I've got plenty Du Maurier books at home. My father owns a bookshop on Brick Lane."

Esther looked surprised. It was as personal as Anna had been with her since they met. Her smile came readily.

"In that case..."

"Just let me know what you think of *Rebecca*, okay?"

"Sure... So you want us to stay in touch?"

Anna pushed her dark-rimmed glasses higher on the bridge of her nose. She seemed to ponder her own suggestion for a while, then shrugged.

"Of course, why not! Unless these awful Nazis kill us before we can take our next breath."

"Shush!" Esther quickly spied around her to assure none of their fellow passengers had heard Anna's harsh German criticism, but the train was packed and noisy. A plump French woman with a red kerchief around her moon-shaped face sat dozing with a wicker basket in her lap from which slender leeks and carrots peeked. Her husband, wiry and wrinkled, sat next to Esther, absorbed in *Le Matin*.

Anna meanwhile continued their conversation.

"I know you were much closer to Océane and Lili. It's not that I was jealous, it's just...that I don't make friends easily anymore...." Her voice trailed off, pain distorting her narrow face amidst the dark, wavy hair. Esther's tender heart was immediately on high alert while she inwardly scolded herself for cold-shouldering the introvert Anna on various occasions during their Le Manoir days.

"What happened?" Esther had to ask, though she wasn't sure it was wise to press the young woman opposite her. Tears lingered on Anna's dark lashes, emotion, she'd not shown before. Then her face became stony and withdrawn again.

"Nothing. Sorry. I shouldn't have brought it up."

"I shouldn't have asked." Esther felt increasingly uncomfortable, longing for their arrival in Paris and no longer treading on the soft toes of this awkward girl. She stared out of the window for a while, glad to see the outskirts of Paris coming into view, the shimmering silhouettes of its greatest landmarks — the Sacre Coeur and the Eiffel Tower — illuminated in the late afternoon sun. Esther almost gasped; it was the first time she laid eyes on this romantic city, and she so much wanted to visit it as Frau Bernstein with Carl. Lost in her thoughts, she suddenly heard Anna's voice come from across her in a whisper.

"My real last name is Grynszpan. We're originally Polish Jews but my parents emigrated to Hanover in 1911. They built up a good life there and my father was the chief editor of the *Judische Rundschau*, a Jewish newspaper. He also owned several bookstores. Then, last summer, we were suddenly told that our residence permits were no longer renewed. Papa's newspaper had already been banned."

Anna's face readopted its pained look and Esther forgot all romantic thoughts of Paris, listening intently to what could have been her own story.

"Only three months later, in October 1938, we became stateless when Hitler announced the so-called "Polen Aktion." Overnight, he ordered us to leave our homes. Like cattle, we were pushed into police trucks and taken to the railway station. In the streets, our German neighbors were chanting. *Juden Raus! Auf Nach Palästina!*'

I remember thinking that our neighborhood, where I grew up and went to school with German girls, was slowly turning into a hostile place. Secretly, I thought that perhaps it was better we went to Poland where we would be more welcome. But my two small twin-sisters Eva and Sarah kept wailing the whole way. I was shell-shocked, tried to comfort them, but when I saw the fear in my parents' eyes, I felt so helpless. We'd lost everything and had no place to go. The train journey to the Polish front was long and horrendous, no water, no food, babies were crying non-stop and old people passing out."

Big tears misted up Anna's glasses as she remembered the horror trip her family had endured. Esther put her hand over Anna's. The stout farmer's wife shifted her position in her dozing state while her husband turned a page of his newspaper. Time stood still only for the two scared Jewish girls.

"Please go on. Tell me," Esther urged her, giving Anna's knee a small squeeze.

Anna put her glasses back on and heaved a deep sigh. "All we had was one small suitcase each. I squeezed the handle of my brown leather suitcase so tightly that the mark was in my palms for days. We knew that everything we had left behind would be stolen by the Gestapo. I asked my father whether we still had relatives in Warsaw, and he shook his head. I'd never seen my intellectual, smart father look so haggard and defeated. My mother was the only one trying to keep her family safe on the floor in a corner of the train, lulling Eva to sleep and then Sarah. Giving us small sips of precious water from a canteen. But the worst was yet to come. When the train stopped at the border, the Polish guards wouldn't let us into the country."

Esther shuddered. She'd thought her and her family's fate hard in Vienna, but it was nothing like what Anna had endured. Yet, they had escaped to England, so they must have been lucky in the end.

Anna seemed to pick up on her trail of thoughts.

"Do you want me to continue? I know it's a terrible story, and the worst is yet to come."

The farmer's wife opened her eyes and burst out in rapid French to her husband, who grumbled back in monosyllables. They were talking about their married daughter, who apparently lived in Paris.

Esther returned her attention to Anna, who was staring down at the cover of Steinbeck's novel. She remembered how Anna had received the brand-new book by mail a month earlier. A farmer in blue dungarees was looking down at a cart in the valley. His wife and young son sitting at his feet. A family fleeing disaster. No wonder Anna was only slowly taking to the new book. Anna resumed her sad tale as the train rolled through Paris on its way to Gare du Lyon.

"There was hardly any help for us after we'd been shoved out of the train. We had nowhere to go and camped out without tents or anything in the pouring rain. My father tried to find us a way into Poland but was refused entrance every time. It got worse by the day. First Eva contracted pneumonia and then Sarah, but there were no doctors or nurses and we hardly had any money. Then a British Red Cross unit set up a refugee camp for us but..."

Anna's voice faltered. "It was too late for Eva and Sarah, delicate girls from birth. They died within hours of each other in their wet little dresses. It was 5 November last year." She sniffed, but held her head high, clearly no longer wanting to cry more tears than already had been shed. Esther didn't know what to say, how to comfort Anna, feeling bad about her earlier behavior toward her.

"My mother never recovered from losing her babies." Anna's voice was toneless, almost mechanical. "Through the Red Cross we got help to get to London, where my mother had an uncle, Uncle Benjamin, with whom we could live.

"Financially, we lacked nothing anymore because Uncle Benjamin is a diamond trader and a bachelor, living in a mansion in Kensington. He paid for my finishing school. Insisted I'd go there. I didn't want to go but with my mother in an asylum and my father only interested in his bookshop, there was little for me to enjoy in London. That's how I ended up at Le Manoir in early January. I don't know what I'll do on my return, but I expect I'll be helping my father in the bookshop or working for my uncle."

Her tonelessness and lack of interest in her future tugged on Esther's heartstrings. They'd almost arrived at the station, where they'd have to find their way to Gare Du Nord with the metro. She still had one more pressing question.

"Why did you change your name?"

"Oh, it's my mother's maiden name and, of course, that of Uncle Benjamin. Does the name Grynszpan not ring a bell for you?"

Esther thought for a moment. Shook her head.

"My father's brother and his wife, Sendel and Riva Grynszpan, were also expelled from their Hanover home and deported to Poland with us. Their son, my cousin Herschel, was studying in Paris at the time. They wrote to him, what had happened. And that's when Herschel..." Anna stopped talking, glancing furtively at the farmer and his wife, who were busy collecting their luggage and had no eye for the two young women at the window.

Anna continued in a whisper. "It was my cousin who killed the German Ernst Vom Rath at the German Embassy in Paris. The retaliation for that murder was what we now know as the Kristallnacht."

Esther clamped a hand over her mouth, remembering too well the devastation to Jewish property that it had led to as far as Vienna.

"Ooooh," she gasped.

"That's why it's safer for me to be Levi. Just in case."

Esther nodded, dumbfounded by Anna's history.

"Well, now you know my somber story and why I usually stick to myself." It sounded almost defiant.

"I'm so sorry," Esther replied, still at a loss for words, "and I'm sorry we didn't talk earlier. But if you want, I can tell you my story on the way to Le Havre. Maybe we can be friends after all? Though it's a bit late."

"Sure!" The wan smile was grateful and gracious in its own way.

11

GOING NORTH

The sea voyage from Le Havre to Oslo seemed interminable. Esther was seasick the whole three days and hardly able to leave her room. Lying in the sour smell of vomit, now sweating, now cold, she thought her last hour had struck. And the boat never stopped rocking. The noise of the ship's engines was deafening, and the cramped little space claustrophobic and stuffy.

There was one small porthole, but Esther had asked the nurse who came to tend to her in the mornings and evenings to keep the lid on the outside shut. She didn't want to see the waves; she could feel their effect on her entire system well enough without having to verify their existence.

It was her very first trip on an ocean and as far as she was concerned, her last. Only for one reason was her sickness favorable. She had no time to fret or worry. Shards of her intense conversation with Anna on the train flitted in and out of her consciousness, as did the teary goodbye on the quay. Newfound friendship nipped in the bud.

"You will write?" Anna's dark gaze, now more understandable to Esther, had pleaded with her.

"Of course. As soon as I arrive in Oslo."

She had had so many plans for when she got on board. Straighten herself out. Be the accomplished daughter her parents had wanted her to become, make Oma proud, grit her teeth over her postponed wedding, be everything to everyone. But she was a miserable mess, afraid of dying of dehydration and weakness. At times, even giving up the will to survive the next hour.

There was a knock on the door, and the Norwegian nurse bustled in without waiting for an answer. She was a tall and spindly woman, maybe in her late forties, her hair in a gray bun, a stiff white apron over a gray dress, a deep line above her long thin nose, hasty blue eyes and impatient movements.

Without further ado, she gripped Esther's pulse and stuffed a thermometer in her armpit. No word was exchanged as Esther gazed helplessly at the strict woman's face. The nurse said nothing. There was no understanding smile, no soft touch. Hers was very different from Océane's treatment after she fainted over her parents' letter.

It crossed Esther's mind that her body was revolting against the trip to the north, but despite her general weakness she brushed that thought aside. Carl would come. He had promised, and she knew him to keep his promises.

"Fever is down." The nurse spoke in clipped English. "You must eat broth."

Broth?

The word alone made her body convulse. But she nodded faintly.

"Salt and liquid," the nurse observed as she pressed on Esther's sunken tummy. A new wave of nausea made her turn to grip the bucket next to the bed. Convulsion after convulsion, but nothing came. It hurt like hell. Tears the only liquid her body could still produce.

"Doctor will come." The nurse got up and left without a further word.

Esther lay panting back on the bed. She wanted to cry, but

didn't dare. Her whole being hurt too much to move even one muscle. She prayed for sleep, the only temporary relief from the agony.

When she woke, the boat was no longer rocking. But there was plenty of noise outside her door. Had the doctor come already? Was she medicated? Slowly Esther raised herself to a sitting position and, though weak and dizzy, she wasn't in as much pain in her stomach as she'd been before. Just a queasiness and a strange pang of hunger.

She listened to the sounds outside. A strange language. Norwegian? It sounded rather rough and raw, but not unpleasant. She could make out the occasional word, which sounded like German. "*Fest tauene Befestige.*" Fasten the ropes! Had they finally touched shore?

The idea gave Esther wings and despite her grogginess, she put feeble feet on the wooden floorboard and rather clumsily got out of her sweaty nightdress and into her travel suit. In her haste, she tore off a button from her jacket and ripped her last pair of good stockings.

Staggering to the tiny bathroom, she lay eyes on herself for the first time in days. The sight in the mirror made her almost back out of the bathroom again. She looked awful. In no way could she appear before her family like this. She was supposed to be their beacon. The one who still had received a good education despite the hardships and drawbacks. She had to shine for them, keep up the semblance of what they wanted for her.

A quick dash of makeup, a good brush of her teeth and a comb through her matted, tangled hair. Mutti and Oma would surely see through this thinly disguised masquerade, but at least she'd made the effort.

Walking down the gangplank, weak-kneed and woozy but also filled with a warm ripple for her long-awaited reunion, Esther scanned the crowds on the docks. A feeble sun now and then peeped through bustling clouds, streaking the upturned faces below her with hopeful rays.

Esther's eyes, trained to spot her Oma, tall and blond, in every crowd, always an exception among Jewish crowds, found herself confronted with a difficulty. Here, almost every other woman was tall and blond. No Oma.

She was glad to see her father standing among the waiting crowds on the quay, but then almost took a step back. It was him for sure, but it also wasn't. He'd lost at least ten kilos and looked gaunt and dejected. Dark rings under his eyes, his shoulders stooped. Norway didn't become Franz Weiss, that was clear. It had diminished him, taken all the jolliness away.

She searched further for her mother, Rebecca, Adam, even Tante Isobel, or that unknown Oncle Frerik. They weren't there. Her father stood on his own. Lost, dazed, not even looking up to meet his eldest daughter's eyes.

"Papi!" she shouted, worming her way through the thickening crowds, bumping into embracing couples and people shouting merry cries of hello.

"Papi!"

Then, she was in her father's arms, feeling his bony frame under his worn suit, but his embrace was warm and wide, as were his words.

"My big daughter! Finally! How your return livens my old heart."

"How are you, Papi, and how is everyone? Where are they?" Esther peeped once again from out of her father's arms, but the rest of the family was nowhere to be seen.

"They are at Tante Isobel's, Bärchen. Don't worry. We're going there now. But it is a long walk. Are you up to that?"

Esther peeled herself out of her father's embrace, looking closely at him for the first time. Besides the loss of all his former weight, there was also a shroud of darkness around him. All his joviality and joie de vivre was gone.

"Are you all right, Papi?" She'd blurted it out before she could help herself.

"Sure, sure!" He waved a tired hand. "But what about you, my dear? Did they feed you well in Lausanne?"

He asked the customary questions, but his mind was clearly somewhere else, somewhere disturbed. Taking her by the hand, he made his way to the docking center where porters were busy collecting the luggage.

"Can't my luggage wait, Papi? The courier service will for sure deliver my suitcases to the house?"

Her father's face remained impassive, but his voice was coarse. "Those days are gone, my dear. We'll have to carry your suitcases ourselves."

No further explanation, factual, fundamental in its change. Esther bit her lip. It was as if the shock of her family's poverty catapulted her into her new surroundings. All her seasickness and frail nerves in the past.

She looked back one more time at the SS *Nordstjernen*, her only link to the past, and took in her new surroundings—this strange new city with its dark-red wood houses and white windowsills. Oslo.

Everything around her breathed and smelled nautical and maritime. All very different from the stately, patrician city of Vienna, with its refinement and cultural heritage. The humid sea wind, combined with the raw language and the robust and tall blond, no-nonsense people around her, made Esther realize she'd arrived in Viking territory. Among the kind of rough-and-tumble guys who'd disrupted her engagement party with their buffoonery. She recoiled inside herself for a moment, feeling homesick for Vienna, and realizing homesickness was what her father was suffering from.

No more suffering. Esther straightened her back and did what she was good at. Saving the situation.

"Of course, we can carry our own belongings, Papi. But listen, I still have some Swiss and French money on me. Do you think we can exchange that at the bank and sit down for a coffee first? I'd really like to hear everything from you before I see the others."

Doubt shimmered in his brown eyes as he took her in, but then they got back some of their former gold flecks. Esther had touched the right chord. Sitting down, a coffee, a chat, his daughter. A life they'd known and fled from. He caved in.

"Of course, my dear. Let's do that first. But I can't be too long. Oncle Frerik depends on my swift return to the shop."

Never letting go of his hand as if she was a little girl again, Esther and her father made their way to the Norges Bank on the Munkedamsveien. As they entered the bank's marble vestibule and he took off his once-expensive-but-now-careworn Homburg, it struck Esther again how desultory her father looked. It made her heart bleed.

Not him! Not her proud father!

Her Papi was a renowned and revered citizen and goldsmith from Vienna. A man with an impeccable reputation and an even more adept professional allure. A rich man, both in wealth and in health. A man of the world. Not this man who let his head hang, trying to make himself invisible, impassable, the two-penny-half-penny man he could and would never be.

They'd lost all their money!

Only then, in that posh bank's entrance, the truth dawned on Esther and she felt as ashamed as her father. Carry their own suitcases, no transport, no staff. And now, unwelcome in the bank. In the old days, the bank had been her father's place of pride and joy. The place that banker Jeremiah Wiesenthal from Wiesenthal & Schmidt would especially open for his best client and personal friend. Franz Weiss.

But now...

"Just wait outside, Papi. I'm sure I can handle it." Esther grabbed her purse and made her way to the revolving door with the gilded handles.

Her father nodded and shuffled back into the dull day, where the sun now refused to shine. Esther gritted her teeth. She would have to be strong. Strong for herself but also for her family. The first thing she'd do was find herself a job and add to the family income.

Resolutely, she went up to the baby-faced office clerk who was eyeing her with a mixture of interest and surprise. She was well-dressed, well-fed, pretty, blonde. Well, she would use it, if needed. All of it. She emptied her purse on the counter.

"How much in Krone?" she demanded, pushing the Swiss and French francs and notes in his direction.

She counted with him to ensure he wouldn't cheat her.

All she had in the world was 150 Krone, which seemed a fortune but was actually less than she'd spent in Switzerland within one month. She carefully stuffed the strange currency in her purse, thanked the brash clerk and, with her heels clicking loud on the marble tiles, made for the door.

She decided she was going to keep the money secret. She would only spend a tiny amount on coffee with her father, and the rest would be for when hard times fell on them. Because instinctively she knew, this was only the beginning.

The beginning of something very different.

12

PAPI'S TALE

"Tell me, Papi, what happened in Vienna? Mutti's letter was deliberately vague. I understood it was because of possible censorship. But we're safe now. You can tell me." Esther was stirring the cream in her coffee with great attention so as not to focus on her father's face.

He remained silent. She would give him time. Around them, the wooden legs of chairs scraped over sanded floorboards, and men and women talked loudly in that strange tongue of which Esther could only make out individual words.

When the silence endured, she glanced in her father's direction. He tried to recover himself. Appear more dignified than he felt. Retrieving the stump of an old cigar from his pocket, she saw him carefully lighting it and drawing in the ashy smoke. Esther cringed. Papi had lost his golden cigar case, from which he would always choose one of his Havanas with great care and a contented smile.

As he cleared his throat, the blue smoke swirled through the air, mixing with the cigarette smoke from other tables.

"It was bad, Bärchen, very bad. I tell myself every morning after waking up that I must be grateful. That my family is still alive, that we're all together. And safe." He put a hand over hers, protectively.

"What happened, Papi?" Her voice was small.

"They set fire to the workshop while we were all asleep upstairs. We had to flee the flames via the fire escape at the back. Could only grab the most essential. The hardest of all was to keep Rebbie and Adam from crying."

Esther's eyes met her father's. He was fighting not to cry himself. Their entire livelihood, all he'd lived for.

"I knew the Gestapo was intent on killing us in our own beds. That's why they couldn't know we'd escaped." He faltered again. "The terrorization had been going on for weeks. Blocking my bank account, raiding the shop. I'm afraid the Bernsteins suffered the same lot."

Esther went rigid at the name of her fiancé but knew she would ask that question later. Now, she needed to know what had brought her father to his knees.

"Thank God, I still had our passports and a little money left. Slept with them under my pillow. Just in case. Your mother and grandmother had a small valise ready for everyone. The threat had been there and to be honest, your mother had insisted on going to Norway much earlier. Maybe she was right."

He took another pull from the tiny cigar stump before stabbing it out in the overflowing ashtray.

"Would you like another coffee, Papi?" It was all Esther had to offer. To her surprise, he consented.

"You're right, my dear. It's best I tell you all before we get home, so it's all done and dusted. We're trying to integrate here as best as we can, but it isn't easy being a beggar."

"Papi! Don't say that!"

"Well. It is the truth. All the assets I had transferred to Switzerland before the war have been frozen. I can't touch them." Her father's voice was shrill, almost desperate. Several Norwegians looked in their direction. Disturbed. German was not a language they wanted to hear in neutral Norway, the difference between the accents not familiar to them.

I'll have to learn Norwegian as fast as I can, Esther thought, focusing on finding a way to survive the crisis, to help her family to decency again.

"I'm so sorry, Papi," she said softly. "You've worked so hard for us. You don't deserve this."

"None of us deserves this." His tone was as bitter as his black coffee.

"How did you get out of Austria?"

"I knew as clear as day we had to let the Bernsteins know we were leaving. So, I sent Oma and Mutti to the station with the children and went over to their house to wake Carl."

Her father halted, throwing her a worried look.

"Go on."

It was hardly audible, the last word ending in a suppressed sob.

"Their shop was raided a few weeks earlier. And closed after. Just like ours. Carl tried to scrape by earning a little money in the same Glassfabrik where I worked before we left. The treatment at the Fabrik was harsh, relentless. No lunch breaks, and for the smallest act of defiance in their eyes, like needing the bathroom or sitting down for a second, they'd keep our paycheck. But what could we do?" Her father stared miserably out of window, remembering the unfair treatment, then resumed his sad tale.

"Meanwhile, Carl Sr had had another stroke, but they couldn't take him to any hospital. No one accepts Jews anymore at the *Allgemeines Krankenhaus*. Or any of the other clinics. You remember how they destroyed our synagogue inside the hospital during the Kristallnacht? No Jew dares to ask for medical treatment since. So, Carl Sr's life is hanging on by a thread."

Franz paused, looking stricken as he spoke of his former competitor, now the father of Esther's betrothed and thus almost family.

"I don't even know if he's still alive. Sarah Bernstein looks after her husband as best she can. I know she's urged Carl to flee the country, but he won't listen. He says he can't leave her coping on her own. Well, there's something to be said for his devotion to his parents."

A silence fell between them. Esther wrung her lace handkerchief between her fingers. A pair of dice landed hard on the wooden surface of the next table. The sudden sound made her jolt. Laughter, cheers. A game, life went on. Was lived.

Also for her.

Also for Carl.

"I know. It's praiseworthy."

What else could she say? It was on the tip of her tongue to ask more about Carl, but her throat constricted. She couldn't. Papi would've told her if he had news.

As she drained the last of her coffee, the first beverage in the new country, she felt the hurt in her empty stomach, in her even emptier heart. Her father seemed to have read her unspoken thought.

"He'll come, Bärchen, don't worry. He'll come!"

She lifted swimming blue-green eyes only to see the doubt reflected in his brown ones. It was too much right now. She had to change the subject.

"Tell me about the journey to Norway."

"Only if you tell me about yours, too." Her father's attempt at lightheartedness lifted her spirits to some extent, and she decided she needed to be a breath of fresh air to her Papi before they went to their new home.

"Not much to tell there. I was seasick during the entire trip. Waves are not for me. I prefer water to be solid. Ice or snow. I can deal with that."

"Well, then you've come to the right country, my dear. Norway is supposed to be glacial in winter. We've so far only had early spring here, but it was cold as marble stone when we arrived. Rebbie insisted on wearing her summer coat underneath her winter coat as an extra layer. Made us laugh." Franz produced a wan smile under his sagging mustache.

Then he looked serious again. "You're like me, Bärchen. I don't like boats either. Going to the diamond fair in New York in 1930 was a-once-and-never-again trip for me. Oysters, immense fruit bowls topped with fresh cream, lamb chops and champagne by the gallon. It was all aboard the SS Manhattan but not meant for Franz Weiss. He lay like a dog in his cabin for two weeks."

Now it was Esther's turn to smile. Some of her father's old vigor returned as he talked about his happier past as a well-reputed gold-smith traveling the world.

"Now, more seriously. In a way, we were lucky as we were one of the last trains the Gestapo allowed Jews to travel on abroad." Franz shook his graying head. "I should have listened to your mother earlier, but I truly never believed it could come to this."

He waved a sad hand around him, conveying he keenly felt the exile, the stateless person he'd become. Thoughts of Anna's story came to Esther's mind as she listened to another hasty retreat. Her father concluded his tale.

"My sister had sort of expected us but hadn't prepared for it, so we took her by surprise. They live over Oncle Frerik's tannery shop on Grønlandsleiret with their two boys, Ole and David. Only a three-room apartment, and our family—now six members—added to that. I've been looking for a place of our own, but it's difficult and expensive when you don't have a regular job and you're a foreigner. Norway is still suffering from the great depression, and their own population comes first. I understand that, but it's quite undoable as it is. I try to stay out of the way as much as I can, helping Frerik in his market stall in the Auktionshallen, but my lack of Norwegian is a drawback." He sighed, scratching his beard stubble, looking dejected again.

"Papi, I'm here to help now. You realize that, don't you? I'm strong; I can work. Maybe I can find work as a housekeeper in a grand house and make use of my expensive education. Plus, it would be one less mouth to feed."

"You're a good girl, Esther, and yes, I'd never thought I'd say it but I'm glad you're back. Mutti has to educate the younger ones, and she's also taken it upon herself to look after the boys so Isobel can work in the shop. I'm sure that we'll manage from now on and soon find a place of our own."

His own pep talk seemed to revive him. As she paid for their coffees—the very first time in her life she'd paid for something for her father—she saw how ashamed he was, and it only strengthened her resolve to become the savior of her family. She'd work so hard, she'd be too tired to even think of Carl and a very different future.

13

A STRANGE NEW HOME

The first test of Esther's conviction came immediately. Dragging her smaller suitcase and her heavy handbag in either hand, she followed her father's back through the busy Oslo streets, one after the other, seemingly without an end. She was exhausted and disoriented. Her heels hurt in her narrow shoes and her beautiful travel suit became crumpled and humid with perspiration. Her hat continued to sink over her eyes. And the people! Men bumped into her as if she was invisible and women with loaded shopping baskets looked angry at her as if she took up too much space on the sidewalk.

A niggling voice in her head kept pushing her to ask, "How far still, Papi?" But her resolution to be her family's anchor from now on prevented her. Then the heel came off her left shoe, and she had to put it in her bag and stumble, almost losing her equilibrium as she limped on.

Just when she thought she could not take another step, her father turned a corner and announced, "Here we are."

Esther put her suitcase down at her feet with a thump. She tried to brush the sweat from her forehead with the sleeve of her jacket, a gesture Madame Paul would have more than frowned upon, but at that moment all etiquette went by the wayside.

"Thank God," she exclaimed. "I know you warned me, but I feel like we've walked for hours. And I'll need to get my best shoe repaired."

"Forget about all that now, Bärchen, and let's celebrate your return."

The front door flung open, and she was in her mother's arms, inhaling her familiar perfume, warm, secure, home.

"My daughter, my daughter," Naomi kept repeating, hugging her close, as they sobbed together, from joy and from stress. Soon, Rebecca and Adam wrapped their arms around mother and daughter to join the family embrace.

"Come inside now," Franz urged them. "You're making a spectacle in the street. I don't think these Nordic folk much appreciate such an outpour of emotion." They all laughed, and Esther felt her mother take her face in-between her soft, warm hands and look at her. There were tears glistening in her dark eyes, but relief and happiness won. Esther was glad to see her mother had at least outwardly not changed much since their ordeal in Vienna.

"Mutti, thank you for everything," Esther whispered. "I've learned so much and I'm sure I can bring it into practice even now."

"Come and greet Oma; she's waiting for you upstairs." With her hands still cupping Esther's cheeks, she mouthed, "She's much worse." The pain of the sudden warning was as sharp as a dagger, but her mother continued in a cheerful voice, as if nothing had happened. "Children, let go of Esther's skirt."

"I will greet Oma in a minute, Mutti. Just give me a sec."

Rebecca and Adam needed her attention. She turned to her sister, who'd grown at least two inches, and pulled her slender, deerlike body into her arms.

"Rebbi, you are so big. And you must teach me Norwegian." Rebecca's smile was as wide as a barn door.

"I will, Es, and you must meet Tore. He's our next-door neighbor, and he can't wait to see you."

"All right, Rebbie, but let's be with the family first." She drew Adam, who'd been watching from a small distance back into the sibling embrace, ignoring her father's snorting about "spectacles in the street."

"How's my brother Adam? Do you like Oslo?"

"It's okay, but some things are funny, like the loads of herring they eat and at least a kilo of potatoes every day. I can say, *"jeg heter Adam og bor på Grønlandsleiret i Oslo."* Do you know what that means?"

"Do tell me!"

With his small chest puffed out, he translated, "My name is Adam and I live on the Grønlandsleiret in Oslo."

"That is fabulous! I have so much to learn."

"Come now, children!" Her father was beginning to become impatient, but something was holding Esther back from walking into that strange house that wasn't theirs. She needed to shed an old skin before she could walk up some stranger's stairs to an apartment over a shop. Too many memories of their luxurious flat on the Prater Strasse played havoc with her.

Rebbie seemed to instinctively understand her dilemma and slipped her hand in hers. *Her little shadow*, Esther thought. How she had missed that silent, watching slip of a girl who felt so deeply and knew her so well. Rebbie looked up to her, the dark eyes solemn and wise. *You'll be okay*, they conveyed without words, and this gave Esther the strength to step into her new skin.

"Come to Oma. She needs you," Rebbie whispered. Adam was already hauling her suitcase to the door, so she followed her family up the stairs, where there was a smell of fried onions and potatoes. Up to new family members, she didn't know, but who were all they had left in the world.

Pulling her black stole tightly around her thin shoulders, Oma stood waiting at the top of the stairs, completely white, straight-backed and statuesque like a Roman statue but with a vacant look in the sea-green eyes.

She's looking backwards, was Esther's first thought. *There's nothing for her here.*

The light eyes—once a reflection of Esther's own—were no longer assessing the measure of a lady her granddaughter had become. Outwardly still that rare combination of sweet and stern, she was inwardly adrift, never to reach shore again.

Esther swallowed, fought the tears, took hesitant steps to this empty shell, remembering the days when, where Oma was, it was home. Oma, who'd been there always when her parents had obligations, Oma the maternal backbone of the family. The memory was bittersweet. Oma was here, and yet she wasn't. What a strange homecoming.

"My Bärchen." Her grandmother's characteristic voice was still strong as ever. At least she remembered. She kissed her granddaughter on the forehead, an old custom, but it wasn't enough for Esther. A raw cry for the past overwhelmed her and against protocol, she threw herself into her grandmother's thin arms. The old lady muttered a confused,

"Come, come, Bärchen, now be strong! It's your wedding day."

Esther exchanged a glance with her mother, who with raised eyebrows seemed to say, "I told you so." Her father slinked down the stairs again, clearly unable to stand the unraveling of his mother's mind any longer.

Two identically looking boys with strawberry-blond hair and pale freckled faces, eyes a deep-blue violet, stuck their heads around the door, taking in the newcomer with interest. Still clasping her grandmother's claw-like hand, the bones thin and brittle as a young bird's, Esther greeted them.

"You must be Ole and David."

"I'm Ole," the slightly bigger one replied, "I'm seven and David is six."

"Boys!" A voice called from inside the apartment. "Come in, and let Esther through."

Still holding Oma's hand, she was the one leading the old lady

through the open door, something that would not have been think-
able only a year ago. They stepped into a middle-class living room
that sprang at her in bright colors and smelled strongly of leather
and shoe wax. Joyful striped carpets on the wooden floor, light
furniture, linen patterned curtains, and an array of comfy leather
chairs. A new type of decoration for Esther, but not unpleasant to
the eye. A coziness she could—somehow—feel at home in.

At the table, also draped with a table runner in yellow, green
and white, sat a young-looking woman behind a sewing machine,
her apron in the same material as the runner. She looked up as her
feet continued to rhythmically push the foot control and the needle
went tack-tack-tack through a leather strip she pushed away
from her.

What immediately struck Esther was Tante Isobel's resemblance to her father, the same broad, jovial face, brown, gold-
flecked eyes, and a ready smile.

It had been ten years since she last saw her aunt waving
goodbye at Vienna station, a young bride-to-be embarking on her
new life in that Nordic country. None of the family had attended
her Oslo wedding to Frerik Gjelsvik.

Esther had been too young to ask why it was all hush-hush at
the time, but had later pieced together that Isobel Weiss was the
first and only one in the family to marry a non-Jew.

Different times, different customs. Now, finally had come the
reunion with her brother and mother, brought about by force of
circumstance.

"Esther!" She exclaimed, "You're here! Sorry for not greeting
you earlier but Frerik has an emergency repair."

She pulled the strap for the leather bag from underneath the
sewing machine, collected the snippets of leather from her lap, and
took off her apron. Then she approached her niece with open arms.
Everything on Tante Isobel was round, so her fleshy embrace felt
welcome and good.

"Now let me look at you, little Madam." She whirled Esther
around as if she was her dance partner, then clucked her tongue.

"Quite a difference from the little girl in petticoats, waving her lace hanky at me as I said goodbye to Vienna to marry my love!" Isobel chuckled and winked. The freedom her aunt exerted was refreshing.

Tante Isobel was light, humorous, flirty. And there came no rebuke from Oma for such light-hearted behavior. To Esther, this fresh aunt with her newly adopted manners was a first hopeful sign in her new country. They'd gone through enough doom and gloom.

"Thank you, Tante!"

"Come and sit with me and tell me all about you. Unpacking can be done later. I'd say lemonade and some Bløtkake. I've baked a fresh one for your arrival."

Tante filled the entire room with her sparkly personality. It made Oma and Mutti reserved ladies-in-waiting. Something in the Weiss blood was very extroverted indeed.

On the invitation of her aunt, Esther took a seat at the table. Adam was lying on the floor with his cousins, racing wooden cars along the stripes of the carpet as if they were lanes. Her mother and grandmother had retired to the leather chairs in the sitting room area, as if unsure where they belonged. Only Rebbie stayed close to her, pulling up a chair next to her big sister.

Clear, though unwritten, demarcation lines divided the ladies of the family. Isobel Gjelsvik was the primary woman here, at home in her own house, and her word law. Not an easy to swallow position for the two proud and distinguished Viennese matrons, though Oma seemed to have let all decorum slip. Mutti was unhappy, pulling on the fabric of her woolen skirt, something she'd never have dreamed of in her own house.

Esther gauged this new hierarchy with her social antennae. What was her role? How best to play it? She enjoyed her aunt's lightheartedness but longed to be in the presence of her mother and grandmother after all this time. Yet she saw no other way than to accept Tante's kind invitation. She smiled apologetically to her maternal protectors.

Her mother smiled back, and Esther prayed she understood her daughter's message.

I'll sort this out for us!

~

THAT EVENING, as they sat around Tante Isobel's large kitchen table draped with one of her colorful tablecloths, the enormity of the change really began to sink in for Esther.

Oncle Frerik, a seven-foot giant with a ferocious mop of ashen-blond hair and steel-blue eyes, took in his rough workman's hands, adorned with black-ringed nails, a heavy book titled *Bibelen på Norsk*. The Bible?

Esther furtively glanced at her elders, whose faces were as impassive as figures of carved ivory. She knew her aunt had converted to Frerik's Protestantism upon her marriage, but had never given it a second thought.

Only Adam seemed to be enamored by the upcoming reading, while the Gjelsvik brothers were kicking each other's shins under the table and got a reprimand from their mother. The rest of the Weiss family—apart from Adam—seemed to withdraw within themselves.

Frerik started reading in a fast, monotonous tone, racing through the words as if the steaming potatoes and smoked herring were of more interest to him than his Lord's Gospel. Adam was counting on his fingers, adamant about cutting the first turf as he broke his tongue over his new language.

"Five, no six!" Adam shouted when their uncle closed the thick Bible with a thud and attached the clasps around it. Ole slipped from his chair to carry the large book to the dresser, where it remained for the rest of the meal.

"Tell me," Oncle Frerik said with a wink to Adam, meanwhile wolfing down the enormous plate of food his wife hastily put in front of him.

"*Himmel* for heaven, *Gud* for God, *fugler* for birds, *dag* for day and *Adam* for Adam." His eyes glistened at his last discovery. "I was mentioned in the Bible today. I'm famous!"

"Well done, first God-made man on earth!" Frerik smacked his lips approvingly. "Now say after me: *I begynnelsen skapte Gud himmelen og Jorden.* That's how *Mosebok* begins or Moses, as you would say. I'm doing my best, wife, reading more from the Old Testament now your folk are here."

Esther was puzzled by the foreign language, the strange and strained atmosphere and the waft of food she wasn't accustomed to. Her uncle kept peering from under his bristly light eyebrows in her direction and that of her family. She had to admit they were all picking their food like nifty little birds, eyes downcast. But the food was good, and Esther's appetite was restored. After not eating properly for days, she was glad her stomach had calmed down. Now, integrating her family in these uncommon surroundings and solving the money problems were her main concerns.

That evening as she lay in the narrow bed she shared with Rebecca, Esther had the first moment to reflect on the strange situation in which her family had landed and how it broke them up. Her mother and grandmother weren't good at not being the mistress of the house. Her father was trying hard to put up a bright face working for his brother-in-law in a business he'd nothing in common with.

Only her siblings seemed to take to the new environment, with Rebbie talking about the friendly neighbors and her new playmate there and Adam having found a common boys' language with the Gjelsvik brothers.

Something had to be done, and it had to happen fast, Esther thought, as she listened to the even breathing of her sister and to the now silent house except for her parents' whispered voices on the other side of the thin wall. She strained her ears but only caught the occasional word—"money", "house," and several times, her own name.

What they were whispering about could only be guessed. She fell asleep with the firm decision that the first thing she'd do the

next day was find work, although she didn't speak the language and
had no formal training in any occupation apart from housekeeping.
Well, for sure, there was housekeeping to be done here, too.

Tomorrow morning. First thing.

I'll save them all.

14

LIFE IN NORWAY

Esther woke with a start, not knowing where she was until she felt the familiar body of her sister next to her. Rebbie! Her heart jumped up; she was home with her beloved sister. Unique Rebbie who had what Oma used to call "an old soul."

But then reality sneaked into the strange bedroom. They weren't snuggled up together in their comfy home at the Prater Strasse. They were in a cold, northern country among strangers, expelled from their hearth and home because of who they were.

Esther lay on her back, letting her mind flit through all the confusing happenings and emotions of the day before. Clear as still water was the oath she'd taken upon herself. Help her family back to who they really were; a decent, God-abiding family who worked hard and owed nobody anything. Stuck in the moment, temporary visitors who'd return to their own country as soon as the borders were open to them again.

She was ready for it. Would learn Norwegian at the speed of light, throw herself into this new adventure and make sure they came out on top. But where to start? She would ask Tante Isobel and Oncle Frerik for all their connections and contact them one after the other until she had a job.

Dressed in her most befitting dress, a navy-blue linen dress with a white collar and cuffs that fitted her like a glove and set off the blond hair and sea-green eyes, she studied herself. Very Madame Paul, said her reflection, but under the circumstances that seemed a safe choice.

Her engagement ring gave her some doubts. Would people employ her if they assumed she'd only stay for a short while before she got married and had to quit? She studied the gold band with the diamonds and decided she couldn't part with this precious remembrance of Carl just yet.

Rebecca had meanwhile woken up as well and was rubbing the sleep from her eyes.

"Sis," she yawned, "where are you going all dressed up like that?"

"To find a job."

Rebecca shot up, her eyes wide awake now.

"A job? Papi won't let you."

"Oh yes, he will, and even if he'd try to stop me, he'd have to kill me first."

"Essie," Rebecca giggled, "what's come over you? You never were one for women's rights."

"That's got nothing to do with me needing a job, sweet one. Papi simply can't earn enough money for the six of us, and Mutti has to look after Oma."

"Can I come?"

Rebecca jumped out of bed and shot into her own simple cotton day dress. "I can work too, you know!"

Esther shook her head. "You're too young, Rebs, and by the way, you have to help Mutti here with looking after the children."

Rebecca pulled a face, tiny wrinkles in her sweet straight nose.

"The boys are boring, and I miss school. My only friend Astrid is back at school now."

"Why aren't you in school? Is it forbidden for foreigners to go to a Norwegian school?"

Esther deliberately didn't use the word Jew. She had enough of being considered Jewish. Protected by Oncle Frerik's Protestantism and living in new country where nobody knew who they were, they had a chance at adopting a new identity. She would not refer to herself or her family as Jewish anymore. Not until Hitler was defeated.

"I could go to school," Rebecca remarked, "but Mutti and Tante can't find a school where I fit in now. I do not yet speak enough Norwegian. Addie's okay; he's still in *Barneskole*. Barn means child. Tante Isobel is busy finding me a language course so I can hopefully go to Astrid's school in January."

"Aha! Well, in that case you can help me find a job."

"How?" Rebecca looked excited and puzzled in equal measure.

"By writing down all the names of the people you've met since you arrived in Oslo."

Her sister's face fell.

"I thought I could go with you to the job."

"No, wisecracker, you can't." Esther kissed her sister's sweet, warm cheek. "They'll think I'm offering you up for child slavery."

A tinkling laughter exploded from Rebecca's lips, a sound so dear and familiar to Esther. Then, with a conspiring look, the younger one added, "I know where we will start. With our neighbors. The Helbergs. Astrid's parents," she explained. "Tore can't wait to meet you. I told you so, didn't I?"

A frown appeared on Esther's fair forehead. "Why would the neighbor's boy want to meet me?"

"He's not a boy, silly," Rebecca chuckled. "Tore's a grown man. He studies at the Oslo *Universitetet*. Norwegian is such a funny language, don't you think?" She repeated, "Universitetet. Tetet. Tetet."

"Okay, that might be a good start," Esther agreed. "Students usually know a lot of side jobs. But write down all the names of other people, anyway. I'm also going to ask Oncle Frerik. And now we're going to have breakfast."

After a light breakfast of ryebread with butter, cheese and jam and two cups of black coffee, Esther with Rebecca on her heels, went down the stairs to her uncle's shop. The smell of acidic tannin and raw hides was sickening. Esther had difficulty keeping her breakfast down in this nauseous odor. Her stomach revolted from the stench.

Rebecca seemed to be already used to the smell of the tannery and skipped in happily to her uncle, who was busy coloring a piece of leather with a red brown paint. The giant Norseman peered at his two nieces over the half glasses that balanced on the bridge of his firm nose before turning back to his painting. His hands were smeared with the brownish paint.

"You settling in all right, Esther?"

Oncle Frerik's voice was deep and loud but not unfriendly. His hands worked on, never resting for one second. "If you're looking for your father, he's already gone to the market."

"Actually, I came for you, Oncle Frerik."

Again, those piercing blue eyes over the rim of his glasses; one quick glance and back to work.

"What can I do for you, Missy?"

"I need a job, Oncle. I need to help increase the family income so we can pay rent for a house of our own. Do you happen to know of something I could do?"

Her uncle shrugged his shoulders while he put the brush on the paint can and took a step back to look at his work.

"Not many jobs to be found for a young girl. Even men have difficulty finding jobs in Oslo. Depression, you know. It's probably easier in the countryside. You know, light farm work or helping with the household."

"Do you know people in the countryside, Oncle?" Esther buckled at the idea of leaving her family again to work elsewhere, but what had to be done had to be done. It would be temporary anyway. Until...

"You could ask Eivind Helberg, our next-door neighbor. His wife's parents have a farm near Søndre Nordstrand, south of Oslo. Maybe they have work."

"I wanted Esther to meet the Helbergs," Rebecca piped in.

"Come, let's see if they're home." She was already pulling her sister's sleeve.

"I'll think on your question, Esther, I promise." Frerik was wiping the paint from his hands with an old rag and looked up as a customer came into the shop. The doorbell jingled merrily, and stuffing the rag in the front pocket of his leather apron, he headed to the front counter in a trot.

"God dag, Per!"

"God dag, Frerik."

Esther followed her sister via the back of the shop to the house next door. Rebecca unlatched one garden gate and slipped into the next. From the back of the house came a tall, silver-colored dog with a black face, his tail curled on his back. Barking loudly, he came racing toward them but then recognized Rebecca and wagged the funny, curled tail. The black snout with round brown eyes sniffed the newcomer with curiosity.

"Hi, Bodil!" Both Rebecca's hands disappeared in the dog's thick fur. He seemed to like her caress but had eyes only for Esther.

"Bodil is an Elkhound," Rebecca explained. "They're the national dog here in Norway."

Friendly but slightly overpowering, Bodil jumped up and put his front paws on Esther's chest. She almost toppled backwards due to the powerful and unexpected jump.

"Bodil, down!"

A stern voice shouted from the house, and down the garden path came a muscle-bound man with swift athletic steps, his rather long mane pushed from his angular face featuring the fierce blue eyes of the Nordic race. Bodil immediately turned his interest to the young man, who grabbed him by the collar and kept him down. The blue eyes were on Esther.

"You!"

They said it at the same time. Facing each other like two cock fighters in the ring, ready to ruffle some feathers. Tore was the first to look away, evading the fiery and furious examination of his reappearance in her life. Esther felt as if he'd physically given her a push. All the embarrassment and disappointment of her ruined engagement dress rolled back to her in that second.

"Why didn't you tell me?" she snapped at her sister.

"I tried to," Rebecca defended herself. "But you wouldn't listen. And you don't have to be so snooty, Es, because Tore is really nice, and he can't wait to apologize to you again."

To her own surprise, Esther laughed out loud. But it wasn't heartfelt. It was hurt, at the ridiculousness of the situation.

"For God's sake, why do I have to run into *you* again, of all people in Norway?"

Tore smiled at her exclamation of horror, a twisted smile as if he'd been invited to dine with a ghost. He replied in a curt, dry voice, "Yeah, I know. I told your sister you'd hate me for the rest of my life."

"You talked about me behind my back?" Esther's indignation only increased at his confession.

"No, we didn't 'talk about you behind your back,' as you put it. You came up once or twice in our conversations. For heaven's sake, Rebecca is your sister. She may talk about her family, may she not?" The whole apologetic attitude disappeared. Tore was angry now as well. Angry at *her*.

How dare he?

Without saying another word, he turned his back on them and strode back to the house. Bodil followed him with drooping ears, tail down.

"Wait!" Esther shouted after him. "I didn't come here to fight over my ruined dress. I came to ask if you know of a job for me."

Tore ignored her until he was at the foot of the wooden steps that led to the porch. He turned, thunder still ablaze in the steely gaze. Had she stepped over the line? She needed the job, needed to make friends, not enemies.

"A job?" he repeated with a tinge of sarcasm. "*You* are asking *me* for a job?" His right hand was caressing the soft neck collar of his four-legged companion. His gaze tempered, became aloof, maybe even suspicious. As if he wanted to say, "I can't figure you out; I don't trust you."

This attitude befuddled Esther. Her whole life, everybody she met had been nice and polite with her. Except for Madame Paul, but that had been part of the Jew-hate and had had little to do with her, Esther. But this man… this man wasn't nice, or polite, or well-behaved, whatever Rebecca thought. It was a complete mystery what her younger sister saw in the man she'd called "nice." It was Rebecca, now, who spoke up in the grown-up way she sometimes adopted.

"Please, Tore, Esther's bark isn't as bad as her bite. May we come in?"

He shrugged his broad shoulders, blew a lock of sandy hair from his eye, then smiled with affection at the younger Weiss sister.

"You know you're always welcome here, Rebs. Astrid can't wait for you to join her at the Fagerborg skole. How are your *norsk* lessons going?"

This chatty, friendly Tore was a completely different person from the surly plebeian who had addressed Esther. She bit her lip. Had she misjudged him? Put him on the wrong foot? What if she'd let him apologize, as Rebecca had said he wanted to? Well, it was too late for well-disposed relations now, but perhaps he would still tell her about the student jobs.

She followed them along the garden path but halted in her tracks. "You are always welcome," he'd said to her sister, but they had both just walked into the house with the dog on their heels without paying further attention to her. It was a new feeling, to be rejected, to have her little sister being favored over her. Not that she begrudged Rebecca a friendship, but to be excluded from it? Just like that?

This country was unreadable to her. Not knowing what to do, she sank down on a garden bench in this stranger's garden, staring vacantly at the abundance of asters, begonias and sweet peas that filled the plot around the bench, their permeating scent perfuming the air. Someone tended this garden well. It was at least welcoming her.

It was as if the long year of separation from her family, her struggle at the finishing school, the sickening travel north and the loss—if only temporary—of her planned future dropped on Esther like a bomb.

She sat there defeated and deflated, more alone than she could ever remember, hanging in-between worlds she hadn't chosen and weren't hers to have and hold. All her earlier determination to save her family by finding employment seeped out of her. *I am small and insignificant. I wonder if God even still loves me.*

"Are you coming, Essie?"

Rebecca's voice cut through her somber suppositions.

Her slender, dark-haired, fifteen-year-old sister was holding open the screen door to the Helberg's residence as if she belonged there, inviting her in. But Esther didn't feel inclined to face more possible scorn from towering Tore. Not now, when she was so vulnerable and her nerves on edge.

"I think I'll just go back to Tante Isobel's."

When she got up from the bench, her hair caught in the thorn of a rosebush, and she was showered with falling rose petals. Cautiously unhooking the thorn from the back of her head, the tiny petals dropped around her like pink confetti rain.

Her tenth birthday party. Papi entering with something in his hand that exploded with a poof, filling the entire sitting room in a cloudburst of tiny pink candies. She and her friends on their knees collecting the sweets.

Breathe, Esther, breathe.

Her feet hurt in the thin-soled shoes, but she wants to get to 100. Where does that dark shadow come from?

With all her force, Esther restrained herself and pushed the unwelcome flashback where it came from.

"Come on in, Es. Tante Liv wants to meet you." Rebecca was raising her voice, cutting through Esther's flashback.

Tante Liv? Was Rebecca addressing their neighbor as if she was family? She certainly was thick with the Helbergs. Smoothing the wrinkles from her best dress and putting the escaped locks of her hair back under the mother-of-pearl hair comb, Esther passed through the screen door that Rebecca held open for her.

The house was cool and comfortable. A red-stone tiled corridor led to an airy, light-filled kitchen, where a blond woman stood kneading dough at a worktop. She brushed a string of springy hair from her angelic blue eyes and smiled at Esther, two rows of beautiful white teeth. Esther thought she looked as lovely as the Goose Girl in *Grimm's Fairy Tales*, a picture book she had held dear as a child.

"Hei, hei. So you're Rebecca's big sister? Welcome to our house. Forgive me for not being able to shake your hand." Tante Liv looked apologetically at her dough-crusted fingers and giggled, a light-hearted sound that escaped like a freed bird from her throat. Esther instantly understood why Rebecca liked to come here. Fru Liv Helberg was fun.

She looked around the homely kitchen as colorful as Tante Isobel's interior furnishing and understood that this must be the Norwegian style decoration. Liv was quick to pick up on Esther's thoughts.

"Come and sit down, Esther. Let me get this dough rising first and clean my hands. Then we can have a chat. I've been looking forward to meeting you. There is much I want to share with you."

Esther was puzzled. Share with her? They didn't even know each other. There was no sight of Rebecca anymore, but she heard voices in another room and a guitar being strummed. Her sister had always wanted to learn the guitar, but Mutti had insisted on the violin as Esther had been taught the piano. Those were the instruments Weiss girls played. A guitar was considered too mundane.

"Don't worry about Rebecca," Liv said. "She and Tore are two peas in a pod. He seems to be closer to his neighbor than to his own sister. I think it's because they share the same sort of philosophical outlook on life."

When the dough lay covered with a hot wet cloth, Liv lit the stove and filled a large metal kettle with water.

"Let's have some coffee as we chat, or do you prefer tea?"

"Coffee is fine." Esther realized it was the first thing she'd actually said.

"My Astrid is very different," Liv continued, undisturbed by Esther's lack of conversation. The latter sat perched on the edge of her chair, still dressed in an outfit in which she'd hoped to get a job.

"Astrid is very practical and down to earth, wants to become a nurse. She's read everything about Florence Nightingale and now believes she can be the Northern angel. Well, I'm just glad she and Rebecca get on so well. There aren't many other children nearby and there's such a big age gap between Tore and Astrid, almost nine years. Not that Rebecca seems to mind either way. She gets on with both of them like a house on fire."

As the water boiled, Liv counted heaped spoons of coffee into the white enamel coffeepot, adding a pinch of salt. Esther watched in surprise.

"You're very different from your sister." Liv stirred the coffee, not explaining in which way the sisters were different. *I'm not my usual self here*, Esther thought, *and it's got to do with that unnerving Tore in the other room. But I can't tell that to his mother. She'd laugh her head off at my indignation.*

Liv had meanwhile put the cups and the coffeepot in front of her on the bright red and yellow oilcloth.

"Let me see if I have some of these *sandbakkelse* cookies for you. If Tore hasn't put his big paws in the jar." Liv giggled again with her bird-like, freeing laugh. She seemed to find most things in life humorous, especially the freedom her children seemed to take. What a conflicting look on pedagogy this was to what Esther and her siblings had been brought up in.

Maybe that was why Rebecca liked to escape to this household. Sitting a little more relaxed on the chair, she accepted both the steaming cup and the *sandbakkelse* that resembled their Linzer cookies but without the jam heart. Esther put white teeth cautiously in a corner of the cookie. The taste was mouth-watering and gone in one other bite. She had another.

"So," Liv continued, the fairy blue eyes fixed on Esther, "I might as well cut right to the chase before these two come and disturb our conversation." She inclined her blonde head toward the voices and the guitar music.

"I have a suggestion to make, but I didn't discuss it with Isobel or your parents for fear they will think I'm being nosy, and besides..." She halted for a moment, a shadow of doubt in the crystal-clear eyes. "Besides, it's not what you are accustomed to."

Esther failed to understand what Liv was talking about, so remained silent.

"My parents own a farm in Søndre Nordstrand."

Esther nodded. Her uncle had told her so.

"My parents are getting old and they're looking for help. Tore goes out often enough to give them a hand, but his studies at the university make it hard for him to be of much-needed help all the time. And Eivind, my husband, works such irregular hours as a police officer. They can't count on him either." She stopped again and Esther saw she felt shy.

"Go on, please."

"Well, you may wonder why my parents don't hire a farmhand, or two, but it's not that they're rich or anything. And they're not very trusting of strangers these days. Norway has too many people with wrong ideas."

Esther frowned. What did she mean? But Liv waved her hand.

"I don't want to get into that political stuff. You and your family have had enough to deal with in Austria, I've understood."

Esther nodded, accepting a second cup of the coffee with the salty taste. Liv continued.

"There is a small cottage on the estate. In the old days, they used it as a hunting lodge so it's very basic and simple, but it has two rooms, one with a kitchen. I had been wondering, seeing how cramped you all live with your aunt and uncle, if perhaps your family would want to move in there. Free of rent, of course, if they help on the farm. There will be plenty of food, perhaps even a small salary. It's mostly a dairy farm, but there are a few acres of good farmland."

Liv suddenly stopped talking and blushed. She let her hands drop in her lap.

"I'm sorry. I shouldn't have brought it up. You're such fine folk. It's just... it's just... Well, would you like another cookie?"

Esther finally rediscovered her manners.

"It's so kind of you, Mrs Helberg. My parents will be so happy. And we're looking for a job and a house, so I'm sure this is the answer."

"But... what about Rebecca and Adam? They've just found some friends here. And your grandmother. She's so fragile. She might not do well in the harsh Norwegian winter out there. It's really very primitive."

Esther rubbed the back of her neck with a cold hand, doubt hitting her. Liv was right. Oma needed care, and the children had to go to school. Should she go on her own? The idea didn't appeal to her, having been away from her loved ones for a year.

"We won't be far, will we?"

"No, it's a thirty minutes' drive by car. I used to go to school in Oslo myself as a child. There's a school bus, and the children are always welcome for sleepovers."

"So, then it's just Oma," Esther pondered.

"I'm sure my parents will accommodate her up in the front parlor during the winter, where they can build her a good fire and keep her warm and dry."

"It all sounds heaven-sent." Esther felt her heart overflow. This good dress she was wearing would serve no purpose anymore. It would be overalls and hard work, but a roof and food. Norway suddenly seemed the best country on earth. They could start afresh. All together.

"I see why you didn't want to bring it up to my parents, but I will," Esther promised the kind Liv. "I'll talk with my mother first as she is looking after Oma."

At that moment, Rebecca skipped into the kitchen, followed by Tore. Esther felt herself go tense immediately again. Eyes the same color as his mother's, but much fiercer, took her in. That attitude.

She'd actually known it the first time she saw him skiing down the Radstädter Tauern Pass and come to a halt, right outside her window. Cocky and cool as a snowbank. And clumsy. Yet his kindness to her sister, and the reverent way he looked at his mother, showed he had a contradictory side to his character.

Esther got up.

"We have to go, Rebecca. We've been away too long already. Mutti will be worried where we are."

"Mutti knows I'm here," Rebecca protested. "She's just glad I'm out of her hair."

"Don't say that!" Esther was the stern older sister now. "Mutti wouldn't even dream of thinking that."

"Well, you've not been here long enough yet, sis."

It sounded too cynical for a fifteen-year-old and made Esther wonder what had happened to the family dynamics. Clearly, Rebecca preferred this family to her own. The move to Søndre would be hard on her.

"Thank you very much for the coffee and the suggestion." Esther took her leave, grabbing Rebecca by the hand and coaching her firmly out of the door. Tore's eyes bored in her back, so she kept her spine straight, as if carrying five volumes on top of her head.

No enemies, she told herself. *I can't afford to be enemies with him when our families become entwined.*

15

THE WARNING

Søndre Nordstrand, November 1939

The last yellow and brown leaves of the oak trees that lined the courtyard of Lindenberg farm whirled around in the November storm. A biting Northern wind was a harbinger of the eternal Nordic winter the Weiss family braced themselves for. No sun in the morning sky, which was gray as a battleship cleaving through the foaming waves.

Head down, hands in her coat pockets, Esther dragged her feet with two pairs of woolen socks in sturdy rubber boots through the rustling leaves, on her way to the red-brown barn where the Lindenberg cows stood in silent rows, waiting for their morning milk session.

The door almost escaped from her grip as she opened it. A sudden gust of wind, fierce and unexpected, made her aware of the grim season. It was dusky and warm in the barn, smelling of hay and cow dung. Two rows of Norwegian reds, mournful eyes in big heads with blinking eyelashes, turned to the human who would relieve them of their full udders. Some mooed in low tones to greet her, swishing the white sashes of their long tails.

"Hello, ladies."

Esther didn't know if cows liked to be greeted, but she was spending so much time in their presence lately—morning and evenings—that some acknowledgement of their daily meetings wouldn't hurt.

Milking the cows and cleaning the dairy barn were Esther's duties since they'd moved to the farm south of Oslo in September. Every family member had their own rough-hand tasks, with little choice or autonomy. But the abundance of food and a roof over their heads made the adults refrain from complaining.

For Esther, the change from the damask tablecloths of Le Manoir to the dung heap in South Norway could not have been more poignant. There was little time to reflect on her new life as she was up before dawn and fell asleep at ten as soon as her head hit the pillow. The cutthroat regime at the sweat of her brow was all she knew now. And accepted. Having no time to dillydally had its advantages. The past was fast dying in the distance.

Esther put her milking stool next to the first cow in the pen and stroked her flank before sitting down.

"Calm down, Bella, it's only me, your clumsy milk maid."

When Romy Gruber, whose father was a gentleman farmer on the outskirts of Vienna, had assured Esther every cow had her own character, she'd declared her friend mad. Now Esther knew Romy had been right.

Romy.

She'd not thought of her friend from the Wasagasse Gymnasium for ages. Romy, the blunt, beautiful, blustery brunette who'd set her up with Carl. Just for fun, but also for love. What had become of her? She'd always claimed she wanted to be a famous movie star, conquer Hollywood, have Gary Grant and Clark Gable fight for her attention. Gosh, Esther suddenly missed her old friend with a pang. Before everything had fallen apart, Romy and she— different as smoke and flame—had shared a special bond.

Never in a million years could Romy have guessed Esther Weiss was milking cows on a cold fall morning on a farm in Norway instead of folding her own napkins in a patrician house in Vienna with a small Bernstein baby in the crib.

"Easy, Bella."

The cow gave Esther a slap in the face with the bushy end of her tail. It almost made the bucket slip from between her thighs.

"Stop daydreaming, silly."

Fresh milk meant butter and cheese and cream for Rebecca and Adam's hot chocolate drink when they returned with the school bus in the late afternoon.

But sometimes Esther couldn't help herself. This moment of relative ease, just squeezing the milk out of Bella's teats in a steady rhythm, always made her sleepy, aware of her body never getting enough rest. Somehow, this half dream state sparked flashes of her former life.

Esther was onto milking her sixth cow when she heard the door to the barn creak open. A gush of freezing wind made Bertha stamp her back hooves and Esther shiver in her anorak.

"Who's there?"

"It's Tore."

She straightened on the stool that made her back hurt in places she didn't know she had.

She looked up alongside Bertha's rust-brown flank as he entered the pen.

"What's up?"

"Nothing, just checking on how you're all doing."

"We're fine."

"You know it means a great deal to me, you helping my grandparents. I can focus much more on my geology course."

"Glad to hear it."

Esther was aware she sounded curt and standoffish, but he'd intruded upon her safe spot, her life with the cows. Tore never failed to make her uncomfortable and unsure of herself.

"I just stopped by to drop off some deliveries from Oslo, but wondered if you'd like to take some hours off. I could show you the Akershus Fortress?"

Esther wondered where this sudden interest in her came from. Why would he want to take her out? Tore was Rebecca's friend, not hers.

"I can't take time off. When I'm done with the cows, I have to help Mutti in the house."

He seemed to sense her mistrust, the gunmetal blue eyes studying her with intent.

"You're right. The fortress was a diversionary maneuver on my behalf. There's something I want to tell you. It involves your family." Esther immediately was on high alert, jumping up from her stool, ready to take action.

"What's wrong with them? Pray tell me!"

Tore held up his hands defensively,

"No, I don't mean it in that respect. They're okay here at the farm, don't worry. I just want to talk through some options with you."

Puzzled, she sat down on the milk stool again and resumed emptying Bertha's udder.

"I'll help you with the last two cows and we'll clean the dung together. Then you could take some time off, correct?"

"Suppose so. If Mutti doesn't need me. Or your grandparents."

Though intrigued by what he wanted to tell her, and also slightly concerned, the idea of being in Tore's presence for a longer time didn't really appeal to Esther.

It was as if this knockabout Norseman always seemed to create an invisible wedge between her sophisticated fiancé and her. He'd been that Jack-in-the-box right from the start of her engagement. Most of all, Tore's constant presence confused Esther. He was too attractive, too present and he was Rebecca's, while she held onto her thin hopes of her own man with both hands.

But of course, she couldn't tell him that. Her family owed the Helbergs so much. She was tied to him, whether she wanted or not.

~

AKERSHUS FORTRESS with its square features and two characteristic apex towers stood gloomy and yet very present in the gray November afternoon. Esther had often glanced with wonder at the all-present medieval landmark since living in Oslo but had never been close. She wasn't sure she wanted to. Tore's remark that he wanted to discuss something about her family was much more on the forefront of her mind.

They'd been silent most of the drive in Tore's Volvo PV 36, a dilapidated, old police car that rattled and groaned through every road bend. Probably a gift from his father, Esther mused. Quite the opposite of Carl's immaculate red Mercedes Benz 170, which he'd owned when everything was still as it should have been.

"Would you like to go inside?" Tore sounded doubtful as he opened the passenger's door for her, and she stepped into the chilly street. Wearing overalls or dungarees most days, she wasn't used to thin stockings and her legs shivered. Pulling her winter coat closer around her, she looked up at the fortress.

"Will it be warm inside?"

"Are fortresses ever warm?" He lifted a light brow. "They're supposed to be sturdy and forbidding, not warm and cozy." The look he gave her made Esther wonder if he was making an allusion to himself, but she shook off the ridiculous thought as soon as it popped up. There was so much going on behind that high forehead with the wild blond locks, but it had nothing to do with her.

Business. They had business to attend to.

"Sure, show me around your royal residence."

"It's actually been more of a prison and a military base," Tore explained as they made their way across the courtyard overlooking the Karpedammen pond. Despite the biting cold and her uneasy feeling, Esther admired the beauty of the structure and the castle's strategic position in Oslo's harbor. An outing? Since when had she been on an outing?

It was just a question of when to bring up the pressing topic. It came earlier than she'd expected. Tore took her from room to room until they were in the castle's chapel where there were no other visitors. As they studied the blue and gold panels behind the altar, Tore sat down on the front bench and for a moment seemed engaged in prayer as he had his eyes closed. Esther slipped into the pew next to him.

She'd only once been in St Stephen's Cathedral in Vienna with Romy but never in a Protestant church. Its cool bareness and simple neatness appealed to her organized mind.

"You must have heard of Vidkun Quisling?" Tore said in a low voice, his eyes still closed.

"He's the leader of the fascist party here in Norway, isn't he? Rebecca told me they'd spoken about him and his party at school. What about him?"

Tore opened his eyes and looked straight at her. She saw the shadow of doubt, which sometimes clouded his clear gaze. As if looking at her gave him some sort of trouble she was unaware of.

"Quisling's a nobody, but he's trying to hook up with Hitler. Wants to get in the Führer's good books. Apparently, he's traveling to Germany in December to see if he and his Nasjonal Samling cronies can come to some sort of agreement with Germany. Quisling presumably claims the Soviet Union is ready to attack Norway and then Great Britain will come to our defense. That's why he wants Germany to intervene, giving Hitler the idea to invade Norway."

Esther looked straight ahead at the golden crucifix behind the altar. "As far as I understood from Rebecca's political science lesson, Quisling got a small minority of votes here. That he's not really a threat?"

"True. Most Norwegians despise him."

"So, what are you trying to say?"

He hesitated, shifted on the hard bench, pushed the hair from his forehead, sighed. "I'm not so sure Norway can escape a disaster, Esther." It was odd to hear him utter her name for the first time. Again, that uncomfortable feeling.

"What do you mean?"

It felt as if she had to pull the words out of him.

"Our country is a strategic asset for the greedy Nazis, certainly spurred on by Quisling's baseless war rhetoric. Think of all our ore and oil. Just what Hitler needs for his war machine. The future of Norway... We talk about nothing else at the university these days. Luckily, we've infiltrated Quisling's Party, so we're well-informed about what the fascists are cooking up. We don't think Hitler cares two fiddlesticks about weak Quisling but he'll certainly be interested in using him as a peon. And we think he will."

"But what does that have to do with my family?"

The blue eyes shot fire.

"Don't you see, Esther? Quisling has been an anti-Semite for years. If we become a German puppet state, your family will be in danger again."

An electric shock went through her. Never again! She had to temper it.

"But you said most Norwegians want to have nothing to do with the fascists in their own country, so for sure they would not surrender. Not like the Austrians did."

Tore was silent for a while. Hesitated again. "Esther, listen. I don't know what you and your family went through, but I know you didn't come to this country out of free will. I know the sacrifice you made."

Again, the blue eyes on her, doubt lingering there.

Stubbornly, she replied, "It will all be over one day, and we can go back to Vienna and I will get mar..."

She couldn't get the words across her lips.

"All I want for you is to be safe and not to have to flee again."

She bit her lip.

"So, what do you think we should do?"

"Get a new name, get the Norwegian nationality."

"What?" Disbelief mingled with horror.

"I know." He shrugged.

"Papi will never accept that. Our name is Weiss, and we will never be Norwegians."

"Esther, please think, now while it is still possible. You should talk to your father. Just in case."

Esther got up, smoothed her woolen coat.

"I appreciate your concern, Tore, but it's really no use. We're here just temporarily. Our real life is in Austria."

"I'm sorry. I had my doubts whether to bring it up. Maybe you're right. All that agitated talk at the university has made me see ghosts. Let's have a coffee, and forget my nosiness."

As they left the seclusion of the chapel, a chill settled on Esther. The seed was sown, the seed of doubt about her family's safety. But she'd taken an oath. *Keep them safe.*

"A coffee would be welcome," she smiled, "and please keep me informed of the political climate, Tore. If ever the situation changes, I promise I will talk with my father. For now, we're just happy to live a simple and tranquil life. It's more than we've had for over two years."

Esther walked back to the car in a state of red alert, wrapping her coat closely around her body, which was strong and healthy from good food and hard work. Vigilance was added to her duties —and vigilant, she would be.

16

LAST DAY IN FREEDOM

Tryvann Vinterpark, February 1940

"Stand closer together. Can't fit you all in!"

From the left, Esther felt Tore inch toward her. Instinctively, she leaned into Rebecca on her right, wondering if she could still swap places with her sister.

"Hold still. Perfect. One more."

They were all staring and smiling at the lens of Oncle Frerik's camera standing on the tripod in the snow. One of the Tryvannskleiva ski instructors was busy taking the family portrait. A rare and special occasion that hadn't even taken place at the first *jul*—or Christmas—they'd celebrated in their new country.

Wrapped in a warm quilt on the front row sat Oma in a fur-laced sledge, flanked on either side by her children Franz and Isobel. Naomi and Frerik with their arm around the waist of their spouses on the outer edge. In the snow at Oma's feet lay the young cousins, Adam, David and Ole. Behind Oma stood the bigger grandchildren, Rebecca and Esther and—on the strict instructions of Oma—Tore Helberg. Not a member of the family but their chauffeur to the Vinterpark, he was also in the photograph.

Tore had protested, but Oma had been tottering on the edge of one of her tantrums so he'd quickly obeyed. Esther had felt strangely uncomfortable with Oma's wish, whereas Rebecca thought it the most natural thing in the world.

Does nobody remember the last time we were in the snow together? Esther asked herself in wonder. The same date two years earlier had been her engagement party to Carl in Overtauern. The one person who'd spoiled her day for her was now standing next to her while her fiancé was God knew where.

She hadn't had a letter from him in almost three months. No answer came to her weekly letters. Only a brief note from Frau Hoffmann in Holland that she'd heard they were still planning on leaving Austria. But she knew no details, and the silence afterward had been deafening.

As Esther glanced down sadly at her engagement ring, temporarily forgetting to smile for the camera, Rebecca nudged her in the ribs. "Spoilsport."

A spoilsport? Was that what she was? Maybe Rebecca was right. This one day, skiing in the Vinterpark was the highlight of their dreary life. The winter in Oslo had been tough, extremely cold, and the work on the farm relentless. But her greatest worry was that Oma was fast sliding into prolonged periods of amnesia interspersed with lucid moments and temper tantrums.

Esther smiled her brightest smile, promising herself she'd enjoy this day. The posing was over. Time to put on her skis and fly down the slope. The snow, the sun, the mountain, it all looked so enticing. How could she be sad? She sent a quick prayer to Carl with the resolve she'd have fun for two.

"Are you racing me, sis?" Adam, his cheeks red from the cold with a woolen hat with embroidered reindeer on them, skied toward her. "Like the old days?"

"Ha, you'll still need a head start, little bro!" Esther cheered, her happy mood leaping to the front like a frolicking rabbit.

"No need for that anymore! I'm almost as tall and twice as strong as you!" Her always slim and short brother had indeed grown tall on the Norwegian diet of whale steaks, potatoes and his favorite cakes and pastries. He was quite the young man now and fluent in Norwegian, almost forgetting his German.

When they got to the top of Tryvannskleiva and stepped out of the ski lift, both Adam and Esther were speechless. The serene beauty of the snow-capped mountain, the slope still covered in fresh snow. The azure blue sky and the powdered snow on the pine trees. But most of all, the silence of nature. It was still early morning. Only a couple of fanatical Norwegian skiers—among them one of Norway's champions, Tore Helberg—had gone down and left some tracks, but the day was fresh and the peace and quiet around the two Austrian young people hit them deeply.

"Look, a deer," Adam whispered, his voice muffled behind the shawl that was wrapped around his mouth and nose. He pointed to a group of deer that stood motionless between the white trees. Their brown skins glimmering in the sun's reflection. A clod of snow fell from a heavily bowed branch. It startled the deer more than the presence of the two humans. They skittered away, showing their white bottoms with the brown tails as they disappeared deeper into the forest.

"It's magical here," Esther whispered back. "I almost don't want to go down. We'll never see it like this again." She inhaled the pine-scented, cold air deep into her lungs, felt the skis under her feet as long wings. Adam seemed to sense his sister's melancholy. He had grown, understood more, was the young man of the family now.

"We'll be okay, Es," he said as he put a gloved hand on hers. " We're safe here! Really, we are. Now, let's go and have some fun!"

Fun!

That's exactly what she needed. Fun! She was almost nineteen now and the past two years had been far from fun. It had been work and work and more work. And though it had led to her family being safe and sound together in a small house on the outskirts of Oslo, plenty of food, and Adam and Rebecca enjoying school, for Esther tomorrow would be as all her other days, getting up at the crack of dawn to milk the Lindenberg cows.

"Ready?" Her brother's dark eyes shone.

"Ready!"

With swift and smooth movements of her hips, she zigzagged down, gaining speed at every turn. The feeling of control over the skis, the wind on her face and the speed. Oh, the speed! Esther forgot everything. Even her brother and the competition. This was like dancing for Esther! This was what being alive meant.

She braked at full speed but with an elegant swirl, just in front of Oma's sledge. Only then did she check where Adam was. She'd won with a big lead. Arriving next to her, he panted angrily,

"Not fair! It was a jump-start!"

"Not true!" Esther argued. "You're just not fast enough!"

"Again?" He smiled, white teeth bared in a ruddy face.

"Sure."

But then Esther turned her attention to her frail grandmother in the sledge.

"Are you warm enough, Oma?"

Her grandmother, bony and shrunken, nodded, a vague smile on her lips. A lucid day or moment. She hardly spoke these days, but her half-smile burned into Esther's soul. These days, to see Oma happy was as rare as a winter swallow. She'd become a handful, grumpy and dissatisfied most days, often refusing to get out of bed and be dressed. Looking after Oma had become Naomi's full-time occupation.

With Oma smiling and safely tucked in her warm blanket, Esther hit the ski lift once again. This time she had to share the trip to the top with Tore. Since their outing to the Akershus Fortress, they'd hardly spoken to each other, but his warning about the Quisling fascist party weighed on Esther's mind.

Though Tore regularly visited his grandparents on the farm, he usually came for Rebecca. Whenever he could, he'd drop her off from school, often accompanied by his sister Astrid.

The silence all the way to the top was slightly awkward—not a new experience for Esther when in Tore's presence. But when he opened the ski lift for her, he remarked, "You're a phenomenal skier, Esther. Would you do me the honor of racing against me?"

Esther gazed straight at him to see if he was mocking her. He was one of the Norwegian national team, one of Norway's top skiers. She had only practiced once in Switzerland. But something in her wanted to compete with him, and he seemed earnest. His eyes, the color of the sky above them, were clear and serious. He meant his compliment.

She shrugged. "Why not? I suppose you want to give me half a slope head start?"

"Not my intention. I'm sorry for this frostiness between us, believe me or not. So I thought we could perhaps shake it off with a good competition. I'll give you a fair chance. I believe in you as a skier."

These were more words than Tore had said to her since their conversation in the chapel. She looked up at him, gauging him. Who was this fierce Viking really, this proud and strong man, who had such a soft spot for her sister? He seemed to care for most of the people around him. Even had patience with her impossible Oma.

It suddenly struck her that one day he could become her brother-in-law, and that realization made her accept his offer. One way or the other, Tore Helberg was in her life. Was there to stay. Maybe one day Carl and she could laugh about it, and they would all sit around the hearth and talk about her ruined sea-blue dress. What it all had led to!

She smiled, a genuine smile, and they pump-fisted their gloves.

"Okay, Tore Helberg, give it everything you got as I won't make it easy on you!"

They set off, pricking their ski poles in the snow with fierce agitation. Until the first plateau Esther kept up with him, and somehow she knew he wasn't making it easy on her, but then she lost more speed and he gained going ahead of her. Yet she gave it her all, diminishing the distance between them as well as she could. Then she heard her whole family cheer her on.

"Come on, Esther, faster, faster!" The shrill voice of Oma sounded above them all.

"Bärchen!!!"

It gave her wings. She fought with all she had, her thigh muscles burning, her back almost bent double, the wind hitting her cheeks under her ski glasses. She fought and fought, not even seeing the track anymore, only the dark patch of Tore's snowsuit coming closer and closer and the voices of her family becoming louder. Her blood sang and her heart raced. Finally, finally, life burst at the seams for Esther as her skis came level with Tore's and they braked at exactly the same time, she one inch before his.

The cheers of her family were ear-splitting and Esther toppled over in a heap of snow, too exhausted to breathe, half-dead and yet never more alive. Adam let himself fall next to her, still shouting. "Esther did it! Esther did it! She beat a champion!"

Tore was towering over her. He removed his glasses and scarf, and his face was one sour smile.

"Miss Esther Weiss," he panted, "you're a force to be reckoned with. I've never in my whole life seen a girl ski like this. I'm going to lick my wounds in the corner now."

"Essie, you must join the Norwegian national team!" Adam cried. "I want to be in the junior team myself next year!"

Sitting amidst her family with her rough farmhand fingers wrapped around a cup of hot cocoa, Esther gleamed with pride. She looked around both sides of the long wooden table with the red-checked cloth at her happy family's faces, and her heart swelled. There was only one drop of pain in it. Carl's absence to join in the fun. Tore was sitting opposite her, looking rather sheepish. Esther felt so boisterous that she couldn't help herself.

"You wouldn't have invited me to the challenge if you'd seriously thought I'd win?"

He blew on his hot cocoa, avoiding her laughing eyes. Rebecca, sitting next to him, nudged his ribs.

"Admit it, Tore. My sis was too strong for you!"

"Wait until I take revenge." He tried to make it sound light-hearted, but Esther could see he was gritting his teeth. Losing was hard for the tall Norseman, that much was clear. She wondered if he'd ever tell his team he'd lost to an Austrian girl.

If only she could ski all day. She would be eternally happy.

Tore announced they would have to leave soon as dusk fell at three in the afternoon in Norway's winters. He wanted to be back in Oslo before nighttime.

"Can we come to Vintergarden soon again? Please?" Adam begged. "This was the most fun day we've had since we moved here."

Oma clapped her wrinkled hands with the long fingers and brown age spots. "Yes! Yes!"

Tears sprang in Esther's eyes. Seeing Oma happy was the best feeling of the day, even better than her revenge on Tore.

17

WAR IN NORWAY

Søndre Nordstrand, 9 April 1940

The unthinkable happened, but it happened anyway. Hitler attacked Norway, that proud Nordic nation, where Quisling's weak but treacherous fascist party had been festering for years.

The shock waves that heralded the end of the Phony War rippled through the country of fjords, fishermen, and fastidious folk like an overflowing wave. After seven months of Allied inaction, the paralysis was over. This demanded an answer, a firm and straightforward 'no' to Nazi Germany.

The fight had begun. Another world war staged, but with unequal combatants.

The Germans had slinked north like thieves in the night with a supremacy of battleships, bombers and tanks, taking Oslo within hours of Bergen, Stavanger and Trondheim, capturing every airfield, coastal fortification and supply of weapons. The Norwegian Army was driven back northward, overruled and defenseless. Defeat was inescapable despite the attempt at delaying actions to give the British destroyers time to steam up from Scapa Flow.

Esther woke to the rumble of battle in the distance and immediately had an eerie feeling that things were wrong. She ran outside in the hour before dawn to look toward Oslo's sky. A red glow of fire rose into the air; the booming of anti-aircraft guns sounded from the fortress. But what confirmed her fear was the wave of German bombers flying low over her head, their Swastikas the gloomy omen of what was awaiting them.

She clapped a hand over her mouth to prevent herself from screaming out, thus upsetting her family. Tore had been right. They'd come here too. There seemed no place in the world where the Germans wouldn't come. Shivering in her nightgown with her winter coat thrown over it, Esther was catapulted back two years in time. Stamping boots through Vienna's streets. Now they came to Oslo.

Rebecca had silently come up to her and stood watching the attack on Oslo with her. Her brown pigtails stood out in the glowing red of the sky. Her face was pinched, her eyes big, and she slipped her trembling fingers in Esther's hand.

"What are we going to do?" Rebecca's voice broke, ended in a sob.

Esther shook herself, remembered her oath.

"Nothing, Rebbie. We're safe here. They'll attack the cities and maybe the ports, but they have no interest in cows and chicken. Really, we're safe here."

How she wanted to believe her own words. She had to.

"Come, let us start our day."

"Will Addie and I go to school today?"

"No, sweetheart, it's best to stay out of Oslo for the time being. Let's wait for Tore to give us more information on what's going on and who's winning. We have no clue. They might still sweep out the Nazis in one swoop. Britain and France and maybe even Poland are definitely going to help us fight for independence."

"I'm afraid, Es." Rebecca squeezed her sister's hand tightly as they went back inside to start breakfast.

"We'll listen to Jens and Inger's radio after they're awake. Maybe the government will make an announcement."

As they went back into their simple house, Esther braced herself for how her parents would react to the invasion of an enemy they seemed to have escaped in vain.

They all sat around the table, wide-eyed and still in their night clothes. Her mother's night cap loosely bound around her graying hair.

"I must go and see to Oma at the big house," was the first thing she said as Esther and Rebecca walked in.

"Do not worry about Oma right now, Mutti. She's probably safely asleep in her cot." Esther put a reaffirming hand on her mother's shoulder. "I think we have to make a plan first."

She gazed at her father, who was sitting with a distant look in his otherwise sparkly eyes, already smoking a cigar, something that would have been unheard of before breakfast in the old days. Was he going to take charge, or leave it to her?

Papi seemed to be less and less interested in acting as the head of the family, preoccupied as he was all day with setting up his small goldsmith business in one of the Lindenberg barns. It was all he lived for these days.

While her mother got their breakfast ready with Rebecca's help, Esther sat at the table with her father and Adam. Adam hadn't spoken a word yet. The angst in his youthful eyes made her choke up. Before being able to speak some pacifying words, she swallowed a few times.

"I think we have nothing to worry about right now."

From the stove, her mother interrupted, "What makes you think that, Esther? For sure, that Quisling is going to be prime minister now, and he hates Jews as much as Hitler."

Esther hesitated, an invisible hand holding her back from speaking the words, but she pushed through nonetheless, not knowing how otherwise to protect her family. "I've spoken with Tore a while ago, exactly about this situation, a German invasion. He suggested to change our last name and become Norwegian."

Her father's fist landed on the table with a bang. The cups rattled on their saucers and Adam whimpered.

"Never! I'm a Weiss and so are you all. We've been Weisses for centuries. And we're Austrians, not Vikings!"

He got up from the table so abruptly that he knocked over the milk jar. A big white blotch fanned out over the wooden table. Esther stared at it. Mesmerized. White, Weiss. She was a Weiss. Maybe her father was right.

"Sorry," he muttered as his wife hastened close with a tea towel to mop up the spilled milk. "I need to work, straighten out my thinking. I'll be back for breakfast later."

He kissed his wife on the cheek, put on his coat, grabbed his tool bag and made for the door.

The noise of rattling tanks going north filled the room as her father opened the front door. For a moment he stood on the threshold, hesitant, shocked, taking in the theatre of war racing past his doorstep for the second time in two years. But then he resolutely shut the door and left.

Adam still sniffed and despite his eleven years, Esther took her brother in her arms, as she'd done when he was a baby. She stroked his dark curls and rocked him softly, while her own heart sank in her body. His hopes for the future were melting like ice, the junior ski team, his school friends, maybe even his wish to become a polar scientist.

"You shouldn't have brought up our identity." Her mother's voice was soft, not accusing.

"Mutti, we have little choice, or do you want to flee again? This time to England?"

"Maybe I would, but we can't. Oma is too weak. We're stuck here, Esther." She brought the porridge to the table and for a moment they ate in silence.

Esther just nodded. Mutti was right.

"Let's at least wait to hear what tidings Tore will bring from Oslo. And we don't have to be afraid that Jens and Inger will betray us. They've told me themselves they despise Quisling's party."

"But what about Tore's father? He's with the police. What side will the police take in case of a surrender?"

"We don't know, Mutti. But the Helbergs and the Lindenbergs knew from the beginning that we were refugee Jews. So do Tante Isobel and Oncle Frerik. They all wouldn't have helped us if they'd been anti-Semites. I think we have good people around us."

"Are you going to teach us again, Mutti, now we can't go to school? But you can't speak enough Norwegian." Adam looked uncertain.

"Maybe schools will reopen soon, son. It's all too early to know. For today, you can play on the farm. As long as you stay out of sight from the road."

Rebecca had been silent during breakfast. She looked forlorn, younger than her sixteen years.

"I hope Tore will come today. He will help us." Her sister's devotion to Tore was endearing, but this time Esther wholeheartedly agreed with her. Tore would be their informant and rock now. She couldn't wait herself for his arrival.

When breakfast was over and Esther went about her normal chores in the cowshed, she finally had time to think things through. *Just like her father*, she thought. She needed that alone time.

Something so strange had happened just the day before. She'd finally, finally received a letter from Carl. And although she'd already read the epistle ten times and cried over it the same amount, she longed to read it again. Even here, amidst Bertha and Bella and the other cows, Carl's letter was in her pocket. She just couldn't part with it.

When the cows were milked and there was a moment of rest before she started cleaning the barn, she sank down in the hay to retrieve the single sheet of paper from its envelope. Kissing it with care so as not to wet the thin paper, she read the words she already knew by heart.

VIENNA, *19 December 1939*

My dearest Esther,

I hope with my whole heart that you and your family are well. Your letter arrived today just after Chanukah and I'm immediately writing back to you, as it might take months before you get this reply. Yours was dated 30 September.

I'm glad to hear you found work on a farm outside Oslo and are with a nice family. From your description, it sounds like you're not bringing into practice your teachings at Le Manoir but I hope the work is doable, though I have a hard time imagining you milking cows and cleaning stables. Let alone planting winter wheat. But what I do know is that you've always been a persevering lady, so you'll make the best of it for as long as we're separated.

HERE, Esther had to pause. He would come to her! He would! A warm wave of relief washed through her every time she read this sentence. Maybe her ordeal would be over soon.

But then the shock hit her.

War had come to Norway. What if the Norwegians couldn't win against the Germans? The rumors of defeat were everywhere. And then there was that treacherous Quisling!

Don't worry, we're Vikings; they won't get us under!

Tore's voice in her head. How confusing. She only wanted to read Carl's letter, disappear in it, drink from its well. Not think of Tore. But Tore was here. He could help. Carl could do nothing for her now. Her thoughts were driving her mad, so she read on.

Life in Vienna has been no fun since you left. My parents are increasingly frail, and I don't think my father will see the end of winter. It may be a blessing after all, as we have had to move out of our house and live with two other families in a small collective apartment. My father clearly indicated that he would like to leave this earthly abode so mother and I can go abroad. He feels he's just a burden on us, which, of course, he isn't.

I am currently looking for work, and I miss the jewelry business. It seems so long ago since I've seen anything beautiful and glittering. And giving you presents was always my greatest pleasure.

Dearest, my mother calls me for dinner, so I have to round off. Please give my deepest respect to your parents and Oma. I was sorry to hear she's not adapting well to the new country. I hope to embrace you this summer. For good!

Be well, Liebling. Stay strong and pray for us. I love you with my whole heart and soul.

Your betrothed,

Carl.

P.S. Mother and father send their regards.

Esther folded the letter in four again and put it back in the envelope. When she got back to her bedroom, she would lay it on top of the other four letters that had arrived from Vienna since she'd left. Her engagement photo, his last present was already fading in the corners. For now, it went back in her coat pocket.

"Carl," she whispered, "Carl, come back to me."

At that moment, the door to the barn opened and for a brief second, she thought her deepest wish had been granted.

She heard a clomping sound. Snow being stamped from boots.

"Esther, are you there?"

Tore. Of course, it was Tore. At this moment—contrary to an hour earlier—the last person on earth she wanted to see.

But here he was, glowing with health, blowing on his frozen fingers. The blue eyes searching hers.

"You've heard?"

She just nodded, too dejected to answer.

"I think we've got a good chance of beating the bastards. I really believe in our Norwegian campaign. We've delayed the invasion so far by sinking that bloody German cruiser Blücher in Oslofjord. The fortress' armaments operated like clockwork, though they hadn't been in use for over a century. You know the last battle we fought was the Swedish-Norwegian war in 1814? No, the Germans won't be able to take Oslo with a snap of their fingers."

Esther wasn't in the mood to hear about the Norwegian capacity for successful battle. She'd lived through an invasion once, and although there had not been any real resistance to her country's occupation, she wasn't so sure the Germans wouldn't get their way up here as well. Tore seemed unaware of her reluctance to talk about the war.

"Our men are fighting at Narvik right now, and we're helped by the Brits, the French, and even the Poles. I wish I'd gone under the arms, but I postponed it until twenty-one because of my studies. Well, we can finally rid Europe of hideous Hitler by showing him what a real battle is."

Only then Tore seemed to become aware Esther wasn't interested in his war cry language.

"Oh sorry. I keep rambling! Forgot you've gone through this before and seen the other side of it."

Esther sighed. "As long as my family's safe, I care little what regime is in power."

"I think you'll be okay here," Tore assured her. "Just stay on the farm. We'll get you all the supplies you need from the city."

"We'll have to discuss matters with your grandparents." Esther grabbed the pitchfork to clear the barn floor between the cows. "They might find it too dangerous to have a Jewish family on their estate."

"Nonsense!" Tore's eyes flashed. "Don't even dare think that! My grandparents adore you all, as do my parents. We consider you family, Esther!"

She faced him. So, he did see her sister as his future spouse? Was that it?

"Thank you. I'm sorry. I have a lot on my mind."

She turned away from him, trying to hide her despair about her own absent love affair. There was no way to explain to him what she missed, what she feared, what she was up against.

He would never understand what it was like to be a Jew and to be afraid you'd never see your fiancé again.

That was what she was up against. Not whether Oslo or Narvik held in battle.

18

THE DEEP END OF DARKNESS

Lindenberg farm, June 1941

"Have you got everything?" Tore asked, as he and Esther walked back to his old Volvo that was parked on the Grønlandsleiret near Oncle Frerik's shop.

She nodded. "I hope so."

"I can always bring extra supplies if needed."

"I know. Thank you."

Tore was balancing a box of summer clothes and shoes for Rebecca and Adam that Tante Isobel had found at the Oslo week market. Her siblings had outgrown all last year's cottons and summer shoes. Esther and her parents would have to do with their old wardrobe. There was no money for anything fancy. Nobody had much. They weren't the only ones. Oma still had her supply of nightgowns and bed jackets, all she needed these days, as she never left her bed anymore.

With head low so as not to make eye contact with the marching SS officers who were taking up most of the space on the pavement, Esther carried her bundle from the drugstore, soap, shampoo, aspirin and plasters and, of course, Oma's pills.

The monthly visits to the capital fell on Esther's shoulders for the obvious reason she could pass for a Norwegian woman, but it didn't make her feel comfortable, despite the loyal escort from Tore.

"Let's get out of here." She was glad to shut the passenger door and hear the old motor start. Life at the farm, no matter how small and limited, was their safe spot, and Esther didn't like being away from her family for too long.

"I agree," Tore endorsed. "I've come to hate my city with the vile Germans bossing us around. Your Oncle Frerik told me he's forced to make all his leather purses and bags for the Gestapo mistresses these days. Norwegians can't afford them and have no use for luxury goods, anyway. The Germans are besotted by his handmade designs. It makes him good money, and he likes that innocent shop front."

Esther wasn't sure she wanted to hear the story. Oncle Frerik and Tante Isobel stayed in touch with them via Tore and his parents, just to make sure there was no direct link to the Weiss family at the Lindenberg farm. Tante Isobel was a Gjelsvik, all traces of her Jewish background erased even from her passport.

Esther sighed a breath of relief as they left Oslo behind them. For security reasons, Tore took the backroads through fields and forests. Esther didn't have to ask why. Leave no trace; shake off possible followers. Though he didn't say much, she knew he was involved in the underground Resistance and had to take every precaution to protect her family, his grandparents and himself.

She wouldn't ask though, like she didn't ask what happened behind the extra door that Oncle Frerik had built in his workshop, where formerly the hides were stacked. But she needn't be told. Oncle Frerik was an amateur radio transmitter *and* a staunch anti-Nazi. Reason enough not to bring it up.

She wanted just to be back with the cows and the chickens and the cleaning of the Lindenberg farmstead. Her life was relatively good; they had no hunger. Just fear. Constant, nagging fear.

"Sunday is Oma's 80th birthday." She didn't know why she told

Tore, but she had been toying with the idea of asking Jens and Inger if they could throw her a small party.

Tore took his eyes from the road and gave her a quick glance. "Impressive! Are you doing anything?"

"I was thinking of ask..."

The words hung in mid-air as he took the last bend and came to the Lindenberg gate. He braked hard. His grandmother, tall and blond like him, still in her apron, was waving her arms frantically at them to stop. Esther was out of the car before Tore had even come to a standstill.

"What's the matter?" she blurted. "Is it Oma?"

"Noooo!" Inger cried, too distressed to talk coherently. She was swaying on her stockinged feet without even wearing shoes. Tore quickly jumped out of the car to steady his grandmother by the elbow.

"What is it, *mormor*? What's going on?"

"They've... they've been taken," she wailed, "the whole family... except for Oma. We hid her in a cupboard." She threw herself in her grandson's arms, shaking all over and unable to stop crying.

Esther felt her knees buckle under her. Her mind couldn't grasp what Inger was saying. A strange droning sound started ringing in her ears. Nausea, breathlessness. She fought to stay clear and upright. What was it that Inger was saying? Her family? They must be safe. They were safe here. She needed to ask for an explanation, but her lips refused to produce coherent words.

"Whe... Whe..." was the only sound she could make. Inger wasn't any better at explaining. She kept crying unconsolably.

"Where's *morfar*?"

From far away, Esther heard Tore ask about his grandfather. Her legs automatically, with a will of their own, set foot in the direction of the cottage. It was a battlefield. Chairs and clothes and pans and books lay strewn over the lawn. The front door hung on one hinge, a gaping wound. She stood for a moment, taking in the cottage. Smoke still rose from the chimney in the kitchen, but there was an eerie, deathlike silence.

Rebecca's blue skirt hung torn on a twig while Adam's science book was ripped in two. Useless, senseless, unfathomable details clung to her retina and clenched together in one word.

Gone.

Her family was gone. She didn't even have to look inside. The silence said it all.

But where were they?

Esther turned around and raced back to the gate. Where her strength came from, she didn't know. Tore and his grandmother were walking toward the farmhouse but turned when they saw her, a wild-eyed and desperate girl. She didn't hesitate. The keys were in the car. She was going to find her family. She, who'd sworn to keep them safe.

It was hard to keep the car on the road while tears filled her eyes, her hands trembled, and her heart almost broke her rib cage in two. Esther also wasn't a very experienced driver, and she had no plan.

Oncle Frerik and Tante Isobel. They would help her. Or should she go straight to the station? Check all trains? But what if they were transported in a truck? Why didn't she ask Inger? She had no details, but knew she had to go straight back to Oslo. Go to Quisling of Terboven herself. If needed. There must be a mistake. Her family hadn't done anything wrong.

They hadn't done anything wrong, except for being Jewish. Oh, why hadn't she listened to Tore when she should have? This was all her fault. But it was too late now.

When she arrived back in Oslo only an hour after she'd left it, doubt crept in. It was busy in the streets, mostly German cars and trucks, but also Norwegian traffic. She knew the way to her aunt and uncle's house, but she felt so ashamed and didn't know how to tell them the terrible tragedy. Again, the idea of the station flitted through her or even Akershus Fortress. Maybe they were taken there?

Oh, the confusion. Why couldn't she think straight?

She ended up on the Grønlandsleiret and ran into her Oncle's shop. She almost backed out immediately again when she saw a high-ranking German talking at the counter with her uncle. Oncle Frerik made a quick gesture with his hand as if to shoo her away and Esther was already outside, ringing the bell to her aunt's apartment as if she would pull the whole thing from the wall.

Her aunt was downstairs in a minute, white-face and teary-eyed.

"Oh my God, Esther, oh my dear God. Tore just phoned us. What are we to do?"

"We have to find them before they're taken to Germany," Esther sobbed.

"Hush," her aunt silenced her, "come upstairs. The walls have ears."

"I want to find them, Tante. I don't have time!"

"I know, but I can't tell you what I know here in the street."

There was no choice but to follow her aunt up the stairs for a moment and enter the bright, joyous living room.

"Sit down."

Esther did as she was told, though perched on the edge of her seat. David and Ole had hidden behind the couch but peeked above it, their freckled faces contorted with terror.

"Listen!" Tante Isobel held a hand on her chest. She had difficulty breathing. "They started rounding up Jews in Oslo last week. Hundreds of them. They put them in trucks and they're transported immediately over the border to Sweden and shipped to Poland where they are locked away in work camps. Our informants in Sweden have followed the convoys and told us so."

"But how did they find our family? We aren't Oslo Jews. We aren't even registered here. Someone must have betrayed us."

"Yes, and we know who it is. Tore's confirmed our suspicion." Her aunt had difficulty talking. Her chest heaved as if she was close to a panic attack.

"Who is it?" Esther was startled by the ferocity of her own voice.

They heard Oncle Frerik stumble up the stairs.

"I've closed the shop early," he barked. "I need to get in touch with my contacts. You know where I am, Isobel. Be on the lookout for the Gestapo."

She just nodded and went to the window, where she stood behind the curtain. Her uncle disappeared again. She heard soft sobbing from behind the couch. Her own tears were nearby.

"What do I do?" Esther shivered uncontrollably.

"Nothing for now," her aunt whispered. "Oncle will be fast. We must just pray that the radio connection works and there are no Germans rattling on the front door with their silly wishes."

At least they're helping me, Esther thought, and a small sliver of hope returned to her. Then she remembered the traitor.

"Who is he?"

"Jens and Inger's neighbor, Harald. He serves for the *Statspolitiet*. An absolute rat."

Despite her distress, Esther noticed her aunt's uncommon use of language. To call someone 'a rat' would have been unheard of before the war.

"Harald Rinnan? You must be wrong. He's one of the most helpful persons I've met since arriving here. Just the other day, he helped me..." Esther's words froze on her lips. "Oh, no!" she cried in despair. "How could I be so ignorant? He asked if we could use more food coupons. Why did nobody warn me about him? If you knew he was a fascist?"

Horrified, she stood looking at her aunt. She herself had let slip they lived with more persons at the farm.

"We didn't know, Esther, honestly we didn't. Rinnan used to be an honorable patriot for years, even part of the *Kommunestyre*. His true face was only unmasked when they started deporting the Jews last week. Nobody knew. That's why he's such a rat."

"I'll kill him with my own hands if anything happens to my family!" The fire flooded back into Esther's veins.

"Hush," her aunt berated her, "there are children in the room."

But a deep anger at the traitor washed over Esther, urging her to take action. *Hurry up, Oncle!*

Isobel pushed the lace curtain further aside, peering down.

"There's Tore in his grandfather's Jeep. He seems in a great hurry. Esther, can you open the door for him?" Her aunt's voice sounded flustered and surprised.

Like an automaton, Esther did as she was told, all the while wondering why it took her uncle so long to find out the whereabouts of her loved ones. Tore stormed into the room.

"Esther, please come back to the farm. Something's wrong with your grandmother. She needs you."

At that moment, Esther's soul split in two. She needed to find her family before it was too late, but now Oma needed her as well. What should she do? In utter despair, she pulled her hair, while both her aunt and Tore came to her aid.

"We'll find them, Esther." That was her aunt.

"We'll do everything we can," Tore added.

"What's wrong with Oma?" She was in tears now.

"We think she had a stroke. She was unconscious when I left. My grandparents had already called the doctor. Don't worry. Doctor Berg is with the Resistance. But she didn't look well. I'm so sorry, Esther. And you too, Fru Gjelsvik."

Her aunt looked stricken down as a broken pillar at the message of her mother's sudden turn for the worse at this terrible moment of distress. Tore handed Esther his handkerchief. She dabbed her face, half aware it smelled of soap and leather. The tears kept coming.

"I'll first drive you back to the Lindenberg farm. Then I'll return to Oslo to help in the search." Tore was taking control of the situation, which was unraveling further by the minute.

"Can you ask Oncle Frerik if he knows anything yet?" Her voice was small and blubbery.

"You both get in the car," her aunt instructed. "Boys, watch the window. I'll ask Frerik if he knows anything and will come out to tell you. I'll be down at the farm as soon as I can."

Everything happened in a matter of seconds.

"Nothing yet," were the last words Esther heard before the Jeep raced down Grønlandsleiret and out of the city.

~

OMA WAS ASLEEP, lying on her back, her white-haired, narrow face sunk deep in the white cushions.

"Not a heart attack, just frailty and stress. All she needs is rest, hot tea and love. And perhaps another day to live." That's what the doctor had said.

Esther sat down next to her bed and put her hand over the wrinkled, liver-spotted hand that she knew so well. The room was serene, very white, with white-washed walls and white linen on the mahogany bed. Even a white carpet on the floorboards.

Her Oma's shallow breath and all that whiteness and quietness suddenly made the noise inside Esther magnified. Her own heart boomed; her head exploded. Papi, Mutti, and sweet Rebecca and Adam. Taken from her in one moment of lost vigilance. Betrayed by a neighbor. She couldn't wrap her head around it.

Without knowing whence it came from, she heard herself whisper Oma's favorite Psalm.

The Lord is my shepherd; I shall not want.

He maketh me to lie down in green pastures; He leadeth me beside the still waters.

He restoreth my soul; He guideth me in straight paths for His name's sake.

Yea, though I walk through the valley of the shadow of death, I will fear no evil, for Thou art with me; Thy rod and Thy staff, they comfort me.

Thou preparest a table before me in the presence of mine enemies; Thou hast anointed my head with oil; my cup runneth over.

Surely goodness and mercy shall follow me all the days of my life; And I shall dwell in the house of the Lord forever.

She sat with her eyes closed, squeezing out the tears through her lashes, when she felt a small pressure on her hand. Her eyelids quickly opened.

Eyes the color of the deep waters fastened on her. Oma was lucid, her gaze steady. Esther's throat contracted. There was so much intimacy and wisdom in those green-blue eyes. They were so peaceful and at ease right now.

Oma didn't know. She should never know!

That was all Esther could think. Keep the truth from this frail soul, who'd seen enough and suffered even more in her life. But she hadn't reckoned with her grandmother's capacity for understanding.

"Always keep Psalm 23 in your heart, Bärchen, whatever will come on your path next."

Esther raised her head to put a kiss on her forehead, which felt dry and cold. "I will, Oma. I promise."

Her grandmother shifted in the bed, took her very green eyes off her grandchild for a moment. "Did you hear what the doctor said?"

"Yes, Oma."

"I'm at peace with my own fate, Bärchen." The old, white lady stayed silent for a while, staring straight at the ceiling. Then with a ferocity that pushed Esther back onto the chair with a shock, added, "Find them, child! Don't let them be murdered by the Nazis. I wish I had the strength to help you, but my time here is up. Help Isobel stay safe."

"No, Oma!" Despair wrenched at her heart. Oma knew. There was no need for hiding anymore what had happened to her son and his family.

"You're all I have left now. Don't leave me, Oma. I can't do this on my own."

The blue-green gaze returned to her. Almost soundlessly, her grandmother whispered, "I saw my Maker this afternoon. I need to go. I pleaded with him to give me a few more hours with you, but I'm on borrowed time."

"Oma, no!" No longer able to restrain herself, she put her head on her grandmother's lap and wept like a lost child. A weak hand caressed her brow.

"Bärchen, Bärchen." Over and over, Oma repeated the pet name she'd given her eldest grandchild. "I fear I have no words of comfort for you. Turn to your God and pray to him for strength."

Esther tried not to cry so she could drink in her Oma's words, carve them in her heart but the tears wouldn't stop, and the defeat was total.

Still, Oma gave her advice that drifted in-between her agony and her fear.

"Trust Jens and Inger who've looked after me so well. Trust Tore; he's a rock of a man."

And then the rhythm returned. "Bärchen, Bärchen, Bärch…"

The voice faltered and fell silent.

The hand fell still.

The room was still.

Oma stiffened under her.

The world was white.

Then it was black. As black as Egypt's night.

19

A STATUE OF STONE

Vienna, 1929

I t is summer, and she is playing with Lise and Charlotte in the back street of their house at the Prater Strasse. Lise has brought her skipping rope and it's her turn to jump in. Lise and Charlotte are counting *49, 50, 51...*

She bounces up and down, in tireless exultation, though her feet in the thin-soled summer shoes are hurting. She wants to get to 100. On and on and on.

Somebody suddenly grabs the rope; it swishes in mid-air, then stops. A big boy, years older, grins at her, two rows of perfect white teeth with a thin mustache on his upper lip. Narrow blue eyes. She recognizes him. Gustav Wagner from the Zirkusgasse, son of the barber. Mean but handsome.

"What do you want?"

She's angry at him for interrupting her record skipping marathon. Heated from exertion, she pulls on the cord trying to free it from his grip, but he hauls it back, ripping it from Lise and Charlotte's hands. The teeth and the smile disappear. His wolflike eyes narrow further. She is in trouble. No one has ever looked so mean at her for no reason at all.

Lisa and Charlotte run away in fear, crying for help. Now she's alone with the beast but still not afraid. She's getting angrier by the minute and kicks him hard against the shins.

"Let go of our rope."

He grabs her arms and twists them behind her back. She screams in pain but continues to fight; a button is torn from her dress but she's not caving in. Not even when her skirt is ripped half-loose from the bodice.

When the rope slides around her neck, she tries to fight even harder. She's not letting this bully win.

"Dirty Jew," he hisses, "I'll kill you and all of your bloody race."

"Noooo." She gags. Her lungs cannot let air in or out. As he tightens the rope, the world swirls like a merry-go-round, colors and sounds all around her. Her ears sing and her mouth is dry. Her tongue hangs loose from her open lips.

Breathe, Esther, breathe!

Someone shakes her arm. Her throat hurts; she wants to vomit.

Let me go!

Suffocating in the heat of the sun. Now she knows it all again! How could she have forgotten Gustav Wagner? It all started with him, the long trek back through her life.

"Esther!"

Who's calling? Papi? It's a male voice. I can't come, Papi. I need to fight that wretched Wagner. I do it for you, too, you know.

"Esther!"

Let me be. I'm learning things here. I can breathe now, though it hurts, but I can't be Esther anymore. Or Bärchen. Or a Weiss. Not for a while.

Who is shaking her arm, talking in her ear?

Don't you see, Papi? Gustav Wagner tried to kill me, just like Harald Rinnan wants to kill you? I won't let him. I'll kill him first. I will kill all of them. All the Jew haters. You'd better call me Jeger, Papi, the Huntress. I've always been just that. I never wanted to be the grand dame of the mansion. That was just make-believe. What Oma and Mutti wanted for me. You tried to soothe me when I came home with my clothes torn, my knuckles bleeding but my eyes shining in triumph. I'd given that little shit a piece of his own. But why didn't you come to my rescue when the lessons started: this is not our Esther. Our Esther behaves, sits straight, is an accomplished lady.

"Esther!"

The voice grows louder, the shaking of her arm more pressing. She stares into deep-blue eyes, the color of the polar sea. She blinks, her brain synapses refusing to make the connection yet. He looks strangely familiar, not unpleasant.

Then another pair of eyes behind round spectacles peer into her face. A tiny prick in her arm. The bespectacled man says in a solemn voice, "Shock. Give it time. Been through too much."

She wants to protest. She can do this. She can fight if they let her.

With the return of consciousness, the agonizing pain washes over her again. They are all gone, and she's alone. She's failed them all. Papi, Mutti, Oma, Rebecca and Adam. If only she could be gone herself.

But she is here. Blazing and alive, understanding her mission.

It had all started with Gustav Wagner ten years earlier. The lady in the making was thwarted again, only to find her true self back. No longer niceties and proper behavior. That was what had led her family to this undeserved fate.

God hadn't given her blond hair and light eyes for nothing. She would fight the Nazis, with skin and hair.

Revenge! Become fearless in the sight of a formidable foe.

Rise above the danger, the deceit, the screaming despair. To become death-defying. If Lot's wife was punished by being turned into a pillar of salt, she'd become a statue of stone. God willing.

Clenching tight fists on top of the crisp linen sheet, she hollered, "I will kill them all!"

"Thank God, she's back!"

It was Tore.

20

THE PREPARATION

A white-faced, impassive Esther came down to breakfast in the Lindenberg farm the next morning and silently took her seat at Jens and Inger's table. Food was an impossibility, but she accepted a cup of black coffee, taking careful, little sips. It stayed down.

"Any news from Oslo?" Despite the seclusion of the farm kitchen, her question was circumspect.

Jens nodded his bristly gray head gravely as he took his eyes from reading *The Bulletin*, the Norwegian illegal paper.

"Frerik managed to contact our man in Stockholm. The Nazis are ruthless. All the Jewish people rounded up in this latest razzia were sent straight to work camps in Poland. They didn't use the railroad but armed trucks to transport them. The convoy set sail from south Sweden this morning. Guerrilla fighters, both our own and Swedes, tried in vain to attack the convoy, but the Germans were armed to the teeth and nobody could come near."

Esther sat straight and motionless as she listened to the deportation of her family being a fact. She nodded slightly.

"We'll have to bury Oma."

Inger jumped in.

"We wanted to wait until you were well enough to discuss that, Esther."

She cringed at hearing her own name.

"I want to change my name. I can't be Esther and I can't be Weiss." Her voice was toneless, detached.

"We were talking about that yesterday evening, girl." Jens folded his paper and hid it under the blocks of wood for the fire. "Inger and I would be happy for you to join our family, but maybe you prefer being part of your aunt's family as she is your only relative now."

Esther shook her head.

"I promised Oma I'd look after Tante Isobel. Nobody should connect me to her. I'd... I'd like to be part of your family for the time being, if I may. So, thank you."

She didn't dare to think for how long. What if the war never ended and her family didn't return? Inger poured her another coffee and added a spoonful of precious sugar.

"Tore has the right connections. A new passport and name are chicken feed for him. We thought it best if you became a Helberg, be his sister, so to speak, as we're too old to be your parents. This house will always be your home, but with the traitors around us, it would be best if you went into hiding for a while. On paper you won't be able to be found, as we'll hide your passport."

Tore's sister? An emotion wanted to flare up inside her, but Esther suppressed it with all her might. His sister she would be. On paper.

With a pinched face, she declared, "I will go by the name of Gunhild as I intend to join the Resistance, so the name of the war goddess suits me."

"Are you sure, my dear?" Inger looked disconcerted, exchanging a look with her elderly husband. "I think you should give it another thought. You're still in shock. Resisting the German occupation is treacherous here. Look at what Harald did. We'd never have thought that possible before the war."

"Gunhild Helberg." She said it aloud, not wanting to hear the name of the man who'd created this crater in her life.

"It sounds solid," Jens agreed. "It will do for now."

~

OMA'S INTERMENT WAS A SMALL, private affair with no Jewish accents. It was just too dangerous.

"One day I'll bring you back to Austria, Oma," Esther promised as she watched her simple coffin being lowered in-between the heaps of freshly turned-up earth in the Protestant part of Søndre Nordgard's cemetery. No headstone, no Jewish prayers, but palpable in everyone was the tension that Rinnan and his *hird*—secret police —might be watching them. Ready to upset the already upset family.

Apart from the undertakers and a quickly rustled-up Protestant priest, there were no other participants. To give potential spies no clue, everyone was standing apart and not talking to each other. Esther, invisible behind her black lace veil, stood in-between Jens and Inger, while Tante Isobel and her family were on the other side of the grave. Tore with his family stood opposite the wiry priest who had positioned himself at the head of the grave, the tips of his worn black shoes stuck in the clunky gray clay. Despite the thin drizzle, the men held their Sunday hats in their hands.

"I am the resurrection and the life, saith the Lord; he that believeth in me, though he were dead, yet shall he live; and whosoever liveth and believeth in me shall never die."

Unfamiliar words to Esther, but she saw her Oncle Frerik straighten his back and close his eyes in prayer. *Whoever prays for Oma, it doesn't matter,* Esther thought. *Any prayer will do these days.*

The tired-looking clergyman held the thick leather Bible in very white, shaking hands. Esther assumed he knew for whom he was paying the last respects, and that he was as afraid of Rinnan's men as they all were.

Esther's mind constantly wanted to drift to her family, God

knew where, but she reined herself in. The physical distance between the only people Oma had known in Norway and the meaningless words the priest mumbled helped her to detach herself from the almost surreal spectacle that took place under her very eyes.

When it was her turn, she scooped some earth onto Oma's simple pine coffin that held one bouquet of white roses—all that had been available in the flower shop. Dry-eyed, disconnected, desensitized.

As the undertakers filled up the rest of the grave, she knew some part of her was saying goodbye to her old self and her whole family, but she was too fragmented and numb to grasp the depth of what was really going on.

She needed to focus on the task ahead. Her only focal point now that she was free. It wasn't a freedom she had sought, on the contrary, but now it was here, she would use it to the utmost.

Jeg heter Jeger.

My name is Huntress.

She could breathe now, though her breath was death.

Although she didn't know how she would prepare her first strike, that it was going to happen was as certain as the movements of the heavenly bodies.

Esther walked away from her Oma's grave, hands curved into fists in her tailored black coat, knowing it was the last time in a long time she would wear anything so fancy.

Bye Oma... Bye Papi... Bye Mutti... Bye Rebbie... Bye Addie!

THE FIRST WEEK after the funeral, Esther's life was filled only with mourning. Going near the cottage was impossible, so she had moved into her Oma's bedroom in the big house and didn't leave it for a week. She was lying in her Oma's bed staring at the big oak tree in full bloom, where blackbirds and sparrows produced a clamor of noise from morning till evening. She heard her cows low for her and Jens starting the tractor.

Though she wanted to get up and help at the farm, her body refused as she cried in her Oma's pillows where the scent of rose soap and lemon drops lingered, from the clothes in her closet to her glass case to the pillowcases.

Inger looked after her as if Esther was an invalid—which she probably was—bringing her soup and hot tea at regular intervals. Esther did her best to keep it all inside, as she wanted to get strong again.

Gray and bent, and normally busy as a wren to keep the big house in order, Inger sat down for a moment on Esther's bed to caress her limp hand. The June light that flooded into her sick room almost around the clock in this Northern country had Esther all confused. Was it morning, afternoon, or evening?

"Tore has sent us two armed men from Oslo." A surprised half-giggle escaped the old lady, and Esther couldn't help thinking how much she and her daughter were alike. Seeing the funny side of compromising situations.

"Why?" Esther wanted to know.

"They're here to protect us from the Gestapo and the *Statspolitiet*. Don't know what use the two good men will be if Rinnan and his gang come racing down here with Jeeps and machine guns, but it's kind of my *sønnesønn* to think of us."

"Are they staying in the house?"

"No, Jens has settled them in the barn. They have a better overview of the estate from there. Been silent though. So, girl, what about you? How are you feeling now?"

"If you tell me what time it is, Inger, I'll get up and help you out."

"No, my dear, it's ten in the evening. We're turning in ourselves now. Tomorrow is another day!"

"I have another question."

"Anything."

"Can Jens or Tore collect everything from the cottage for me and store it somewhere? I can't look at it right now."

"That's already done, dearie. Don't worry. We've emptied the cottage and sealed it for the time being. Your family belongings are safely stored in our attic. We've just kept your clothes and personal belongings downstairs so you can sort them yourself when you're ready."

"Thank you." Tears welled up in Esther's eyes, and Inger hastened to offer her a handkerchief. "I will."

She knew she would only take the book Anna had given her, *Rebecca*. But she would even wrap up her engagement photo and ring, and put them away. She would not lay her eyes on the few family heirlooms that had come from Austria until the war was over and she was reunited with her family.

"*We're not meant for happiness, you and I.*" The quote from *Rebecca* forced itself on her. Esther stood still and thought about it for a second, then resolutely said, "I'll need other clothes. Only pants and shirts in dark colors and sturdy shoes. Could you phone Tante Isobel to ask her for that?"

"Heavens, girl, what for?" Inger sighed, the gray eyebrows questioning.

Less forceful, Esther replied, "I'm going to ask Tore to help me join the Resistance." And more defiantly she added, "And if he refuses, I'll just do it on my own. I must do something, Inger. I have to take revenge and help free Norway from these monsters."

"The idea seems to bring some color to your cheeks, dear, so who am I to keep you back? You've lost enough as it is. I probably would've done the same if I was your age."

"So, you understand?"

"I understand, but I don't agree. It's very dangerous. Never have we experienced what we're going through right now. Not even when the Swedes and the Danes were calling the shots here." She giggled again. "Well, that was way before my time. Of course. Norway has not been in armed battle since the Dano-Swedish war of 1813."

Esther had to agree that the idea of fighting the enemy energized her, but it would also be hard to leave this lovely couple and the farm that had at first been such a haven to her family. For a short while.

"I'll get up tomorrow and milk the cows."

"Sleep first and see how you feel in the morning." Inger pressed her hand for the last time and got up. Agile and elastic for her old age.

Esther lay awake until dusk settled, and the farm fell silent. Unable to sleep, she sneaked out of bed and sat on the windowsill. In the distance shimmered the light of Rinnan's farm. She concentrated on it, slowly forming a plan in her mind.

"I'm coming for you! You'd better watch out for Gunhild!"

"GUNHILD!"

Not used to her new name yet, she didn't look up but continued squeezing Bertha's teats, marveling at the powerful stream of white liquid the loyal cow produced.

Tore surfaced next to Bertha waving a red Pass Norge at her. Her new passport.

"You've got it?" Despite herself, her face lit up but fell immediately again. "I wish we'd done this a year ago for my whole family."

"It wouldn't have made much difference, I'm afraid," Tore remarked, as he leaned his tall frame against the doorpost of Bertha's pen. "But I'd for sure like to know where the leak was that made Rinnan find out you were Jewish. Which brings me to the next thing. We have to find you a safe house. The protection we brought in will be blown to smithereens if the Germans catch a hint of you being here."

Esther stroked Bertha's flank. She knew he was right, but it would be hard to leave and live the life of a refugee, always on the look-out. She knew it was her destiny. She was—more or less—ready for it. As well as she could be.

"I know, but you have to help me with some things."

"Sure." He smiled, obviously glad she'd accept his help.

"Is the door closed?"

"Yes."

Dropping her voice, she announced, "I need a gun and I need to learn to shoot. I want to become a guerrilla fighter."

"Es... Gunhild, no!" Tore looked shocked.

"Shut up!" she snapped. "I am no longer the girl in the aquamarine dress on the arm of a rich jeweler from Vienna. That girl is dead."

Esther got up from her milk stool, upsetting Bertha, who was sensitive to her mistress's sudden anger, and swished her tail with agitation. She stood in front of Tore who was a good head taller than her, but seeing her rage, he backed away from her.

"You know I'm strong. You know I beat you on that slope. The Resistance needs me and I need the Resistance. I can kill and I can sabotage. But I have to learn how. I have nothing to lose, Tore, and I want to kill. No, I need to kill. It's my only drive now."

He was speechless, slowly shook his head. Clearly couldn't wrap his mind around the change she'd undergone. She saw he tried to understand, look for arguments to change her mind, but she shook her head in return.

"Nothing can stop me now, Tore. Either you help me, or I find someone else via my uncle who will supply me with a weapon."

"Of course, I'll help you, if you're sure you want to do this." His voice was coming from somewhere deep inside of him. He seemed touched by her determination. Touched. Then she saw admiration. Something in his gaze told her he knew she would fight with the same *gründlichkeit* with which she'd embarked on all the projects in her life.

Caving in, he let his long body drop on a stack of hay bales, tapping the place next to him. "We'll have to talk quietly just in case."

She sat down, aware of his nearness, but for the first time not intimidated or uncomfortable with it. Tore was Tore. He would help her, and all the rest was unimportant.

"I'll bring my gun tomorrow and we'll practice in the tractor shed. Put up some bales of straw to muffle the sound. It will only be a first line of defense for yourself. I'll try to get you a gun of your own, but we're low on weapons all around. We're waiting for supplies from Britain but they take ages to be delivered. I can't give you mine; I need it myself."

Esther stood watching him, wide legged, ready for action. Outside, the cows lowed in the fields; birds chirped merrily in the chestnut tree and a fly buzzed busily around her head.

She shrugged. "Okay. Just continue to do your best for me."

"If you're really keen on joining our cause and learning how to fight, I can help you sail to the Shetland Islands. That's where our so-called Linge men are trained. The good thing about sending you there will be that you're out of Rinnan's claws. After your return, I'll make sure you get posted somewhere where nobody knows you."

"But what about your grandparents? They can't run the farm on their own."

"Don't worry about that. There's so much unemployment right now. People who refuse to join the Nasjonal Samling, teachers, civil servants, union workers, they're all fired and desperate for a job. I'll see to it that my grandparents get help."

This put Esther's mind at ease, though some part of her still hesitated about leaving them. It felt good to know that Tore was trustworthy, someone she could turn to for help. But who was he really?

"What is it exactly you do in the Resistance, Tore?"

"I can't tell you that, even if I wanted to, but let's say I'm one of the linking pins between the Home Front and the Government in exile in London. So, I'm not really out in the fields fighting, if that's what you mean."

She gave him a sisterly nudge.

"So, you're telling me you're the office clerk and I'll be the tough cookie in the field? What a change of gender roles." Despite herself, she had to giggle at the idea.

There was tenderness in his next words that she couldn't miss.

"You're immensely strong, and the name of Gunhild adorns you. But know that despite the fact I'm sitting indoors doing the paperwork, I'll keep an eye on you, Miss Helberg."

Somehow, this promise calmed her troubled heart because she believed him.

"How long will my training be?"

"About six weeks. If you can sail next week, you'll be back by August."

"August 1941." It sounded surreal.

ESTHER WENT about her shooting lesson with the same tenacity with which she'd impressed Monsieur George walking the Le Manoir salon with books on her head. And Tore, though an opposite character from the affected Russian gentleman with his silk cravat and perfumed whiskers, was a similar enthusiastic and upbeat instructor.

"Try again, Gunhild! Good shot, girl. That's it. You're a pro!"

Esther didn't stop, until she was able to hit the inner circle of the practice target pinned to the pile of bales. Her index finger burned like an evil fire from constantly pulling the trigger of the Kongsberg colt, and her ears rang with the never-ending bangs. Yet she wouldn't stop, wouldn't give up.

"I have to get it right. I can't afford to miss." She forced still more concentration into her trembling hand and held her body rigid to beat the fatigue.

"What do you mean?" Tore grabbed the gun from her when she wanted to recharge, forcing her to take a break.

"You can tell me," he added in a softer voice.

"No, I can't. I just want to learn this as fast as I can. What other weapons do you use, rifles or knives, or what?"

"What's gotten into you?" Tore still held the Colt away from her, though Esther made an attempt at grabbing it from him.

"No," he said firmly, "I'm not giving it back until you tell me."

"You don't think I'll shoot myself, Tore?" she sneered. "I wouldn't have to be so precise if I wanted to get rid of myself."

"Though it's been a concern of mine when you asked about the lesson, no, that's not it. I think this has to do with Rinnan, right?"

It was as if he'd pricked a balloon and deflated her. Was she that transparent in her motives? But then she heard him say,

"It's been going through my mind as well, E. To kill the bastard, but it's way too dangerous. He's a constant visitor to Terboven and Quisling at the Stortinget, you know, the parliament. If anything happens to him, they'll let the *hird*, the secret police loose on us. So get it out of your head. For your own sake and that of our brothers and sisters in the Resistance."

She listened carefully to him and saw his point. Yet Rinnan had to bleed for what he'd done. On the exterior, she'd agree to steer clear of her target, but inwardly— no, she was out to take revenge, no matter what. Then why was she biting her lip? Some part of her felt horrified at the thought of how far she might go, the risk it was to all of them.

She forced herself to say in a voice that didn't sound like her own, tight and terse, "I promise. So will you let me shoot now?"

21

THE REVENGE OF LISE LUNDE

Esther's first gun, an Enfield No. 2, lay in her hand as smooth and settled as if made for her. The dark-red wooden grip felt solid, and the short barrel made her long to shoot someone at short range.

"It took me an awful lot of bribing to get hold of this second-hand British gun. So many of us want to be armed these days, but the Resistance can't lay their hands on enough weapons. One of the reasons we're not very effective in our guerrilla war against the Germans and the NS, I'm afraid," Tore explained.

Esther ignored his scarcity remark. She was concentrating on hitting target after target with effortless grace, cocking and releasing the hammer in rhythmic movements after every shot, as if she wasn't trained to lay tables and host dinner parties.

"So, this one has a spurless hammer and is double-action only?"

Tore laughed. "Where did you get that knowledge?"

"Your grandfather gave me his encyclopaedia, so I looked up all the different weapons. I'd hoped for a British one. I'd actually hoped for exactly this one. Can I keep it?"

"I was just telling you I had to bribe someone to hand over his gun to me. So, yes. But you should thank me for it."

Esther stopped her shooting actions, lowered the revolver, and gazed straight at him. His eyes were smiling.

"Never mind," he said, "as long as you promise not to do anything foolish with the Enfield. Here's the gun belt and your ammunition."

"Thank you, Tore." For a moment she stood undecided if she should show more warmth, be a better friend, but those emotions were dangerous, and she'd rather hold them at bay.

He got up, stretched his long limbs.

"Well, keep your new toy out of sight. You sail Tuesday next. Tomorrow, Nils will come down to help on the farm. He's a botany student at my university but needs to lie low for a while. Nils is one of my best men, first-class organizer of the underground *Bulletin*. If you talk with him, make sure it's out of sight and out of earshot of everyone. I don't want to endanger my grandparents."

"Do they know Nils and what he does?" Esther couldn't help asking.

"They do. My grandparents need to stay out of public sight as well, especially with Rinnan in the neighborhood. So please be careful, will you?"

"Promise." Esther secured the belt around her khaki pants and tucked her gun away, then covered it with her gabardine coat. "Anything else I need to know before the trip?"

"No, just be prepared. Travel light. I could drive you to Bergen, if you want."

"Can you? How far is it?"

"About 300 kilometers."

"That would be great, but can you spare the time?"

"As a matter of fact, I have to check in with one of our agents in Bergen, so it works well for me too. We'll travel unnoticed in a neutral car during the day, arrive in Bergen toward evening. The Scotland ships can only sail out in the brief hours of night, no lights, low engine." Tore hesitated a moment, clearly wondering if he should give her more information just yet.

"Go on."

"The German occupation is strongest along the entire coastline. They're still building what they call Festung Norwegen, as part of the Atlantic Wall that goes right to the south of France. You won't believe your eyes when you see it. Fortifications like anti-aircraft batteries, bunkers, tanks, infantry forces. They for sure believe the Allied invasion will happen on our coast and that it can happen any day soon. They're still building the wall busy like ants, night and day.

"How many ships have gone down?" Her voice sounded steady, but concerned. So far only seasickness had been her worry. This was much bigger.

"I won't lie. About 30 percent, but you're sailing with Hemrik and he's the best skipper we have. It'll be a tricky trip, anyway. Second thoughts?" The blue eyes rested on her with more warmth than she could muster.

"No! Let's do it." She didn't want his concern. It only strengthened her resolve to face the danger.

She turned away from him, determined to pack her backpack and go.

TRICKY, Tore had said. Everything was tricky in Esther's life these days and she would have to learn to live with that.

Dressed in her darkest clothes, her duffle bag ready next to her, she lay on her bed and stared into the darkening sky outside her window. Bertha lowed once, as if saying goodbye. It was strangely enough the only thing that pulled at her heartstrings.

The cows, both before and after, had been her solace and support. Their warm bodies, the mournful eyes and always that sense of recognizing her, even in her darkest hours. The cows had been the only creatures she'd allowed entrance to her heart, and now she had to say goodbye to them as well.

Esther's heart and mind were strangely tranquil. For some

reason, her life had never seemed more straightforward and clearer. No one else to consider, no one else to care for, no one left to love. Not even Carl, who faded more and more into the shadows. No time to worry about him, dead or alive. Staying alive herself was her only drive now. A quick glance at her watch with the tiny torch Tore had given her. Five to twelve. Time to go.

Soundlessly, she went on her stockinged feet down the stairs, cursing every step that creaked under her weight. She stood still, held her breath, listened. Nothing. Sneaking out the backdoor, without even leaving a note for Jens and Inger. It was too dangerous. She had one note in her pocket, and that should suffice, explain it all.

The road was dark, no moon, an overcast sky that hid the stars. Through the deep night, weak dance music came to her ears in shards, and it made her halt. He was still up. That complicated her mission, as he possibly had guests. She'd counted on finding him in his bed.

There was no turning back, so she put one foot before the other until she came to the entrance of Rinnan's estate. Electric lights and jazz music flooded her way. On the driveway stood a jumble of German Mercedes's brotherly next to black Volvos.

"Why didn't I check earlier?" Esther thought in a panic, seeing her entire plan fall apart. She'd researched the whole situation so carefully but had not considered the possibility that Rinnan would throw a party on a Monday night.

Without having an alternative, she ducked behind the rhododendron bushes and hid her duffle bag there. She unclasped her gun belt and stuffed the revolver in the pocket of her coat. Then she waited. Checking the movements of the guests on the patio and in the brightly lit rooms of Rinnan's house.

There was no other option but to wait, despite that this meant losing precious hours while darkness was her best disguise. She'd hoped to cover the distance to Oslo on foot before daylight. To get away from here as far as possible and to intercept Tore, who would pick her up at the farm at six. Now she was forced to stay in the neighborhood and lie low near the road, trying to draw his attention, with all the danger of being sniffed out by Gestapo dogs.

Highly alert, she took in the platinum blonde women in their cocktail dresses being swirled around by SS officers and Norwegian fascists. It surprised her to hear songs like *In the Mood* by Joe Garland and Gershwin's musical *Shall We Dance*. Music that had been forbidden as *Entartete Kunst* in Vienna. Here, the Nazis seem to have fewer such scruples.

All the while, Esther's eyes sought Rinnan, who at first didn't seem to be present at his own party. She'd found out about her target as much as possible without raising suspicion. A single man of thirty-three, in a liaison with Sonja Hagelin, who was also romantically involved with Quisling's right-hand Jonas Lie.

Where was he?

The music worked on her nerves, and the grass in which she sat was damp. Suddenly she perked up. Rinnan entered the bright sitting room with Sonja on his arm. He marched over to the gramophone and abruptly silenced the last notes of Gershwin's dance tunes. Couples stopped dancing in mid-air and looked surprised.

One man shouted, "Hey, what are you doing, Har? My sweetheart has a lot more swing in her hips yet."

"Enough for tonight, chaps!"

Through the open doors, Esther heard Rinnan break up the party resolutely. "There will be a real ball on Friday, and you're all invited."

Amidst cheers and the clinking of glasses, the guests thronged outside, shouting goodbyes, and slamming car doors. Engines roared. Sonja got into the car with Lie.

Esther was on her toes now, following every move, making sure she saw all the guests really disappear. Two waiters in white tunics and black trousers started clearing the mess. Rinnan came out on the patio and lit a cigarette. At intervals, the red tip of his cigarette glowed in the dark like a small fireball.

How long before the waiters were ready?

Finally, she saw the two men get into an old van and drive away.

And then her luck was with her. Rinnan was still sitting on a wicker chair on his patio with a glass of liquor, smoking one cigarette after the other. Totally at ease.

Like a cat, Esther slinked near, her ears thumping and feeling like every step she took made the sound of an elephant foot.

Was he armed? A shiver went through her. If so, she had to be faster. She cocked the Enfield inside her pocket, cringing at the metal sound, but Rinnan seemed deep in thought and unaware of the intruder until she was right before him.

Black hair, black clothes, black eyes. And a broad forehead. Good.

"This is for my family."

The bullet exploded in his forehead. She cocked again and aimed at his heart.

He gazed up at her, an astonished, not-understanding look on his face that turned ghastly.

"I am Esther Weiss and you deported my family. I'll kill you all."

He sank to his side, the glass dropped from his hand and shattered on the tiles. The cigarette smoldered a hole in his black pants. The smell of burning flesh.

He was already dead.

She pinned the note on his bloody chest and ran back to the rhododendron bushes. There she listened. Nothing but the hooting of a night owl startled by the two shots.

It was done. Now, to get away as fast as she could.

"I loved you, Harald, but you cheated on me with Lie's whore. I can't forgive you. I hate you and that's why I killed you. Lise Lunde."

Let them sort out this crime of passion among themselves. It would be an interesting find. But more importantly, it would erase all traces to the Resistance.

Esther grabbed her duffle bag, feeling like whistling a song. She felt better than she had in years.

22

IT BECOMES REAL

"**W**hat are you doing here in the ditch? You haven't...?"
Tore's scrutinizing gaze fixated her, as Esther threw the duffel bag onto the backseat of his Volvo and climbed in the passenger seat. She was too tired to argue, but the fact he asked if she'd killed Rinnan meant he didn't know the answer. The murder of the head of the *Statspolitiet* hadn't spilled to the capital yet.

"I don't know what you're talking about. I was awake early and thought I'd come and meet you." She sank back in the old leather seat with satisfaction. Though the night had not been cold, the grass had been wet and her bones were sore.

"Why are your clothes wet?"

"Oh, please drop it, Tore. I walked through tall grass."

"Um."

She closed her eyes, too knackered to keep them open, hoping he would let her take a nap and stop asking his nosy questions.

"If you were so wide awake at the crack of dawn, it's strange you're now sleepy again."

He wouldn't let it rest. She looked straight at him, feeling how her fiery anger rose to her green gaze. He kept his eyes on the road, the strong, regular profile not showing a trace of misgiving. Esther sighed. It was so hard to be angry at Tore; he never seemed to do anything wrong. And that thought making her even angrier.

"All right, you busybody. I killed him, so put your foot on the pedal and let's get the hell out of here."

Cursing under his breath, he accelerated, and the old Volvo spluttered and took off.

"They won't find him for an hour or so, and I made sure there's no link to the Resistance. I left no traces, so give me a break and let me sleep for an hour or so."

"Sleep? Are you crazy? Do you know what danger we all are in now, Esther?"

He must be really angry, using her real name. But she wasn't having his anger, nor his scorn.

"I don't care what you think. The guy had to die. I told you there's no link to any of your men. I enacted it as if it was a crime of passion."

"They won't buy it! Every time a German or one of Quisling's men is murdered, they take revenge by killing random young men, sometimes up to one hundred men per mishap."

Now Esther was wide awake. Was it true? She frowned, didn't grasp it. Tore remained silent, concentrating on getting through Oslo and onto the road to Gol.

"I'm sorry." They said it at the same time.

"I didn't know," Esther added, her voice smaller than the point of a fine needle.

"You couldn't know, Esther. And I should not have lost my temper with you. I wanted to use this trip to instruct you as best as I can on how to work within the organization."

"At least he's dead and can do no more harm."

"That's true. But how do you feel about that? Having killed your first man?"

Esther tried to think straight, but couldn't. Some part of her registered she should feel something, if only relief, or remorse, but it was strangely quiet in her soul.

"I'm not feeling much. I'm just hungry and tired. Does that mean I no longer have a soul? Am I putting my own needs before everything else now?"

As she huddled further in her coat to forget hunger and sleep, Tore pointed to the glove compartment.

"Open it. I brought supplies for the trip."

Her eyes widened as she saw a bar of Cadbury ration chocolate and a thermos flask of tea.

"Chocolate! Where did you get hold of that?" Delight in her voice.

"One of the perks of being in touch with the Brits, I guess. You can have all of it if you promise to bring new bars from across the pond." She was aware of his deliberately light tone and grateful for it, but the heavy question of the dead man continued to hang in the air. After she'd eaten and drank the tea, she decided she would come clean with him.

"What do you think it means, Tore, that I don't care two fiddlesticks about having killed Rinnan? My indifference does worry me, though. It's totally opposite of who I am and how I was brought up. Is it just the possession of a gun in my pocket? Am I a criminal now?"

Tore laughed his characteristic full laugh that reminded Esther of his mother's. Seeing the humor in atypical situations.

"So many questions posed before the oracle at once, Esther. Well, let me disencumber you. According to your own observations, I'd say you still have a soul. And now close your eyes and have your nap. I'll wake you up when we're nearing Geilo, where we'll take a brief stop. Now shush!"

With a vague smile, Esther fell asleep. Somehow, the way Tore took control of situations comforted her pained soul. Although she still thought him cocky at times, with only a sweet spot for her sister and his family, she basked in the care he took of her. And there was so much she had to learn from him in this new life.

∼

ESTHER WOKE TO A FAIRYLIKE COUNTRYSIDE. Crystal-clear lakes, pine-green forests and sapphire blue skies. The road was narrow and meandered through hamlets with wooden houses painted in green, yellow, and blue. Children played by the roadside and women in traditional dresses stood chatting with each other. No sign of war, of woe or worry. She was sure she'd never seen a prettier sight and her heart sprang up. To live like this, in a peaceful community and just go about your own life in freedom!

She must have thought aloud, because Tore's voice cut through her daydream.

"Don't let what you see at face value delude you, Esther. Resistance is springing up everywhere, and these women could as well be talking about the laundry as sharing the latest illegal press bulletins or planning a meeting of the forbidden trade union later tonight. We don't know. But women are our main clandestine workers at the moment, especially in the small communities where well-known resistance figures are easily tracked down by the secret police or the SS. Somehow women can more easily remain under the radar."

Esther took a last glimpse of the group of four women standing close together as the Volvo sped past and out of the hamlet. For some reason, it brought her current job into focus. 'Clandestine' was the word Tore had used. It was a shedding of her old skin of notability and order. She was a cold-hearted assassin on her way to a life undercover. And yet she could not imagine another life anymore.

"Is that the reason you want me in the organization?" She cocked her head, a half-smile on her face.

"No. I don't recruit anyone. You wanted it yourself, Gunhild, and that's why I want to make absolutely sure you get the best possible training and don't do stupid things on your own anymore." The vehemence was back in his voice. "I can't stress it enough in how big a pickle our country is, fighting two enemies, one from the outside and one from the inside. We can't have random lynch parties going on. We're too vulnerable and dispersed to fight effectively unless we're disciplined and understand what we're doing."

He sounded rather schoolmasterly, but she accepted the sermon. He was right, of course; he knew the country and its people best. She wanted to be effective, perhaps even earn his praise. She might have beaten him on the ski slope, but his knowledge of this freedom war was far superior to hers.

Learning on the job was Esther's forte, so she fired her next question.

"How do the different Resistance groups communicate with each other?"

"With difficulty, and sometimes not at all. The coordination committee is in Oslo. We constantly try to reach as many different groups and cells as possible scattered from Kristiansund in the south to Varanger Peninsula in the very north. The local groups consist of people in all walks of life—journalists, clergymen, teachers, lawyers, defeated military men, fishermen."

"And women?"

"Yes, especially within the teachers' organizations there are many women who joined the 'Standfast' struggle last fall. All the teachers were put under pressure to join the Nasjonal Samling for fear of losing their jobs. So many protested that Terboven and Quisling couldn't fire them all. So, the Standfast was successful. That's also when teachers started wearing a paperclip on their lapel as a symbol of protest."

Esther listened carefully, storing all the information away for later. Something nagged at her, the politeness of it all. The seeking of a solid and cautious structure, which would take years to implement. They didn't have that time. The Germans had to be overpowered somehow and their prisoners freed. Every day counted. All she wanted was her Papi and Mutti and siblings back.

Mowing down all those rotten apples with the single swing of a machine gun seemed a much better tactic to her. Tore must have felt her restlessness surfacing again.

"You can fight, Gunhild, as long as you're willing to follow the rules."

"But I am very un-Norwegian in this?"

"Not at all. There are many who think we need to show more armed resistance, especially among the Milorg, the Norwegian military, that was defeated. You'll meet many of these men in the Shetlands."

The deep-blue eyes held hers for a moment. "But you're un-Norwegian as a woman. Your fighting spirit, which I've had the honor of being defeated by, is tremendous. Is that Jewish, Austrian, what is it? I can't place it."

Esther thought for a moment, then shook her head.

"Though I wanted to fight injustice and bullying as a little girl, that spirit was thoroughly discouraged by my formidable mother and grandmother. I truly believed I was the pliable goody-two-shoes going to get married. Some part of me still believes in that fairy-tale. But fate pushed me over the edge."

She drew in a deep breath. "I've always had a great need for physical action that I've tried to curb in order to be a lady. If I let loose that wild side, I'd ramble on the piano for hours on end, dance like crazy or go skiing down Radstädter Tauern Pass over and over again. I guess I'm just restless."

She stopped, abruptly. Aware she'd never been so open with Tore before. Hated herself for it. It was none of his business. She heard him say the words she didn't want to hear. Not now, not ever.

"I saw all of that the very first time I laid eyes on you, Esther Weiss."

The words were spoken. Couldn't be taken back. She with a cup of Darjeeling tea, awaiting her fiancé, readying herself for a totally different life. He'd raced into her life and never really left.

"Then help me get my family and my fiancé back!" She almost spat the words in his face. Anger flaring up at this impossible man in this impossible situation. Everything impossible.

Tore didn't speak for a while. Concentrated on the road. A quick glance in his direction showed the muscles of his cheek working fervently. In the same low, soft voice, he finally responded.

"I'll do everything in my might to help you reunite with your family, Esther. I promise. Everything. You know how fond I've grown of Rebecca. My heart hurts every second of every day, knowing I failed her and you and your family."

Now she looked straight at him, her own anger subsiding.

"You did nothing wrong, Tore. You were the one who warned us, and I should have pushed through. I'm to blame. Not you."

"Oh, no, you're wrong there, girl. I knew this country, and I knew the direction it was heading. And I knew what you'd given up coming here. You, above all, should have been safe in my country. We failed you all."

"Let's drop it, Tore. Putting the blame on anyone but the real culprits won't help us. Instead, tell me what I need to know now we're in this together."

She looked out of the window and for the first time saw the beginning of the famous fjords rise before them. A majestic scenery of bays and inlets and coves, patches of lagoon-blue and pearly-gray water, white-foamed waves crashing on the rocks deep below them.

This was pure life, nature in all its glory of freedom and power. They were right on the edge of the world and Esther felt it in her bones. Freedom on the other side of the North Sea. Freedom as if they could touch it with their hands.

"Aahhh!" she exclaimed, wonderstruck by a blend of beauty and blue funk. The sea was wild, and she had to cross it.

"You like it?"

"It's ... I have no words for it. I never knew such landscapes could exist."

"Oh yes. This is where the Vikings got their itches. Had to master the waves." Tore laughed freely.

The outskirts of Bergen loomed up in the distance. Rows of similar wooden houses in different colors built on a myriad of peninsulas. The water almost to their doorsteps. Both a folkloric and a mythical town. Unlike any town Esther had ever got a glimpse of.

"You're okay?"

Caring Tore showed his face again, but she now was grateful he asked. Soon their ways would part, and only God knew if they'd ever see each other again in this war. She was about to become a mini-Viking herself. Totally alone, ruling the waves.

Small fishing vessels and sailing boats lay strewn over the harbor, bobbing up and down wildly as they pulled on their anchors. They were so tiny; they would rock even wilder on open sea. The remembrance of her first experience with seasickness was still fresh in her mind. How tough would be tough?

"Here." Tore retrieved a small bottle from his coat pocket. "I heard you don't really have sea legs. This might help. My grand-mother makes them herself. It's a combination of sour honey, herbs and wine. Used to give it to Astrid, who always got carsick. Don't eat much before you go on board. Just some dry bread, and take little sips of Inger's potion. It might help. But then again, it might not." He handed her the bottle.

"Thank you, Tore. You're always so thoughtful."

"Ah, that." He waved his hand almost irritably. "Now, before you go, some last instructions. As I told you already, the ship will sail out as soon as it's dark, but listen to the skipper's commands at all times. It's going to be extremely dangerous during the entire cross-ing. Not just the Nazi surveying planes and anti-aircraft. The entire trip is always tedious because of the dangerous weather. It can be nasty as hell before you reach the Shetland islands."

Esther couldn't help shivering. Thinking again of dying at sea instead of in battle. Capsizing and dying in the ice-cold water? She tried with all her might to focus on what Tore was saying, but her stomach was queasy and her throat dry. She was aware she was wringing her hands.

"Just listen to Skipper Helmik. He'll keep you safe. Like most of the Shetland bus skippers, he's a local fisherman. They've put their vessels at the disposal of the resistance. They're not trained military men, but they know the sea as no other. They are armed with light machine guns concealed inside oil drums placed on deck. On the out journey they take civilians and soldiers and bring back trained fighters and secret agents from the SOE, radio transmitters and weapons."

"How long will the journey take?" Esther tried hard not to sound too jittery.

"About two or three days. Depends on the tide. When I went in April, we did it in forty-eight hours. But I sailed from Ålesund."

"You made the trip as well?"

"Yes!" He chortled his peculiar laugh. "I know you think I'm just an office clerk, Gunhild, but I did my training, too. Don't worry. Though I'm more specialized in intercepting phone calls and finding the right radio waves, that sort of technical stuff."

The idyllic scene of the enchanted coastline chilled further in Esther's eyes. The reality of war, the tiny cogwheel she was in it. There was no way back. How badly she'd planned all this, diving into danger head on. Her courage would have to come from some-place, but for now she was as adrift as a pinnace in peril.

"We're here." Tore parked the Volvo on the side of the quay next to other motor vehicles, some of them German jeeps.

It was a busy late afternoon on the docks. People came and went, SS officers in their green uniforms smoking and watching the crowds move. The cobbled quay was scattered with fishnets, some of them being repaired, some hauled on to trawlers ready to sail out. Men in yellow oil suits with boots attached to them, big beards and weather-beaten faces paid no attention to the SS officers, but a strange tension hung in the air. As if everyone was acting out a play instead of doing a real job.

"What are they doing here?" She couldn't help asking.

"What do you think? Keep an eye on boats being made ready to sail out. Don't worry, your boat isn't lying here. I'm going to intro-duce you to Helmik. Not his real name, of course. Remember, never real names. And you don't know mine. If you're caught—which by Heaven I hope not—you know too many real names already. So forget them. You go as Gunhild Helberg but will come back from Lunna House with your code name."

She nodded, mental notes going into her brain synapses faster than the speed of light.

"Helmik will take you to the M.B Herny. It's a medium-sized fishing boat, and he's a very experienced skipper. Did the Shetland bus a dozen times already. I trust you with him."

Esther grabbed her duffle bag and followed Tore over the cobblestone to the gray-haired giant with a black beret and full beard. He smiled a toothless smile as he saw Tore approach him.

"Good to see you, fellow! Brought the Miss, I see?" Eyes the gray of mercury gauged her from top to toe. He looked doubtful.

"Let's go inside," he continued in his clipped voice, clearly a Norwegian accent Esther had difficulty following. "Get away from some dirty ears." It was clear who he meant.

"I'll have to be going again, Helmik. Still got to drive up to Lille-hammer tonight."

"You've got a mighty long drive there, son, but one glass of ale and some bread and herring has never killed one hungry man that I have met."

Tore smiled. "True."

They walked a few streets when Helmik entered a café called *Skipperstuen*. The same jolly atmosphere as on the quay, but with the same strain. Again, Germans sat at the tables, but there was so much noise that they could talk without being overheard. Esther was overtaken by sadness; the long day behind her and the uncertain night before her. She picked on her food while the men ate hearty meals and talked incessantly. She was grateful for the cup of coffee and the slice of cake Helmik shoved her way.

Before she knew it, they were outside and going in yet another direction.

"Helmik will take you to a safe house where you can rest until departure, Gunhild. I'm leaving you two now."

Please don't go! Something in her begged, but she knew she would never say it aloud. She bit her lip, trembled. Before she knew what was happening, she was drawn into a bearhug and held tightly.

"Be well, sister! I'll try to pick you up, on your return." She wanted to be held in the safety of that embrace that smelled of beer, cigarette smoke and leather for eternity, but he'd already released her. Tapped her on the shoulder one last time.

"Take care of her, Helmik. She's still green. Contact me when you know who's bringing her back and where."

"Count on it, son. I'll take care of the Missy, don't worry!"

And Tore was gone. Walked away with those big strides, not looking back.

"Come on, Missy, no time for those sad doggy eyes. We've got a trip to prepare." The bristly eyebrows wrinkled in a jocular manner, clearly to make her laugh. The blue eyes twinkled underneath. Helmik certainly was a larger-than-life character, amiable, but with a steely reserve underneath his navy skipper's sweater. Just the kind of man to help her overcome her fear of dying at sea.

23

CHOPPY WATERS

"**S**tay low in the boat, and sorry for having to throw a tarpaulin cloth over you." Helmik grinned, showing his toothless mouth under the gray beard as he covered Esther with a piece of material that stank of fish and sea water. It didn't bode well for her queasy stomach.

Together with the only other female on board, Helmik had created a makeshift bed for them on the floor of the tiny cabin. The rough boards were made somewhat less uncomfortable with a pile of horse blankets that were itchy but warm.

As they had gone on board, Esther had made out nine other shadows that would be her fellow passengers for the next couple of days. Two men looked like they were in uniform, a young couple and two indistinctive men. The skipper was assisted by two young fishermen who quickly took off their bright yellow oil suits for sailing out.

To Esther, they were only silhouettes with no history but one common goal, to safely cross the 230 miles to Lerwick. She tried to make herself as comfortable as she could and wondered when the tarpaulin could be removed. It was hard to breathe underneath it.

"I'm Hilde," the young woman next to her whispered. Real name or not was not a question to ask.

"Gunhild," she whispered back, as the boat rocked on the wild North Sea, though still at anchor in sight of the harbor. Holding tightly onto the small bottle Tore had given her, Esther didn't dare to ask more.

"I've secured some chloral hydrate pills," Hilde said in the dark. "If you want one, let me know. It'll help you sleep."

The briny scent of the ocean, paired with the sweaty odor of too many people packed together in a confined place, already made her nauseated. The constant rocking of the boat was far from soothing, either.

"Thanks, but shouldn't we stay awake and be prepared?"

"What can we do? Very little, right? If the Germans get us, they get us, asleep or dead. Does it matter?"

"Should we ask?"

"No, my husband knows I take the pills to make the crossing. He'll let Helmik know. So?"

"How long do they work for?" Esther wasn't sure whether she should tell Hilde about the potion. The idea of sleep and not being aware of the danger and boat movements was very tempting.

"Depends. You best take two. It will knock you out until daylight, and we'll be at some distance from the shore."

"In that case, yes please."

"We'll wait until we've covered the first miles. Then we can throw off this stinking cover. I wouldn't want us to suffocate in our own spit."

The ship's engine started, and at very low speed the boat tonk-tonked toward open sea. Above them there was no talking, no movement. The only sound came from the engine and the bow cap hitting the waves. Nausea rolled in and Esther unscrewed the bottle. The taste of the liquid was surprisingly sweet and agreeable, and it seemed to work. She could at least control the physical discomfort, so she didn't have to vomit. Not yet, at least.

To blot out the perilous present, she concentrated with all she had on bringing Inger's friendly face with the gray bun and bent back before her mind's eye. Seeing her stand at her kitchen top, preparing her herbs while chatting with her, with Oma. Such friendliness and open, warm-hearted balance. Then Tore's face appeared with vivid clarity before her, the blue gaze telling her to stay calm.

They are so kind, she thought, biting on her tears, *so kind to strangers. I must take an example from them.*

"Here," Hilde said, sitting up and throwing the tarpaulin aside. "Enough is enough." She unscrewed a flask and offered the luke-warm tea to Esther, putting two pills in her hand in the dark.

"Thank you." She swallowed and gave the flask back.

"Sweet dreams."

Hilde certainly had a touch of the ironic. Somehow, she reminded Esther of blurt-it-all-out Romy. As she settled back on the blankets, fully dressed, with her boots on, she pulled another blanket over her. The boat rocked like crazy, but she minded little. She went with the movements, and they swung her to...

Something crashed into the side of the boat. Over the roar of the engine and the waves, a plane rumbled overhead.

"Stay low," Helmik shouted. "Get out the gun."

Esther shivered, wide-awake again.

"Will we sink? Have they hit us?"

"Sounds like it." Hilde seemed neither surprised, nor affected.

And then she knew. Fear was no option. Her body drowsy but her brain awake, Esther grabbed her gun and moved the few steps from the cabin onto the deck. All was dark and moving sea. The silhouettes down on their stomachs. The only light came from the wingtips of the disappearing Messerschmidt. She felt silly—her gun was going to do them no good. What did she think? Shoot at a plane?

On her belly, she tiger crawled to Helmik at the wheel.

"Are we okay?" She had to ask as he seemed to be concentrating on ploughing the waves and nothing else.

"You here? What are you doing?"

"Are we okay?" she repeated.

"Sure. For now. They may come back with more. It's always a gamble, Missy."

"Is the boat still whole?"

"Hans is checking it. Now, go back downstairs."

Esther felt silly again, but then Helmik added, "You're a brave lassie. You'll do fine with them Scots. Now, try and grab some sleep."

AFTER TWO DAYS AT SEA, it was a strange, surreal experience to see the coastline of their destination sketched on the horizon. As she crawled on deck, Esther realized she'd survived her first Shetland Bus crossing without scars. It could be she'd gotten used to the rocking of the boat, but more likely the paralyzing fear of the German bombers returning made her body forget all about seasickness. It was also possible that Inger's potion *did* really work. Whatever it was, Esther felt fine enough and was, relieved, at times rapturous.

Without asking permission, she made her way up to the wheel-house of the fishing boat where Helmik stood with one hand on the wheel, while slurping coffee from an enamel cup with his other.

"Morning, Missy, seems like we've made it. Glad Tore won't be up my tailpipe for feeding you to the fish or the Jerries."

"Morning, Helmik. Have you been up all night?"

"What you think, lassie? Do I look like I did?"

Unsure what his age was, but gauging from his grayness certainly over fifty, Esther had to admit he didn't look tired or ruffled in the least. He was whistling *Ja, vi elsker dette landet*, which she had learned was the Norwegian anthem.

"You look fine, Helmik. Amazingly fine."

"Must be the lady's company." He winked at her, his bristly eyebrow going up and down.

Esther took to studying the display with interest and was glad she recognized the chronometer. The other equipment was a puzzle to her. Helmik's steady, calm presence made her feel safe. Through the small windows that were splashed white with salt, she could discern land coming nearer, the piers that led to the harbor stretching toward them like long, thin arms of welcome.

"Can I try?" She pointed to the large wooden steering wheel that seemed glued to Hermik's right hand.

"Sure, lassie, if you want. Gives me time to fill my pipe."

He showed her how to hold the wheel. "Not too anxious. Give her some leeway."

It was a masterful feeling. She was steering the boat to safety. Helmik seemed totally absorbed in his pipe, but Esther knew he studied her every move, never letting his attention slacken.

"I think you Norwegians are fabulous," she said, enjoying the power in her hands. "I was brought up thinking you were all buffoons and walked around with knives between your teeth." She had to giggle at her own thoughts.

"Who says we don't?" He puffed his pipe and blew out the aromatic smoke in big swirls, an enormous grin under his mustache.

"Sorry," she said, "but you're all so steadfast and stout-hearted. Aren't you even a tiny bit relieved we arrived safely?"

When he didn't answer, she took her eyes from the bowsprit and glanced at him. The smile was gone, and now he did look tired and old.

"I am, Missy. I thank *den gode Herren* every minute on my arrival at *Hjaltland*, as we used to call the Shetlands. I don't know if He listens but so far, the M.B Herny has made the crossing three times to and from without problem. That's not the fate of many of my friends." He looked haggard again and then resolutely stepped in to take the wheel from her to steer the ship into Lerwick harbor.

"Can I stay with you until we arrive?" She just couldn't part from this rock of a man yet. He seemed not only able to master the waves, but also held some supremacy over the enemy.

"You stay here, Missy. I like your company."

She had a friend, and they both knew it. A friend in war is a friend indeed.

24

THE TRAINING

On approaching Lunna House in the late June sun, Esther felt as if she'd stepped back in time and entered Jane Eyre's era. Almost a century later, she appeared to be walking into a Thornfield Hall type of mansion, with the deserted moorlands around it. The building had a desolate look, as if it was hiding a terrible secret. But this time the secret wasn't a lunatic in the attic or an impossible love affair. There was nothing romantic or fictional about Lunna House, despite its exterior. It hid hard-boiled exercise and intelligence training. A grim reminder of war on the other side of the North Sea.

Yet Esther felt she could breathe freer here than she'd been able to for years. Finally, outside the claws of German occupation. Here, free spirits ruled the roost, and nobody would mind she was Jewish. Not that they would guess with her passport stating she was Gunhild Helberg. She inhaled the early evening air, filling her lungs. Two mourning doves skimmed past her, and wings stretched out, landed on the rooftop, two tiny silhouettes against the summer's evening light.

I've killed a man. I'm no longer innocent. In the freedom she now found herself experiencing, this realization hit Esther hard. *What is to become of me?* Her legs kept walking like an automation toward the sprawled-out mansion, the straps of the heavy duffel bag cutting into her shoulders, her heart thumping like mad. Nobody was aware of her agitated state. They all trudged along, tired and hungry.

Esther was alone with her conscience, the recent events overtaking her weary body and mind like a hammer blow.

Coo-oo, coo-ooooo, coo-ooooo.

It sounded so sad, so forlorn. A line from *Rebecca* came to mind. *"Accidents happen so easily, even to the most experienced people. Think of the number killed out hunting every season."* Rinnan's death was only that, a freak happening to the world, a baptism into guerrilla fighting for her. *Swallow it, girl. Many more will follow.*

She quickened her pace, interpreting the quote as a reminder that this was part and parcel of her duty now.

Be a free spirit. The first free spirit she encountered was a giant of a Scotsman, who introduced himself as Captain Bill, their trainer. He was wearing the khaki battle dress of the British army, belted and with a gun slung around his shoulder, but Esther could easily picture him in a tartan kilt and boots, standing high on the cliffs, his long, dark mane waving in the wind, scanning the North Sea for Nazis to skin alive with his knife.

"Welcome to Lunna House, ye all," Captain Bill greeted them in his Scottish brogue. He adopted a laid-back attitude, but the hawk's eyes spoke of no-nonsense and missed nothing. "Ye'll be dealin' with me for yer six-week training but make no mistake. There's a selection after every week. Most of you won't even make it to the second week." Esther felt the piercing eyes resting on her and she blushed, fists in her pocket.

Wrong there, mate! she thought, but lowered her eyes to hide her anger. She'd show him she would complete the training with flying colors. But when she glanced around the dining room that looked more like a cheerless village hall, she saw all the other participants were men, some twenty of them, in battle dress or still in suits, in their prime. Eager expressions on taut faces. She was the only female of the group. No wonder he'd given her that look.

Esther stood taller. The men in suits didn't appear muscular or trained in guerrilla fighting either, so she had as good a chance as these white-collar city dwellers.

"I know most of ye have traveled a long distance over the past few days, so today ye can use to settle in and explore my terrain." Captain Bill bared his white teeth in a grin at 'my terrain.' He was clearly proud of his training facility. "Tomorrow mornin' at six sharp, I expect ye all here for yer first trainin'. Start with a survival trip. It'll be fun. Good night, for now." Another grin, a booming voice used to giving commands.

From the surrounding languages, Esther pieced together the group was a mix of young Norwegians who'd arrived like her by boat, some young Scottish officers, and the suit men were mainly codebreakers and radio experts from England.

Esther got a small room of her own in the attic, which she was happy with, glad to lie down on her small bunk bed without the constant swaying of the ship. The movement was still in her bones but helped to rock her asleep.

The next morning, she woke to a glorious day, sun peeping through the small skylight. A bluebird was singing a merry song outside her window. Though all spoke of peaceful nature, she knew there was no way to forget the war, nor the reason she had made the trip. But for a few more moments, she lay on her back listening to freedom until her heart became heavy again.

"I cannot rest, not until..." she muttered as the remembrance of her family creeped into her consciousness. And where was Carl? She didn't expect to hear from him until the war was over. Until. Until. Nobody knew how long it would be. The rumors about the German and Polish work camps were awful. Too awful to be believed. She shuddered.

"Don't go down that line of thought. Focus on today. The earlier we beat the Nazis, the quicker you will be reunited with them."

Slipping into her camouflage clothes and clasping her holster and weapon under her coat, she rattled down the stairs on her sturdy boots and entered the room that had served as a dining room the day before.

When she opened the door, she was surprised to see a woman standing with her back to her, staring out of the window over the rough terrain. Khaki overalls hiding her slim posture, long black hair in a ponytail. She turned and faced Esther.

"Sable?"

"Esther?"

They stood gaping at each other, not understanding how this was possible.

"What are you doing here?' they asked at the same time.

Uncertain, unbelieving, then crossing the distance between them. Walking into an embrace, hugging each other tightly.

"I'm Bill's girlfriend," Sable explained. "So, you went to Norway after all? But what are you doing here?" The next moment, Sable held Esther's Enfield in the air with a triumphant smile on her attractive face.

"Heavens, girl, what would the Sphinx have to say about this?"

"How did you do that?" Esther looked puzzled.

"Because I'm Bill's girlfriend," Sable joked. "No, because I'm good. I'm an SOE agent, doll." She handed her back the gun, which Esther shoved in its place.

Sable took Esther by the hand and led her to the two leather armchairs in front of the extinguished fireplace.

"I can't believe it. This is providence," Sable observed. "I've been waiting for an opportunity to do something back for you after you saved my life, and God has granted me this opportunity. I can train you, girl, and you'll be the best agent in the Norwegian resistance."

Esther remained silent, temporarily too overcome with emotion. Then she blurted out, "My family has been deported. That's why I'm here. I have nobody anymore."

"What about that fiancé of yours?"

Esther shook her head. Sable slipped out of her chair and sank at Esther's feet.

"Oh no, oh no, oh no!" She kept repeating, "The bastards, the rotten bastards! We'll get them, Es. Each and every one of them."

"I've killed one already." Esther couldn't help herself. She knew she shouldn't talk about it but somehow Sable's presence, a girl from her past with whom she'd made peace, opened the floodgates and she had to tell her everything.

"Wait!" Sable waved a slender hand. "I'm going to find Bill and tell him you and me are taking today to catch up and get you in the right shape. He'll understand. We need to get you mentally strong before you can embark on this important mission. You do get that, don't you?"

Esther nodded while Sable left the room in search of her Captain.

They walked the beaches, hands in pockets, and talked for hours. Though Sable was friendly and certainly complaisant, she'd not lost her overbearing and bossy demeanor. She just used it now for another cause instead of getting herself in trouble with boys and school authorities. But there was very little of why she herself was actually in the Shetlands, involved in the training of secret agents. Despite her baggy clothes and sailor-type cigarette in the corner of her red lips, she was still every inch Lady Sable Montgomery.

It nagged at Esther that the inequality between them still carried on, so she decided to nip it in the bud. She was clearly becoming a more straightforward, cut-the-crap Norwegian herself.

"We've talked a lot about my motives and why I should curb my feelings of revenge and channel them to intelligence and smart decisions, but why are you actually here, Sable? I'd more likely pictured you at the Moulin Rouge in Paris or maybe the casinos of Monte Carlo."

It was as if she'd hit the raven-black haired girl in the face. Sable stood stock-still in the sand, pasty-faced and played-out. Esther already regretted her question, ready to apologize. After all, it was none of her business and Sable clearly belonged to the Lunna House staff. But the light-blue eyes sought Esther's face, and she saw insecurity in them, disbelief, and a strange longing. To confess? To her?

"I'm not my mother!" Her tone was bitter, not angry.

"I didn't mean that. It's just that I'd like to get to know you better."

"So, you still don't trust me?" Sable kicked the tip of her boot into the wet sand. "Well, I guess I don't look very trustworthy. And I certainly didn't behave like that in the past."

"As Captain Bill trusts you, I trust you, too. That's not it. It's just ...that you seem to hide something, but maybe I'm reading way too much into it."

Sable drew in a long breath between half-closed lips, then fished a packet of Lucky Strikes from her pocket and placed one in-between the full lips. She looked askew at Esther as she lit it.

"You're way too sharp, Miss Gunhild, and you know it."

"I'm not trying to be sharp, or anything. And you don't have to tell me if you don't want to."

Drawing a long and deep pull on her cigarette, Sable made an impatient movement with her hand.

"Well, as we are in the middle of nowhere and there are no unwelcome ears, I might as well tell you my story. I've got a kid. A girl. Already had her before I came to Switzerland."

"Heavens, I didn't know you were married." This was the last piece of information Esther had expected.

"I'm not married." Sable stared out over the gray sea that rolled its powerful waves over the strip of sand. The tide was rising.

"Then where is she?"

"I don't know. They took her away from me at birth. I named her Davina, but she probably now is Gertie or Marie or something else drab. She was given away in adoption and I was packed off to Switzerland."

"But how?" Esther's mind couldn't fit the pieces of the puzzle. "Who did that and why? What about the father?"

"Who did that were my mother and her then boyfriend. The father never knew I was pregnant."

"Why, Sable? Why didn't you tell him? He would've married you."

"Oh Esther, you're such a goose. No, he wouldn't. I don't know why I told you all this. I never tell it to anyone."

"Does Bill know?"

The blue eyes flashed. "No, and don't you dare tell him!"

Esther backed away from her sudden fury. "I never would. So why did you tell *me*?"

"Because you asked. I thought you'd care." It sounded defiant and dejected.

"I do care, Sable, of course I do. I'm so sorry."

"Isabella will be three this week. I have no clue where she is. If she even knows she's not with her birth parents. Probably not, and probably for the best. But it might explain to you why I flipped at times at Le Manoir. And I shouldn't have taken it out on you. I know. Like I shouldn't have told you this now, but there's something so darn disarming about you."

"Come here." Esther took the cigarette from her fingers and stamped it out with her shoe. "Come here!" *Words wouldn't help now*, she thought, as she pulled the slim, dark figure in her arms and held her in a tight embrace. What she expected happened. Sable's body shook as she cried against Esther's chest. She let her cry for a long time, just holding her, then finally spoke in a gentle tone.

"Cry as much as you want, Sable. It's okay. We both hurt so much, so much. But we'll get through it. I will get my family back and you your little girl. Maybe not during the war, but one day this hell will be over, and we will be reunited with our loved ones."

"But how?" Sable sniffed. "How can I find out where my little girl is?"

"Well, you've come to the right profession, dear. You must tell Bill if you're serious with him. Then trust the intelligence services. They are so smart. People everywhere can be tracked. Just start at the hospital where she was born. Trust the process. She's legally your child and now you've reached adult age, you can claim her back."

The crying had stopped. Soon, Sable restored some of her former equilibrium. Peeking at her watch, she said resolutely, "Back to base. We've earned a proper lunch and then we start the training. Thank you, Esther. I knew you were gold from the very first moment I laid eyes on you."

Though her heart was sore for both Sable and herself, Esther accepted the compliment with gratitude. Hand in hand, they walked up the path to Lunna House.

"I'm glad I confided in the right person." Sable sounded all perked up. "But I know I still owe you an explanation, how I got so deeply involved in Resistance work. Don't worry, I'll tell you all. We have plenty of time."

THE FRIENDSHIP with Sable only deepened over the weeks and sustained Esther during the merciless hardship of the training.

The first week was all about survival, trekking with heavy rucksacks for eight to ten hours per day, until her feet were full of blisters and the muscles of her legs too tight to move another step. They slept under the stars, having to make their own camp, search for food and cook it over fires. It sounded adventurous but was actually an ordeal after having been on the move all day. She was almost too tired to taste the rabbit meat when it was finally cooked.

The curt and critical Captain Bill was always spurring them on, from daybreak till dusk, asking just that bit of extra exertion from the participants that they didn't have. It was then that Esther learned to lean on Sable, while she saw the last shadows of Ladyship and shenanigans disperse in her friend.

In everything Sable was Captain Bill's right hand, showing a strength and tenacity uncommon in her slight body. Mentally she was even more formidable, checking on people who fell behind, dressing wounds, pricking blisters, holding pep-talks where Bill just grumbled that they had to get on with it and stop whining.

But always, always she supported Esther, helped her to become stronger, more confident, more independent, more self-sufficient. Through Sable, Esther became a fighter worthy of representing the Norwegian Cause. It forged an unbreakable bond between them, a love deep and loyal like women can have.

The second week, to Esther's relief, they stayed at Lunna House and learned decoding messages and radio transmitting. But it was all quite technical and she was bored after a while.

"This is not your thing, is it?" Sable came to stand behind her while Esther was messing with the wires and trying to connect the dots. She threw it aside, frustrated.

"No, it's not. I don't know what Tore sees in it. Though the survival trek was arduous in the end, it's much more my thing. I'm also looking forward to gun protection training. I love that."

"Who's Tore?" One black eyebrow rose, and for a moment they were just two girls. Esther shrugged.

"On paper, he's my brother. He's actually my sister Rebecca's friend." Her face grew gloomy, mentioning her captured little sister. Sable was quick to throw a slender arm around her.

"Tell me about him."

"There's little to tell." But Sable's eyes bored into hers, so she told her that Tore would be waiting for her when she returned to Norway and find her a position in the movement.

"Good!" Sable clapped her hands. "No office job for you, Miss Gunhild, no typing, no radios, though you must learn the basics when you're out in the woods or on the ski slopes. We'll get you trained to join the male-only Norwegian Independent Company."

"Oh, I've heard of them. That's Magnus Linge's Company, isn't it? He's a real hero in Norway. Did you know he was a famous actor before the war?" Esther's eyes shone.

"Yes, I know Magnus well," Sable continued. "The Norwegian Independent Company was set up after Operation Claymore in the Lofoten this March. Magnus didn't think it was a successful raid, but what he didn't know at the time was that the Allies managed to capture a set of rotor wheels for the Enigma machine, and its code books from the German armed trawler Krebs. The Nazi naval codes are now cracked by women at Bletchley Park in England. With these codes, our convoys know how to avoid U-boat concentrations."

"That's amazing. I'm learning so much here, but I don't think the Norwegian Independent Company will take on women."

"True, they only have one female member, and she's a nurse but she's even forbidden to learn how to parachute."

"So, it's useless to try. I'll have to opt for courier or newspaper distributor, that sort of thing. By the way, Tore said he was going to find me a position when I return to Norway, and he'll never agree to me joining the Norwegian Independent Company." Esther frowned. Her genuine passion was to fight and forget the past. All of it. Live only for surviving the next hour, a bomb in one hand and a gun in her other.

"You'll have to disguise your sex. Cut off those girly curls and hide those curves. Brave women before us have done it. And so can you." Sable stood before her in her overalls, hands on slender hips, a provocative look on her pretty face.

"Hmmm... I'd still have to consult with Tore."

"Why? Does he own you? Come on, Esther, one phone call from Bill and that's settled. Norway direly needs good fighters. They're trained here at Lunna House and at Drumintoul Lodge in Scotland. Your Tore knows the quality of the commandos we deliver. He'll bark but he won't bite."

Esther began to feel a lot better and decided she would try even harder to become a good commando.

"One more thing before I leave you to figure out these field communication systems," Sable said. "You'll have to come back here in a couple of months. There's another combined Allied raid planned for the end of this year. Our Winston simply loves showing Hitler the weak spots in his coastal defense. These pinpricks are just the start. Can't tell you more about it, but it will be coordinated from Scotland and from here so if you want to be part of the party, you'll have to cross again."

"No problem. I'm working on my sea legs." She hoped her resolute nod showed her she was up to the task.

~

FOUR WEEKS LATER, Esther stood before the giant Captain Bill with slight Sable at his side.

"You've done great, Gunhild Helberg. Your code name is Jeger as Sable told me you've seen this name in a dream. Though I'm not a dreamer, I believe in their power, so Jeger it is. We'll see you back in October. Stay safe and whole until then."

"Thank you, Captain Bill. I will."

She and Sable hugged each other tightly, but without tears. Esther was glad to know she would see more of her new friend soon. She turned on her heels to follow the other agents to Lerwick harbor. In her rucksack, she had three more British guns, two radio sets and the latest instructions for the central committee in Oslo.

She felt special and needed, but her joy was complete when she saw the toothless smile of Helmik next to the M.B Herny.

"Hello, lassie,. I was told to come and collect a special cargo. And I'm in need of a good shipmate in the wheelhouse."

"At your service."

It was a salutation with a grin.

25

OPERATION ARCHERY

27 December 1941

tanding on deck amidst the commando troops that steamed up toward Måløy, Esther shifted uneasily from one foot to the other in her crude commando uniform. That it was an ice-cold, pitch-black night and the North Sea wild and capricious was her lesser concern. She was afraid to be unmasked as a woman, after all. For weeks she'd practiced a forceful swagger and had adopted a noncommunicative, angry look that held the other commandos at bay. But she had to cooperate and might have to answer questions, at which point her female voice might betray her.

In all other ways she could be on par with the men; she'd built muscle and resilience against cold and hunger. Fear was something from another lifetime. She could fight in combat, throw mortar fire as cover, and shoot straight with anything from a Wembley revolver to a Lee-Enfield rifle. The latter was swung over her shoulder, while her combat helmet sat securely on her short, blonde hair.

The months of training had made her face lean and the lines hard. Though she could not sport a mustache or beard, there were other men like her—still boys—who went to battle as beardless as they were born.

Her group politely broke up to let the commander of the Norwegian Armed Forces in exile, Captain Magnus Linge, in their midst. Esther tried to get as good a glimpse of him as the darkness permitted, struck as she always was at his exemplary presence.

How he did it she didn't know, but Captain Linge appeared distinguished even in the heat of war. Though dressed in the same khaki uniform they all wore, on him it looked as if it was a battle costume, styled and fitted in his favor. She felt the piercing blue eyes with their serious look resting on her for a moment. He knew who she was; she was sure of it.

"Men, latest update after the delay at Sullum Voe, due to the bad weather. Glad you all could enjoy some unexpected Christmas celebrations there, as I don't expect us to see any twinkling bells or stuffed turkey for the next two days. On the contrary."

He drew in a sharp breath, making eye contact with everyone in turn. Esther felt a shiver go through her. The last instructions. Within hours, she would be in combat, real combat.

Linge continued, "We're currently having perfect weather conditions, so that seems like a good sign. Here are the latest details about our combined Allied attack. At sea: eight naval forces, including a destroyer and a submarine. In the air: nineteen Blenheims of Bomber Command with their flight protection, ten Hampdens for smoke laying or bombing with Beaufighters flight protection. On the ground: Operational Headquarters, Special Service Brigade, a detachment of the Special Service Brigade Signal Section, all ranks of the No. 3 Commando, two Troops of No. 2 Commando, a detachment from No. 6 Commando, officers from the MI.9 War Office, a Press Unit of correspondents and photographers, and last but not least, us: Royal Norwegian Army. Total military personnel: 51 officers, 525 other ranks. And I'm your commander. As you all know."

He laughed a dry chuckle, but every commando looked up at him with deference. After Operation Claymore in March 1941,

Major Linge was an absolute hero. Stunned by the size of the operation, Esther listened carefully and felt her heart swell. She was one of them!

Then everyone's attention was drawn to a lot of merriment going on among the press unit. They were all posing for a photo on deck, while one of them worked with a large flashlight to create enough light for the photo.

"Extinguish that at once!" Linge barked as the press men dispersed, still laughing among themselves. "don't know what they're getting themselves into, drinking and partying like this," he growled. Directing himself to his men again, he added,

"We're tacked onto Group 3, consisting of 105 Commandos. We assault the Island of Måløy. Smoke bombs dropped from the aircrafts will disguise our arrival. Our task is to mop up after the bombardments. Round up and arrest Nazi survivors and Quislings, complete the demolition and then cross the short stretch of water to join the fighting in South Vaagso. Is that clear?"

A muffled "yes" was the answer.

"Any questions?"

"What happens in case of casualties, Captain?" someone asked.

"In case of minor injuries, you help your fellow men; there will be dressing stations, and every group has a medical team. In case of death, the stretcher bearers will collect the bodies. Dead Germans and Quislings are left where they are. Of course." Again, that dry chuckle, but Esther had the eerie feeling something bad would happen to some of them. It could be her, but it could be any of them.

"That's all, men. Take a moment of rest before we land. Sergeant Helberg, follow me, please."

Esther straightened at hearing her name. It was a shock. Gunhild had been changed to Gunnar, but her last name was still Helberg. On stiff legs, she followed Captain Linge to his hut.

Inside the cramped place, he took off his helmet to show a mop of combed back black hair. The blue eyes took her in with interest as the crease between his eyes deepened. He looked like the celebrity he was, and it made her uncomfortable, a commoner. Linge sat himself at his writing desk and lit a thin cigar.

"So, you're Tore's brother?" He waved away the smoke, as she nodded. "I know we're not supposed to know each other by name, but there seem to be a couple of people around who're closely looking after you. Does the name Helmik ring a bell?"

She nodded again.

He leaned in her direction and pointed to a chair stacked with earmarked novels.

"Just shove them on the floor; we need to talk."

Esther gingerly grabbed the pile of novels and arranged them in a neat row next to the chair. Ibsen's *Peer Gynt* play was among them, as well as a couple of Shakespeare's plays.

"Would you care for a cigar?"

Now she was forced to speak. With her head bowed down, she mumbled, "No thank you, Captain."

"So why does a Jewish girl from Vienna think she wants to take part in a commando raid with Norway's toughest fighters?"

She didn't dare to meet his eyes. It was all over. Found out, after all. He'd known who she was all along. Of course, this man knew everything. Then why let her come along? Or would she be shipped off to Oslo, as soon as they set foot on the island? Confusion muddled her brain. There would be heavy fighting where they landed; she couldn't just hop on the next bus or train.

"I'm sorry, Sir, what do you mean?" It was a very weak excuse. He leaned even closer. She could smell his breath, smoke, and coffee.

"Esther Weiss, daughter of a Viennese goldsmith who's been deported to Poland, with the rest of his family. Except for you. You escaped. Of course, you're angry. Don't worry. So am I. I'm an actor, for Heaven's sake, and I was just a reserve in the army. I've not been reciting Ibsen's Peer Gynt for two years but acting on a war stage instead. Not for fun, I can tell you." The dry chuckle followed. Esther still stared at her hands, red from wringing them in confusion.

"I'm sorry, Sir. I don't want to compromise you, or the team."

"Stop your sorries, Jeger. We need you!"

"What?" She looked up, hope in her eyes.

"I may not be as smart as I look, but I recognize a fighter when I see one. Of course, it's all rather uncommon, and the secret is between you and me. That's why you stay close to me today. All the time. You can add me as one of your protective circle, so to speak."

"Thank you, Sir."

"Name's Magnus, not Sir. Simply Magnus unless you're under command. Then it's Captain Linge. Understood?'"

"Yes Si...Magnus. Thank you."

"I'm surprised at your meekness now, Jeger. From what I've been told, among others from Captain Bill, you're a mean fighter and a class A shooter. I need you to give us sniper cover, okay?"

"Yes, Captain."

"Clever!" He chortled, coughed.

"Now take a rest, use my sofa. I'm not letting you out of my eyesight, Jeger. Oh, and in case I forget or don't have the time anymore, I'm mighty proud of you. First woman ever under Norway's command. Well done."

"Thank you, Magnus. And yes, I'm lost for words by this sudden exposure. That's why I may come across as timid. But you can count on me. One hundred percent. I don't want any special treatment. I'm battle ready."

"Good to hear. Now, let me learn my lines in case we conquer the Nazis today. Or at least keep every Nazi along the Atlantic wall nervous for the rest of his days in power." With the familiar chortle, he picked up a novel and started to read. Esther lay down on the sofa and closed her eyes. Though she was far from sleep, it was good to shut out all impressions for only a brief moment in time.

THE CONSTANT, legato sound of the Scottish piper accompanied them as they sailed into the fjord with the mountains on both sides rising like steep, shadowed walls. Overhead, the drone of the British planes was an almost comforting sound on their way to drop their bombs, while the Navy ships flanked them as protective big brothers, booming their cannons as a warm welcome to the Germans.

Certain her eardrums would burst any second from the constant bombardments and explosions, Esther let herself sink from the barge into the ice-cold water that came to her waist and, wading through, followed the backs of her compatriots in the pitch dark like a row of black ducks. As she clambered onto dry land a little later, slippery with ice and snow, the thick smoke, dropped from the planes to form a curtain that disguised their arrival on Måløy, made her eyes water and blurred her vision. All hell had broken loose. Both in the air and on the island. The Germans, for sure, realized they were coming for them.

A firm hand helped her up the rocky shore and she, in her turn, grabbed the hand of the man after her. From there, they moved as one body, following Linge, who stayed close to her all the time. The relentless bombardments continued, followed by explosions and barracks and wooden houses going up in flames. Group 3 was ready to face the enemy. Fear or hesitation was no longer an option.

They had set the stage. Now they had to act.

"Duck!" His command was hardly audible over the noise. It happened in a split second. Esther felt Linge throw himself on top of her, as she went down flat on her back in the sand. A bullet whizzed overhead. *Damn*, was her first thought, *I should have seen that one coming.*

"Sorry," she breathed, lying still, "and thank you."

"No worries, Helberg, you'll get the hang of it. Make sure you watch all sides, not just ahead of you. Eyes in the back of your head. Remember." He rolled off her, and dusted his pants, looking somewhat embarrassed, clearly aware of her sex. As she got back on her feet, she swore to not let that happen again. *You can count on me,* she'd promised. It wasn't supposed to be an empty promise.

Yet in that short instance, Magnus had shown he was part of

her protective circle and that meant a lot to her. As Esther followed his fast-moving back toward the burning town, her heart filled with a deep sense of gratitude. Magnus Linge would not let her down and she—as Gunnar Helberg or Jeger—wanted to fight by his side and under his command until the end of the war. He was a mentor now, but he could very well become a good friend. Of that, she was certain.

As they came closer to the Germans, slipping on the snow-covered path, they stayed close together, their rifles ready to fire. The incendiaries paved the way, as they got closer to the burning town. In the approach of dawn, Esther saw the radio division set up their equipment to stay in touch with the other groups by the side of the road, but they marched on. A British destroyer steamed up close by in the bay. Everything looked gray, smoky apart from the licking flames that stood out like bright orange tongues. They gave off heat, and she started sweating in her uniform. Cold sweat, but still sweat.

"The street fights will soon begin, Helberg. Are you ready?" Magnus's voice sounded over the roaring snipers and the cracking fires. "Though it looks like most of them are barricading themselves inside. Easy-peasy. They will burn to death."

"Yes, Captain."

He was right, there were no Germans yet, but they approached with vigilance, every synapse of their bodies ready for action.

Two Quislings, men in suits with hats as if going on business, had been sniffed out and surrendered themselves. German planes appeared on the scene, one of them immediately going down as it was hit. It suddenly looked like there wouldn't be any fighting. Germans who ventured outside quickly surrendered, even coming toward them with white flags. Esther rejoiced. It looked like the raid was going to be very successful with little bloodshed.

She gazed at the hated Nazis with their arms over their heads and their swastikas on their uniforms as they were accompanied by British commandos to the waiting ships. Then, groups of Quislings under gunshot were carrying stretchers with wounded men, including the German commander, who was also wounded. Was it already done? It was confusing.

Close by, an ammunition barrack exploded and crumbled before her eyes like a matchstick box. Debris flew everywhere, clouding the already smoke-filled sky. The pungent smell of gunpowder burnt the inside of her nostrils. They all had black-smeared faces and a layer of dust on their uniforms. The normally pristine white snow was completely black.

They were now approaching the German headquarters set up in the town's hotel, which they quickly surrounded. Cameramen following them on their heels. Esther had no time to think. All her senses were on high alert as she shot on every moving German and fatally hit at least two. This was the place they had to capture fast and ruthlessly as the seat of the German command had to be wiped out completely. All around her, there was a burst of snipers and hand grenades. The Germans fiercely defended their headquarters, their last hope.

With Magnus by her side, Esther ran toward them. Next to her, one of their commandos was hit in the back and collapsed almost on her feet. She ran on, keeping Magnus constantly in her sight, and looking at all sides as he had instructed her. She held a hand grenade, ready to throw into the open door of the hotel. Flames were already licking out of the roof.

The next scene happened in slow motion. She knew she had tried to throw herself in front of Magnus's body as he had done for her but was too late. A German aimed his rifle and shot the captain in the chest. Her wounded cry rang over the noise.

'Nooooo! Captain Linge! Noooo!"

"Go on, Jeger, do your duty!" Linge shouted as he collapsed, and though in doubt, Esther ran on in red fury to throw the grenade straight at the killer. He exploded before her eyes, then disappeared in a jet flame, as the hotel came crashing down on him. Esther sprang back, toppling over her own men, aware the Germans were being swallowed alive by the fire. But more came from other streets, so she turned on her heels and was given no time to see how

Magnus was doing. Lying on the ground in a pool of blood, he was still giving her instructions.

"Watch the left side of the hotel, Jeger." She kept shooting in one direction, then the other, mowing every approaching German down. But they kept coming, giving her no time to sink down near Magnus. As long as he kept instructing her, he was alive. Soon, stretcher bearers would come and see to his wound. She just had to make sure no one could come near him. Her Enfield was empty, so she grabbed his gun and kept going. Where was their Group?

"Assist me here!" she cried at the top of her lungs and then saw she'd been backed up by her own men for a while.

"Captain Linge is down, stretcher bearers needed. Now!" she cried again, longing with every fiber of her being for this fight to be over so she could take care of Magnus. Finally, the stretcher bearers came, and she gave them cover as well. Backing away while facing the Germans and still mowing them down as the sharpshooter Tore had trained, she meanwhile grabbed one handle of the stretcher, one eye gauging how her commander was doing. Not knowing why or what she was saying, she kept talking to him.

"You'll be okay, Captain. Easy-peasy, remember?"

Bringing her face close to him, she saw he was still breathing, though with a rasping, irregular breath. His tunic was stained with blood, the once so forceful blue gaze glazed.

"Proud...of...you...Jeger. Win...the...war... for...me."

His head lolled aside.

"No!" She shrieked wildly, "No, Magnus! We were supposed to look after each other. Not you! Not you! I can't win this bloody war without you!" Her face was white; the morning wind blew the tears from her eyes. Still holding the handle of the stretcher, she looked back in a mist of tears at the scene of their fight. A town turned into a burning heap of scrap.

"I will, Magnus. I will win the war for you!"

She followed the other bearers, reaching the barge in a trot. He was gone. Didn't need medical attention, but a grave. The tears kept coming, streaming down her face, tears of pain, of defeat, of anger.

The raid had been short and successful, but it taken their best man. Her first combat with her first friend.

Was this what the war meant? Only losing people and never winning? She felt so much loss as she boarded the ship with the dead body of their commander. The entire Group 3 stood stiff and silent. Esther knew what to do. When in crisis...

"In honor of Magnus Linge, I'm going to ask the Home Front to rename the Norwegian combat garrisons the Lingen Compani," she announced in as clear a voice as she could muster, wiping the last tears from her cheeks. Her face and hands were black with dust and gunpowder, and she smelled like war.

As if naturally taking Magnus's place as their leader, she took off her cap, shaking loose short blonde curls, exposing her female face. The rest of the men stood gaping at her in disbelief, but she could see the admiration gleam in their eyes. They'd witnessed how she'd fought to make sure their wounded commander wasn't captured by the Nazis, to be given no funeral at all.

"Yes, Ma'am."

IT HAD BEEN a Blitz attack that had totally surprised the Germans. It had taken the Lingen Compani only thirty minutes to overpower the enemy, kill and capture dozens of Nazis and Quislings and—sadly—have their captain and two other commandos killed. A couple of their men wounded. A perfect raid by all standards but one. The first ever dent in the German superiority of occupied Europe. One that would boost the Allied morale for the raids to come.

And yet.

Kneeling next to Magnus's stretcher, Esther felt only sadness. What did a boat full of prisoners mean? What even did the joy of Norwegians fleeing German tyranny mean, boarding a ship to freedom in Scotland? The catch might be great; the loss was greater. One of Norway's finest freedom fighters had died in an otherwise victorious raid.

They had come to destroy the German garrison stronghold on Måløy together. Now she was alive, while he had died. She gave him a last salute, remembering her promise to win the war for him.

"I'll mourn you later, Magnus. I have to conquer Vaagso for you first."

And so, the new Lingen company under command of Gunhild Helberg steamed up the fjord to the next German garrison. While another piece of Esther's mortal heart died, her resolve was all the stronger.

26

BACK IN OSLO

Oslo, January 1942

The room was cold, the world was cold, her heart was cold. Esther lay curled up under three blankets in an anonymous apartment somewhere in West Oslo; she didn't even remember the name of the apartment complex or the street name. She never saw the other inhabitants.

In the two weeks she'd been back in Oslo, she'd changed safe houses three times. And on this lusterless, dark morning in early January, she'd probably see the last of this dreary place as well. Someone had leaked her name during the Måløy raid and instead of returning to the Shetlands to prepare for the next attack, Gunhild Helberg had been ordered to lie low in Oslo for a while to keep out of sight of the secret police. They'd cracked down on so many of the people on the coast over the winter.

Waiting wasn't Esther's strongest point. The first fight, however tragic, had given her an appetite for more and a goal. Now, she was pinned down in limbo with just her thoughts and her bleeding heart.

Her heart bled, for her family, for Magnus and for all the

Norwegians who were shot, tortured, deported. Very few of them escaped the claws of the Gestapo or Quisling's secret police. Everyone was hungry. The winter was endless. And she? She was restless.

A new assignment had been promised via a courier, but for two weeks nothing had come, and waiting time was the worst for Esther. It meant remembering what could only best be kept at bay by loud and incessant action and sleeping badly.

The brief hours of day changed to night as the flick of a switch and she had nothing to do, could go nowhere, saw no one. Listlessly, she flipped the pages of *Rebecca*, a name that hurt her every time she read it. Plus, this Rebecca, Daphne Du Maurier's Rebecca was a horrible woman. Nothing like her own sweet, intelligent Rebbie with her brown eyes and dogged adoration for that tall Norse Tore.

Rebbie, Rebbie, Rebbie!

Why do I keep toting along Anna's favorite book? she wondered for the hundredth time. The writing was good, but Esther found the story so sad. Everyone seemed guilty of something except for the nameless heroine. Maybe her Rebbie was that nameless heroine. She, Esther, certainly had a big, bloody stain on her soul. There it was:

"I suppose sooner or later in the life of everyone comes a moment of trial. We all of us have our particular devil who rides us and torments us, and we must give battle in the end."

Should she give in? Stop this thirst for battle that took only the best of them? And she missed Tore. Through that same courier, she'd tried to get a message to him that she was in the capital, but he hadn't knocked on her door.

Enough of this whining, she told herself, *and I'm done waiting.*

She threw the covers off and got into her dark camouflage clothes. Thinking about Rebbie suddenly made the urge to find out if any message had filtered through from Poland or Germany extremely urgent.

Despite the simple message to stay put inside the apartment

until either taken to another safe house or instructed to get to place X for the next mission, Esther couldn't obey any longer. She simply had to act, get on the move. All this secrecy, being an anonymous link in an unknown organization, made her balk.

Disoriented in Oslo, which she'd never been given the time to get acquainted with, she marched through unfamiliar streets for hours, frozen hands in her pockets, her woolen hat deep over her ears, shoulders hunched. Gunhild Helberg. Despite the blizzard of snow, despite people being arrested or even shot before her eyes, despite the knowledge she should not endanger her only remaining family, she plodded on, had to know.

Upon turning a familiar corner, it was a great relief to finally see the street post Grønlandsleiret, and in the distance the sign plate of her uncle's leather shop *Gjelsviks Skinnbutikk*. But nearing it, she stopped in her tracks. It was boarded up. Someone had in black letters scrawled, *Communist, Jew lover* and the Star of David on the boarded-up windows and door. It was ridiculous. Oncle Frerik was no communist; he was a practicing Christian. But the word *Jew* hit her like a meteor.

This must mean his underground press center and radio station had been disclosed. His marriage to a Jewess revealed. Were they deported too? Or worse, murdered? Esther had a hard time breathing, though she instinctively slinked to the other side of the road. *Don't give yourself away, demonstrate no emotions, not even now*. But she had a hard time breathing, and her legs wanted to give way underneath her. Ignoring the shiver as cold as a coiling water snake that ran up her spine, she walked on. Casually, incognito, while her heart screamed murder.

She was no longer the wild girl who killed traitors on the spot, though the heat of anger and the useless pain were the same. The two smug SS officers parading outside the closed shop would be an easy target. Her hand moved to the Enfield under her coat, but she walked on. How she managed, she didn't know.

The next moment, she was staggering up the garden path she'd once gone up with Rebecca three years earlier, feeling incredibly weak. Yet she found herself banging on the backdoor of the Helberg's house with all her might.

"Don't let them be arrested as well!" she prayed. Relief flooded through her when she heard Bodil's watchful bark. A little later, Liv's blonde head peeked cautiously around the corner.

"Esther? You here?" Frau Helberg exclaimed worriedly, "Come in quick!"

Bodil pushed his wet snout into her hand. Automatically burying her frozen fingers in his thick collar, she remembered how Rebbie had loved this dog, this family, this house. She couldn't help herself, but flung herself in Liv's arms and cried.

"Oh girl, oh girl," Liv kept repeating, 'I understand Tore's not informed you yet. Oh, girl. Come in and get dry and warm. I'll make you some tea."

Still crying and clinging to Tore's mother, Esther followed her to the kitchen where she'd sat down on that day after her arrival in Oslo. No Rebbie and Tore playing the guitar and laughing in the next room. The house was very silent. Bodil had retreated to his mat and lay down, sad eyes taking her in. Liv busied herself with the tea.

"What happened to my uncle and aunt?" Esther summoned all the strength she possessed to ask the question.

"I'll tell you after you've had some warmth in your body. You look frozen to the bone. Let's get you warm first."

The hot tea calmed her somewhat, though her teeth clattered against the porcelain rim. Liv had peeled off her winter coat and wrapped Esther in a warm stole of her own. Then she grabbed both her hands, the light eyes full of concern.

"We don't know who betrayed them. The Gestapo or an *agent provocateur*. We never seem to know how people are given away. We only hope we're not the next one. Nobody saw. They came last night. We didn't even hear anything. They were taken like thieves in the night. Then this morning they came to board up the shop. I tried to get hold of Tore, but like you he moves from place to place, and I haven't seen him in over a week."

"So... so... you don't know where they are?"

Liz slowly shook her head, a sad and shattered expression on her face.

"I wish I could tell you. We seem to be glad just to save our own skin for another day. The movement is so dispersed because of the incessant attacks by the Gestapo and the NS. Every time there's a form of central organization, they round up some of the central contacts and we go without information for weeks. It's so frustrating."

Esther nodded, numbed.

"I know. I shouldn't even be here. I think..." Her eyes welled with tears. "I think I sensed something because I was supposed to stay where I was but now... but now... I don't even know if I can find the place back where I was staying."

"Dangerous as it can be, you're staying here tonight. If we're lucky, Tore may show up and he'll know where to take you. If not, Eivind will try to find out. Now finish your *sandbakkelse*. It's no real comfort, but something sweet will do you good."

"Thank you, Liv. How are you doing? And how are Inger and Jens? I miss them, you know. We... we had a great time together at the farm."

"I know, dear girl, I know. Though we're all suffering and under a lot of stress, thank God we're still all alive, doing our thing. Even my Astrid throws her weight behind the Cause, stenciling the *Bulletin* and distributing it around Oslo on her bicycle."

At that moment, there was a quick succession of raps on the back door and Liv's eyes lit up.

"Tore!" She ran to the door to let her son in.

"Can't stay long, Mor. Just delivering the newspaper for Astrid to distribute tomorrow," Esther heard him say.

"Come in for a moment. See who's here," his mother urged. Esther sat up more upright. They hadn't seen each other for over a year, not since he'd dropped her off in Bergen for her trip to the Shetland Islands. It was strangely familiar to hear his voice, as if he lived inside her, hidden in some deep crevice of her heart.

"Tore!"

"Esther?"

She stood, balancing from one foot to the other, hugging Liv's stole around her shoulders. He looked different, tired, skinny, slightly hunched but the steel-blue eyes, full of light, searched her face. Like automatons, they moved toward each other, affected, uncertain. She felt his muscular arms around her and let herself be hugged, held, upheld. Like her, he was trembling, as overcome as she was.

"Esther," he said again, softly, from deep within him. Then held her more lightly, as if she was breakable, which she wasn't.

"I'll leave you two alone for a bit; go to the sitting room to talk. I'll start dinner and will keep an eye on the door. Tore, you show Esther our hiding place, should you need it." Liv took control, giving them space and time.

"I really ought to be going back to Headquarters," Tore observed hesitantly, "but I'd hoped to see you, Esther. I want... I need to talk to you, so yes, Mother, I'll stay to dinner and go back straight after."

They sat on Liv's blue and white striped sofa, awkwardly together, closer than they should.

"How have you been?" Tore didn't meet her eyes but lit a cigarette and inhaled deeply.

"I just found out about my uncle and aunt. Do you know anything?"

"We tried to get information on them through all our contacts. There are signs your uncle is still in Oslo, being held at Bredtveit Prison. But that's not sure. We're trying to get hold of Paal Bergson, who is the director of the prison and poses as an NS man but is actually on our side. Recently, he's been under scrutiny from Quisling's men himself, so he has a hard time feeding us information about the prisoners. If your uncle is held there, it most likely means torture, though." Tore threw her a quick glance. Esther winced.

"Your uncle was the chairman of the national retail trade union and an active opposer of the so called 'new order.' Immediately after Terboven's *coup* on 25 September 1940, he helped set up the paper *Fri Fagvevegelse* for a free trade union. He was both editor and distributor. So, the Gestapo will try all means to find out what he knows." She winced again, a lump in her stomach. Torture— they all knew they faced it, but who could stand it and for how long?

"And Tante Isobel?" Esther hardly dared not ask.

Tore sighed.

"You've seen the signs on the boarded-up shop. Doesn't bode well. All Jews who weren't able to flee to Sweden or go into hiding have been deported to Germany or Poland. Someone who knew she was Jewish must have tipped off the secret police. I'm so sorry, Esther, and I know how hollow my words sound."

Esther couldn't answer. She just swallowed something in her throat that wouldn't go down, again and again. Now they were all gone. She had no family left.

"We are your family, surrogate family, if you want and for what it's worth." It was said almost inaudibly.

Abruptly, Esther got up.

"I have to go. There might be a new mission for me. Have you heard anything?" Her hands disappeared in the pockets of her combat pants, curled into fists.

"Sit down! We must talk."

But Esther couldn't sit. She marched the pretty Helberg sitting room up and down, up and down, a pent-up energy that needed an outlet.

"All right, I'll stay a while. You can talk as I pace."

"I'd rather see you pace than sink into misery." Tore lit another cigarette, his tall frame bowed forward, a stress-line between his eyes.

"They've buried Magnus Linge at Vestre Gravlund here in Oslo. I thought you might like to visit his grave one day."

Esther turned on her heels, looked down on his slumped body.

"You knew Magnus as well?"

"Of course, everybody knew him. They've actually changed the name of the Norwegian Independent Company after him. It's the Linge Company now."

"Really?" Somehow this message was a little balm on all the wounds.

"What's more," Tore continued, "the whole Norwegian team has praised your bravery. Killing the Germans who hit Magnus during the attack of the headquarters on Maløy and not flinching one moment. Tit for tat. That's why I'm told they've got a new secret mission for you, which will demand further training in England for a while. You've made it as the first female commando, Esther! I'm so proud of you."

"Really?" Her vocabulary seemed reduced to one word.

"Yes. I'm glad I'm the one to tell you because I hadn't expected to. Didn't know you were in Oslo too."

"I've been twiddling my thumbs for two weeks here, wondering what was going on."

"I think they want to get you across the border to Sweden this time and fly to London from there."

"London?" The monosyllables kept coming.

Tore patted the couch next to him.

"Do sit down for a moment, Esther. Your pacing and silence make me nervous."

"It makes me nervous that you always seem to know where I'm going when I don't." She was aware she was warding him off in an unfriendly manner.

"I told you I'm part of the Coordination Committee that's in touch with our government in London. We get the messages, but the people in the field are the real heroes. People like you."

She sat down on the edge of the sofa, feeling a mixture of pride and exhaustion. How long could she carry on with this pressure? The answer was 'as long as it takes.' She knew, sank back, closed her eyes for a moment. She was so tired, so homeless, so rootless.

A warm hand touched her forehead. A stray curl was pushed back. It felt good, intimate, but on opening her eyes again she saw something in Tore's gaze she didn't want to see. It was there again.

Rädstadter Tauern Pass, their first meeting in Oslo, his goodbye in Bergen. The blue eyes probing her soul. She couldn't handle it. Not now, not ever.

"Don't."

The tone was friendly, the undertone clear. He withdrew his hand, mumbled "sorry."

"Dinner's ready!" Liv shouted from the kitchen.

"Will you be okay, Esther?" Tore asked as they got to their feet.

They stood facing each other and slowly, very slowly she nodded.

"I will as long as we both stay alive. I can't handle another person disappearing from my life."

He put a hand on her shoulder, brotherly now.

"I will do my best if you do too. I want to help you find your family... and your fiancé when this bloody war is over."

"Thank you, Tore." She grabbed his hand and kissed it. "Thank you, for everything."

27

A NEW MISSION

17 October 1942

A cold haze enveloped the Scottish Highlands, hiding the mountain peaks in a slurry gray blur that blended in with the snow-laden crevices. The sky had also dissolved in the Scotch mist, but somewhere overhead spotter fighters cruised toward the North Sea. Most likely Bristol Blenheims on their way to take aerial pictures of Norway, Esther thought. She could distinguish the spins of the propellers vaguely over the roar of the engine.

She brought her skis to a standstill and listened, leaning on the poles. The roar faded and was followed by a rare moment of silence from human activity. The mountains given back to nature, the crack of a branch, but for the rest stillness. Within and without stillness in the cold, white world.

Her Secret agent training called SOE training—for which operation she didn't know—had been even tougher than the one in the Shetlands and lasted throughout the summer. She needed this moment away from everyone, alone with nature which had become her best friend, though never to be trusted. After all, it was

Sabbath. Not that anyone at Achnacarry Castle cared or knew. It was her moment of reflection. Her remembrance of what once was. And who had been at the center of her world, her family, their life in Vienna... and Carl.

Heavy drops of water plonked from the pine branches onto her helmet. Plop, plop, plop. A sudden gust of wind made the newly fallen snow whirl around her, stick to her white watertight overalls. From across the gorge, the low grunting of a red deer buck echoed. She was alone in God's world. Was he still looking after her? After her loved ones?

Angrily, she pushed the ends of the poles in the snow and skied away.

No going back there!

Evening came sneaking in like an uninvited guest, but Esther knew the terrain around Achnacarry backward and forward, having crossed it on foot and on skis many times. She could see the lights of the castle in the distance and went faster, suddenly longing for a cup of hot tea and company.

"Help!"

The cry was below her, a shallow but steep ravine.

"Help!" A male voice. Though her first reaction was high alert, she immediately reminded herself she was not in a war zone. This was a comrade.

She unclasped her skis and lay down on her stomach, peering down into the dusk.

"Who's there? What's wrong?"

"It's Per. I've broken my leg."

Per? One of their own company?

Esther was already retrieving her survival cord from her ruck-sack, while she shouted down, "Do you think I can haul you up? Can you grab the rope? Use your good leg to get up against the wall?"

"Sure. Just throw it."

Esther looked for a place to wind the rope around and was glad to see a sturdy birch.

"It's coming."

She waited until she felt a tug on the other side and started pulling with all her might. Her strength came naturally to her these days. Plenty of nutrition and heavy physical training had made her strong as an ox.

Soon, she saw Per's contorted face appear over the ridge.

"Easy now," she instructed. "Hold your hands there, and I'll pull you up as carefully as I can."

Minutes later, she was carrying the Norwegian on her back while holding her rucksack and skis in her hands. He winced and cursed all the way, but she ignored it. A broken leg could be mended.

"I'll get Doc Smith to you directly."

Kicking open the door with her snow boot, she deposited Per on a plush sofa in the castle's hall, and went in search of the doctor, who had his office in the former scullery down the hall. She marched over a long paisley carpet, along mauve wallpapered walls hung with oil portraits of the castle owners down to the Middle Ages but had no eye for all that luster.

"Thanks, Jeger," she heard Per shout after her. "You're an amazing commando, you know."

Shrugging her shoulders, she made for the doctor's office. All these compliments, they were great for sure, but she was dying to get back into the fight.

AFTER DINNER ESTHER wanted to turn in when Anton Tronstad, their commander, ordered her to his private room that was also his office. Tronstad had confiscated one of the grand parlors and she sometimes thought he would've enjoyed being the Lord of the castle, how he paraded around there over the expensive mahogany parquet on his sturdy boots and khaki uniform, or took up a pondering position at the large bay windows smoking his pipe and overlooking his grounds.

She was surprised to see the always zippy and go-go Norseman looking clearly out of sorts. Thinking back if there was anything she'd done wrong, she couldn't recall. She'd fought hard for her position in the men's group and had earned it. Never claiming femininity as a reason not to be able to carry out an order, and she was the best skier of them all. Even better than Tronstad, though by a hair.

"Jeger!"

"Yes, Major."

"When was the last time you did a parachute jump?"

Esther's heart sprung up. Did this mean she was close to action?

"Six weeks ago, Major."

He nodded, looked down at the papers in front of him. Still not happy faced. It was a map of Central Southern Norway. The rugged terrain around Hardanger Plateau. What on earth was going on there?

"Sit down, Jeger. We need to talk."

She did as she was told, pushing aside all thoughts of irregular behavior, now only full of anticipation of what he had in store for her. The tall, lean man—probably in his mid-twenties—pushed aside a mop of light-brown hair that fell over his forehead. The shiny blue eyes, which always seemed hyper-focused at any object that came into view, rested on her, clearly gauging her aptitude for the job at hand.

With two elbows on the table and a line between those hawkish eyes, Esther felt scrutinized, as if under a microscope. A trickle of sweat ran down her neck into the woolen vest she wore under her combat blouse.

"Do you know how to operate the B2 radio set?"

"Yes, Major."

"Did you take the demolition class?"

"Yes, Major."

"No injuries, illnesses?"

"Not that I'm aware of, Major."

The blue eyes went to the maps and documents on his desk. He turned a page, seemed absorbed in reading, but then spoke without looking up.

"Per Johansen's fall today is mighty untimely. We'd planned a mission for tomorrow night, in which he was scheduled to take part. Why the idiot wanted to say goodbye to his Scottish lass and fall in a ditch is beyond me. But it happened and his lights are out."

Tronstad paused, gave her a quick glance, assessing her expression. Esther remained deadpan. Instructions would follow and she would carry them out. One way, or the other. She just hoped it would be in Norway.

"If the weather behaves itself, four men—me included—will be dropped on the Hardanger Plateau. As it's full moon, we must jump tomorrow night. Already missed a couple of months, but we really should be on the ground before winter hits even harder. Our target is the hydroelectric power plant at Vemork."

Norway? The plateau in Telemark? She knew what it meant. In hush-hush voices, the talk had been about the heavy water plant for months. Something—nobody knew exactly what—was produced there that the Germans could use for a very dangerous bomb. Four men. Who would be the other two?

Her eyes met his. He looked pained, uncertain, which gave him an almost boyish look.

"I don't want to do this, Jeger, and on the other hand, I want to give you a chance. I've heard nothing but good things about you, and I've seen your work. It's as good as that of any of the men. But..."

She drew in a breath. Now it would come. She was a woman. Weak, needy, a burden. What would it be?

"...you're a bit too fanatical for my taste. It's your drive to kill, to eliminate Nazis and Quislings that worries me. I don't know if you have your anger under control."

Esther was aware she was gaping at him and quickly shut her mouth. Her being a woman was not a problem; her hate was. Without knowing if it was her turn to talk, she had to interrupt to defend herself.

"I know, Major, and I've been working on getting my anger under control. I swear I can do it."

He nodded, and the etch between his eyes lessened to some extent.

"I've seen that too. Strangely enough, it's one reason I want to recruit you. Your fighting spirit is so mighty. This is going to be one of the toughest missions in the war so far. The will and the spirit will be of even greater need than physical fitness or endurance."

A silence followed. The grandfather's clock on the wall struck eight. The striking of the hour seemed to help Tronstad reach his decision.

"You're the best person for the job, Jeger. The other two are Claus Nielsen and Arne Rønneberg. Claus is our radio man, and Arne is our explosives expert. I command and read the maps. I expect you as the fastest skier to be our eyes and ears. Alright?"

"Certainly, Major Tronstad." Esther felt a surge of adrenaline, fear and excitement wrapped in one. Only one more day. She was chosen out of so many agents. As a woman. Her heart swelled with pride. Defending her adopted country, slaying the Nazis, whatever gruesome plan they had with that power plant. She was on it.

"Good!" Tronstad shook her hand with a firm grip. "We're a team, so no ranks, and certainly no last names. Just call me Anton. Only use first names when we're on our own. Otherwise, it's the code names. I'm the Grouse, Claus is the Swallow and Arne the Seagull. You will just stay Jeger because it fits you."

"I know, Maj... Anton."

"Let me call in Claus and Arne. They're in for a treat they didn't expect." He winked at her, but she saw a shadow of doubt glide over his clean-shaven face. Would there be protests against her participation from them?

∽

ESTHER SAT STILL as a statue when the Westland Lysander took off from the RAF airfield near Inverness. They were accompanied by two more planes, which protected the Lysander on the flight across the North Sea. Weather conditions were good, and she could see small bobbing lights from the fishing boats deep below in the ink-blue water. Whether they were really fishing boats, or Shetland Buses, remained a guess.

She was aware of the extreme silence inside the aircraft with Anton sitting next to her and Claus and Arne opposite. The dynamics had certainly changed with her sudden appearance in their tight friends' group. In particular, Arne had been opposed to the idea of bringing her in as the 'fourth' man.

"A girl, a blonde girl?" he'd scowled. "Are you out of your mind? This is supposed to be the most dangerous and most important action in the entire war."

It had taken some stern talking by Anton to shut him up and accept that the friend of his youth, Per Johansen, was replaced by a Jewish girl from Vienna. He had shut up but unwillingly, and it had created a tense atmosphere.

Esther continued to gaze out of the small window and concentrate on the mission ahead. She would show she wasn't a burden but an asset, if it was the last thing she did in this life.

"Are you ready?" Anton nudged her rib, as if guessing her thoughts.

"I am. Couldn't be more prepared."

"Good. It will take some orientation when we're on the ground. First, we locate the package with the skis. I count on you. Your vision is superb."

"Thank you."

She glanced across at Arne and saw he looked unhappy with the compliment Anton had just given her. It would take a lot of work to show him she was nobody's favorite. She was Jeger. She would answer commands, but she was no man's girl. There was only one man in her life, and he was God knew where. If he was even still alive.

Suddenly, Esther missed her engagement ring with a pang of pain. It lay hidden on its velvet cushion in the little box at Jens and

Inger's farm. The last place where her heart had been alive. Even Carl's letters were hidden in the attic in Sønde Nordstrand. It was too dangerous to carry anything with her from her old life.

Just one thing, one single hope. *Rebecca*. Stored in her backpack. The one tie to her former life that posed no danger, held no clue, just the last gift she'd received from a girl just like her.

She'd read the book so often now that she could almost recite it by heart. The sentences drifted into her mind at unexpected moments and provided a strange sort of anchor in her whirlwind life. As she sat still inside the plane, her lips formed the words, without sound.

"If only there could be an invention that bottled up a memory, like scent. And it never faded, and it never got stale. And then, when one wanted it, the bottle could be uncorked, and it would be like living the moment all over again.

Life would never be as it had been before the war, but she did all this for one sole reason. To defeat the Nazis and reunite with her family. Hopefully marry Carl.

But no one knew how long the fight would go on. It meant pushing all thoughts of belonging aside to concentrate on the mission ahead.

Below them the maze of fjords showed up, vaguely illuminated by the shine of the moon and the German searchlights. They left the sea and the inlets and soon flew over mainland Norway which was a vast white landscape covered in snow.

Staring down at her adopted country she hadn't seen for months, it was hard not to feel conflicting emotions bubble up. From the shifting of the men in their seats around her, Esther understood she wasn't the only one going through a mixture of elation and grief. Elation for the country they loved and grief for the way it had been brought to its knees.

No thinking of that now!

In the dark, she felt Tronstad's eyes resting on her, felt his encouraging smile. She was part of a new team, and she was ready for it.

Esther checked her watch. Almost one a.m. It wouldn't be long now before they left the relative seclusion of the aircraft and floated down in the frosty night. She had learned to withstand cold temperatures of minus twenty degrees Celsius, and their protective clothing was of the best material.

"Cold, hunger, exhaustion, it is all of no matter to me," she reminded herself. "I will pull through and at some point, we will win. We have to."

MINUTES later she was floating down like a martial eagle, the icy wind biting her cheeks, her sharp eyes scanning the fields below her that were wrapped in shadows of dark forests and patches of white snow. The wind sang in the ropes above her; the tangy scent of the pines rose to tickle her nostrils. It was magical, and she wished it would last forever.

Magic Norway! And no German in sight.

Her parachute worked like clockwork while she watched as the three other enormous balloons floated nearby in perfect silence. A new but exhilarating emotion flooded through her as her feet touched the ground. To fall on home ground from the sky was unthinkable, wonderful, inexplicable.

The feeling of being homebound was so strong that she spontaneously thanked her God for the opportunity to return and do her bit. God, who played such a tiny part in her life these days. But some feelings were just too big for a tiny person.

She plonked in the fresh snow with a soft thud and routinely pulled in her parachute to fold it. The moon gave just enough light to see what they were doing. A cloudless night, hardly any wind. As she approached the others, she scanned the area for their luggage and equipment.

Soon she hoisted her thirty-kilo pack on her back and clicked on her skis. The three others also worked in silence, but when they were ready to move, there seemed confusion about their exact location. All three men were from the Telemark region where they had landed, so knew the land like the back of their hands.

It was not until Anton used a strong expletive that she understood they were completely off track.

"At least a week's journey away from our target."

"We bloody can't change that," Claus observed. "So, let's get going."

Esther didn't know what to feel or think, but her body—although it was the middle of the night—had but one wish. To ski for as long as it would take to arrive at their first stop for the night. The most appealing option being a rest in an abandoned cabin, but most likely it meant sleeping outdoors at a temperature of minus 25 degrees Celsius.

28

THE TEAM

The bitter wind, incessant snowstorms, hunger, and freezing temperatures were nothing compared to the physical exhaustion and pain Esther encountered. A body that didn't want to operate anymore when the mind still spurred it on. And yet, from somewhere she didn't know she possessed, the strength came to prick her poles in the snow and ski another few stretches. Hour after wretched hour, from pre-dawn till late in the evening, when they would set up camp and she could finally drop the thirty-kilo package off her back.

It was over a week now that they had been traversing the polar conditions on the Hardangar Plateau, but Anton had still not given the ultimate sign they had arrived at their first destination.

She, who had to be their eyes and ears, strained both senses for the brief hours of daylight that late October granted them, not just for stray Germans but for potential food, a reindeer for dinner, or even a wood grouse. Then, when dusk fell, she had to work like a Trojan, either going up in front or covering their back, depending on where Anton wanted her. Her Enfield ready to be fired, often securing them the meat for the evening dinner.

The Hardangar Plateau was an endless white moon landscape

that stretched to all sides as far as the eye could roam, a region lost to the world at last, at least to human occupation. A perfect place to travel unseen but an unforeseen wilderness, even to the trained mountaineer.

"Watch out!"

Her shout came too late, a thin cry evaporating in the terrain's vastness. She jerked her skis aside and narrowly avoided landing in a patch where the snow had become ice water. Claus, who followed her, fell straight into the pit, howling as he went head under.

"Set up the tent now, Jeger," Anton instructed, "and heat it as hot as you can." He already knelt at the side of the ice to help Claus scramble out. Despite her utter fatigue, Esther worked furiously with Arne at her side. They had Claus, who'd stripped to his under-wear with the help of Anton, inside the warm tent in under ten minutes.

"Narrow escape from drowning, or hypothermia," Anton observed, as they all slurped hot tea and saw Claus slowly return to his normal self. Esther was wide-eyed with shock and kept apolo-gizing, until Claus said through clattering teeth,

"St... stop it, Jeger. Be... because of your warning, I... I was the only m... muttonhead to fall in. You s... saved the others."

They all chimed in and praised her vigilance. Their genuine thankfulness warmed her heart. Finally... definitely... Esther felt they'd now accepted her as one of the team.

"Let's bivouac here for the night," Anton decided. "It's best to keep Claus warm for a couple of hours more, and we've made good progress anyway today. It looks like tomorrow we'll reach our last post."

Esther could not have been more grateful for not having to ski another mile in the dark and the cold. But it didn't mean they could rest on their laurels. There was dinner to cook and another attempt at trying to send a message to the headquarters in London. So far, Claus had not been able to emit a radio signal, which they all knew would stress the command center in Baker Street. They failed again.

"Tomorrow is another day," Claus sighed, glad to slip back into his sleeping bag. It was twenty-five degrees below zero outside their tent and fifteen degrees below inside. The coldest night so far.

They lay inside their sleeping bags around the gas lamp that was now their only source of light and warmth, drowsy from the long day but eager to tell each other stories. In the past weeks, Esther had learned so much about the background of these mountain fighters, their time at elementary school together, their families, their first loves.

She'd listened, absorbed it all, a land and customs so different from her own and yet sounding so wholesome and real. Scouting, ski trips, ghost stories around the fire, hunting and fishing. It had a charm and simplicity that spoke to her heart, and she felt more and more at home in this Nordic country with its blond, blue-eyed giants who were straightforward, honest and incredibly brave.

"Your turn, Jeger. We know so little about you." Arne picked up a piece of dried apple from his food package and threw it in her direction.

She caught it and frowned.

"I've got nothing to tell." In her self-conscious state, her cheeks reddened. A state of confusion she hadn't felt for quite some time. But the men wouldn't hear any excuses. Her warning of the ice patch had once again changed the dynamics. The men were interested in the girl behind Jeger.

"Come on, Esther," Anton invited her, using her real name for the first time.

"What do you want to know?" She still tried to ward them off.

"It's rumored you're a Jew from Vienna," Claus, square and the darkest of them, probed, his light-brown eyes taking in the effect of his words on her. "Is it true?"

She shrugged, not knowing if it would be safe to reveal this secret even here, with no German or Quisling around for miles.

"You can tell us, Esther," Anton helped. "I know your story through our mutual contact Tore Helberg, but the others don't."

"You knew?" Esther glanced at her commander.

"Of course, I need to know the background of my men... and women," he added.

"It's true," she began hesitantly. "I was born in the Rothschild Hospital in Vienna on 6 June 1921 as the eldest daughter of Franz and Naomi Weiss. My parents owned a goldsmith atelier and jeweler's shop on the Prater Strasse." She hesitated a moment and then added quickly, "I have a three-year younger sister, Rebecca and a six-year younger brother, Adam. My father's mother—we call her Oma—also lived with us and came with us when we fled... moved to Norway."

She looked at their faces in the dim light and saw they were listening to her, spellbound but unaware how sharp the pain was to tell *her* story. Their stories had been all about complete families living together in houses nearby, whereas she had nothing, her hands empty, her soul shredded.

But somehow, these men, with whom she'd trained for months and now fought the elements for weeks, pulled the words from her lips. Maybe sharing it would lessen the pain, dam in her anger.

"I was... am engaged to the son of another Viennese jeweler, Carl Bernstein. After our engagement, because I was still only seventeen, I spent a year in Switzerland learning good housekeeping at a finishing school."

"What? You? You're kidding us?" Ash-blond Arne, with his ruddy skin and quick wit, slapped his thigh. It made Esther chuckle as well.

"Yes, it's true. I come from a high-class family. And even though the Jewish community was under severe pressure after the Anschluss, when I left for that posh school, we never imagined it would get out of hand as it did."

"True," Anton agreed, "we never in our wildest dreams thought Hitler would attack Norway but with hindsight, we've all been too blind or too trusting."

"Well, tomorrow you can deck the table for us, Esther!" Claus joked. They all laughed. But Esther soon adopted a more serious look again.

"Strange thing is, I really enjoyed all the knicks and knacks of learning how to run a mansion. I totally envisioned that life then. Had a great year, although the headmistress was horrible and a Jew hater. We called her the Sphinx. I made some great friends there, whom I hope to meet again after the war."

"You already reunited with Lady Sable Montgomery, didn't you?" Anton seemed to know everything. Esther smiled, thinking of her raven-haired friend in the Shetlands with fondness.

"Yes, I did."

"I know that beauty!" Claus clacked his tongue.

"She's not for you, mate! Got that Scot hanging on her fingertips," Arne reminded his friend.

Suddenly they were no longer commandos but young people fighting together for the same cause.

"So, what happened, Esther? What made you change into a hard-boiled fighter?" Claus's tone had softened, understanding she was coming to the hardest part of her story.

Esther looked down at the stick in her hands, with which she'd been stirring the embers in the fire. Her fingers clamped the wood more tightly. Her appetite for the apple was gone. She cleared her throat. Out with it. These were friends, ready to take on one of the deadliest actions with her. She might be gone tomorrow. They should know her story.

"I was still in Switzerland when the war broke out, and I couldn't return to Austria because my family had moved here in the spring of 1940. Carl had to stay with his elderly parents in Vienna. We thought... we thought we would be safe here with my uncle and auntie who lived in Oslo." Esther swallowed hard. They, too, were gone, with their small sons.

"But... well... you know what happened with the Jews. We were betrayed." She took a sharp breath. "My whole family was deported while I wasn't home. Gone without a trace. My Oma—who had been hidden by friends—died of shock some days later. And I..." Her eyes were bright orbs of hatred. "I swore I would take revenge and that's what I've done."

"You killed Harald Rinnan, didn't you?" Anton's voice sounded almost gentle as he asked it.

"Holy smoke, was that you?"

Three pairs of eyes looked at her with admiration, but Esther bent her head, not feeling as proud of that first kill anymore as she'd been just after committing it. Now she knew how immature and rash she'd acted. It could have ended badly for her and many others.

"You've got to love a girl like you, Esther Weiss!" Claus spoke the words with reverence.

"Thank you. I'm learning." She felt a need to play down his declaration of love. It was slightly over the top.

Anton, who'd been laying on his side smoking his pipe, suddenly sat upright. Slapping his forehead, he exclaimed, "Why didn't I think of that before?"

"What?" they all asked together.

"Could you still walk in high heels, Esther, or are snow shoes and skis the only footwear you're comfortable in?"

"What do you mean?" She laughed at this sudden change in the conversation.

For a moment, Anton seemed absorbed in thought, the wrinkle between his fair eyes deepening.

"After this mission, of course. The greatest threat to the resistance movement now are the informers and *agent provocateurs*. At the beginning of the war, we Norwegians were quite stupid ourselves, having no history of intelligence work or resistance. We were way too open about our actions, which has led to many arrests and executions. We didn't take enough security precautions. Now we're much better at this, but we could do with an agent who dresses up and infiltrates in these circles to pinpoint the rotten apples."

He looked straight at her, and she saw the urgency of his request. Tore had said as much. The Norwegians, despite their ardor and tenacity, remained vulnerable to the onslaught of the Gestapo and the traitors in their midst.

"I can walk in high heels, and I can kill with one shot. Lynch, if needed." She said it through gritted teeth, feeling the surge of anger flooding through her again. This was the work she'd yearned for. Would it finally be given to her?

Anton nodded.

"You know, Esther, always on command. The Home Front is already accusing the Linge Company of running the military show too much on its own. What the central committee in Oslo overlooks, in my humble opinion, is that it's not the Linge Company that is in command of the sabotage and intelligence actions. That's run by the SOE headquarters in London. I agree with the Home Front, though, that coordination in all our missions big or small must always be taken in the light of the severity of Nazi reprisals. Too many innocent Norwegians have already been killed as scapegoats for our actions against the Germans."

"I promise I will only work under command," Esther replied, "and I hope I'll also still be doing teamwork. I enjoy being with you guys."

"We like having you, Jeger. I'm sorry I doubted your capacities at first." Arne gave her a lopsided smile.

"Apologies accepted."

Compassion and companionship bridled some of the perpetual pain.

29

THE GREAT SABOTAGE

They set out at dawn the next morning, a blood-red strip at the horizon heralding another glacial day. But Esther felt better than she'd done in weeks. The men had boosted her morale, given her a reason to believe in herself and in this mighty cause.

Just when the sun, red as fresh bull's blood, had freed itself from the earth and started the rise of its short span across the firmament, Arne halted in his tracks. His three followers braked in the automatic and synchronous rhythm they'd become used to. Esther was in the rear. Anton's white breath plumed in the frosty air. One pole raised high, he shouted.

"We've done it! First part of mission accomplished. We're at Møsvatn."

For a moment, she thought she'd misunderstood him. There was nothing in front of them of any significance. Just that vast whiteness which was their constant travel companion, bulky shapes meaning big boulders or tiny hills. But he pointed to something that looked like a roof, half-hidden under at least a meter of snow.

It was a hut. And a hut meant sleeping indoors instead of in a tent or a bed dug out in the snow. If only they could stay there for a day or two, she could regain her strength. Esther cheered with the men as they set out to dig out their new habitat.

As soon as they got inside, they arranged their belongings and started a fire to dry their clothes and sleeping bags. A little later, a new cheer sounded. It was Claus. He'd found a couple of rods lying next to the hut and connected them to serve as an antenna. Finally, he managed to make the much-needed contact with London. Not only did the SOE want to know the team was ready to strike, but they also needed the latest details before targeting Vemork.

Esther listened in, always fascinated by the ease with which Claus operated the transmitter. She held her breath when she heard the secret question roll out seconds later.

"What did you see in the early morning of 5 November?"

With a smug face, Claus replied with the requested answer, "Three pink elephants."

They all cheered again. It wouldn't be long now.

Anton, who'd been collecting wood outside, came in to warm his hands by the already roaring fire. The hut, small and sparsely furnished, radiated a welcome heat. They savored every spec of warmth they could get. And even though the place was cramped, and stank of wet socks and boiled potatoes, it was cozy enough. Esther warmed her stiff fingers around a cup of tea, blowing on the steaming brown liquid. A rare moment of bliss in a blizzard of turmoil.

"Time to contact our local man, don't you think? Get the latest details as we wait for more from London?"

They all sat down to a cup of real coffee when Esther asked, "Isn't it time I knew a little more, too?"

Anton smiled at her, the blue eyes shining in a myriad of tiny lines.

"I thought you'd never ask!"

"I can be patient if I need to," she grinned, "and I needed to show I was worthy to take part, I guess."

"True." He scratched his two-week beard. "We'll invite Einar Skinnar here, and then we'll all have a meeting."

"First, tell me what heavy water is and why it is so dangerous in the hands of the Germans?" Esther insisted, "I know there have been Allied attacks on Vemork before, so it must be really high on the agenda that we blow up the entire factory."

Anton grinned, brightening his face which had grown tight and serious over the past days. The cold and uncertainty seemed to sometimes hit him. Esther felt he could do with the nudge.

"Ha, I'm not a scientist so I don't know the exact details, but as far as I understand, the technology itself is straightforward. Heavy water is separated from normal water by electrolysis. It deals with a slight difference in the speed at which the reaction proceeds. To produce pure heavy water, you need a large cascade of electrolysis chambers. Loads of scientists are busy with a race to make a super effective and devastating bomb for which they need this heavy water. Already before the war, Norsk Hydro was the heavy-water supplier for the entire scientific community." He grinned again. "Well, how was my first lecture as a don't-know-what-I'm-talking-about professor?"

Esther giggled. "I think you underestimate yourself, Professor Tronstad. The ignorance is all mine. I fear I understand very little of it all, but I remember my father talking about Jewish scientists who were actually developing an atomic bomb for Germany before the war. They haven't been so smart after all, arresting the right brains for the business."

"Agree, agree! It's a well-known fact Jewish scientists are... were superb. Also, here in Norway." He scratched his beard again, looking uncomfortable at his own words.

"I see. Thank you. I know enough." Though she didn't understand the how and what, it was enough to know the production of this heavy water had to be stopped.

Anton spoke up with a bit of a roguish look, which lit up his formerly taut expression.

"We won't blow up the tanks. We demolish the operation chamber, which is located in the basement."

There was a knock on the door, and all hands went to their guns.

"It's me, Einar!"

A sigh of relief.

Einar Skinner was an older man, with thinning grey hair and a droopy face. He was clearly a good acquaintance of the three friends as there was plenty of back-slapping and joking accompanied by big beardy smiles, before they sat around the rough wooden table and the earnestness of the matter came up.

At first, the newcomer looked with suspicion at the girl in their midst, but her three companions almost tumbled over each other to talk about her in superlatives. The ardor with which they now considered her one of their own made her almost blush. Skinner held up his hands in defense.

"All right Missy, you seem to have some fans, so who am I? But don't come telling me afterward that this was the toughest job you ever did."

"I'm quite prepared, Sir." She hoped it didn't sound too huffy.

"Einar's the name. I've never been called 'sir' in my life, and I'd rather keep it that way."

"So, what do you know, Einar?" Anton asked with some impatience.

"London asked me to observe the German defenses of the area since the summer, and that's all I've done. Only a couple of weeks ago, the German commander-in-chief in Norway, General von Falkenhorst, came to visit the plant. Shows the Germans suspect a British attack, but seemingly they expect it to come from the air. A garrison of just forty men is stationed in the village of Rjukan. There are twelve security men at the dam and about twelve near the main plant. Their numbers have been reduced after the summer. Why, I don't know. Also, most of the guards are elderly or infirm Austrians under the command of an elderly captain." He looked almost comical at this last utterance.

Esther perked up at hearing about her fellow countrymen, but then slumped back in her seat. They were with the enemy; of course they were. They had nothing in common with her and she would kill them if she had to. Einar continued as the men smoked, and the hut filled with a blue haze that made her drowsy.

"German commandos sometimes pass through Telemark but also leave again. I believe there must be Gestapo agents in the area, but I haven't been able to locate them. I'm sorry."

Anton waved an energetic hand.

"Go on, fellow. We want to know what you know, not what you don't know." Skinner didn't seem to take offense and continued in his humdrum voice.

"The Germans have erected three iron hawsers across the valley to prevent low-flying bombing raids from reaching their target. On the ground, most of the defenses are positioned in such a way as to prevent an assault from the ridge above the plant. That must be where they expect the attack to come from. Most of the minefields and booby traps are placed to protect that side of the plant. They've also got searchlights on the roof and a nest of machine guns near the entrance."

"Pretty detailed briefing."

Anton liked order and overview. It was what Esther liked about him. They were similar in that respect, and despite her sleepiness in the warm hut and buzzing voices, she drank in Skinner's words and stored them all in the compartments of her brain for when she had a need for them.

Skinner tugged on his pipe.

"As you know, there's a single drawbridge across the gorge that goes straight to the plant. It will be hard, if not impossible, to cross there as it's guarded, night and day. You will always be in full view approaching in that way. Have you figured out how you want to get to the wretched thing?"

Maps were spread out on the table and for the first time, Esther actually saw the long rectangular building deep in the valley that they had to put out of order. At the back of the building were pipelines that went up the steep slope amidst pine trees. If they couldn't use the bridge, they'd have to descend the steep slope and cross the riverbed. But the thickly forested sides rose almost vertically from the narrow crest. An impossible climb down... and up. She looked at the men's faces. Quizzical expressions all around.

"We have no choice." Her voice sounded firm, which surprised and embarrassed her. She wasn't in charge. Four pairs of eyes looked up at her. A stretch of silence. Disbelief. Then Anton nodded. Spoke the word.

"You're right."

"Sheer suicide!" Arne protested.

But the dice were cast.

THE NEXT EVENING, with the help of a meager moon, they found themselves at the ridge of the steep slope looking down. In vague shadows deep below, the greyish building stood as if innocent. They checked all the details Einar had given them, two pinpricks in black on the bridge, the guards, the searchlight going over the sky every ten minutes. For the rest, a low humming of the machines and the silence of the night.

"Ready?" Anton checked their state. "So you know your roles—Esther, Arne and I go inside, while you guard the bridge and the entrance, Claus. We must make sure you can contact London. Rightly or wrongly."

"Yes." Three answers.

"Very last orders. After the raid, we climb up on the other side of the mountain where we've not left any traces yet. They'll come after us with everything they've got, so we must be faster than light. As soon as we're at the top—if we make it—we separate. Esther and Arne, you go to the Swedish border with at least a few miles between you, I go south, and Claus goes north. Burn every part of your map that you've covered. Leave no traces. We'll be in touch in a few weeks via Tore in Oslo.

"Good luck."

They looked at each other, an unsung prayer in every heart.

The steep climb down was treacherous and incredibly difficult. They went slowly, needing to find their footing and also listen for any suspicious sounds. But the valley seemed asleep and they the only creatures inching closer to their target. Esther was grateful for the physical training and exercise she'd had, but she was panting heavily with her rucksack and skis on top, weighing like the entire world. They didn't speak, needed all their concentration, but kept a constant eye on each other. One wrong move, and an injury was close.

Slowly, ever so slowly, the distance between the top and the riverbed became smaller and the factory closer.

In the still night, they could hear the guards stamp their cold feet on the bridge and the sonorous grunting of the machines that produced that dangerous liquid.

They stood still, catching their breath, and silently thanking the dry bedding under their feet. Part one of the mission, which had taken them two full hours, was completed. Claus slinked away from them in the direction of the bridge, and Esther followed Arne and Anton to the back of the building.

Anton motioned them to bury their backpacks and skis under a layer of snow and dried leaves. Before she knew it, he'd cracked a small basement window with his boot and noiselessly piled up the glass shards. One by one, they weaseled themselves through the small window frame. Esther was the last to go through, quickly getting back to her feet.

They found themselves in a white-tiled, low-ceilinged space with several open compartments. The floor was laid with brick-red tiles, so moving around had to be done with the utmost care not to make a sound. The basement was dimly lit by small electric lights along the walls that shone on the equipment, which, to Esther, looked like huge boilers.

They quickly spread as planned. Anton monitored the control room, a glass-paneled room on an elevation where a guard sat nodding in front of several screens that beeped and pinged. All his muscles tight, Anton was ready to jump up and strangle the man, if necessary. Arne and Esther moved stealthily toward the center room, which was the main operation room for all of Vemork.

Even in the moment of extreme focus, it struck Esther how easily they had gotten in and how brilliant their plan had been. One guard, asleep. The Germans, for sure, had not foreseen an attack here.

No time to think, though, only to act. As Arne tied the ignition for the time bomb together, she struck the match. A small blue flame turning yellow. The seconds now counted. Three minutes they would have between now and the explosion. This match meant life or death. Never had an act in her life counted so much.

Yet she was deadly calm, ready to die if it was her time, praying only that their mission would be successful, that people soon all over the world could sleep peacefully in their soft beds again, the beast that was Naziism eradicated with this resistance bomb.

The last thing she heard was the sizzling of the wax cord as she ran for her life, not caring for the sound of her footsteps that would be the least of the Nazis' concern when the inferno hit.

30

THE FLIGHT

In the same order they'd entered through the hole in the glass, they exited and ran as never in their lives, away from the expected blast. One second to grab and adjust their packs and as Claus joined them again, four tiny black figures climbed the steep mountain, under cover of night and pine trees.

With hindsight, Esther didn't know what came first, the sky-high fireball, or the blast of the explosion. Both threw her against the snowy ground, grabbing a branch of the nearby tree not to slide down again. Her ears rung, her eyes blinded, parts of cement and bricks landing on them. Sirens went off, dogs barking, men shouting gruff German commands.

"Hallelujah!" Anton said in a low voice. "Come on, faster now. The hounds are after us."

Esther didn't look back on the havoc of destruction they'd created down in the valley. She only wanted to go up, up, up, to the top of the ridge, slip into her skis and flee to Sweden. If anything was capital punishment, this was it. Fatigue, fear, fetters, all were gone. And no remorse, none, for the lives of those they must have taken. Just the hope the plant would never be operational again and heavy water in German hands no longer an Allied nightmare.

They shook hands at the top, frozen gloves clamping each other in a last farewell.

"Be well and rely on your maps," Anton said as goodbye.

"See you in Oslo, Jeger," Claus added.

"You're my partner-in-crime," Arne smiled.

"Thank you, guys! You've been the best of friends. Good luck and stay safe."

"We'll meet at Tore's!"

Those were Anton's last words.

But would they?

Again, Esther didn't look back. The first fifty miles she had to cover were engraved in her memory. Only after them she would take the time to check her route.

After she'd gone for some miles through the dark, she got the eerie feeling something was wrong. There was no direct reason, but her highly strung feeling made her sharpen her senses even more. She would soon leave the pine forest and cross an open space, so it was even more important she remained unseen. Then she heard it again. Swoosh, swoosh, someone on skis. Following her. She went even faster, stayed close to the rim of the forest to find out what was going on, and then she spotted him. A German soldier, in full uniform, coming closer.

Esther sped up, knowing she had to cross the open space now so as not to get off track. She had no choice. Getting her gun ready, she flew as fast as she could, but somehow the German was reducing the distance between them. It was now down to one mile.

He was faster downhill; she was faster uphill, so she sought the uphill spots but to no avail. Soon she would have to start firing, but doing it at high speed and backwards wasn't the most helpful position. A bullet whizzed past her.

Now!

She fired. Missed. It almost threw her off-balance as she kept skiing at a madman's rate. He shot at her again. Missed too. The sound of the gunshots rang in her ears, a vibrating echo that she tried to ignore but left her temporarily deaf. It made her miss his next bullet that was really near, closer than he'd been before. A grim warning.

Her case seemed pretty hopeless. Sweat started running down her forehead and into her eyes, blurring her vision.

"Damn it, concentrate on your torso and legs, Esther," she instructed herself as she tried to recover her essential sensory perceptions. Reduced eyesight, no vision. She'd been trained by the best agents to work under these harsh conditions. Learned to trust every fiber of her body, feel the surroundings with all her cells.

She was doing just that, but still he was winning terrain. Gritting her teeth, Esther made one last furious attempt to fire at her pursuer, her skis pointing north, her upper body twisted in his direction. She didn't expect any result. Her position was just too disadvantageous.

A yelp, clear and whining through the still landscape. By God, she'd hit him. But was it going to be enough? No, it wasn't. Pang. Another bullet from the German, and this one grazed the sleeve of her insulated overalls. She registered it had gone through the outer layer, but there was no pain. Good—in and out of the material. No time to check it. She was okay.

Anger rose at the man's persistent patrol, so she looked over her shoulder one more time to aim at him and get it over and done with. Bingo, she'd hit him again.

"I'll get you, you wretched fellow," she grimaced, and luck shone on like the weak wintry daylight fighting to rise over the horizon. He finally went down in the snow and the shots stopped. Glancing back a few more times, she assured herself he'd not be getting up anymore. *That'll be your punishment*, she thought grimly.

Esther hoped she wasn't injured, but upon checking at her first stopping point, found a cut in her upper arm. She mopped up the blood, then bandaged it as well as she could with just one arm and hurried on.

At the next checkpoint, she got rid of her uniform, burned it together with her first map and got into her civilian clothes. Now she was Gunhild Helberg again, skiing long-distance for fun. Well, fun? Exhaustion, hunger and loneliness set in. It was still over one hundred miles to the border.

Her arm throbbed. All she wanted was to lie down and sleep, but despite her innocent appearance as a woman, SOE safety precautions prescribed she couldn't do anything of the sort. She had to report in Sweden. If she was stopped by the Germans and found carrying detailed maps and a message for London, all hell would break loose. Not just for Gunhild Helberg.

Yet she longed with every fiber of her being for home. Home? She had no home. For as long as the war went on, this white wilderness was her home. To keep herself occupied, Esther hummed songs to herself, Austrian nursery rhymes. She thought of food she'd enjoyed as a little girl, Sachertorte and cream pies. But she did not think of her people.

Her thoughts swirled to Tore, wondering where he was, whether he was still safe. The golden-maned boy who one day hopefully would marry her sister. She saw his eyes before her, blue as the West Indies lagoon, a color she'd once admired in a picture magazine. Honest eyes, open and friendly, but holding some force back.

What was it? Why couldn't they simply be friends?

Silly, you are friends. Didn't he tell you he'd still be there for you after the war?

"After the war." She spoke the words aloud, a white plume rising from her lips. True, a few cracks were surfacing in German's almighty power. But they were so tiny and their hopes so high. Hitler's desperate campaign against Russia? It sure resembled Napoleon's madness trying to conquer that vast country. Africa was being recaptured by the Allies, and Mussolini was faltering. Yet the power of Quisling and the Gestapo in Norway were unabatedly strong. And where was the promised Allied invasion? Would it come in the new year, in 1943?

As Esther's thoughts hopped from one subject to the next, she knew her arm was getting worse. The growing red stain on the white sleeve forced her to acknowledge the bleeding hadn't

stopped. Her flesh burned and throbbed. Her training told her to
take this seriously. There was no way she could ski all the way to
neutral Sweden with this arm without seeing a doctor. An infec-
tion would kill her. She would soon have to stop and have it
properly treated. That's when a brazen plan developed in her
brain.

As the first fuchsia-colored clouds announced the new day,
Esther reached the town of Veggli, which meant she had covered
one hundred kilometers during the night but was still at only one-
third of her trek to safety. She had no choice but to ask for help.
Hopefully she'd put enough distance between Vemork and this
small town not to be connected any longer to the carnage her team
had wreaked at the heavy-water plant. It was always a risk, but a
risk worth taking. She would pose as a wounded solo female skier.
Not a straightforward story to believe this wound, but a stray
hunter would do.

Sitting down on the boardwalk under the shelter of the local
bakery, she took off her skis and had to support her wounded arm
with the other. She was in great pain. Glad to see a woman with a
shopping basket pass by on the other side of the street, Esther
called out to her.

"Fru, can you please help me?"

The woman looked up, a vigilant look in her eyes, but after
some hesitation approached the wounded traveler.

"Who are you?" she asked, spying around her with suspicion.
Esther cursed the German accent she clearly still had in
Norwegian.

"Don't worry," she said in a soft voice, spotting the paperclip on
the woman's lapel as a sign she was a member of the resistance.
"I'm with you but I'm wounded. I need a doctor."

The elderly woman, who sported dove-gray eyes and a round
face over which her skin spanned like a blossoming apple, scrutinized her a little longer.

"Where are you from?"

No details, Jeger, no details.

"I'm traveling to Sweden after a mission. A German shot me in the arm." She bared her teeth. "But he's worse off."

The woman chuckled.

"Then you're good folk. I'll get you to a doctor, but first you come to my house and I'll get you some breakfast."

The next hours were a bluish-white blur, shaped by strange sounds and prickly scents and unclear orbs, a vague pain tugging on her right arm. Esther hovered between consciousness and unconsciousness, a kind of floating in which her legs were heavy with skis and her heart still beat, but her brain didn't function.

Some part of her registered a German field doctor inspecting her arm, but she was too weak and too delirious to protest it. The round face of the woman who'd taken her in and put her on a sofa hovered behind the German. She clung to that one image, hoping against hope that the woman would keep her identity safe and let no one inspect her luggage.

Then she slept.

The sleep of the innocent, no longer aware of or resistant to danger. But danger still found her, even in her sleep.

She entered a prison with rows of square barred windows and a heavy metal door. It clanged shut behind her. Finding herself in a barren field covered with skulls, she focused on stepping around the skulls on her way to a white door that stood open. Brown light came from it. She wanted to turn, but the metal door was closed, and she had no other option than going through that door.

She didn't want to, felt trapped. Death all around her.

Then the brown light was in her, and her heart stopped.

Carl stood in the middle of the empty space, a stone floor, stone walls, no windows. He was very thin and wore a striped pajama. He was hacking the stones on the floor with a blunt shovel.

"Carl?" It was a soft question, her voice lost in the hacking, like the thumping of her heart. He didn't look up. "Carl?" she asked again, not sure it was him. He raised his head, and she saw his eyes were empty sockets. A raven flew through the opening where his eyes had been, flapping her way.

Esther screamed.

Someone shook her good shoulder softly. A glass was put to her lips. The round face and a warm voice saying, "*Stille, men barn.* Be still, my child."

It took Esther an entire week before she could continue her journey to Sweden. Fru Rønneberg looked after her with love and care and never exposed the patient to further danger.

After all, she was Arne's mother. Another link in the endless chain of paperclips.

31

A WELL-DRESSED ATTACK

Oslo, March 1943

As the black Mercedes climbed the main road of Bygdøy, a peninsula west of Oslo, Vidkun Quisling's majestic villa came into view, standing white-walled and red-roofed on top of the hill for God and all men to admire.

It was a blowy, sunny evening in early March. Nature still found it difficult to awaken after the long, grim winter. Humans felt the same. Where the snowdrops bent their heads as they peeked through the thawing snow, humans drew in their chins. With heads bent down, they didn't look up to admire the blood-red sun setting over Oslofjord but stared at the toes of their worn shoes, their stomachs grumbling and their morale low.

The promised Allied invasion had never come. Instead, hunger, suppression and terror were the Norse's daily bread. Only the Nazis and Quislings still partied into the wee hours. No one else had the energy, or the lust, to dance, or even to laugh out loud.

Villa Grande—which Quisling had renamed Gimlé after some Nordic mythological fantasy of his—raised high above the surrounding residential buildings as a flagship. Esther looked at the traitor's lair with mixed feelings. A part of her wanted to blow up the whole caboodle. Another part of her hated this mission that would force her to converse with the people she despised most in the entire world.

Perhaps I was never cut out for the diplomacy Oma so wanted to drill into me, she thought. But thoughts of Oma only triggered sadness.

Esther clutched her tinsel yarn purse and tentatively felt the seam in the cuff of her left sleeve. Hidden there was tonight's mission, which could or couldn't work. To distract herself, she rearranged the folds of her gold lamé evening dress over her knees. Her hired dress was highly uncomfortable after years of combat boots, male shirts, and pants. The thin, stretchy material and low-cut neckline made her feel like an exposed doll, fragile and defenseless, despite the hidden arms she carried, along with Arne, her partner-in-crime sitting next to her on the back seat of the chauffeur-driven German car.

Arne was equally dressed up in a black tuxedo and bow tie but seemed hardly bothered by his overnight change from commando to fancy civilian. He exuded a waft of cologne and expensive cigars. Smells she thought she'd never associate with her outdoorsy friend and fellow fighter.

Esther studied him sideways, saw how his sharp eyes missed nothing as they scanned the habitat of their foe, but the look on his clean-shaven, ruddy face was unfathomable. She knew how good he was at deadpan expressions and how fearless he was. Arne Rønneberg could bluff himself out of any peril by going straight to the enemy and claiming he was their most ardent supporter. Only to get around them as they stood in his way to his next mission.

Having taken in all information he needed, he answered her gaze, slightly raising the blond eyebrows. She answered him with an equally wry smile. They didn't speak. They could work with hand signs and facial expressions.

The German driver, a jolly man with a red, rather alcoholic expression, was tapping the beat of some German song with one hand on the steering wheel, now and then glancing in the back mirror at these odd Norwegians who seemed rather sour and silent on their way to the great state ball.

But he got his bulky body from behind the steering wheel to open the back door for them. Esther gathered up her skirts and put one high-heeled, suede boot tentatively on the gravel.

"*Viel Spass*, enjoy your evening" the chauffeur grimaced, "*Herr und Frau Magus.*"

Esther gave him a haughty nod, pulling her fur cape around her shoulders and taking Arne's proffered arm.

"Ready?"

"Always."

Esther activated herself to her usual state of high alert as they thronged among the other guests in evening dress on their way to the main entrance. The buzzing of the German language all around her slightly unnerved her, unaccustomed and allergic as she had become to her native tongue.

Arne gave her arm a light squeeze. Having done a variety of missions together over the first months of 1943, they now knew each other inside-out, his awareness an extension of hers and vice versa. They truly were partners-in-crime, ever since their first mission in the basement of the heavy water plant.

Maria Quisling, coiffed with pretty waves in her dark hair, the dark eyebrows perfect and strong and her Russian face doll-like and sharp, stood in the luxurious hall to welcome her guests. Her husband, tall, bulky and with his usual surly look stood at her side, his probing eyes scanning all the faces that passed before him.

Esther had to swallow twice as she stood in line to greet their hosts. Her throat was dry, her hands squeezed tight the handles of her frilly evening purse. Arne's hand on the small of her back, a reminder of their mission.

But being in the nearness of this horrific traitor was much harder than she'd expected. Her urge to pull up her gun from her boot and shoot him between his traitor eyes right before all these hypocrite guests was almost too strong to resist. She was a fighter, not a calm society ma'am anymore. She had no patience with niceties and lies. Those days were gone.

Mutti and Oma had meant well but had been born and bred in a different era. Perhaps in their world, polite manners and good breeding had still found fertile ground. Now were the days of the street fighters with grazed knees, a fierce fight for freedom, and a well-loaded gun.

Sorry, Mutti. Sorry, Oma. I hope you forgive me for what I've become.

Esther stood straighter, disentangling herself from the cobwebs of the past, but wondering if she could still pull it off. Being a well-bred *and* well-armed show pony. As captain Gunhild Helberg, she'd sworn alliance to the Lingen Company and the Norwegian military. She was under strict command not to do anything foolish.

"Easy now!" She reminded herself as she let her fist relax, "Quisling is not your target tonight. Not yet."

When it was their turn to shake hands with their hosts, Esther first grasped Fru Quisling's smooth, soft hand and braced herself for her husband' s cold, dry grip. It was done before she could have more emotions about it. No questions about their identity. Not that it wasn't carefully constructed, right back to Catholic Vienna, if needed.

The evening started with a formal dinner of about fifty guests, both Quislings and Nazis sitting at one incredibly long, beautifully decked table. Esther couldn't fail to detect this, thinking with a strange pang about her table setting at Le Manoir with the sweet Océane by her side. That evening, when they'd first met Lili.

Her friends. Where were they? Had Océane become a doctor, and Lili followed her dream to fight the Nazis? They wouldn't have recognized soft-hearted, well-mannered Esther if they bumped into her. She was all muscles and tautness under her glittery dress, armed to the teeth, right in the Lion's Den as one of Norway's most hard-nailed agents. The Esther Weiss they'd known had died years ago.

Arne tapped her wrist, and she shook herself from her straying thoughts, a nasty trait that sometimes manifested since her arm injury in November. A split second of distraction. It could be deadly.

Reichskommissar Terboven, lean, mean, and steely, sat at Maria Quisling's right hand while her husband sat at the head of the table. Terboven, as always in the hated uniform with the Nazi insignia and the ridiculous billowing pants above his shiny black boots, was even more dried out than Esther had expected, easily one of the vilest and most cold-blooded creatures this terror regime had produced.

As she chewed over his personality, it flashed through her that bad people like Terboven were probably not born that way but given the opportunity developed hate systems that could bring entire nations to their knees. Yet, she needed to find his Achilles' heel. Everybody had one, but especially an ice-cold fish like Joseph Terboven.

Esther smirked. His weakness was right there under his own eyes.

The married *Reichskommissar*, who'd conveniently left his wife Ilse Stahl, Joseph Goebbels's former secretary and mistress, home in Germany. To Quisling's party he'd brought his latest conquest, the glamorous, dark-haired Norwegian-Swedish Sonja Wigert. Esther had difficulty not to cast her a sly smile. The attractive actress, whom she'd met in Sweden, was firmly on their side. Wigert was a formidable spy. And soon—hopefully—Terboven's destruction.

It promised to become an interesting evening.

The seating arrangement was perfect, thanks to hired footmen, who'd been carefully selected by Tore to make sure risks were kept to a minimum. The Head of the Norwegian SS, Jonas Hagelin, was flanked on either side by Arne and Esther. Tonight, Arne played the role of the cash-rich Swedish banker Marius Magus with a keen interest in backing the NS, accompanied by his adorable, aristocratic wife, Ursula von Hügel-Magus.

Arne's fluent Swedish, combined with his private school

upbringing, made him the perfect man for the role. Esther also threw herself into the position of lovely decoration for her husband with all the flair she could muster.

"There you go, mean Madame Sphinx, how I would love to see your snooty face now. Your little Jew dining with your favorite Nazi friends. Thank you for the etiquette lessons." She took a sip from the crystal water glass, pinky raised and smiling amiably. What a charade it was. If it hadn't been so deadly serious.

The Resistance movement had had Hagelin on their radar for a long time. As head of the *Statspolitiet,* he was responsible for the arrests, detention and deportation of the Norwegian Jews and as leader of the *Hird*, the Norwegian SS, exercised torture and terror that was often more barbaric than of their German counterparts. As Minister of the Interior in Quisling's Cabinet, he was one of the most hated men in all of Norway.

Though everyone expected Hagelin to soon be replaced by another Quisling crony, it was high priority to deal Hitler's puppet regime a sensitive blow. Better a Norwegian than a Nazi. If a setup was even suspected, there would be fewer reprisals. And it was a known fact that Hagelin had weak health, having survived two heart attacks recently. The man was a drunkard with no self-care, tottering on the edge of death, anyway.

A small push was all he needed, and Esther was as ready as a primed cannon to be the catalyst in his ultimate downfall. Her first task demanded stealth and cunning, but she didn't have to do it alone. A trusted waiter—code name Igor—stood right behind her chair, ready to pour the wine after she'd emptied the contents of her seam into her own wineglass. As she worked half hidden in the wide sleeve of her evening dress, nobody noticed.

The cooperation was seamless. Placing the glass nonchalantly in the row of other glasses next to her plate, she knew she, together with Igor and Arne, would keep the lethal glass under strict surveillance.

Content with stage one, she turned to her table companion and swallowed her disgust for Hagelin's puffed face, the wispy baby-blonde hair around a balding skull and the squinting pigs' eyes. But like a true Madame Paul pupil, she entertained him in a sunny voice with a fabricated story about her father's Schloss in the Austrian Wildspitze mountains.

Most of her attention, though, was focused on his wineglass, the contents of which disappeared in his substantial stomach at a rapid rate. She sipped from her water glass as she talked, now and then picking at her food—decadent thin slices of roast beef with more garnish than she'd seen in years, meat she'd not seen anywhere near her plate or that of her fellow fighters since eternity. It was only the hors d'oeuvre.

"Keep talking," she told herself. The evening was still young and small talk prevalent. The so-called real talk, her occasional husband's backing of Quisling's government, would wait until the main course.

It seemed to drag on for hours, but finally a whole pig was brought in and placed in the middle of the table under the shouts of many *oohs* and *aahs*. Fru Quisling beamed with pride in her turquoise brocade evening dress, squeezing her husband's meaty hand in delight. Hagelin's eyes shone like the inner sanctum of hell.

The man sure likes his meat, Esther thought, as his large hands picked up Fru Quisling's delicate silver cutlery and he dove into his next plate. Esther tapped Arne's arm behind the minister's back.

"*Geht's gut, Liebling?* Everything all right?" she asked in a honeyed voice. Their code.

"Certainly!" Arne answered promptly as he took over the conversation and started unfolding his financial plans to the guzzling Hagelin.

Inch-by-inch, Esther pushed her wineglass toward her victim. Behind her chair, she felt the waiter's eyes following her every move while scanning the other people at the table. It was comforting to know she had a friend standing there. But every second counted. She had to work faster as Hagelin's glass was almost empty, and he would soon snap his fingers to order his fourth glass.

Arne did what he could, talking and talking, but the minister's only interest at this point of the evening was filling his stomach to the brim with food and liquor.

Just when Esther had almost reached her goal of exchanging their glasses, he grabbed his own glass by the stem and held it up. She had no choice but to go for the worst of two scenarios. They were running out of time. One quick glance around the table. A soft clearing of the throat behind her chair. No one paid attention to them.

"You can have my glass, Jonas dear," she whispered as seductively in his ear as she could, "and even more of me if you want later."

The audacity of her own suggestion shocked her, but the beady eyes, deep in their flesh, were full of gourmand and greed.

"What about your husband?" he whispered back as Esther quickly shoved her glass of wine in front of him and picked up his glass.

"He doesn't care," she whispered back, as she held up Hagelin's glass for the waiter to fill.

A deep sense of satisfaction settled on her as she put his glass firmly next to her plate and watched him down his Socrates' cup. Now, all her hopes were set on the working of the extreme dose of calcium to trigger the failure of his weak heart. There was no guarantee. None.

Gelatin fruit with ice cream was served, and Hagelin downed two more glasses of sweet dessert wine with his oversized helping. The clock ticked. Esther felt sweat beads trickle down her neck. Why had she been so stupid to give him special attention? There had been no need. Was she playing a losing game?

The police officer had even squeezed her thigh twice, and she had not dared to slap his fat hand away. After all, she'd offered herself to him. Focusing on her plate, she tried to keep some of the dreadful gelatin on her spoon and was angry with herself for seeing the trembling of her hand. She didn't dare to look at Arne, felt Igor's eyes in her back. It would be too risky for them to come to her aid. And after all, this was her mistake.

People were getting ready to get up and go to the ballroom. The assembly was already loud and rowdy because of the free flowing of wine and liquor and the likes-know-likes, slap-on-the-back-old-chap ambiance. Hagelin was still sitting in his chair, drunk as a drum and half hanging against her bosom.

Breathe, Esther, breathe!

No flash, nothing. Gustav Wagner's spell was long broken. This was a physical threat of another order. She was a grown woman, fully conscious, and he a grown man. She could handle this. But how? Would she fight him if it came to that? She was strong enough to floor him with only half of her capacity, but Hagelin would certainly have her arrested if she refused him. And what then?

He collapsed like a ponderous pudding, suddenly and without a sound.

Esther heard herself shout, "Help, a doctor!" as she kneeled next to the unconscious man and began pulling on his uniform jacket. People came to stand around them when a gruff voice in German admonished them, and the crowd made way.

"*Aus dem Weg! Ich bin Arzt.* All aside, I'm a doctor."

Esther rose to her feet, wringing her hands helplessly as she looked down on the Army doctor checking him.

"*Zu spat!* Too late."

The words were music to her ears. Especially spoken out in her mother's tongue. But there was also a pang of guilt. She slinked back from the scene, dabbed her eyes with her handkerchief. Then took Arne's arm and went to say goodbye to their hosts. There was certainly not going to be a ball now.

It was ever so easy to slip out of Villa Grande in the confusion after the sudden death of Jonas Hagelin.

When will my conscience return? Esther mused. *I'm as bad as they are.* Stepping into the cool evening breeze, it somehow soothed her troubled heart.

"Can we walk back, at least some part of the way?" she asked, hearing her voice was coarse and sounded unnatural.

"Sure," Arne agreed, "and don't think I don't know what's going on inside you at this moment. Same here. We'll never get used to it, Jeger. We're doing unnatural things in unnatural times, but one day, when this all is over, we'll be civilized again."

He still held her arm and she let him.

She nodded in the dark.

Civilized.

32

THE BIRTHDAY PARTY

Oslo, 6 June 1943

"We cannot let your birthday go by without a small celebration." Tore, who was sitting at her desk near the open window, looked up from his writing to fix her with those all-seeing blue eyes that never made her know quite where to look. Esther was lying on her bed, listlessly thumbing through *Rebecca*, not at all in the mood for a party. She pondered as she read, *"I believe there is a theory that men and women emerge finer and stronger after suffering, and that to advance in this or any world we must endure ordeal by fire."*

It wasn't just theory; it wasn't just fiction. She'd experienced it herself, though very differently, from Du Maurier's nameless heroine. She was so much stronger today, so much more herself than the days at Le Manoir, when she and Anna Levi were cooped up in that attic room. The book Anna had given her... It still made no sense, but it was a comfort, something that tied her to another Jewish girl before the war.

For the past months, she'd been living in a small apartment just off Kirkegata in the heart of Oslo. Her studio was on the second floor in an apartment block that was mainly used by SS officers and overseen by one loyal janitor.

"The best place to hide is in plain sight," Tore had said, when Esther—after the Hagelin's assassination—had told him she needed a breather from the heavy resistance work.

Tore had been right, of course. Neither the Germans nor the Quislings had an inkling that the innocent-looking blonde girl who took out her bike to ride the city every day was, in fact, Jeger. One of the fighters who was at the top of their list to catch. The work was simpler, being a courier for the Home Front, but it was also boring.

Esther longed for the end of the war. Longed for Vienna.

She sighed.

"What did you have in mind?"

Swinging her legs to the floor, Esther sat up, pushed the blonde curls that had been growing longer again in the past months away from her face.

"You only turn twenty-two once. And you've been down in the dumps of late."

"How do you know my exact birthday?" Her voice was sharp.

"Remember, I had to hide your passport in my grandparents' attic?"

"Aha, you had a look."

"So, what do you think about inviting your Linge boys and Sigrid, my secretary? Just for a couple of hours?"

"Wouldn't it be dangerous? I mean, it's already a risk you being here." Esther looked doubtful.

"Remember that on paper I'm your brother. I can visit my sister. Though I agree there is danger to it. The Gestapo is really closing in on the inner circle of the Home Front. But Portner Sveri will notify us when something unusual goes on."

Suddenly Esther thirsted for young people and light-hearted banter around her. Life was so bleak and especially on this day, flashes of her wonderful birthday parties kept popping up. Mutti standing in the doorway with her birthday cake with eight burning candles; Papi singing *Zum Geburtstag viel Glück*, unable to carry any tune but with all the gusto of his jovial personality; Oma accompanying him on the piano. And later Carl showering her with gifts, earrings he'd made; a warm kiss on her neck after he'd fastened her new necklace.

"What's wrong, Esther?"

Without noticing it, her eyes had filled up with tears. She brushed them briskly away with the sleeve of her blouse.

"Nothing. Memories."

"I know it won't take the hurt away, but my mother made you some *sandbakkelse*." Tore retrieved a greasy paper bag from his backpack and placed it on the table. In a lackluster voice he added, "There's so little we can do for you, Esther, but we're trying."

Esther got up and filled the water kettle.

"I know, I'm sorry. You and your family have been so good to me. Let me make us some tea and eat your mother's cookies. And please thank her from me."

"I also brought you a small present." He looked almost shy.

"A present?" She was aware she was parroting him because this gesture made her uncomfortable. The eternal dilemma with this tall, generous boy-man. She turned her back to him to busy herself with the tea.

"I'll open it in a minute."

She looked at the parcel wrapped in deep red paper with the pink ribbon that Tore had put next to the bag with the cookies. Another wave of emotion rippled through Esther, and she cursed herself for being so unstable. Her only present this year. From Tore.

"What is it?"

"Well, you'll have to find out by opening it." He took a sip from his tea, and it felt as if she could sense he regretted having brought something for her. The atmosphere was certainly strange and tense.

With unsteady fingers, she untied the ribbon, then unwrapped the silk paper. A small rectangular box painted with colorful flower motifs in bright reds and blues and yellows smiled back at her. It was at the same time beautiful and very Norwegian.

"Rosemaling," Tore explained, "it's a traditional folklore way of painting here. I hope you like it. It's just a small thing I saw in the window of an antique shop last week, and it seemed perfect for you."

"It's... it's beautiful." Esther had to swallow. "It's precisely why I love this country so much. You live under such harsh conditions, but you always surround yourself with so many bright and happy colors. It lifts the spirit. Thank you, Tore." She smiled at him through misty eyes.

"I'm glad you see it that way. My only reason for getting you a birthday present was to cheer you up a little, not to make you uncomfortable."

For a moment, they drank the tea in silence and nibbled on Liv's sandbakkelse. Esther couldn't stop glancing at her new box. Somehow it made her happier than she could ever remember having been happy with a present.

"Now, about the party." Tore brushed the last crumbs from the corners of his mouth. "Shall we do it?"

"Sure, why not. But I have nothing to offer. No drinks or snacks."

"Don't worry about that. It's all arranged." He looked at her with a smug expression on his handsome face, the light-blue eyes twinkling.

"What do you mean?"

"I organized it just in case. But I told everyone to not be disappointed if you said no. We know this is a burdened day for you."

"Tore, you didn't?" Despite herself, Esther burst out in a merry laugh. That he would go to the length of throwing her a party without letting her know... He was so full of surprises.

"I've promised to look after my little sis," he winked.

"You're only my senior by two years!"

"Every year counts."

"All right, big brother, and what time do our friends arrive?"

"I told them to be here at eight unless they heard from me before."

Esther jumped up, all action and happiness, but suddenly stood still again.

"I've got nothing to wear!"

Tore went to her closet and stood with his back to the closed doors.

"I've even thought of that, but I have to warn you. I've found one of your dresses and hung it in your closet when you were out on your bike. But... but I realize it's very selfish of me." He stopped, gazed past her. Esther looked puzzled but still full of zest, cried out,

"For heaven's sake, Tore, what are you talking about? You're not telling me you've also bought me a dress?"

"No, no, of course not. It was in the attic at the farm. It's this one." He opened the door, and Esther saw her blue engagement dress hang among her ordinary clothes. The sea-blue silk shone like a precious summer sky among her camouflage outfits.

"Tore...why?" She was confused, chilled.

"Let me explain, Esther. The first time I saw you, you wore this dress, and I ruined it for you. Will you shine in it one more time? Just... also to celebrate our special bond."

Stunned, she stood next to her dress, feeling the fabric, flooded by memories of that snow-filled February day in Radstädter Tauern. She turned to look at him. Saw the raw emotions in his face. Hadn't Rebecca told her that Tore only wanted to apologize? Had she ever really forgiven him? It was forgiveness that filled her heart now and thankfulness for this man, this friend who never again had stepped over the line, who wanted her to do... What? She didn't know. Her heart was torn. She was engaged; he was Rebecca's.

Yet she grabbed both his hands and pressed them warmly. Looking into his eyes with a quivering smile, she said, "I'll wear it for you, Tore. After all, the poor dress never made it to my engagement."

"Thank you, Esther, that means a lot to me."

"And now back to work," she mocked, to lessen the tension.

"What are you working on, and what will I have to take to the station before the party starts?"

"You're probably right. I promised to write this directive that has to go out to all youth organizations, schools and churches all over Norway."

"I know I shouldn't ask what it is for, but I've got my suspicions. Is it the mandatory signing up of young men to fight on Hitler's Eastern Front?"

"Indeed." Tore was serious again. "Next stage in this bloody war. Recruiting Norwegians to fight for the Nazis. It's a serious law that Quisling is pushing through. Just like with the Standfast in 1941, we'll have to rise *en masse* to stop this idiocy. If all Norwegian youth refuse to go under the arms, Quisling will get a piece of Terboven's mind, not us."

"Okay, understood," Esther answered, her mind more on her upcoming party, the reunion of friends than the squabble between two hideous men. "I'll let you get your eloquence on paper. You're so important in this movement, Tore, and it makes me want to do more again myself."

"Soon, Esther. First, your party. Oh, and getting this thing to the station after I've microfilmed it."

"At your service, Herr Helberg," she joked, taking her dress to the bathroom to see if it still fit.

"It's all right, Esther, you can take the film first thing tomorrow morning. Just realized there's no night train to Stockholm tonight," Tore shouted after her.

EXACTLY AT EIGHT 'o clock that evening, the doorbell buzzed, and the porter announced her guests. Waiting until two SS officers in their battle-green uniforms had descended the stairs and left the building, Esther raced down to meet them. She beamed at the sight of her friends Anton, Arne and Claus standing under the porch in light summer clothes, their faces tanned, and their bodies fit and agile.

"Come in! What a surprise!"

"*Gratulerer med dagen!* Happy Birthday." Anton shook her hand firmly. Then Claus and Arne. They all smiled at each other. Their bond unbreakable since Vemork, but they hardly saw each other. It was exceptional that Tore had managed to get them all together.

"Quickly inside," she urged, routinely checking the surroundings for possible informers.

"We're loaded with beer and wine. Also got hold of crackers, cheese and fish pasties. Used all the coupons we had!"

"You shouldn't have," Esther smiled, her mouth already salivating at the thought of such delicacies she hadn't tasted in years.

The men were following her up the stairs when the doorbell buzzed again.

"You go on in," she announced, "Tore and Sigrid are there. I'll see who it is."

She waited for porter Sveri to give her the green light. Her eyes widened when she saw her new guest.

"Helmik!"

"It's me, all right, lassie!" The grey-haired skipper stood grinning from ear to ear. "Come here and give your old friend a hug!" Esther closed the distance between them and disappeared in his bearhug. He smelled of Aquavit, and fish, but she didn't care. The rough wool of his sweater pressed against her cheek and for a brief moment Esther felt safe, guarded from the war, scooped up by life.

"Thank you for coming!" she murmured.

"It coincided with me being in Oslo. Great planning by the Almighty." Helmik raised his eyes to the sky and released her from his embrace. "Now, show me where the party is!"

Sitting around her table, Esther felt lifted by friendship and festivity. She knew Sigrid least of them all, but she was a kind, rather silent girl who studied geology at Oslo Universitet as a cover-up for her resistance work. Tore had told her Sigrid was one of the

fiercest anti-Nazis he knew and that she carried out her resistance
work with a nonchalance and fearlessness that was mindboggling.

Esther studied her, and feeling she wanted to get to know her
better, asked, "Have you ever been outside Norway?" It seemed like
a silly question, but she couldn't come up with anything else. Sigrid
looked at her with fawn-brown eyes behind her round spectacles.

"Yes, I've studied a year at Oxford and lived in Stockholm for six
months doing research assessing soil liquefaction potential."

"Oh!" Esther sat back in her chair and felt catapulted back five
years in time when Océane had told her she studied medicine.
That feeling of inadequacy regarding her own academic perfor-
mance nagged at her. "That's amazing. I mean, I guess, if you know
what that is."

"Don't worry," Sigrid laughed, "it sounds more interesting than
it really is. Besides these days, all I do is stenciling and transporting
microfilms in my underwear."

They both giggled, but then in a more serious tone Sigrid
added, "I can't wait, though, to go really back into geology. It's my
passion. I come from quite an academic family, I guess. What about
you? If you want to talk about it. I understood from Tore that it's not
been easy for you." Sigrid's empathy was heart-warming and Esther
blossomed under so much kindness.

The men had meanwhile started the beer and were having an
animated conversation among themselves until Arne shouted, "We
need some music. And dancing. I want the first dance, Jeger!" His
eyes danced before his body did, and Esther giggled. It was always
so easy to get along with Arne. She never felt with him the tension
that always crept up between her and Tore.

Tore protested.

"I want the first dance."

"You'll have to arm wrestle me, brother!" Arne told him.

"Stop it," Esther cried, half laughing, "I'll decide myself with
whom I dance first." And she pointed to Helmik, who already got to
his feet and clapping his hands above his head, cheered, "Music, we
need music!"

Esther saw the look Tore gave Arne but had no time to worry about it as Helmik was already swirling her around the room to Glenn Miller's "The Man with The Mandolin."

"You look dazzling in blue, lassie." He winked. "All the young lads are head-over-heels for you."

Esther chortled. "It's just the alcohol, Helmik. Tomorrow, they will have forgotten me."

"You're wrong there, las..."

The door to her apartment crashed open with a bang. The needle of the gramophone screeched to a yammering halt. Two menacing Gestapo officers stood in the doorway, their guns pointing straight at the party guests.

33

IT'S ALL OVER

Esther awoke in a fetal position on a cold stone floor with dim light filtering through a tiny barred top window. She couldn't open her right eye, and her entire body hurt. It took her a while to remember how she'd ended up in this place. And when she did, she closed her good eye too and curled up in an even tighter ball. Her right ear tintinnabulated with an irritating and persistent low ring. Her stomach felt like mush.

She was in Grini Detention camp.

It was all over.

She lay a few moments trying not to move a muscle, just breathing raspy, quick breaths that hurt like a burning furnace. The fog in her head had to settle, her body fighting to stay alive. She waited, being trained for this on the Shetlands and in Scotland. As soon as her mind was clear, a plan would form, and she would be in charge again.

Question one. What had she let slip during the interrogation? Nothing, she thought proudly, she'd said nothing until she'd lost consciousness. Then there was the obvious gap in her memory, but no prisoner could talk having passed out. She had not betrayed her friends.

The first part of her inner investigation cleared; Esther moved her attention to her brutalized body. First, she tried to move her legs and found she could uncurl her stiff limbs. They felt sore all over, but every part could move; no bone was broken. The pain was most excruciating in her abdomen and face. In a flash, she saw the butt of a rifle hit her forcefully, accompanied by the wide grin of a lanky Gestapo officer.

"*Sprich*, Gunhild Helberg! Talk up! *Wo ist* Tore Helberg! You know where he is!"

They knew her false name. They were looking for Tore. Of course, they were looking for Tore through her. So it meant he'd escaped. Had the others too? Where were they?

Then her party flashed back to memory. Yes, she'd been alone in her apartment. The men and Sigrid had played drunk dummies and arm-in-arm had stumbled down the stairs, singing silly songs and falling over each other in a tangle of playacted intoxication. They'd slipped through the Gestapo's fingers in the assumption Esther would be safe as well. An innocent party, a narrow escape. But what about Tore? Was he here as well? He'd still been there when the SS was already banging on her door. Why did her memory fail her at such a crucial moment?

Her mind raced further before her interrogators would put their claws on her. What could they have on her? Of course, the Måløy raid where she'd been exposed. But had that traveled all the way from the north to the Gestapo in Oslo?

Esther sat up with difficulty and pulled her sea-blue dress over her battered knees. Through her good eye, she could see the pleated front was splashed with her own blood. The dress was soiled all over again.

"Ich habe...ich habe," she stuttered, not looking at the two black-clad officers across from her. "I was celebrating my birthday, just an innocent party with some friends. We got slightly drunk, and I apologize... for the noise we made. But it was an innocent party."

"Don't fool us, Helberg. You know we searched the flat, and

your brother had been there that day. And where did you get that accent? You sound as Norwegian as my sister in Heidelberg." She heard one of them snicker and peered through her eyelashes as she tried to desperately remember all she'd learned in her training about interrogations and torture. *Let them talk, find out what they know, spot their weaknesses, play everything down, but don't play too innocent.*

They'd searched her flat. In the party's buzz, Tore had forgotten about the directive and the microfilm, which were still lying on the sideboard. Signed by him in the name of the Home Front. Her arrest was simple and maybe she was just the bait, not a suspect herself. Not yet. So with all she still had in her, she had to protect Tore.

One thing was as clear as the bruised back of her hand. They'd known Tore was there, and they were looking for him. How could she find out if he'd escaped? They'd probably provide her with that knowledge themselves. Her hand went to her mangled stomach, and she retched, spilling the last contents of wine and fish pasty over the dirty prison floor. The taste in her mouth was of iron and sour spittle.

When her body stopped its involuntary dry heaving, she forced herself to breathe a little slower and deeper, needing to know if she'd broken any ribs. It was a meager consolation that the Nazis seemed to only have inflicted a gigantic bruise inside her body. Esther was unable to establish any further damage, and her abdominal muscles worked despite the pain. Damage to her organs seemed unlikely.

Esther thanked her teachers in silence for the medical training she'd had to scan her body in a situation like this, where no doctor looked after her wounds, and she had to do what she could herself even without supplies like bandages or pain killers.

Next, her attention went to her face, caked with blood and dirt. One eye felt like a balloon and wouldn't open. The right side of her face ached and throbbed. The result of another blow with the rifle.

With both hands, she tentatively examined her face. Her lip was torn; her teeth clattered non-stop against each other, but were still in her mouth. She remembered two blows against her face, then the punch in her stomach that had made her pass out. The Gestapo had had little success with their first interrogation, so she would have to brace herself for more.

"I need to get up from this cold floor."

Trying first on all fours, she got to a standing position but was so weak, she quickly staggered the two steps to the narrow bunk bed to sit down. An almost irrepressible need to relieve herself made her longingly look at the cracked chamber pot in the corner, but she wasn't sure she'd make it without collapsing again.

Her head spun, the headache splitting, her belly throbbing. The cell was chilly and damp. Her body quivering like a reed. She pulled the horse blanket that lay folded on the bunk bed around her shoulders and sat as still as she could. Trying not to think of her bodily needs.

The next hours, or days, were all that mattered. If she could hold on not giving away information, the others had time to get to safety. How to hold herself under the next round of torture. How not to break. How not to hand these Nazis new fighters through her. She wished she was stronger, but she had only one weapon.

Her hatred.

Would it be enough?

The test came soon enough. The door to her cell opened with a screeching sound, and in the dim light stood the lanky Gestapo officer with his mean grin.

"Gunhild Helberg, our minx warrior," he snickered. He pointed the barrel of his gun toward her. "*Aufstehen!* Get up!"

She did as she was told, huddled in the rough, woolen blanket and suppressing the involuntary shaking of her body as best as she could.

"*Vorwärts, marsch!*" he ordered, prodding the barrel of his rifle in her back. Esther almost fell forward, but he gripped her roughly by the elbow and yanked her upright. Trudging along, covered in the blanket, her bladder almost bursting from the sudden move, she stumbled through the narrow hall.

"*Links!* Left," the guard behind her ordered. They entered a square room with a wooden table and two straight chairs. A single lamp hung over the table. Stone floor, stone walls, no windows. A heavyset Gestapo agent sat at the table smoking a cigarette, the smoke swirling up in light-grey shards. The winged eagle and skull on his high cap gleamed in the light.

"*Hinsetzen!* Sit," the man behind her said, pointing to the empty chair, but Esther kept standing.

"Can I... I please use the bathroom?"

"The bathroom?" The man at the table bared narrow-set teeth under his thin mustard-colored moustache. "Are we getting posh here?"

"Please."

"All right, I don't want you to mess up here. Sergeant Fehmer, don't let her out of your sight and bring her straight back here."

Esther had never used the bathroom with another person watching her and, for a moment, feared she never could.

"Control above all," she ordered herself, as her legs shook, mentally preparing herself for what was in store for her. Struggling back into her panties, she felt a calm settle on her. She could lose herself, her body, her life but she would not give in. Not now, not ever.

Facing the man with the big cap and the narrow teeth, she took in his features so she would never forget. A small mouth, a thin moustache, flabby cheeks with a twitch left, narrow, brooding eyes. In his forties, sickly but mean as a graveyard dog. Not the best man to have opposite her. He lit another cigarette, seemed absorbed in reading her file.

After long minutes of silent smoking, the narrow eyes of difficult-to-distinguish color fixed her, tested her, gauged her strength. She looked him straight in the eye. Always the best tactic, Captain Bill had taught her in the first months at Lunna House. Don't show fear; show power and you will feel it.

You want to play the silent treatment? her eyes said. *Go ahead, I can play it too.*

She won the first round. He lowered his eyes. It took guts to intimidate a female prisoner. This man didn't have it, contrary to the lanky one who seemed to have no conscience at all.

"You claim you're Gunhild Helberg?"

"Yes."

"We know you are not Gunhild Helberg. Tore Helberg has one sister, and her name is not Gunhild. But let's play along with your tune for a while." He raised his eyes to meet hers again, only to calculate the effect his revelation would have on her. Esther was prepared for this, actually embraced it. She'd better be the Jew Esther Weiss here than Tore's relative.

The lanky one kept pacing the room, throwing menacing looks in her way. There was no escape. There was only inner strength to carry her through.

"Why do you doubt I'm Gunhild Helberg?"

A fist landed on the table, so hard the man hurt himself and became even angrier.

"Shut your mouth, you German whore! I ask the questions here."

He brought his face closer to her, and she smelled his breath, rotten eggs with stale tobacco. Her stomach heaved.

In a low, slow voice, he articulated, "You-get-one-chance! Where-is-Tore-Helberg?"

"I don't know."

"Liar!"

The man was stupid enough to bang the same fist on the table. He obviously liked to work himself up into a frenzy. *Not as good a thing*, Esther thought. Hadn't Anton taught her that anger was toxic, blinded you, made you do the wrong things?

"He was in your apartment yesterday. His papers were found in your flat."

Everything counted on her words now.

"He came to my birthday, Herr Commandant, as my brother,

but I know nothing of his whereabouts." Her mouth was dry, and the headache made it hard to stay alert.

"I thought we had already established that Tore Helberg is not your brother but your lover."

The unexpectedness of this remark threatened to bring her off balance. Esther clenched her jaw not to retort with the truth. Don't show them anything.

"Well, you've had your chance, and you didn't take it. Sergeant Fehmer, she's yours!"

Esther went rigid. The butt hit between her shoulder blades, and she slumped forward. Pain shot into her neck and shoulders. Her hands landed on the table to support herself. Despite herself, tears sprang into her eyes. Of anger and pain, equally.

The commandant, who still was nameless to her, walked around the table and shouted in her deaf right ear.

"Are you going to answer now?"

"I don't know where he is."

It was the truth. Like all of them, Tore moved from safe house to safe house.

The pain between her shoulders dulled. Esther's mind worked fast. They seemed not to know of her own resistance work, but did they know her real identity? Jens and Inger would be in danger too, if they knew who she was and where she'd lived.

"You leave us no choice!" The sturdy officer remarked with mock regret.

He is the kind of Nazi who would wash his hands in innocence, always and everywhere, Esther thought with disgust, as the rifle hit her back twice. Hard.

This time she moaned, broke into sobs.

"Good," the leader said, "we're getting closer! Get her up." He himself sat down at the table again. She felt herself being lifted from the chair and as she stood, the punching started, over and over again, until she fell in a pool of her own blood and couldn't get up anymore.

"Who are you?" Sergeant Fehmer hollered in her face.

Soon she would have no other choice. The torture was unbearable. Her real name seemed the lesser evil. Let them deport her to Germany. Keep her friends safe.

"I'm... I'm Esther Weiss... from... Vienna. A... Jew," she blubbered.

Another kick with the black boot, in her side, against her thigh.

"Dirty Jew, where is Tore Helberg? Tore Helberg! Tore Helberg!"

She would not tell them.

Not. Ever.

Esther passed out as they were still screaming his name in her face. With a sigh of relief, she accepted oblivion.

Take me to Mutti and Papi. Bring me home.

34

A MIRACLE

E sther dreamed that someone was lifting her up and carrying her to the light. She felt weightless and full of anticipation. Soon she would see God and be reunited with her family. Wrapped in a soft, warm blanket, her body filled up with a golden glow. It felt luminous, lustrous, an all-compassing love that made her smile.

A soft breeze on her temples, a powerful body carrying her. Then a voice saying,

"Be careful. Put her down here!"

It was a human voice, not a voice of the angels. The language was Norwegian. Esther was puzzled, tried to open her eyes but couldn't. She wanted to open her mouth but couldn't. Someone felt her pulse.

"She's coming around." Vague memories of that voice. Who was it? The smell of bleach and antiseptics. A hospital?

"Esther?" Another voice. Also, familiar.

And then she knew.

Tore!

What was he doing here? Where was she? She had to talk, make them know she was alive, but her body refused and so did her brain.

"It's all right. Don't try to say or do anything, Esther. I'm Doctor Berg. Do you remember me?"

Someone took her hand, squeezed it softly. She tried to think. Doctor Berg and Tore. But there were more people in the room. She could sense it.

"We're here too, Esther. Jens and Inger. You're safe now."

Safe from what? What had happened? It felt so odd she couldn't move, but there was no pain, just a total lack of strength in her bones and muscles.

"She doesn't remember yet." That was the doctor's voice.

Remember what?

"How long before she can be transported? We need to get her across the border as quickly as possible." That was Tore. Where did he want to take her?

"And you too, young man! You're both in danger any minute you stay here longer." That was Jens.

It was odd how they were talking about and around her, but the oddest of all was how she was suddenly back on the farm with Jens and Inger. Was it a dream, after all?

She felt the doctor come closer.

"Listen to me, Esther. I know you can hear me, even if you can't talk back. I know your memory is temporarily gone, and that's as well. You're sedated, so you have no pain, but the pain will return. You're in danger, so we must start moving you tonight. I have no choice. I'll supply your friends with enough painkillers and fluids for the journey. You will make it; you will heal. Just give it time." He gave her hand another little squeeze. She felt the pressure, but in a numb sort of way.

Her head wanted to nod, thank him for his kindness, though his words didn't make much sense to her. In the same light way as before, she was lifted up and carried away.

The next thing she noticed was the humming of an engine. Her body was swaddled in blankets but rocked softly on the bed she was lying on. Her hips and back hurt, her head felt like a balloon, and her mouth was dry. One eye opened a crack. It was dark. She was woozy, strangely detached from the pain in her body. She tried to lift her arm from underneath the blanket, and surprisingly she could.

Something moved on the floor next to her.

"Esther?"

His whispered voice.

She couldn't answer but moved her arm in his direction. He took her hand.

"Do you need anything?"

He was sitting close to her. Through the crack, she could see he had lit his torch, shone it on her face. She pointed to her mouth.

"Water?" He quickly grabbed the canteen and dropped a straw in it. Held it to her mouth. She tried to suck on the straw, but her lips had no strength.

"Wait!" He put an arm around her and lifted her upper body, then put the canteen to her mouth. She swallowed. It tasted like iron, but the liquid smoothed the rough inside of her mouth and throat.

"Enough?" He put her down tenderly again and tucked the blanket around her. Switched off the torch.

Tore was with her. Somehow that soothed her troubled state, but there was a loud voice yelling his name in her ear, telling her she shouldn't be near him. Her presence brought danger to him. She wanted to tell him but couldn't. There was nothing she could do about it right now.

The hum of the engine, the water, pills, soft sliding food and lulling sleep and Tore. Esther didn't know for how long. But it seemed endless. When the pain was too much, she raised her hand. She was only thirsty, never hungry. Sleep was best.

"Esther?" Someone tapped her arm. "Esther, we're here."

Here? Where is here?

The next thing she knew, she was being hoisted onto a stretcher and two medics hurried across a long courtyard with her on it. Swedish? They spoke Swedish, which might mean they were in Sweden. It was all the same to her.

A week later

Esther was sitting on a bench in a secluded garden listening to bumblebees buzzing around the magnolia. A large red-and-white striped parasol above her head shaded the summer sun. A fly had landed in her lemonade on the garden table in front of her. She was wearing a dress she didn't recognize. The only thing she recognized was the volume of *Rebecca* on the table. She would recognize the lovely cover everywhere. Opening it randomly, she read, "*You have blotted out the past for me, far more effectively than all the bright lights of Monte Carlo.*"

A tiny, black spider with perfect little limbs marched along the edge of the table in her direction. Esther followed the insect with her eyes, weary, suddenly saddened. There was no need to kill it now. Rebecca wasn't here to be afraid. As if knowing its fate was safe, the spider went down along the table leg and disappeared in the tall grass. Gone... without a trace.

At that moment Tore came sauntering toward her, a smile on his face, his long, short-sleeved arms tanned and his hair even more golden in the shine of the sun. He did blot out the sun, and she couldn't help but smile back at him. He was so alive and handsome. Esther shook herself; it was just good to see him despite the anxiety she had about his safety. It never quite left her. She was convinced she endangered him more than he knew. Her memory was still failing her.

The Swedish doctor had said it was time she remembered. Or it would be gone for good.

"Hi," she said, suddenly bashful in his presence that never left her untouched. She was so vulnerable now and he so strong and loving.

"Hi!" he replied, dropping his tall frame in the chair opposite her. "How are you feeling today?"

"Okay, I guess, but Doctor Arnemo says I should start remembering what happened. He's afraid I'll have permanent brain damage."

"Do you want me to help you, Esther?" The blue eyes looked open to questions. "I mean, I don't know what happened to you in Grini prison, but I have an inkling. I know all the rest."

"Grini prison? Was that where I was?" She tried hard to remember.

"Yes. Do you remember your birthday party?"

She folded her hands in her lap. A pain shot through her abdomen. It made her cringe. She remembered.

"Helmik. Dancing."

"Yes, you were dancing with Helmik."

"Where is my box? You bought me a lovely painted box? What did you call it?"

"Oh, Esther." He grabbed her hands across the table. "Rosemaling it's called. I'm so glad your memory is coming back."

"Where is the box?" she asked again with more urgency in her voice.

"I think it is still in your apartment. I'll ask Portner Sveri to go look for it. Don't worry about the box."

"I'm afraid, Tore." Her voice was tiny now. He got up from his chair and came to sit next to her on the bench, his arm around her shoulder.

"I understand, Esther. Horrible, horrible things happened to you. Your brain is just trying to protect you from the trauma."

She nodded, feeling as if she was staring down a misty ravine, knowing she would have to take the leap and jump in. But in the mist lay one certainty. She had been brave.

"Shall I tell you how we rescued you?"

"Yes."

"It didn't take us long to find out you were in Grini. We have our contacts there inside the prison and got hold of them straight away. So, we knew you were... um... treated badly, and that we had to act with haste. That either you would snap, or they would deport you. But that wretched Fehmer and Kerner were on duty for four days in a row and kept their hawk's eyes on you so we couldn't act."

Tore waited as one of the nurse assistants came their way with the trolley with fresh drinks and sandwiches. Esther smiled up at the young Swedish girl, readily accepting both. Her appetite had returned.

"Go on," she said after the nurse had served them and started pushing the rattling trolley to the next patient in the hospital garden.

"Two trusted Gestapos—yes, even within the German prison systems we have accomplices—signaled us to be ready to pick you up. They covered you with a sheet, giving the appearance you'd died so no-one checked when a coroner showed up with a coffin." Tore rubbed a hand over his face. "I'm sorry about that part, Esther, but we couldn't take any risk."

But she took it with a surprised chuckle.

"Me in a coffin? What an excellent idea."

"I'm glad you think so. I thought it rather morbid."

"Thank you, Tore!" She leaned in closer to him, and he gave her shoulder a squeeze.

"Ouch!"

"Sorry!"

"It's nothing. My body is healing well. I'll soon outski you again."

Now it was his turn to chortle, "That's the Esther I like!"

They sipped their lemonade, fell silent. The torture returned to her in flashes until all the pieces of the puzzle were whole.

Her voice was hoarse but steady when she finally spoke. "I gave them nothing about our cause. I'm one hundred percent sure of that. Only my real name and my race. It seemed the best way out of my tough luck."

Tore sat still as a leaf on a windless day, listening to her words with piety and reverence.

"After your arrest, everybody who was at your party went into hiding anyway, just in case. But you do realize the magnitude of your sacrifice? I now finally see why the Linge Company was so keen to have you as one of them. I guess... I somehow underestimated you. It's just that you're so... sweet."

"I'm not sweet by any measure, Tore, and I'm not done yet. As soon as I may, I'll be back in Norway, back to fighting."

He looked at her as if he was trying to fit the two sides of her personality together in his mind. Meanwhile, the sun disappeared behind a cloud but then reappeared with even more radiance.

It was the summer of 1943.

"No, Esther, you can't!" Tore's face contorted with worry. "You're not going back. It's way too dangerous. They'll deport you to Ravensbrück straight away."

"Oh yes, I can go back. And so can you. I've seen you getting restless here, biding your time in Stockholm as you were looking after me."

"No, I haven't. I can as easily work from the Stockholm Legation as from Oslo." His voice didn't sound convinced, though.

"Liar."

"Okay, you're right, the call up for young people in the German Labor Effort is becoming our major concern right now but..."

"So, we'll return to Norway as soon as the doctors discharge me." Esther's voice was resolute, but her hands gripped the wooden lattice of the bench beneath her. She made her voice sound upbeat as she added, "Oh, and something else. I don't want to talk about what happened inside Grini. You know the stories well enough. It wasn't any different for me. In the end, it's only physical bruises. They will heal. They haven't broken my spirit. All I want is to focus again on getting the Nazis out of our country, quislings included."

It may have sounded more dapper than she felt, but she meant it. Every word. Until the sun shone in freedom over the Continent again.

Our country.

Did she feel more Norwegian than Austrian now? Yes. She'd learned to love both the country and its people. They suited her temperament.

.

35

THE LAST MISSION

In March 1944, the recruitment of thousands of young Norwegians as German cannon fodder in their losing war was in full swing. Although Tore's Home Front Office did all they could to convince both the Government in London and key figures and organizations within Norway that a catastrophe was about to take place, not many people seemed to take this desperate German recruitment act seriously.

The Labor Service, or AT as it was called, was just another of Quisling's megalomanic plans inspired by the Nazi occupation. Ultimately, it would crash on the resilience of the Norwegian people, like the mandatory membership of the NS had done, the fascist education in the classroom, and the breaking of the power of the underground press. In name, Quisling might be Minister President and gleefully rub shoulders with Terboven, or even his idol Hitler, yet neither his own people nor the Nazi regime thought as highly of the man as he did himself.

Esther could sense Tore's frustration with the lethargy and disbelief around him. Everybody seemed to have become war-weary. The will to fight, or even just to oppose, slackened. Norwegians were hungry, terrorized people, hardly believing anymore in an Allied invasion coming to their doorstep.

Messages of victories over the German armies happened in faraway countries—Italy, Greece, Russia. Meanwhile, Germany's ally, Japan, reigned with almighty rule over the entire Far East.

Germany's terror in Norway in 1944 was at its peak, scarring almost every community large and small. There was hardly a resistance cell, civil or military, that hadn't lost one or more of its members. Half of the Linge Company had been wiped out, men she'd trained with, like that unfortunate Per whose place she'd taken in the Vemork assault. But so many others she and Tore knew. Good men and women. Cold-bloodedly shot, tortured till death, sent to die in Polish or German concentration camps. By the thousands. Esther prayed every day for her close-knit group of fighters, Helmik, Claus, Anton, Arne and Sigrid. And of course, always Tore.

No wonder the people of Norway had had enough. They'd suffered for four years from the inside and the outside, constantly having to be watchful in two directions: the Gestapo or the NS.

The far-reaching effects of sending Norway's youth *en masse* to fight for the enemy was something only a few people foresaw, among them Tore. Germany was losing and the wounded animal was becoming rabid and rushed. Esther knew she needed to do something, something drastic. So, she sent a message to Anton via a trusted courier.

"It's not enough merely to stop recruitment to AT. We must destroy the registers for the service. According to our sources there are 80,000 to 90,000 men on that list. They will be used as the most important instrument for the Nazis in the event of a mobilization. Can you imagine our own men having to fight against our Allies for the liberation of Norway? We simply must stop this!"

Esther deliberated whether she should discuss her plans with Tore but bided her time. Linge Company was incorporated in Milorg, the Norwegian military organization, which in its turn resided under the overall Allied command. It wasn't just a matter of walking into the building where the lists were kept and setting it on fire. It was what Esther would love to do most of all, but she understood this wasn't how it worked. All the resistance groups worked together now—in Norway and abroad—to hit the ground running with free and well-organized people should the German power finally collapse.

Esther was lucky. Soon, clearance came from both Milorg and London that the registers could be destroyed in an act of sabotage. She didn't have to tell Tore; he knew himself, being the spider in the web of it all.

They didn't meet in person. It was too dangerous. So she sent him a message, via a box they used in one of Oslo's banks, that she was ready to carry out the mission and would await instructions with whom and when.

Tore answered.

"It will not be enough to destroy the main registers. These registers are kept on a punch-card system. If necessary, the AT management can reconstruct the cards with the help of the records in the ten counties and Greater Oslo. So, it's going to be a comprehensive sabotage. Find out where the main registers are kept and what security measures are in place. And be careful."

Esther met her contact, a man called Harald, three days later. Harald was a spindly man in his fifties, greying hair under a bowler hat and dressed in a long, beige trench coat as if he was an Englishman. He was fidgety and too thin. They took a walk in the Palace Park, a lush, tree-filled park where King Haakon had resided before his chaotic flight from the Germans in 1940.

"What have you found?" Esther went straight to the core of the matter. His squirmy personality worked on her nerves, and she was afraid they would draw the attention of the Waffen SS, with which the park swarmed. She couldn't afford to stand out in the center of Oslo, despite short black hair and glasses that hopefully provided enough of a coverup.

"I know the businessman who owns the punch-card machine that is used for the AT enrolment. He's reliable, so that's good."

Harald swung his thin beige arms in an exaggerated way, while he walked really fast and slurred his last words. It was crucial she caught everything he said, so Esther moved closer to him, which clearly made both of them feel awkward and apprehensive.

"Sorry," she mumbled, "I can't keep up and we have to talk in low voices."

"I'll be done in a moment," he offered, never slowing down and slumping the beige arms at his sides.

"The business owner also happens to know the AT officer in charge of the enrollment, a man called Viggo. Viggo's told him that the registers are stored in three places, but the majority are in a vault on the top floor of the AT headquarters next to Oslo Town Hall. Viggo should be reliable, and he's willing to store all the registers in the vault at the beginning of May under some pretext of security. There are only two keys to the vault, of which Viggo has one. I've arranged for you to meet him, but there is one but. It may be a trap, so make sure you're armed and have someone to cover you."

He'd spoken so fast and soft that Esther wasn't sure she'd heard everything so repeated the most important phrases. Harald just nodded.

"After Viggo's given you the keys—front door, department and vault—and the map of the building, he must immediately be transported across the border to Sweden. When the Germans find no signs of trespassing, he'll be the first one they'll be looking for."

"It will be arranged."

"That's all." Harald was gone without even saying goodbye.

"Well, you have all sorts in this movement," Esther mused. She was happy with the valuable information he'd given her. Ready for her next attack.

Through the box in the bank, Esther received the following letter from Tore:

"The Labor Service recruits have been told to assemble in the middle of May 1944. In most parts of the country, they have been warned not to do so by a barrage from our organization. The anti-AT committee has

been producing information material around the clock to notify everyone
the real reasons the Germans have for this recruitment.

"This will be the touchstone for the attitude of the Norwegian people,
and the result of the action will determine the line to be followed for the
future in the struggle here at home. So we're breaking down the AT from
the inside in addition to destroying their national registration system here
in Oslo. Everyone is on high alert both in the Home Front and in the
Government in London. But so are Quisling and the Gestapo. This is our
ultimate test. Thousands of young men will have to go into hiding in the
forests anyway over the summer.

"The action is to take place at midnight on 4 and 5 May."

Esther clasped the all-important keys in her fist inside her coat
pocket. Just four innocent-looking keys—front door, department
door, anteroom and vault. Yet they felt heavy, carrying the burden
of so much responsibility. They represented the fate of Norway's
male youth. Their lives were now on the line, forced to fight on the
wrong side, prolonging the war in Hitler's desperate attempt to save
his Third Reich.

It was the evening before the attack, an unusually balmy
evening for early May. Esther needed to get all the information she
could about the AT headquarters and its users. Which offices were
still illuminated? Who went in and out at this time of night?

Her cover on the watch was a young girl called Ursula—not her
own name, of course—whom Esther had once met during her time
at Drumintoul Lodge in Scotland. One of the few other women
commandos. A trained secret agent and a sharpshooter like no
other. But they pretended not to know each other, keeping a suitable distance. Two girls enjoying the evening air, a late stroll
before bed.

A Gestapo motorcycle patrol rushed round the corner, lit up
everything, obviously on the hunt for someone. They passed by,
shouted something about pretty girls, vanished at high speed
around the corner. Esther's fist tightened.

TWENTY-FOUR HOURS LATER, the same scene repeated, but Esther now had a hand grenade in her handbag and a loaded Enfield gun in her pocket. She walked slowly but steadily across Rådhus-plassen, the square in front of the Town Hall, so as not to draw attention to herself. Ursula followed her as a shadow.

This Thursday the night porter, a reliable man, greeted her as she walked in. He put three fingers in the air. Then made another three. Three SS officers in the building on the third floor.

"*God natt*, Larsen," Esther greeted him in a chirpy voice, but her heart sank. Third floor was the floor where she needed to be. Was it a trap, after all? But there was no time to waste, and she started climbing the stairs to the third floor, rehearsing the story she'd made up in case they asked what she was doing. With her smart dress, heeled shoes and fancy handbag, she'd get away with the secretary story. But the cyanide pill in her bra was a macabre reminder she could not be caught again.

The three SS officers were playing a game of poker in a side office, clearly stationed there to protect the vault with the Labor Force registrations. They looked up as she took the last step of the stairs and walked down the lobby.

"Just adding some files to the vault," she shouted to them in German, tapping her bag.

"Go ahead," one of them shouted back. The men were clearly more interested in their game than in the strange time of night for a secretary to come and do work outside office hours. Esther kept her ears wide open for any move on their part to follow her to the door of the antechamber. She made sure she rattled the keys audibly. The Germans remained where they were.

Now she would have to work as quickly as she could. The keys worked like clockwork and the vault, laden with files, was opened within seconds. She listened again. Laughter. "*Ich bin dran*, my turn, Big Blind," she heard but there was no shuffling of chairs. She removed the safety pin from the grenade and threw it on top of the papers so it wouldn't make a sound. She quickly closed the door, locked it. Then walked rapidly out of the anteroom which she left open.

Calling a jolly *"Guten abend, Herren!"* she sped down the stairs. They didn't even react.

"Outside, Larsen," Esther yelled as she raced past his lodge. He followed on her heels, saving his life. The escape car, an inconspicuous old Volvo, stood ready with Ursula at the wheel. A tremendous explosion thundered behind them as the whole of the third floor of the AT Headquarters spat apart.

Esther looked back at the third floor which already stood ablaze, flames licking from the exploded windows. It was not a pretty sight, but she hoped it would save the lives of thousands of young men.

"I'm sorry," she muttered, for the first time feeling she'd killed three innocent Germans as collateral damage to the sabotage. But the act had been successful. Tore would sleep a little lighter tonight. And she?

"To Sweden," she ordered. "I'm afraid this has to be my last mission from within Norway."

36

DO IT, GERMANS, LAY DOWN YOUR ARMS!

T hroughout 1944 and the first half of 1945, the war dragged on indefinitely for the people of Norway. Despite Allied advances on mainland Europe after their successful landings on the Normandy coasts in June 1944. Despite Soviet troops crossing the frontier in Finnmark, the very north of Norway on 25 October 1944. Hitler's thousand-year Reich was creaking on all fronts, but the yearned-for German capitulation continued to flounder.

In an all-torn-up answer to beat their retreat, the German troops began practicing scorched earth tactics in West Finnmark and North Troms, destroying the property and businesses of over 40,000 inhabitants and deporting them south with the help of the NS authorities. The magnitude of the people's devastation, destruction and despair only slowly trickled to the Home Front in Oslo and the Stockholm Legation, where Esther was stationed.

The country was in an utter maelstrom, with the Gestapo and the State Police sending a flurry of black-clad men down on the resistance members. Never before in the war had torture and murder been more prominently executed by the dying beast called Nazism. While the beast growled and killed, the Norwegians held their breath. Shuddering at the gruesome reports that filtered from the concentration camps and prisons.

Esther's task was to streamline the civil 'export' between Norway and Sweden. With the growth of the hope of a German defeat, the resistance movement had grown exponentially, but so had the grip of the Gestapo on their members. Many of the prominent people, some of whom had been active since the start of the war, had to be helped across the border into neutral Sweden.

But most of the guide routes were discovered, and the dapper guides and their 'refugees' executed. It meant a constant search for new guides and pathways through the forested terrain in South Norway. Being busy with her new assignment helped Esther forget she'd much rather go into active sabotage within Norway all over again. But the signs were on red. The movement forbade Jeger's return to active service until the end of the war.

Her constant worry was Tore's fate, which hung in the balance as well. She'd received several messages that he was top on the list of most-sought resistance members, but despite an arrest during a street check and mishandling by the State Police in which he'd broken his arm, he'd so far stayed out of the Gestapo's clutches. But for how long?

"I won't waver. My job here as leader of the Home Front Secretariat is too important," he'd written, and Esther could do nothing but pray for his safety.

In all the frenzy and fragmented information, there was one very persistent and frightening rumor buzzing around. Norway would be used as the center of the scene of war by the dying regime. The entire country was going to be kept hostage in exchange for more favorable terms of surrender. A horrifying thought, but very plausible.

AND THEN, finally, the day came Esther thought would never arrive; a date she was sure would be ingrained in her memory forever. 30

April 1945. Adolf Hitler killed himself in his beleaguered Berlin bunker.

Now it would all be over soon.

It had started with the Austrian Adolf, and it would end there. A twelve-year reign of terror. No one was going to take over; not his dummy Doenitz, nor humbug Himmler, not the terrible Terhoven. Ultimately, they'd all been nothing but Hitler's pawns, fabrications of the biggest monster humanity had ever produced.

It was over, despite Grand-Admiral Doenitz being appointed successor and head of the German armed forces. She was going back home. Now.

Esther tore her black wig off her head and shook her blonde curls free. It felt like a liberation of its own. The metal-rimmed glasses disappeared in her pocket. She was Esther Weiss again, ready to retrieve her real passport from the Lindenbergs' attic.

"I'm heading back to Oslo!" she announced to her colleagues at the Stockholm Legation.

"You can't! The war's not over. The Germans still crack the whip in Norway." Ursula, who'd stayed with her after their AT mission, tried to stop her.

"You can come with me if you want or stay here. Either way, I'm heading for the train station. Mind my words. It won't be long now!"

"Do as you please, Gunhild, but for heaven's sake, wear your disguise."

It was the last thing she heard as she rambled down the stairs, collected her rucksack and set out on foot in the chilly morning to *Stockholms Centralstation*.

Esther arrived at Oslo's *Østbanestasjonen* on 1 May. Somehow, the picture in her head didn't match with reality. She was so cheerful to be back after almost a year, her heart wanting to celebrate and her soul wanting to prepare for the search for her family.

But SS officers were marching up and down the platforms in their green uniforms as if they still belonged there. Outside on the Jernbanetorget Square, the Gestapo raced around in their jeeps and on motorcycles, stopping and harassing Norwegians as they had done for the past five years. Oslo was far from a festive mood; all its inhabitants experienced was the same-old, same-old oppression and atrocity.

She had changed. She had breathed the free air of Sweden, not having had to look over her shoulder all the time, staying in the same apartment during her entire stay, even having enough food in her belly almost all days. It would be her task to bring the spirit of freedom to her downtrodden, exhausted compatriots.

Starting with Tore.

She found him in his underground campaign quarters, in an unfinished cellar space under a block of flats a little way from the city center. He was sitting at an improvised camp table typing rather frantically on a black Remington typewriter, with his back to her. As it was cold in the underground quarters, he had wrapped a woolen shawl around his shoulders. His blond hair needed a hair-cut, and his brown corduroy blazer was frayed at the elbows. But it was Tore all right, straight-up and working on the cause. His long frame bent in an arc of dedication.

Two other people from the secretariat, Sigrid in a long gabar-dine coat, frizzy hair peeping from under a man's hat and a student Esther recognized as Tore's right hand, Anders Sanengen, sat at a short distance away, discussing some papers and smoking ciga-rettes. A radio set in the corner spewed nonstop news bulletins, both in English and Norwegian.

"Hi, Tore," she whispered, so as not to disquiet him. He turned, had to focus as he was staring against the light. Blinked, squinted, the blue eyes alert. When he recognized her, his expression changed from great delight to even greater concern. He got up from his chair, knocking it over in his haste, and closed the distance between them in two big strides.

She was in his arms, feeling the fabric of his coat against her face, as the shawl tickled her nose. His heart beat warm and vibrant under her ear.

"*Min Gud*, Heavens, Esther, what are you doing here?" Concern had clearly won, but he held her tight, his head resting on the top of her head. She felt the magical strength of his arms around her, the unspoken delight of being reunited after the longest separation since the beginning of the war. She almost let go, sank into the embrace, but corrected herself. Peeling herself free, she answered him.

"You don't think I'd want to miss out on Norway's liberation? Not for the world. I want to be here with you when Norway's flag waves from Akershus Castle again and the hideous swastikas are taken down and burned to ashes." Smiling up at him, she saw his concern melt. Hope and happiness had won.

"Oh Esther, it's so good to see you in the flesh again. How have you been?" He still held her hand as she went over to greet Sigrid and Anders.

"I've been okay, sort of lazy compared to my first years in the movement. Never want to do an office job in my life again. I missed the great outdoors, but it was a good thing I had to slow down. Never completely recovered to my full strength after Grini. The Linge boys would call me a cream puff if they saw me like this." Esther said it with a dose of nonchalance, but she saw that the frown deepened between Tore's eyes and a muscle twitched in his left jaw.

"Rotten bastards. Let's hope this idiocy is over soon and we can have you examined properly. Well, you heard I had my tiny portion of manhandling by the Gestapo as well?"

"I did. You must tell me how you escaped. You are a cat with nine lives, having been at the center of all the fun for five years and never forced to flee the country."

"Do you want to know my secret?" He grinned at her with the face of a joyful boy. The exuberance she'd seen in him since that first time in the Austrian Alps, quite un-Norwegian in a way.

"Of course, but will you tell me?" She loved the lighthearted tone they could now adopt.

"It's easy as pie, Miss-Phony-Helberg. I'm just too plain to stand out. If you knew how many romances I've seen blossoming throughout the war." He nodded his head toward Sigrid and Anders, and Esther could see their heads were very close together, the papers they had been discussing forgotten. "But everyone over-looks me, girls and Gestapo alike."

"Oh, shut up, you!" Giving him a friendly nudge in the ribs, she added, "There's nothing plain about you, Mister-Real-Helberg. I'm sure throngs of girls have been pining for your attention. You just never notice it as you're always tapping away like mad on that thing." She pointed to the Remington with the half-finished article.

"You think so?" His head askew, he pondered her words.

"You'll be fine, Tore." As she spoke the words, her heart ached for her own future in which she would have to try to find Carl. Most days, she kept the agonizing fear at bay, but it crept up on her in the nights. Where was he? Still alive? Maimed? Or perhaps he'd even forgotten her. She shook herself.

"Let's not waste time," she said, interrupting her unwelcome thoughts. "What can I do?"

"We'll have to find you a place to crash. It's extremely dangerous now, so we all must be extra vigilant. You can get penalty of death just for crossing the street in front of a Gestapo jeep. Everyone's tense like a greyhound before the race."

"Where do you sleep?"

"Here."

"Can I sleep here, too?" Esther looked around the underground quarters. It had only one camp bed but, if needed, she could sleep on the floor. During her winter trek to Vemork with the Linge team, she'd slept in worse conditions.

Tore looked doubtful, but then slowly nodded.

"The safest plan. I'll ask Anders to get an extra mattress for you."

❧

4 AND 5 May came and went. The German forces capitulated unilaterally on the entire northern continental front. But not in Norway. Nothing changed in Norway.

The young people in the underground shelter, packed in coats and shawls despite the spring weather above ground, stared at each other in despair. The radio their constant companion in these frightful hours and days.

What about Norway? Was their country, after all, going to be used as collateral? The fear was real, fed by the contradicting messages from both the BBC and the Norwegian broadcasts from Stockholm.

Denmark was free, as were Holland, Great-Britain, Belgium, France, and all the countries around the Mediterranean. Even Poland and Russia, but not Norway.

The reports that came through their contacts were equally grave. There was much disagreement among the leading German officers, no one really being in charge anymore after the collapse of the regime and Hitler's death.

In the early evening of the 5th, there was a rap on the door. The signal was correct but carried out with great urgency. Tore went to see what was going on, his gun pointing at the door; pocketing the weapon again when a trusted courier shoved a message in his hand and disappeared again at high speed.

Tearing open the message from the Coordinating Committee, he read aloud,

"The Commander of the Home Forces, Jens Chr. Hauge, has received a telegram from General Eisenhower, instructing the German Commander-in-Chief in Norway, Franz Böhme to get in touch with SHAEF.

The Government-in-exile has telegraphed credentials to the Home Front leadership, which empowers them to do what is necessary to maintain good order pending its arrival back on Norwegian territory in the case of a German capitulation."

Tore stopped reading and turned up the volume knob on the radio set. A lot of cracking and beeping emitted from the old wireless but on finding the wavelength, they all listened with bated breath. It was true. The ball was in Böhme's court. What would he and Donitz decide?

Again, nothing happened for another couple of days while all over Europe, Esther imagined people dancing in the streets, getting drunk with freedom and a truckload of alcohol. The wait and the tension were almost unbearable. The May days in that Oslo cellar dragged like sluggish Roman snails.

On 7 May, Tore gave up his restraint to stay put. Grabbing his briefcase and stuffing it with his papers, he shouted, "I'm going to see what's going on at Headquarters. We'd better make a head start with forming that interim government. The Germans are kaput!"

"I'm coming with you," Esther announced, and for once Tore didn't protest.

As she sat on the back of his bicycle with him peddling fast toward the committee's assembly point in the west end of Oslo, they were met by a procession of children with flags, singing Norwegian songs. Flags were likewise draped over the balconies.

The moment had come. But had it? It was still not peace or even an armistice. But Oslo's people no longer could be held back. Tears streaming down her cheeks, Esther grabbed the fabric of Tore's coat and yelled from the top of her lungs, "We are free!"

"Yes, we are! Or, we will be in a matter of hours," he cried back, swerving on his bike in pure extasy.

Yet something held her back from total release. The day seemed fragile as an eggshell. All could still go awry. She yearned for the message of capitulation with every fiber in her body. *Do it, Germans! Lay down your arms.*

On arrival at the Home Front headquarters, they found it in a total frenzy. It was an atmosphere of seething activity and agitated talk. The radio blared over the sea of human voices; telephones rang. The air was blue with smoke and smelled strongly of stale coffee. All fear of a Gestapo or *Statspolitiet* raid seemed over.

Esther saw how a group of people thronged around Tore, the men with their shirt sleeves rolled up and their ties thrusted inside their shirts; the women elbowing their way through the men to get closer to him, cigarette in hand, white blouses tucked into smart navy or grey skirts. Secretaries. Esther had to smile. Tore was popular enough among the ladies, but he had absolutely no eye for them. Instead, he was discussing the draft victory proclamation he'd composed, ready to go on the front page of the *Oslo Press* the next day and be broadcast on the State Radio.

"But there's no capitulation yet!" someone cried.

"The Allied Military command that is to take over from the Germans isn't on Norwegian soil yet!" another shouted.

Tore made a quieting movement with his hand, and some of the cacophony subsided.

"We as the Home Front and civil administration must be prepared for taking interim control. That's why the proclamation has to be sent to the press and the radio station with the message to inform the country as soon as the capitulation is a fact," he assured them.

"But what if they print it too soon?"

"But when, oh when? We've been waiting so long?"

The discussion went on and on. At some point, the voices subsided to the background and Esther felt herself in a strange bubble. She was Norwegian, and she wasn't. That liberty was about to happen to her adopted country was clear. But for her the war wouldn't be over. Perhaps it would just begin.

37

PEACE. AND NOW?

The black fingers of the office clock on the wall crawled at a snail's pace to 8 May 1945. Esther was sitting on the edge of a table in the Home Front Headquarters playing with a glass paperweight and swinging her legs. The Norwegians were still involved in their discussions over the immediate future of their country. She was tired, tense and tetchy.

"I'm never good at having nothing to do," she reminded herself. "I wish there was something. Wring that stupid General Böhme's neck, or storm the German headquarters. Why are they taking so long?" But Tore had said that their contacts were sure the capitulation was about to be formalized at midnight. She looked at her watch. Two more hours.

Somehow all the bustle surrounding her threw her back on herself, on her extreme journey from a shy Viennese fiancé to a fierce freedom fighter in some of Norway's most crucial years in history.

At this hectic moment, no one paid particular attention to her or asked her advice, but everybody knew who she was. Tore had told them with pride that she was one of the Linge commandos, who'd actually fought with the illustrious Magnus Linge in Operation Archery. These office people, who'd spent most of their resistance years coordinating all the events from the capital, treated Jeger, as she was still called, with great respect.

"Your war decorations are going to be much fancier than mine," Tore had joked during her convalescence time in Stockholm, when he had kept her company. She'd shrugged at the mention of military medals, not caring two fiddlesticks for them, but now his words came back to her as she watched him in agitated discussion.

If there was one person who should be decorated to the brim, it was Tore Helberg. He'd never taken a day off, had never thought about himself for all the five long years of the war. She had come and gone, taken breaks, been away in other countries for many months, away from the theatre of war. But Tore had only been with her in Stockholm for two weeks, and then still he had been working.

He deserved a break, but that immediately gave Esther a troubled feeling. She wanted him with her in her search for her family. He'd promised so much, but she decided she couldn't ask it from him. He had a right to celebrate with his friends and family, rejoice in Norway's end of terror. For as long as he wanted. Finally, free to do as he pleased. He'd mentioned longing to finish his degree in geology, and become a polar explorer.

I'll sneak out on my own as soon as I can, she thought. She would go to Jens and Inger to pick up her valise and her passport. Some money was still stored away at the farm that would pay for the trip.

The trip. That was the least of her worries. To find her family. How and where? She really didn't know how to go about it.

"Esther!"

The world around her exploded.

"Hauge has done it! He's talked with Böhme before the arrival of the Allied military mission. He's convinced him to surrender with the promise we will not direct our arms at the Germans."

Tore grabbed her by the waist and danced wildly with her through the crowded office. Caps were thrown in the air and the

national anthem *Ja, vi elsker dette landet*—Yes, we love this country
—spontaneously came out of all mouths.

Esther was taken up in the merriment, and it totally gripped
her. She laughed and cried and kissed Tore, who continued to hold
her tight, his face one big grin that would not part from him,
though the blue eyes cried. The release was ecstatic, orgasmic.
People didn't know whether to laugh or to cry, so did both at the
same time. So much pain, so much loss, so much sacrifice.

All the people from the Home Front left the office in a daisy
chain and flocked into the streets, where they were joined by ever
more citizens, who were carrying flags and singing songs, though it
was the middle of the night. Esther held firmly onto Tore's hand,
not wanting to lose him in the crowd. Somebody thrusted a megaphone in Tore's direction.

"Talk to the people; tell them it's real."

He was hoisted onto a makeshift platform, people cheering at
him. Esther was pulled up next to him and, grabbing her hand, he
raised their arms together in the air. Another salvo of cheers.

Do they all know me? Esther wondered, *or is this finally for Tore?*
Television crews came from out of nowhere, Norwegian broad-
casters who had been illegal for the entire war.

"Speak, speak!" The crowd roared.

Tore put the megaphone to his mouth and, suddenly, silence
reigned. Esther watched his profile. The blond mane, the strong
nose, the intense eyes. He loved his people. He was Norway. And
she? She loved Norway, too. The words he spoke vibrated in her
inner self, and she knew then that what he said would make him
immortal in the eyes of his compatriots.

*"Never have we had more at stake. Our very existence as a people
was threatened—legal security, intellectual freedom and the dignity of
man, our entire cultural inheritance, everything that makes life worth
living."*

More tears, more cheers. He squeezed her hand. She didn't
want to shed anymore tears. She wanted to be dry-eyed as she said
goodbye to him. Her days with Tore were over. She hoped she

would see him on her future visits to Norway, but for now she had to let him go.

Don't linger on it, Esther. Just do your duty and find your family.

EARLY THE NEXT MORNING, with Oslo still wrapped in its intoxicated liberation sleep, Esther set out by bus toward Søndre Nordstrand. She had no time to lose, but was also not looking forward to what lay ahead of her.

Tentatively letting the knocker tap a few times on the Lindenbergs' front door, she braced herself, forcing a smile on her face.

"Esther!" Inger, completely white-haired now and bent like an old stick, stood in the doorway, opening her skinny arms in a wide gesture. "*Mitt kjære barn.* My dear child, God bless, is it really you?"

Esther let herself be taken into the skeletal embrace, her tears flowing freely, both of exaltation and of ache. Shocked at the change in her old protector, Esther let herself feel the warmth of her embrace. How old had she become herself? She'd certainly aged more than the five years the war had taken. Twenty-four. She felt more like forty-four. Well, nothing exterior was important. Only what she felt—her love for this remarkable old lady.

"Inger, how have you been? I'm so glad to see you. How's Jens?"

"We're good, we're good! Glad it's finally over. Do come in. We hadn't expected you so soon."

"Well, you know me," Esther said wryly. "For me, it's not over yet."

"Come in first, dear girl. I'll put the kettle on. No talk of sadness right now."

Jens was sitting in an easy chair near the fireplace in the large, cozy kitchen, his ear glued to the radio and with the *Oslo Press* spread open on his knees.

"Our grandson is an important man now," the old farmer beamed, his eyes twinkling in exactly the same way as Tore's, "and we've been told on the bush telegraph that you've been very heroic as well, Esther. They call you *Jeger*, right?"

Esther shook Jens's free hand and was motioned to another easy chair by Inger, who started busying around them making coffee. It was good to be back in the old farm living room, where time seemed to have stood still. No furniture upside-down, no chaos, no sign of Nazi influence.

Just the familiar bright-clothed sofa and carpet, the potted plants in the window. Geraniums in full bloom. How was it possible? Everything seemed to affect Esther at this moment, even the fact flowers would bloom. She felt she would soon dissipate into a sobbing mess if she didn't fall back on both her finishing school and her commando training.

This was not the time to fall apart. She smiled back at Jens, a genuine smile.

"Not anymore, Jens. I can be Esther Weiss again. I actually came to collect my real passport." She looked rather forlorn.

"Ahh, yes," Jens observed, turning the volume on the radio down and folding his paper. "I wish we could do more for you, Esther, but Inger and I are too old. Tore's promised to help you with your search, hasn't he?"

Esther felt herself go rigid. She would have to explain she was only staying for a day, needed to board the train tomorrow before Tore would come and search for her.

"He did." Her voice was small. "But it's too much to ask from him right now. I'll go to Vienna on my own."

Inger stopped her work to intervene. "I don't think that's wise, my child. You don't know what you'll find. You need someone strong with you just in case."

"Please. I've thought it through. I'm sure I'll find people I know back in Vienna, and they will help me. I want Tore to rebuild his life here."

Inger shook her head. "You're a good girl, Esther, but I don't think it's wise."

"Well, I've made up my mind, but I promise I'll be back. I'm just taking the bare essentials from the attic. That is, if it's okay to leave our other belongings here for the time being?"

"Nobody uses that rat-infested attic," Jens grumbled as he slurped his coffee, "and I think the wife is right. It's too much hassle on your own, Esther."

"Please," she begged again, "I need to do this on my own. Don't tell Tore I'm here in case he phones."

The old couple exchanged a knowing look. Headstrong girl, nothing to be done about it. Esther hesitated a moment, then changed the subject.

"After the coffee, I'd like to pay a visit to Oma's grave. It's been way too long."

"We've kept it tidy for you. And Inger puts fresh flowers on the tomb every other week." Jens scratched the gray stubble on his chin and added in a soft voice, "We've thought so much of you all the days of the war. Prayed every night that the rest of your family members have come through."

"Thank you, I'll go now." Esther got up, unable to stand any more emotion. Inger understood what Esther needed.

"Look, I've got the daisies ready in a vase. Was planning to go today. Liberation day. Now you can bring them."

Grateful for the distraction, Esther walked through the budding fields to her grandmother's grave in the small graveyard in the village. Never in her whole, long life could high-class, sophisticated Oma Weiss have fathomed she would be buried in Søndre Nordstrand and not next to her husband at the Viennese Jewish cemetery in Seegasse.

The grave looked neat and tidy, as Jens had said. Esther bit hard on her lip. She didn't want to cry anymore. Crying hurt and made her unstable.

"I need my wits around me now, Oma. Please watch over me as you've always done. Keep your *Bärchen* safe, and let her bring our family back to Norway. I think I'll leave you here anyway. We'll all come. We'll all come back to you."

The soft wind rustled in the willows; a tiny rabbit jumped in-between the graves in her direction. It sat still, ears up. Curious round eyes taking her in. It was like a sign.

"I'll go now, Oma. I have a long journey before me, but I've shown I have strength and stamina. Now I need it most of all."

The wind rustled a little harder. The rabbit hopped away, showing its cute bobbing white tail as it disappeared in the bushes. White. Weiss.

They were the Weiss family.

Laying her hand on the white marble headstone, Esther found herself whispering the Kaddish in Aramaic, stealthily looking around her, but no one would understand a word she prayed anyway.

"Magnified and sanctified is the great name of God throughout the world, which was created according to Divine will. May the rule of peace be established speedily in our time, unto us and unto the entire household of Israel. And let us say: Amen."

"Bye, Oma! With God's will, I'll be back, bringing the rule of peace."

When she returned to the farm, Inger had laid the table for lunch and insisted Esther sit down and eat with them, but she had no appetite. Though the smell was delicious—freshly baked bread, apple compote, homemade cheese and pickles—it felt as if she was carrying a heavy stone in her stomach, and nothing else would fit in.

Inger wanted to hear no excuse as she patted the plush upholstery of her dinner chair.

"Sit down for a minute, and stop being like a cat on hot bricks. I'll help you get prepared after lunch, but first you need to get something of substance inside of you or you'll collapse before you've even set out."

Esther had to smile at the old lady's ardor. She was so sweet, in fact so very much like Oma and Mutti, though they would say it in posher words. So, she obeyed. The food tasted good, better than she'd had in all the war.

"See," Inger gleamed, "I know better what you need than you

know yourself." At that, she exchanged a knowing wink with her husband.

"I'll need to see if I can find my important papers in the attic to take with me to Vienna." She sighed. It would be hard, very hard.

"Do you want me to go up with you?" Jens was dunking a piece of bread in the cinnamon apples.

"No, I'll be fine. Thank you."

∾

It was Rebecca's violin case, Adam's electric train set. A present from Tante Isobel and Oncle Frerik on his twelfth birthday. Her mother's hat box, clothes, bric-a-brac they'd collected in the two years in Norway. Books. Photo albums. And the scent. The scent of home. Esther swallowed and swallowed, fighting her way to what she was looking for. Her father's briefcase. Documents she might need.

She was looking for their passports, but they weren't present. Had they taken them with them after all?

Finally, she emptied the contents of her father's briefcase in her valise without looking at them. The keys to their house on the Prater Strasse tinkled among them. On top, she put some clothes for the journey. Her hand hovered over the box with her engagement ring and the photo wrapped in a cloth. She took a sharp breath, then chose. The photo would stay behind, but the box with the ring went into her suitcase.

Finally, she put the *Rebecca* volume on top and closed the metal clips of her small valise.

∾

An hour later, Esther sat back in the bus that would take her to *Østbanestasjonen* where she would board the train to Gothenborg, then Copenhagen, Hamburg, through Germany to Austria. Her valise and her loyal war rucksack sat on the seat next to her.

Her mind was blank, her emotions calm. She could do this. Amidst all the euphoria of the liberated people, she could travel south to find the truth. *"I had built up false pictures in my mind and sat before them. I had never had the courage to demand the truth."* The sentence from *Rebecca* sprang to mind. This was what she was. A post-war girl plucking up the courage to confront the truth. It wouldn't be pretty; it was going to be ghastly.

Breathe, Esther, breathe!

She'd have to have the courage to face the truth of rumors about gas chambers, prisoners emaciated and ill, in striped pajamas, piles of shoes, heaps of extracted golden teeth...

What was the truth about rumors that six million Jews were killed? Men, women, children?

It couldn't be true. It couldn't. And yet, after all she'd seen in Norway, she knew the Nazis were capable of everything.

38

THE TRUTH

The train was late, but nobody seemed to mind. Around Esther, people were dancing, Aquavit bottle in hand.

"The King is on his way back home!" An elderly man shouted, throwing his hat in the air! "*Lenge leve kongen.* Long live the king!" People clapped, laughed, cheered.

Esther checked her watch, afraid she would miss her connection in Gothenburg. Finally, the old train rattled into the station and stopped at her feet. She would be glad to be inside, away from the festive crowds. Her head rang, and she felt nauseated. The old wound in her stomach acted up. *Damn Nazis*, she murmured, as she placed her valise inside the train first and then hoisted herself inside.

"Esther!"

He came running toward her in his shirtsleeves, a frown on his face. Before she knew what he was doing, he'd jumped on the train that at that moment set itself in motion. Esther saw he was slightly off-kilter. She'd never seen Tore drunk before.

She almost panicked. "What are you doing?"

"What are *you* doing, you mean?" he slurred.

"Tore, you must get off the train at the next station."

"You thought you could get rid of me that easily, Jeger?" He was drunk and angry. A Tore Esther had never seen before. As he slumped next to her on the seat, her thoughts raced.

"Did your grandparents phone you?"

The wink they'd shared.

"Yeah, they saved me, or rather they threw me in at the deep end. I suppose I'm in your bad books now, because you didn't want me to come?"

"You weren't thinking of coming with me like this? You haven't even got a coat, or clothes." Esther was at a loss.

Tore sat up a little straighter and rather pathetically thumped himself on his breast.

'I've got everything I need here, my heart and my passport!'

"Tore, no!" She shook her head. "You can't come with me like this."

He seemed to sober up suddenly. Grabbing both her hands in his, he said in an urgent, low voice, "Look at me, Esther, and tell me you don't want me to come. Really don't want me to. Then I'll hop off at the Swedish border. I promise."

At first, Esther couldn't meet his gaze. Her hands trembled. Despite his drunkenness, Tore's message was clear and simple. *I'll come with you if you want me. Yes or no?*

She had wanted him to come. Her reason for preventing him to go with her had been his right to his own life. But he said he wanted to. She raised her eyes, realizing she was crying. Her "yes" was muffled, laden with heartache. It was hard to look deep into his eyes, eyes she knew so well, who told her the story she wanted to hear, but couldn't. He held her gaze, all haze gone, then gave her hands a little squeeze.

"Then I don't want to hear another word about it. I'll get myself some necessities on our first stop." He looked at her coyly. "Before I raced to the station, my mother tucked a purse in my pants pockets. So, I lied. I've got a little more than just my heart and my passport. Now let me take a nap."

He slept with his head on her shoulder, the deep sleep of intoxication. Esther stared at the changing landscape in southern Norway without really seeing it, feeling the weight of his head on her and listening to his light snoring. She tried to think, make sense of herself, but couldn't. As always, not being able to act but being forced to sit still in a corner was not Esther's forte.

Was she glad he was coming with her? Or would it only make things more difficult the moment her heart would be broken in two? Because that was what she expected. Tore had always barged in, right from the start, demanded her attention, made himself heard. Loud and clear. But he was kind and thoughtful. And he'd been so fond of Rebecca.

Suddenly, it was as if she heard Oma whisper in her ear.

"Let it go, Bärchen. Accept his help. It is genuine, but what's more, you need him. You cannot walk through the valley of the shadow of death all alone. May God bless you both."

ESTHER AND TORE arrived at Wien Südbahnhof on 15 May 1945 after an arduous and upsetting journey through Denmark and Germany. Especially the days in Germany had been horrific, the people defeated, their cities bombed, an atmosphere of suspicion and revenge.

"We've done it!" Tore, donning a new summer coat, strapped his new rucksack on his back and grabbed the handle of Esther's valise.

"I can carry my own stuff," she protested, also hoisting her rucksack on her back, but the truth was she had only eyes for her city and ears for the familiar singsong Austrian-German voices around her. Esther was home. After six years abroad, she could finally breathe.

"You're okay?" Tore scanned her face, the line between his eyes deepening.

"Sure! I just have no words for all that's going through me."

"I can't imagine. Must be so much. Anyway, I have a plan," he

said as they disembarked and walked down the platform toward
the exit at Landgutgasse.

"Okay, tell me. I've come up with dozens of plans, but I keep
changing them."

The sight of the beautiful Schweizergarten, the green park that
lay opposite the station, made Esther halt in her tracks.

She was skipping rope in the park, Adam on his tricycle and Rebecca
with her own small pink bike. A picnic on Sunday, Oma under a white
parasol, Papi smoking a cigar lying on a checked cloth in the grass. Mutti
reading a novel.

Flashes, so many flashes, they came with every step she took.
Her breath faltered. She felt dizzy.

"Let's sit in the park for a bit," she gasped. "I need some fresh air
after this godforsaken journey."

Tore already set course to the park on his long legs, her valise
under his arm, checking if she was following him.

They sat down on a bench near the big pond.

"I have so many memories here. We came here often. We all
loved this park."

She knew she had to let him in, share her burden, but how and
in what? The spring sun shone down on them. Around them, the
Austrians were slowly waking from the torment of war. Esther had
to move with the tides, even if she wondered if she shouldn't have
stayed in Norway and picked up her life there.

"You can tell me everything. You know that, don't you?" Tore lit
a cigarette, though he hardly smoked. It moved him, too, Esther
could see that. And it made her feel even more helpless.

"What was your plan?" She eluded his offer for the time being.

"I think we should check into a hotel. One you have no memories of. That is unrelated to either your Jewish background, or
collaboration with the Nazis. Could you think of one? Though I'm
far from a professional in these matters, I think it's important you're
on neutral ground to face all of this." He waved his arm in the air as
if encompassing all of Vienna and what it symbolized for Esther.

She nodded thankfully. "Good idea. I think we could try *Austria*

Classic Hotel Wien. It's on my street, the Prater Strasse, but it *is* owned... or at least it *was* owned by the Jewish Scheiflinger family. I just... just would like to be close to home."

"Let's seek out your classic hotel then, when you're rested enough."

Tore was already up from the bench, stretching his long body to shake off the travel fatigue.

Walking into her own street with her small valise containing her family papers was hard, much harder than Esther had expected. Her knees were like jelly and the stone was back in her stomach. Every step, every cobblestone had a memory, most of them happy and carefree.

Her oppressed mood was reflected in what she saw around her. Craters where houses had been bombed away, rubble everywhere, people scurrying around hungry and with scared eyes. Not jubilant Norwegians with song and Aquavit.

The streets were patrolled by heavily armed Soviet soldiers in khaki uniforms, who whistled at the girls and didn't seem very different in their menacing presence from the Nazis seven years earlier. But they had brought freedom. Had perhaps liberated her family from the camps.

She looked sideways at Tore, who walked with his particular frown that things were not okay. A pang of ache jolted her. He should be celebrating up north, not going through another hell with her here.

As if he guessed her somber thoughts, he gritted through his teeth, "I'm glad you don't have to endure this on your own, Esther. It's not a pretty sight for sure. Never knew it was this bad for the people down here."

"Only for the Jews, and now the collaborators pay the price. As they should." Esther's fighting mentality was suddenly kindled by the sight of the post-war scene. She welcomed the adrenaline shot it gave. It felt much better than her defeat.

"Here we are." But then she looked doubtful again. Soviet officers with long machine guns guarded the entrance to the old hotel.

There was no sight of well-coiffed ladies in evening dress on the arms of gallant men in tuxedos drifting up the stairs to a Max Steiner evening of film music by the *Wien Philharmonic Orchestra*. The proud hotel, damaged by bombs itself, exuded gray drab and the total absence of music and gaiety.

"*Ist das Hotel geöffnet*?" She addressed the young mustached Soviet in German.

"Not for guests!"

Esther's face fell. "Oh, I'd so hoped..." Her voice trailed away while the foreign officer stared intently at her.

"*Papiere!*"

She handed him her passport.

"Are you a returning Jew?"

"Yes, but not from the camps. I fought with the Allies in Norway."

"And he?" The young officer chewed his thick mustache, pointing to Tore.

"I'm Norwegian, also did my bit in the war." The officer inspected Tore's identity papers with interest.

"Crossed into Finnmark October last year. 10th Rifle Division. We recaptured Kirkenes."

"Incredible!" Tore shouted. "Thank you so much. What's your name, if I may ask?"

"Lieutenant Shcherbakov." The Soviet clicked his heels and saluted. "It was my pleasure, just feeling bad about not being able to stop those bloody Germans from their scorched earth tactics."

"I would love to buy you a drink when you're off duty, Lieutenant Shcherbakov." Tore was clearly touched meeting one of the first liberators of his country. Shcherbakov exchanged a few words in Russian with his colleague.

"Come on in! We'll find you a room at the hotel. It's one of our headquarters now, but I'm sure we can fit you in."

Esther looked up at the soldier with gratitude and suddenly felt the weariness in her bones. She needed to rest, gather her strength.

They followed the Soviet into the lobby, which was filled with soldiers sitting at tables playing cards or reading Russian novels. They seemed very relaxed, their heavy boots on the Art Deco coffee tables and their rifles stacked in the corner. There were no ifs or buts about the Russians being lord and master in Vienna now.

"Will this do?" Shcherbakov had taken it upon himself to get them a room. He pushed open one door on the first floor, small with two single beds and a view of the inner courtyard.

"Wonderful, thank you." Esther looked longingly at the bed near the window. Her head throbbed, all the triggers and emotions proving too much for her.

"You lie and rest for a bit while I go down with our new friend and scrape us together some food, all right?" Tore had dumped his rucksack and Esther's valise on the floor and was already back at the door.

"You're sure?"

"Sure as pie!"

The door closed. She was alone. Finally. But she had no time to plan or think. Her brain shut off, and she slept.

It was dark when Esther woke. The room was silent, but there was noise in the corridors and the courtyard. Raw Russian voices, a new language, new people in her country. Turning onto her back, she stared for a while at the pattern that the lights from outside made on the ceiling. A vague smell of dust and old furniture hung in the room. Some part of her was at peace, home where she belonged, but a larger part was drifting, not knowing who she was or where she was going.

Awake now, though still groggy and disoriented, she slipped from underneath the duvet and switched on the overhead lamp. The room gave up its shadows; they were only inside of her now. The side of her head near her right ear still throbbed, a cruel reminder of Grini, but Esther resolutely opened her valise. Placed *Rebecca* on the bedstand, her clothes in the cupboard. Her father's papers in a heap on the bed. She opened Anna's book randomly and her eyes were drawn to a passage, as always befitting of her state.

"I stared at them, impressing them forever on my mind, wondering why they had the power to touch me, to sadden me, as though they were children that didn't want me to go away."

Papi's papers. His children. His legacy.

Most of her father's papers were from the shop and the atelier, his diplomas, the purchase of the house and workshop, her parents' marriage certificate and all their birth certificates. There was one closed envelope with Esther's name on it. Only her name written in her father's business-like handwriting.

She turned it around, hesitated. When had he written this, and why hadn't he mentioned it to her? It surely looked important, but somehow, she wished she'd never found it. It didn't feel like a good omen. Her father had clearly not left it in sight of her to find.

Should she open it now? Maybe he had meant it for her to read after his death. But what if it held important information that she needed to know now?

After much dilly-dallying, Esther got out her pocketknife and carefully removed her father's seal. It was a short letter in her father's characteristic square handwriting. She read:

Oslo, 15 February 1941

My beloved daughter Esther,

When you read this letter, it means your Mother and I have passed, and you are our legal successor. As our eldest child, I appoint you as sole executor of our will.

Here are the things you need to do. Our will is positioned with Advocatfirma Biering & Østvedt at the Keysers gate 15 in Oslo.

Esther stopped, torn between reading on and putting the letter back in the envelope. Her father might not have passed, and she wasn't supposed to read it yet. But her logic told her it was best to know as much as was possible before the search. Just in case. So, she continued.

I have instructed Paul Biering to assist you with everything you may need. Most of our liquidity and gold is safeguarded with Dreyfus Banquiers in Zürich, through a Jewish bank. I trust Switzerland will remain neutral and unoccupied for the duration of the war. Please divide all deposits equally among you, Rebecca and Adam.

As far as our house and workshop on the Prater Strasse are concerned, you have the papers and keys to prove they are yours. The original copies of all documents are with the solicitor's firm.

May God bless you on your journey, my child.

Your Father,

Franz Abraham Weiss

Esther stared at the letter; her mouth half open, trying to grasp the official tone and meaning of her father's words. The responsibility hoisted onto her twenty-five-year-old shoulders. Dry-eyed, clear-minded, her father's daughter. He had known. He'd foreseen it all, taken his measures. A businessman, always a businessman, wanting his family to lack nothing. Not this generation, not the next.

A love so deep, so warm and vibrant flooded through her as she sat on the old bedspread in the Austria Classic Hotel, only a stone's throw away from her father's shop. How he'd slaved for them, for his wife, for his mother. Always wanting the best for them.

And now?

She knew. Just like he had known, but she still hung on with the slightest sliver of hope. Still fighting the stone-cold truth.

39

PASSION

Tore entered the room, just when Esther was putting her father's papers back in her rucksack.

"I've brought you some *Apfelstrudel*." He placed the greasy paper bag on the small table and smiled at her. Another flashback tossed Esther back like a cork at sea. Her birthday two years earlier. Tore putting a greasy bag on the table. His mother's *sandbakkelse*. Her arrest.

She grabbed her head with both hands.

"I don't want to go crazy."

Tore was at her side in two strides, grabbing her by the shoulders, his grip gentle and yet firm. As he was.

"What is it, Esther? Please talk to me."

She let him hug her, needed his comfort, just for a little while.

"I'll be okay," she murmured against his chest, "I just keep having flashbacks. They derail me. I have to stay focused on finding my family."

"I'll help you with whatever you need. Tell me about the flashbacks, if you can."

"I can't. Even if I wanted to. They're like snapshots in short exposure film. I can't grasp the images, they flit in and out of my mind but when they're there, they are so sharp, like needles. I suppose I'm just tired."

"Sit down and let me grab you a coffee. The trolley is just outside in the corridor."

Tore was right. The coffee perked her up, and the *Apfelstrudel* was delicious. Esther licked the sugar from her fingers, which evoked another flashback of a lanky Gestapo officer crushing her hand while she clenched her teeth so hard, she wouldn't scream. She had difficulty opening her mouth to take another bite, but somehow she managed. She needed something in her stomach to have a little more resilience.

She cleared her throat, deciding to do as Tore asked of her. Open up, share her burden, though it didn't come easy.

"I found an important letter from my father among his papers. It involves... uh... his will in case he is no longer with us."

Tore said nothing for a while, seemed to search for words. "That must have been so hard. No wonder you're knocked sideways."

"His will is deposited with a solicitor called Biering in Oslo."

Tore's blue eyes lit up. "Oh, I know him. He's also my parents' solicitor. Fine fellow. We'll visit him when we get back." Then he stopped. "Or do you want me to pay him a visit him in case... in case you stay here in Vienna?"

She shook her head.

"No, I didn't mean that. It's of no immediate concern right now."

"So, it was just upsetting to read a letter as if your father is no longer here?" She felt Tore's concerned gaze on her.

"Yes. It made me wonder if I should read it at all, but as the envelope only held my name, I thought I'd better know the contents. He's put all he could safeguard in a bank in Switzerland." Esther raised her eyebrows in doubt. This was all so heavy and difficult.

"Then it should be safe there until you know more." Tore tried to sound upbeat.

"I'll try to tell you what's happening to me, Tore. You're making all this effort just for my sake, and I'm all over the place." She sighed, feeling conflicted as usual with this gentle giant.

"That's exactly the reason I'm here with you, Esther. By the way, while you were resting, I found out a thing or two by talking to our Soviet friend." Tore's face was serious, but he was clearly dying to tell her his news.

"Go on."

"Dimitri—that's the Russian guy—gave some tips on how to search for your family. The people who've been liberated from the concentration camps were repatriated as soon as they were fit enough to travel. Those who couldn't or wouldn't go back home—the so-called 'non-repatriables'—have been placed in camps. Usually by nationality. They're called Displaced Persons Camps."

Esther listened intently as she paced the room, fingers entwined at her back. A trace of hope in her chest, but doubt still wrinkled her forehead.

"But we won't know which camp to go to."

"The Red Cross should have those lists. Dimitri is willing to help us, but I didn't want to give your family's names without asking you first." Tore took a sip from his coffee, his eyes following Esther's nervous pacing between the window and the table.

"That's very kind of him. But what if they are... dead?"

"According to Dimitri, it's too early to expect a comprehensive list of the deceased, but bulletin boards are placed at stations and near synagogues where survivors go every day to read the names. Also, with this the Red Cross might be able to help us." Tore's eyes glimmered. He was so eager to help, but still Esther felt unsure about the whole procedure.

In a pensive voice, she replied, "I just don't know where to start. I fear the worst."

Tore poured her another coffee.

"Come and sit down for a minute. I suggest we start tomorrow morning. Take a good rest today. Oh, and I did one other thing." His expression was a trifle sheepish.

"What?"

"I... went to check out your house. You said number 24?"

Her eyes flitted to his face, alarm and anticipation struggling for first position.

"And...?"

He held off.

"It looks all right, not bombed or anything."

"But...?"

"Someone's living there. I saw a young couple come out of the front door with a baby carriage. They looked... un-Jewish."

Esther shrugged, acting as if disinterested, but in reality, her heart was pounding madly in her chest. Not her house, not her parental home, not now. She didn't want to hear about a strange family living there, so she waved it off with an impatient movement with her hand..

"No matter! I'll deal with that later. I got my father's papers to prove it's ours. But not now! Please."

"Sorry." Tore sounded affected as well. "How tactless of me to bring it up."

But Esther said in a toneless voice, "You couldn't know. You just tried to help. My parents fled to Norway just before they would've been evicted from the Prater Strasse. Carl wrote to me later that he and his parents were forced out of their house and had to move into a ghetto just for Jews. His family shared a two-room flat with two other families." And she continued with more anger, "Germans and Austrians were already confiscating our houses before the war. We were second-rate citizens then."

She got up again and resumed her pacing.

"Sometimes I hate this country and want to leave as soon as I find my family. It doesn't feel like home anymore. But we'll deal with my family's possessions later. It's the least of my worries."

We. She'd used *we.* Well, she was sure she couldn't do this part without Tore. Everything hurt, even the thought of strangers living illegally in their home.

"I agree! Family first, *Jeger!*" Tore presumably used her code name to boost her fighting spirit. She gave him a wan smile and mouthed 'thank you.'

That night Esther lay awake for a long time, trying to find a sense of home that was elusive, adrift in a city she felt she could no longer connect to. If, at that moment, she could have taken the train back to Oslo, she would've been very tempted. She now knew her real life lay there amidst the fjords, the Nordic temperament, the simple yet natural lifestyle.

Vienna was old, a remnant of the past, too stylized and sophisticated.

Vienna was just a mission. Esther's very last mission in this wicked, wicked war.

THE MIDDLE-AGED LADY at the *Österreichisches Rotes Kreuz* at the Vienna General Hospital was friendly, but extremely overworked.

"Have you been to the station? Have you been to the Stadttempel Synagogue? Those places first, please. We get so many requests. I'm not sure I can help you."

Esther had spread her family's birth certificates and most recent photos on the counter, but the secretary hadn't looked at them. Esther's heart sank. Didn't the woman understand every step on this path was painful and she, too, had no patience or time to lose?

Tore stepped in.

"We understood you have lists of people who returned. And perhaps people who didn't. Could we have a look at those lists ourselves? We won't bother you in your work."

The woman looked at Tore as if he'd bitten her.

"Of course not. These lists contain personal details. I'm not allowed."

"We only need to look at the list with W. The Weiss family. Nothing else." Tore had his foot in the door and was going to keep it there. Esther was thankful to him.

"Please," he added, "it's her whole family, Madame."

Tired eyes went to Esther's face. The kindness shone through the weariness.

"Alright, then. Five minutes. And don't take that ledger out of my eyesight. Keep it right here on the counter."

The moment the secretary put the heavy ledger in front of them, Esther felt herself go weak as a lamb that couldn't stand the weight of its own wool. Tore put a steadying arm around her waist.

"Do you want me to look? You can sit down on that chair in the corner, if you like?"

"No. I need to know."

She went through the alphabet to the dreaded W.

Franz Abraham Weiss, died Auschwitz 15 February 1942, cause of death: gas chambers

Adam Franz Weiss, died Auschwitz, 20 December 1941, cause of death: gas chambers

Naomi Bella Weiss-Aronson, died Ravensbrück, 15 April 1943, cause of death: exhaustion.

Black, a black world, forever black.

THE NEXT THING Esther knew was a white world. A high white-ceilinged, white-walled room with white curtains. She was in a bed, with white bedclothes, wearing a white gown.

She was alone.

She would always be alone.

They were gone, dead, murdered, exterminated. Gassed!

Her beautiful, always smiling, freckled brother whose soul was as pure as gold and who was free of all human sin. Mutti, caring, correct, strong-willed. She'd never said a bad thing about another person in her life. Too well-bred and exemplary. Jovial, warm-blooded Papi, who'd tried so hard to save his family and had failed.

Why?

Esther screamed at the white walls without words.

Why?

What had they done to deserve this? What in the world?

Slowly, she came back to a world that would never be the same. She'd feared it but had not believed it until the blue ink in the ledger had given her the truth she didn't want, couldn't cope with. The letters in that ledger were all she'd ever have left of them. Proof they lived and died.

But why was Rebecca not on the list?

And where was Tore? Whoever had put her in this bed had meant well, but it was time to leave. To find Rebecca and to find Carl.

Shuffling out of bed, she looked around the room. Voices in the corridor. The door opened.

Tore, his face ashen and evading her eyes, came in, followed by a doctor.

"Ah," the doctor stated, "I see you have recovered. Let me just check you."

"No need, doctor, thank you. I'd like to go now. I have to find my sister."

"But you are in shock, Miss Weiss. We'd better keep you here for the night. Just in case you have another breakdown."

"A breakdown? *Herr Gott!* I've just lost my family, and you babble about a breakdown? What are you, a psychiatrist?" She was vaguely aware she was taking out her anger on the innocent doctor but couldn't help herself. Someone had to take the blow.

"Where are my clothes? I have no time for this nonsense! Or do you want to lock me up here? Haven't you had enough of locking up and killing Jews?" Her voice must have been extremely loud, because an alarmed nurse looked around the door.

"Do you need anything, Doctor Wiesenthal?"

"No, we're okay here, Nurse Frida, you can go." The doctor spoke in a gentle, sing-song voice, clearly used to dealing with traumatized patients.

Esther's mouth fell open at the mentioning of his name. He must be Jewish! How was that possible?

"Please sit down," the doctor said, authority in his voice but of a friendly kind. Esther sank back on the bed. Tore kept standing like a statue in the middle of the room. He seemed in shock as well.

"I see my name calms you down and I'm glad of it." The doctor's voice was even, steady. "You are correct. I'm a psychiatrist but I'm a doctor, first and foremost." He stopped for a moment, took a breath. "I have survived three concentration camps, Esther. I've lost my wife and my three young children. Do you want to know how I survived?"

Through her eyelashes, Esther glanced at the young doctor who had pulled up a chair opposite her. A deep shame washed over her. How had she dared to shout at him like that? A man who'd gone through exactly the same as her family. The only difference was that he had survived.

She couldn't answer, sat like a mummy.

"It's okay. I understand your anger and you haven't offended me," he said. "Even in the camps I was a doctor, and I tried to help my fellow prisoners as best as I could. As soon as I was strong again, I came back to my hospital to work. I thank God for my passion, medicine. And that's all I can say to you, Esther. Find your passion; it will keep you alive. It will pull you through this dark night of the soul. Find it, whatever it is."

She nodded, just a slight movement of her head.

"I'm so sorry." Her voice sounded unnatural, not belonging to her. *Passion.* She told herself to remember that word. For later. When it would matter.

The doctor kept sitting in the chair, just looking at her, then cleared his throat.

"I told you I wanted to keep you here for the night. I had my reason for that, but now I'm having second thoughts. I have something for you that will help you in the search for your passion."

She didn't react. Didn't know what he was hinting at. Maybe a book or some study.

The doctor turned to Tore, who snapped himself out of his trance.

"How are you feeling, Herr Helberg? You seem out of sorts, as well. You must be a good friend of the Weiss family?"

"I am, doctor. So, it pains me I cannot help Esther reunite with her family."

"There's more to it than just that, isn't it?" the physician remarked.

Tore looked as if he wanted to speed out of the room and never return. Even Esther, in her grief, registered he was behaving in a strange, un-Tore-like way.

"Sit down, fellow, and tell us what is bothering you."

Esther looked from the doctor to Tore, who staggered to the other chair in the room and slumped down on it. He looked sick, even closed his eyes. For a moment, the sight of him like this made her forget her own misery.

"Tore, what's wrong?" All this time he had supported her, but now the stress seemed to overwhelm him. The doctor took charge.

"Never mind, Herr Helberg, let me take the burden off your shoulders. I see it's too heavy for you."

The doctor sighed.

"Another reason I wanted to keep you here, but it's a day of truths, so to speak." The doctor's light-brown eyes rested on Esther, and she braced herself for what was to come.

"What Tore tried to tell you was that he opened the ledger to the letter B. To check what had happened to the Bernstein family."

Esther's eyes widened. She held her breath. The doctor shook his head, saddened, compassionate, disheartened.

"I knew. I always knew," she blurted out. It was a half-truth to scaffold the truth of the thin hope she'd carried in her heart all these years. The pretence she'd known Carl wasn't ever coming back to her, would sustain her now, pull her through. Deny the hope, and you deny the pain.

In a whisper she added, "after his last letter, I couldn't wear my engagement ring anymore. I think I knew then." She kept repeating 'I knew then" as a mantra, and it did calm her somewhat. Maybe some part of her *had* known. Was it the moment she watched his navy jacket disappear in the crowds at the Swiss border? Was it? What did it matter now?

Carl was also gone. Gone. Gone!

The enormity of her losses couldn't sink in, not yet. What had the doctor said about passion?

"So why would you want to keep me here, doctor? I think I can manage. Tore will help me."

"Because there is more." He scrutinized her face now, more soul-doctor than medical man.

There was a slight tap on the door.

"Come in!" The doctor called, his eyes never leaving Esther's face.

A young nurse looked around the door, held out her hand and over the threshold stepped...

Rebecca.

Skeletal, almost bald, huge-eyed Rebecca. Tentative steps, looking back at the nurse who gently nudged her forward.

Esther sank to the floor on her knees, crying, "My God, My God, thank you, thank you."

And she understood what the doctor had meant about passion.

A fierce, animal love roared like fire in her chest.

She had a reason to live.

To love.

To love again.

40

THE LONG ROAD TO RECOVERY

"I remember laughing aloud, and the laugh being carried by the wind away from me." — Rebecca

SHE WAS SO THIN, so breakable, and yet her eyes shone with the depth of wisdom she'd always had. Ever since she gurgled in her little crib, tiny hands grabbing fistfuls of Esther's blonde curls.

Rebbie.

Esther hardly dared to touch her, afraid she would bruise that precious, brutalized being all over again.

"Rebbie," she whispered, "is it really you?" Unaware of anyone else in the room, Esther stood before her sister, overcome by a primal urge to embrace her only surviving family member but not daring to.

There was something aloof and adverse around her sister, as if she no longer belonged to this world. And though Rebecca made eye contact with her, she did not seem to share Esther's longing for physical contact.

"Essie?" It was more a question than a statement. Rebecca's voice was as thin as her body, but deeper than Esther remembered.

"Can I hold you? I need to hold you, Rebbie?"

Esther looked from the doctor to the nurse, asking them permission to do what should have been the most natural thing on earth. Doctor Wiesenthal nodded, so Esther took her twenty-two-year-old sister ever so cautiously in her arms. Rebecca didn't move a muscle, didn't answer her embrace.

Esther almost panicked, still keeping her arms around that strange-smelling, skeletal being. A waft of hospital antiseptics and cheap washing powder, light as a thin-boned bird, her skin rubbery and tight. Esther's heart broke all over again, but she had to accept that this impersonal girl was deeply traumatized, as yet unable to find her way back to some form of life worth living. What was her own trauma compared to what her sister had gone through? Nothing!

Please come back to me, Rebbie!

Rebecca wriggled out of her embrace, turning to Tore, who stood by the window. "Tore, is that really you?" Her voice had some of its former buddy-buddy quality.

"It's me, Rebecca. I'm so damn glad to see you." All the love of the world vibrated in Tore's reply.

Esther tried holding on to her sister, but she slipped out of her arms and ran to Tore, clamping her matchstick-thin arms around his waist. He held her, loosely, lovingly, and over Rebecca's head made a grimace at Esther that said as much as "I'm so sorry."

Rebecca started babbling straight away. "Did you bring your guitar, Tore? I've missed playing with you."

"Esther?" the doctor addressed her in a gentle voice. "Your sister will be safe with Mr. Helberg for the next minutes. Could you come with me to my office? I promise I'll take you straight back here."

Esther had a hard time tearing her eyes away from the once so lively and outspoken wisecracker, a glimpse of whom was now returning. She followed the doctor to his office. The soles of her feet wouldn't lift from the linoleum floor, while her heart wept.

Doctor Wiesenthal didn't pussyfoot around the difficult reunion.

"Don't take your sister's incapacity to be glad at seeing you again personally. I think it's heaven-sent that Mr. Helberg is with you. Rebecca has told me a lot about him, and he might well be the catalyst that helps her connect again with the world." Esther let her head hang. She was so disappointed, and the doctor's words didn't make it easier for her. Tore could have what her sister needed.

"Do you want me to tell you what we know of your sister's time in the camps? So, you have an idea before she's able to tell you herself, which may be a long time?"

Esther nodded, staring numbly at her folded hands in her lap. Drained, devoid of emotion, an emptiness so vast she didn't know a person could still breathe and feel dead at the same time.

"We know nothing about Rebecca's time in Auschwitz, where she must have arrived with your parents and your brother in August 1941. Your father and brother were sent to the men's camp, and your mother and Rebecca to the women's camp. At the beginning of 1943, your mother and Rebecca were transported to the Ravensbrück women's camp, north of Berlin. At the time of their arrival, your mother was already very weak and ill. Rebecca tried as best as she could to look after her, but lack of medical care and hygiene proved fatal for your mother."

The doctor ceased his monologue. It was clearly a huge wrench to retell a terrible tale, one he'd gone through himself.

"Just tell me the facts." Esther's voice was shaky, but resolute.

"After your mother passed, Rebecca had a small ray of luck. There was a female guard at Ravensbrück—her name was Angela Plagge—who wasn't as bad as the others. She'd found out that Rebecca was a great violinist, so she arranged that she could give concerts for the camp commanders. Rebecca was still treated badly and not given enough food, but *Overseer* Plagge definitely helped your sister to stay alive. Rebecca talks about her time in Ravensbrück but refuses to talk about Auschwitz, so I fear there's a big trauma there." The doctor's hazel eyes rested on Esther.

"How... was she liberated?"

"With the Red Army on their heels, the SS sent the female prisoners who could still walk on a death march toward Mecklenburg, clearly to erase evidence of what had happened in the camp. Many died on this last march. The handful of survivors were found by a Soviet scout unit on 30 April. Rebecca was immediately admitted to a Red Cross hospital near Mecklenburg, where they saved her physical life. When she was strong enough to be transported, she was brought to Vienna. She arrived about a week ago, so I've had little time to work with her."

"Does she... know of our father and Adam?" It was hard to mention their names.

"Yes." The doctor nodded. "I saw no reason to hold that information from her. And Rebecca wanted to know. She made that very clear."

"So, you think it is normal that she doesn't want to be close to me right now?"

"Yes, I do. See it as too much sunshine. You need shade. Rebecca needs to shade her fragile heart from the rawness of love."

"How long?"

Helplessness fought with reason.

"I don't know, Esther. Every patient is different, but I think we made a big step in the right direction today. Rebecca now has someone to hang onto, though I understand you had wanted to be that person. Give it time. Come every day, and slowly, very slowly build up your sister bond again."

"I want to go back to her now." Esther rose from her chair.

The doctor's eyes fixed on her.

"One more thing, Esther. You need help too. You've suffered the same losses. And you've had to live with the uncertainty about your family for years. I'm also here for you. We can do this together."

Esther stared at the white hospital wall, her mind blank, simultaneously feeling everything and nothing at all. For the first time, her training proved a handicap. Her first reaction was to wave the doctor's concern away. She could handle this. Esther Weiss could

and would always fight if given a cause to fight for. And that was
Rebecca now, only Rebecca. Not her own journey, up until this
point.

And yet, that big black blanket of fear that hung over her and
over all of Vienna. She felt the angst would suffocate her, especially
in the night.

The doctor must have sensed her inner struggle because he
said in that kind, sing-song tone, "Esther, you cannot help your
sister when you don't take time to acknowledge your own pain. It
has to be done, and the sooner the better. You want Rebecca to have
a chance at a normal life again, don't you?"

"Of course!" It came out angrier than she meant. Looking into
his wise, tranquil eyes—a man who certainly had had to fight his
own demons—she added more softly, "Thank you, doctor. You're
right. I might need help too. I always feel because I was a trained
commando during the war and was arrested and tortured myself,
that I'm stronger than I think. Rebecca certainly is my Achilles'
heel. I need to be another kind of strong for her. Not combat strong,
but soft strong, and I don't know how to do that anymore."

Doctor Wiesenthal nodded, but then looked thoughtful again.

"I still only hear you wanting to live for someone else. You'll
have to learn to live for yourself, too, Esther. And living, *really living*,
means learning to mourn. There is no backdoor out of grief. You
must go through the fire and come out the other side. You know I'm
not talking empty talk. I know myself how difficult, how impossible
it is to accept our loved ones are no longer with us." The compassion in the doctor's voice grazed on her mettle.

She pressed her lips together. Blinked.

"You're right. I accept your offer for help. Thank you again."

"When I'm around here at the hospital, just drop in. No need
for formality. Those days are gone."

Esther found Tore and Rebecca still engaged in conversation.
Tore was telling her of his time at the Home Front. Rebecca sat with
her legs tucked under her on the bed, wrapped in a warm blanket
and sucking on a Sherbet lemon; the bag with yellow sweets lay

next to her. She smiled as Esther entered the room, the beautiful smile that used to light up her sweet, almond-shaped face. Esther's heart swelled. Could it be?

"Hi, Essie." That was Rebecca. Esther shot Tore a grateful smile and he grinned, while his eyes were serious.

"Esther and I better go back to the hotel now, Rebecca. May we come back tomorrow?"

She screamed 'no' inside, having only had a few seconds with her sister so far, but she was dead-tired, suddenly unable to stand on her own two legs. So much had happened in so few hours.

"You're right. We'll be back tomorrow, Rebbie. Maybe we can go for a short walk together."

"Maybe." Rebecca's eyes glazed over, all her attention still turned toward Tore, her body limp and lifeless like a rag doll. The vague disinterest of her sister was too much for Esther. She swayed on her legs, more broken than she'd been in the entire war. Her only living sibling unable to connect with her.

Rebbie, please!

THAT NIGHT TORE held a fully dressed Esther in his arms. She needed to feel another alive human against her, for comfort, to know she was not alone. He held her close to him, let her cry, rage, exhaust herself.

There were only two of the Weiss family left now. And she would never be Esther Bernstein. How could she come to terms with it? It was too big, too finite to grasp.

But she slept, finally, drowning in her own tears, never wanting to wake up again. Unless... unless there was Rebbie to fight for and Rebbie wanted her.

Esther awoke in a damp dread that permeated the entire room, all of Vienna, the whole world. Anger replaced grief and then became blood-red hatred again.

Tore let her be, let her manhandle whatever she got her hands on. Wringing her shirt in her hands over and over until it was a gray rag. Pacing the room, and then collapsing on the bed again to sob her heart out. Then getting up and punching her pillow in anger.

Vaguely she realized this was what doctor Wiesenthal had meant when he'd said she had to grieve too. This immense well of bereavement and broken-heartedness had taken her over, forcing her to face it head-on. And this was only the beginning. A beginning that felt it would never end. It would only end when she finally lay down to die herself.

Death!

Briefly, it seemed an attractive solution that morning. Easier than the pounding pain that raged through her. A rage that ultimately served no purpose.

They would never come back. Not one of them. Ever.

Through the mist of her misery, she heard Tore say from afar, "Esther, Rebecca will be waiting for you. Do you think you cou…?"

She looked up through her tears. He was sitting at the table, white-faced and solemn, but inviting her with a gesture of his hand. She smelled coffee and bread.

Tore.

In all this agony, he never was anything but kind. He was… What was he? He was bliss.

Esther tried to calm herself, rubbed her eyes, and readjusted her clothes. She got up on weak legs to stumble toward the table.

"Thank you, Tore."

"Stop thanking me, Esther. You needn't."

Her heart was clearly a wide-open wound now because at that moment, a deep compassion for this loyal man washed over her. He seemed so desolate, so powerless, this formidable resistance fighter.

"Oh yes, I do." She managed a smile, but was shocked to see his blue eyes fill with tears. Rebecca was his Achilles' heel too.

She placed her hand over his.

"I'll be okay; we'll be okay!"

"I'm sorry." He blew his nose and poured her a cup of coffee.

PALE AND WASTED, Esther sat in the hotel's breakfast room, which was buzzing with Russian voices and the clanging of cutlery on plates. Some upbeat dance music blared from two speakers in the corners. Waitresses hastened between the tables, serving sausages and black coffee.

Tore had excused himself for a moment to chat with the Soviet he called Dimitri. Esther assumed he was still extracting information from the soldier. She sat fiddling with a piece of bread, in a moment of lull, dull emotions she welcomed amidst all the extremities of her feelings.

"Fraulein Esther? Esther Weiss, is that you?" She looked up from crumbling the bread. Frowned. One of the waitresses in a black dress, white apron, white headdress stood looking at her, serving tray in hand.

"Helga? Helga Müller?"

"Yes, it's me. *Mein Gott*, Fraulein Esther, you're alive?" Her mother's former maid looked stricken yet elated. The years and the war had not been friendly to her. A graying bun and ashy skin. But the eyes still had that resolute shine Esther remembered so well.

"How are you?" They asked it at the same time.

Helga clutched the empty tray under her arm, scrutinizing the daughter of her former employer.

"What's with your family?"

Esther shook her head. "I've just found out yesterday that only Rebecca has survived."

"*Mein Gott.*" Helga's hand went over her mouth. "*Mein Gott*, Frau Weiss und Alte Frau Weiss. I've had the best years of my working life with your family. Those wretched Nazis. But they'll pay for it, I tell you, they'll pay for it!" She clenched her fist and shook it in the air.

"Oma died in Norway; she was spared the ordeal of the camps," Esther said tiredly.

Helga sighed. "A small solace."

"And how have you been these years?" Esther needed to change the subject, the heaviness of it all.

"I've survived. That's all. I'm glad that Third Reich nonsense is finally over. I sometimes believed I was the only German who didn't hang onto Hitler's coattails, but of course, that isn't true. Yet life will never be the same."

Esther nodded, glancing at Tore. Though she was glad to see Helga, she yearned to go back to the hospital.

"Wait," Helga said. "Do you have a minute? I've got something for you."

"What is it?"

Helga had her stricken look again.

"I tried to help the Bernstein family after you left for Norway. It was too horrible what happened to them. Old Mr. Bernstein thankfully died before the worst, but Carl and his mother were evicted from their house."

"Yes, I know, he told me in his letter." Talking about Carl was very, very hard.

Helga continued, "I kept visiting them in the ghetto, just bringing them some food I could spare. Until they were deported to God-knows-where. But just before they were forced to leave, Carl gave me a note for you. I put it in an envelope and kept it for you. In case you would come back after the war. And here you are. Thank God! I've got it in my room here at the hotel. Do you want me to fetch it?"

Esther nodded, but had no voice to answer.

Helga hurried away and came back with a small white envelope. Esther tucked it in her coat pocket. She would read it later.

"Will I see you again?" Helga urged.

"Of course. I don't know how long we will be in Vienna. I'm here with a friend." She pointed in Tore's direction.

"Him?" Helga frowned. "Wasn't he the one who spoiled your engagement dress?"

Despite herself, Esther burst out in laughter. "He is indeed. His bark is worse than his bite, though. Tore's family's been very good to us in Norway. And Tore adores Rebecca."

As if he'd heard his name, Tore came toward them, clearly surprised to see Esther in animated conversation with one of the waitresses.

"You!" Helga prodded a tapered finger almost into Tore's chest, who shied away from the anger she radiated.

"I plead not guilty," he joked, but Helga kept up her stern look.

"You ruined the girl's beautiful day, do you realize?"

Confused, Tore looked from Esther to the fuming waitress.

"She's talking about my engagement dress," Esther clarified. "Helga used to be my mother's and grandmother's maid."

"Oh, I'm so sorry." Tore looked guilty. "I guess there's nothing I can do in your eyes, Madame, to undo my terrible crime?"

"It's okay, Helga, I've long forgiven Tore. We've fought together against the Nazis in Norway, and we've become good friends."

Helga eyeballed the tall Norseman with suspicion. Esther could see her brain cells working fast.

"We're friends, Helga, just friends!"

"All right. I'll see you again soon, Fraulein Esther." Tore got a nod. "Got to get back to work." Helga scurried out of breakfast room.

On their way to the hospital, Esther felt Carl's letter burn in her pocket.

"Have you got a minute?" She sank down on a bench in a public garden.

"Sure."

Staring at the blank envelope, she hesitated, but then quickly tore it open. The note was written on the backside of a ration card. His handwriting was hurried and untidy. The ink blotched, but she could make out the letters.

10 August 1941

Dearest Esther,

I must leave soon and am not sure what will happen to us. Things don't look good. We're leaving for Poland.

In case I can't come back, I have one wish. If you ever marry and have a daughter, please let her have my ring on her engagement. That way, I will still be a part of you.

I love you always,

Your Carl.

Esther burst out in tears. Tore quickly sat down next to her.

"What happened?"

She handed him the note.

"*Kjære Gud!* Dear God," he exclaimed, "come here, girl." He pulled her close, let her cry. "He must have been such a nice man."

"He was," she sobbed, "he was."

41

RÄDSTADTER TAUERN PASS

December 1945

F rost had bitten into the tall windows of the apartment on Währinger Gürtel in Vienna's 18th district. The ice flowers made a lovely, lace-like pattern on the windows. Soft snowflakes, whirling in the wind, clung to the icy patterns and stuck there.

Inside the apartment, Helga opened the soot door of the coal stove and added a shovel of coal. The stove roared like an untamed lion. The fierce eastern wind immediately sucked the flames into the chimney. Quickly shutting the stove door again, Helga brushed the gray-white flakes from her arms and hands. The small Mika windows radiated an orange-red light.

Esther and Rebecca were sitting opposite each other at the dinner table, playing a game of chess. Esther's chin rested on her hand as she studied the pieces on the board, while Rebecca sat leaning against the back of her chair, squinting through her eyelids, seemingly relaxed and detached, but all too ready to strike.

"Have you done all the shopping for Sabbath, Helga?" Esther broke her concentration to take charge of her little household.

"We're expecting a special guest." Before Helga could answer, Rebecca cheered.

"Checkmate!"

She clapped her hands in glee. "You shouldn't think of trivialities when you play against me, sis! That always does you in."

Admitting her defeat, Esther simpered, "Even if I gave it my all, you win, Rebs. You're just a master at chess. Too strong for me." She raised her arms in mock despair. Rebecca loved winning, and Esther loved everything that made Rebecca happy. She looked across the table at her sister, the soft brown hair in short curls now, dimples in her lean face, the dark eyes glittering with mirth. She was wearing a dark-green merino dress that hugged her slender frame and covered the horrific tattoo on her lower arm.

As always, as her eyes rested on her beloved sister, Esther felt tears well up, but these days the sadness was mingled with deep joy.

"I did," Helga assured her. "I'll make you girls your favorite dish. The *challah* breads are ready. I'm just not pleased with the skinniness of the chicken I could buy at the market, but it will have to do."

"Another game?" Rebecca asked eagerly. "It's still morning. Our appointment at the hospital is only in two hours."

"All right!"

Rebecca was already putting her white pieces in order on the board. Helga left for the kitchen.

"Who's the special guest?" Rebecca lifted one eyebrow as a question mark.

"It surprises me it took you so long to ask," Esther jested.

"Well, it's never anyone I know, so why should I care?"

"You know Doctor Wiesenthal. You knew him before me," Esther retorted.

"Oh him, that's not a surprise." Rebecca drew a face which contorted her pretty features.

"Rebbie! He's been so good to us, and he has no one to celebrate Sabbath with. We owe him."

Rebecca couldn't help pulling another face. "I think you've fallen in love with your psychiatrist, sis!"

"Hush, Rebecca! Nothing of the sort. You should know better than that."

"All right, don't bite! I'm just afraid you'll end up an old spinster!" Rebecca rolled her eyes.

Esther planted her elbows next to the board on the table, temporarily forgetting the game. She gazed intently at her only surviving next of kin.

"We should both be finished with our therapy before the end of this year. And you're so much stronger now. Have you given it a thought where you would want to live?"

Rebecca's dark eyes lit up.

"I don't know what that has to do with your 'special guest but yes, I have." She added nothing more.

"Well?" Esther toyed with her queen.

"I'm not saying it." A serious expression slid over her sister's features. "I don't want to go anywhere where you wouldn't be happy, Es. We have a good life here now, thanks to Papi's diligence and care. Helga's been our absolute prop and stay, these months. And yet..." Her voice drifted off.

"Yet?" Esther almost held her breath. Was her sister feeling the same she was feeling?

Almost inaudibly, Rebecca whispered, "I miss Norway."

Esther blew through her teeth, a gulf of relief flooding her veins.

"So do I! And that's my surprise. Tore's coming to visit us. He's arriving tonight."

"Tore?" Rebecca jumped up from her chair and started dancing wildly through the room, "Oh, I missed him so! Did the government let him go?"

Esther felt herself smile all over. She was overjoyed herself.

"Yes, his *Departementet for sosiale saker* will be run by his deputy Sigrid Grannes for the time being."

"Oh, I'm so, so happy!" Rebecca wouldn't stop dancing. "Can we go to Rädtstadt with him? Just for a week? Where we originally met him?"

"Would you like that?" Esther pondered the option and then quickly added, "I think it's a brilliant idea. Get some skis under my feet again and, of course, beat Tore!"

"Yes, yes, yes! Oh, Es!" Rebecca swirled toward her sister and collapsed in her arms, laughing, crying, incredibly vivid and alive.

Hand-in-hand, they stood stamping their feet on the platform for international arrivals at Wien Südbahnhof. Both were wrapped in thick woolen coats, hats, shawls, and gloves, looking like two polar explorers. Vienna was readying itself for an ice-cold winter. Esther felt her heart thump wildly in her chest and wondered why she was so elated.

Tore had said goodbye to them at the beginning of June when Rebecca's initial reserve toward Esther had slowly melted. The new interim government had offered him the position of Minister of Social Affairs, and Esther had seen the longing in his face. Being a member of the first post-war Norwegian cabinet was the greatest triumph of his years of striving, much more than any medal would do.

"Go!" The sisters had agreed in union. "Go after your dream, Tore!"

But now he returned, writing he missed his girls and longed to see them for prolonged Christmas holidays.

THE TRAIN slowly came to a caterwauling halt. Screeching doors opened, passengers from the north thronged out, carrying bulky suitcases. Some with skis. The skiing season was just about to open. Esther craned her neck. Where was he? Rebecca spotted him first with her quick eyes.

"Tore!" She boomed over the noise. Rebecca's thin camp voice had gained its strength and melody over the past months, but Esther thought Tore would recognize her sister's voice from the end of the earth. Rebecca let go of Esther's hand, running full speed toward the tall Norseman, who dropped the bag he'd been holding and opened his arms. Esther watched, feeling a pang of jealousy for their open affection for each other, then corrected herself. She walked in their direction, small, slow steps, to give them time to welcome each other.

Over Rebecca's head, Tore's eyes locked with hers. The blue shone like a precious diamond, glistening with a single tear. There was so much love in those eyes, more than her heart could take, and she stopped in her tracks. People began bumping into her, scolding her clumsiness.

With Rebecca still tucked under his arm, he picked up his bag, and heavily loaded as he was also carrying a rucksack, closed the distance between them.

"Rebs, let me go for a moment as I greet your sister."

"Sure, I'll hold your bag for you." Rebecca released herself from her friend and smiled at Esther. A victorious smile, or at least that's how she read it.

"Esther, my Esther." His voice was thick with emotion as he took her in his arms and held her, kissing the top of her blonde head. "How have you been, my dear one?"

"All right, I've been more than fine, Tore, but it's absolute bliss to see you." She couldn't help herself but melted in his arms, forgetting the obstruction they formed on the platform, her sister's happiness, her own fear.

Never love another man again!

She felt he didn't want to let her go either, but the pressure of their surroundings forced them apart. Esther's cheeks were red from confusion and embarrassment. Tore was Rebecca's and Rebecca was Tore's.

She quickly hid her red cheeks under her shawl and said in a chirpy voice that sounded insincere to herself, "Let's get home. Helga is waiting with the dinner."

~

A week later

A late dawn peeked its head above the snowy Radstädter Tauern Pass. Cold red sun, crisp new snow, a cerulean blue sky. A perfect day for skiing. Esther woke with an avidness she hadn't felt in years.

A holiday.

Who'd have thought it possible that she could be on a holiday? With her sister and her best friend! Even the absence of her beloved family and fiancé could not kill her joy. Their spirit was with her here in the inn, even as she lay awake in this rustic bedroom with its checked curtains and beamed ceiling, her sister's even breathing in the other bed. This was home, her family's sacred place.

Felix, the Himmlhof Innkeeper and his now middle-aged daughters, had not stopped shaking their hands and praising "Herr Gott" for their return. Rebecca thrived in the mountain air and now even took part in their skiing competitions.

Esther was happy but...

There was one thing that pressed her down as she lay in her comfy bed listening to the Inn coming alive. She had to tell Tore it was all right to propose to her sister. Rebecca had been waiting for this moment since she was fifteen, and it was clear Tore only took her fragile health into consideration with his delay. Rebecca was strong enough and wanted to return to Norway.

Esther would follow them and find herself a job. She'd always be close to the two people in her life who meant the world to her. Be part of their family, godmother to their eldest child. Then why was she crying? Why were the tears dripping down her temples onto the white pillowcase?

SCINTILLATING white slopes sparkled like precious diamonds before her eyes. For a moment, Esther stood to admire the perfect slope with a small red dot in the valley waving at her. She adjusted her skiing glasses and checked the fasteners on her skis. Tore waited patiently.

"You're ready?" He grinned, but she couldn't really see the expression behind his dark glasses. Rebecca had chosen to wait down in the valley.

"I want to hold the stopwatch this time. But I bet Esther will win," Rebecca had announced before Esther and Tore went up in the ski lift. Esther had thought it odd. Rebecca always took part in their first morning competition, only opting out when she became tired in the afternoon.

There had been a strange tension in the lift on the way up. Esther had wondered if he and Rebecca had quarreled but didn't dare to ask. Tore had been distant, fidgety.

I'll race him as hard as I can; that will put the fire back in him, she thought.

"I am ready to beat you, Mr. Tore Helberg," she declared, pricking her poles next to her skis.

The smile didn't leave his face, but his jaw twitched.

"Never in a thousand years, Miss Esther Weiss!"

They went down, fast, passionate, keeping abreast for the first half of the slope. Then Esther felt she was losing speed and wondered what happened. She fought herself back, closed the distance between them again, constantly keeping the zigzagging Tore in her vision. But he was beating her more and more, no matter how much she urged herself on.

I'm not as strong as I used to be, she thought. *But I will not give up. I never give up!*

Yet Tore beat her. Crossed the finish line three ski lengths before her. Panting, her hand in her waist, her spleen aching, she accepted her defeat. For once, Tore had been the stronger of them. Rebecca was jumping up and down with glee.

"Take my stopwatch, Tore!" she cheered.

It happened so fast. He was on one knee before her in the snow, his eyes gazing up at her timidly but full of that boundless love.

"What are you doing?" Esther's eyes grew huge.

"Esther Weiss, would you do the honor of becoming my wife?" He clicked open a small box, what Esther had thought was the stopwatch. She looked astounded from Rebecca to Tore in the snow. Rebecca was wildly nodding yes.

"But..." she began, "but it is you and Rebecca? It's always been..."

"Shut up, sis!" Rebecca put two fists in her waist and stood wide-legged next to Tore.

"Tore's my best friend, but he's to be your lover, your husband."

"But..." Esther's lip trembled.

"Don't let the poor man lie there in the snow until he's frozen," her little sister commanded. "Just say yes or no. Simple as pie."

Esther stared at the beautiful ring with a heart-shaped emerald, the color of her eyes, that first dress.

"But Tore," she said, wiping the tears from her cheeks with her gloves, "Tore, do you want to marry *me*?"

"I do, but only if *you* want to have *me*, my dear." His voice was solemn, slightly unsure.

She stretched out her hand and pulled him up.

"I do. With all my heart. I fell in love with you on my birthday in 1943. I knew then you were the one but never dared to dream you would love me back." She hesitated. "Or that I would be - you know - available."

He held her, tenderness and strength in one, all that Tore was. Warm lips sought hers, waited for an answer. His eyes staring deeply into hers. Passion, friendship, survival. His voice held all of it as he answered.

"I wanted you from the first moment I saw you. Throwing cocoa over you was my only way of making sure you'd never forget me."

She kissed him back. Crying, laughing and crying again.

"Oh Tore, oh Tore. I love this life. I love you!" She motioned to Rebecca and pulled her into the family embrace.

"I guess you played a part in this, you little devil of a sister?"

"Phew," Rebecca sighed, "I'm not one for matchmaking. I tried to get the two of you together in Oslo in 1939. And where are we now? Almost 1946. No, not my best job."

They all laughed. Cried and laughed again.

"And the ashes blew toward us with the salt wind from the sea," Esther quoted.

EPILOGUE

Helga Müller followed the Weiss sisters to Norway and dedicated her last serving years to looking after Jens and Inger Lindenberg. On the farm, she became acquainted with farm hand Leif Berg and eventually married him. Lindenberg farm—with permission from daughter Liv and the rest of the family—was inherited by Helga and her husband.

In the summer of 1946 Esther, Océane and Lili were able to reunite at À La Petit Chaise on the Rue de Grenelle in the 7th Arrondissement in Paris and stayed lifelong friends.

Esther also continued to correspond with Edda Van der Falck, Anna Levi and Sable Montgomery.

Tante Isobel Gjelsvik died in Auschwitz in November 1943, but Oncle Frerik survived Grini prison and returned to his leather business on the Grønlandsleiret. Their two sons Ole and David, who'd been staying with Frerik's sister, returned to their father after his release. As their only other surviving family, Esther and Rebecca stayed close to their uncle and cousins.

Tore's parents, Liv and Eivind, were overjoyed with their son's engagement to Esther. Daughter Astrid remained Rebecca's lifelong best friend. Dog Bodil lived until the ripe age of fifteen.

Skipper Helmik, Anton Tronstad, Claus Nielsen, Arne Rønneberg and Sigrid Gannes also remained resistance friends for life with the Helbergs. Arne gave Esther away at her wedding, which finally sealed the lid on Tore's fear that she loved Arne instead of him.

Doctor Chaim Wiesenthal became a renowned survivors' psychiatrist in Vienna and London. He wrote many widely read books on the topic.

Rebecca studied music at Oslo Conservatory and married the Jewish Norwegian poet and concentration camp survivor Ben Adler. The family was completed with son Adam and daughter Yasmin. From the early 1950s, Rebecca traveled the world to lecture on Holocaust awareness.

Esther and Tore were married in Oslo in a combined Protestant/Jewish ceremony in January 1946. Their marriage was blessed with one daughter in 1948, Naomi Liv Helberg.

Tore remained Minister of Social Affairs in the Norwegian Cabinet until 1949 when he returned to Oslo University to finish his geology studies. He eventually became the director of the Norwegian Polar Institute.

Esther specialized in skiing lessons for war victims. The Helbergs bought a resort in Tryvannskleiva, which they named the 'Franz and Naomi Weiss Recuperation Center.' Esther also remained a reserve commando in the Norwegian Military until 1956.

All the surviving and killed Norwegian Resistance fighters who made their appearance in *The Norwegian Assassin* were decorated with the highest war medals by King Haakon in 1947.

The spirits of Oma, Franz and Naomi Weiss, brother Adam and Tante Isobel were forever in everybody's hearts. Never forgotten were all the other victims of the concentration camps in Poland, Germany and Norway.

The Norwegian Resistance fighters—the real heroes of this book—many of whom have given their lives for the freedom of their country, are honored by the people of Norway until this day.

~

I HOPE YOU ENJOYED Esther's harrowing journey through WW2. You've just finished the 4th book in *The Resistance Girl Series*. Three more will be following. Among them Sable's story in *The Highland Raven*, of which you can read the first chapter on the next page.

BUT BEFORE YOU TURN THE PAGE, I would like to stress that the Norwegian Resistance movement played a vital role in Norway's and Europe's liberation from the yoke of fascism in WW2. Would you like to know more about the REAL heroines and heroes in this fight?

You can.

I wrote a brief introduction to the Norwegian Resistance movement, which you can download it for free by clicking this link: The Norwegian Resistance 1940-1945. (Ebook) You will also receive all the inside Hannah Byron news via my newsletter.

Rather read more of my fiction for free? Sign up for a free copy of Doctor Agnès by clicking on the title. (Ebook)

And a big **Thank You** for reading my latest novel.

Warmly,

Hannah Byron

~

SNEAK PEEK: THE HIGHLAND RAVEN

CHAPTER 1 ALL THE RAIN IN THE WORLD

Alnor Castle, Scotland, January 1938

Brittle, raw sleet pelted the leaded windows of the library in the east wing of Alnor Castle. The twists of storm and deluge caused the delicate, colored glass to creak in its leaden panels, shooting an icy draft along the floorboards of the spacious, book-filled room. Three open fireplaces that roared like the devil were not sufficient to produce a favorable temperature in the Victorian chamber.

Even though it was merely three o'clock in the afternoon, the lamps had been lit above the reading table to keep the gloomy weather out. The Art déco lampshades with their zigzags in ruby red and sapphire blue cast a flirtatious shimmer on the oak table below but provided little light. Still, fire and lamps established a veneer of coziness.

The rainstorm shielded the normally stunning view from the library over Loch Fyne with its emerald water, arched shoreline and the Arrochar Alps across the loch. None of the familiar sights were visible today, but even if they had, it would've made no difference to Lady Sable Montgomery who, wrapped in her mink coat, sat at the table.

Two slender fingers with tapered, coral nails fastened around the gold-inlaid fountain pen. Prominently at the top of the cream sheet of paper, Sable had jotted in her childish script.

Herr Von Henkell.

Now the pen hovered over these three words and with an angry scratch Sable crossed out 'Herr'.

Shifting in her chair, she stifled the clatter of her teeth while a deep shudder rushed through her body. The delicate jaw, half-covered under a mass of silken black hair, was clenched, but her cornflower-blue eyes were dry, even though red-rimmed. She paused a moment and suddenly the words jumped of their own accord from her Parker, criss-cross over the pad, like an illustration of poorly drawn grasses, showing rhyme or reason.

Drecklig.

I hate you all.

No right.

Mummy's Lover.

Swine.

Burn in Hell

Dirty Paws.

It was MY ba...

She ripped the page from the writing block and crumpled it into a ball that landed with a precise arc into the fire. Sable got up from the table with such animosity that the antique dinner chair toppled on its back. She dealt it another kick as she marched to the fogged-up window.

"No!" she hissed, pressing her heated forehead against the cool glass. "You'll not paper me into submission. Not now. Not ever. I detest the lot of you and I'm out of here."

But how? Sable felt the dry palms of panic tighten around her neck. How was she, at nineteen, going to break free from here? Without her allowance, snubbed by society like a bad apple? Not even her charming features and fashionable dowry would help her out of this pickle. And it wasn't like Freddie Frinton-Smith would be coop-a-hoop to wed her now, not even when his father's estate was facing extinction and the Montgomery money would be like lavish water on a withering plant.

"No!" she repeated firmly. "I'm not marrying Freddo; I'm not marrying anyone. I'll stay at Alnor until Dad gets home. He'll supply me the money. He'll have to. Then I'll leave for good."

"The scandal, you know!" Sable cocked her head, her voice affected and high-pitched, mimicking her mother.

With her index finger, she drew a heart on the damp glass with a smaller heart inside, hastily wiping it out with her palm.

"No!"

The third 'no' was loud and clear. Turning her back to the window and leaning against the windowsill, Sable scanned her father's library in the dying light of the winter afternoon. Apart from the crackling of the fire and the sleet that beat the windows like popping corn in a pan, the room was quiet, far away from the bustle of the grand kitchen and mother's cocktail party. This wing of the castle was hushed in silence. As if Sable had strayed into Sleeping Beauty's realm, where all the inhabitants were comatose.

"If only," she grimaced, "If only I had the power to make them sleep eternally. All of them. That would be their deserved revenge."

Her father's bookcases ran along three walls, many of the volumes dating back to the 18th century, thick brown leather volumes silently collecting dusk and musk but filling the cases from floor to ceiling. In between the bookcases the sad deer heads with dead eyes spread their antlers to the stucco ceiling.

Except for the cleaning maids, nobody ever entered this place anymore. Not after the Earl Archibald Montgomery, 6th Baron of Alnor, had separated from his adulterous wife a year earlier, and made his London house on Cavendish Square his permanent residence.

Then how on earth had she, Sable, landed here? She'd sought solace, sought the distant presence of her absent father. Once this had been his favorite room, the cornerstone of his ancestors' literary collection. His proudest inheritance. Once upon a time. High-brow Daddy, who lived for books and hunting parties.

Dad. Talcum, tweed, and tobacco. She could smell his scent to this day. Her small hand in his, lying side by side on a knoll of grass, stalking the gigantic stag Dad called Christopher.

The memories were bittersweet. Even Dad had let her down, left her in care of her uncaring, selfish mother. Knowing she would be ruined by her, just like flapper girl Misty Fletcher had ruined him twenty years earlier.

Did he love her that little?

"Sable?" Nellie's docile voice sounded from the door. A soft knock. Sable's hackles were raised. Spying around her, it crossed her mind to slip behind the velvet curtains and pretend she wasn't there. But her body failed her, as transfixed and frozen as her mind.

"Oh, there you are. What on earth are you doing in here, my dear? It's freezing and your mother is asking for you." Nellie, silver strands in her once frisky, blond hair, her small eyes fluttering both guilty and innocent, looked up at the young Lady, nervously rubbing the palms of her hands on her navy, silk skirt.

Sable stared at the maid, hard, not moving one muscle while the blue eyes flashed. *How dare you!*

The wimpy maid, one of her mother's latest useless additions, cast her colorless eyes to the floor. "Will you come, Lady Sable? It would cause so much less trouble."

"No! I want my tea here. I actually want a bed made up here in the library for tonight. Tell Butler Simms to bring the foldable bed down and my bedding. You can bring my nightwear!"

The light-gray eyes flashed quickly up before going down to the carpet again at the sight of the red-tapered finger pointing at her like a loaded gun.

"You can't, Lady Sable, it's unheard of." It came out in a nervy whisper.

"What happened in this damned place is what's unheard-of, Nellie. Now, do as you're told. I'm waiting for my father to return."

"Yes, Ma'am. At what time would you like your tea, Ma'am?"

Irritated by the maid's 'ma'am-ing', Sable sneered. "Now! And make sure no one disturbs me here until I've spoken with my father."

"But Lord Archibald might be held up in London. It may be days before he returns." The guilt in the maid's voice made Sable cringe, and she felt the blood rise to the roots of her hair. She breathed in and out, trying to calm herself. Nellie had only been sent here to smooth ruffled feathers and would likely to be sent packing by the whimsical Lady of the house if she failed in her mission to get a grip on the obstinate daughter. The maid looked so miserable on her spot on the Persian carpet, Sable strode over to the table, grabbed her pen, and scribbled across the pad.

"Mother, it is my express will to stay in the library until Father returns. Nellie is not to blame. I don't want to see you and I think you know why! Sable."

Tearing the sheet from the pad, she folded it in four and handed it to the help already shrinking away.

"You don't deserve this favor from me, Nellie, but I hope it'll cover your spineless back."

"Thank you, Ma'am."

"Out!" The red finger flashed once again in the maid's direction. Nellie backed out in a hurry; her soft-soled shoes soundless as a burglar's.

Sable turned to face the window, her shoulders sagging, a tremendous sadness enveloping her soul. Jamming her fists in the pockets of the mink coat, she stood, realizing she'd always been alone but never so much as now. The hole in her body was a size larger than life.

She felt beaten, backstabbed, bastardized.

Sleep came in fits but gave no respite. Sable didn't know if lying awake on the uncomfortable bed with the slates pressing into her back was better than the brief intervals of unconsciousness. She'd promised herself no more crying but, in the night, in that unfamiliar library with the wind howling around the west corner of the Scottish highland castle, the memories pressed upon her as grain is crushed by millstones.

She'd long lain awake hoping to hear the familiar screeching of the Roll Royce's tires on the gravel, a sign Dad had answered her cry for help. Being able to hear his arrival had been Sable's other reason to choose this outpost of the castle, but after midnight it was clear, he'd not return tonight.

A dozen outrageous plans flitted through Sable's restless mind, from a tour through the outback of Australia, to studying Art in New York. Anything to get away from England and Scotland, from Mother and Von Henkell. But Sable cared little for adventure trips and even less for art. She knew it was naïve, but she'd never considered her future in any seriousness.

"Well, it isn't easy to know what you want when you're dragged from one boarding school to the next, spending your holidays with parents whose only engagement is being at each other's throats and not being endowed with any special skillset yourself," she thought not without self-deprecation.

High time to change it. But what did she want to do? In all honesty, she didn't want to do anything. If there had been a Sleeping Beauty pill that took her out of this world until everything was nice and normal again, she'd gobble it up.

As the gray morning brought a fresh dose of sleet and shallow light, Sable finally fell asleep. The dreamless, deep state of oblivion she'd begged for. When she woke, it was in a confused, blurry state, her eyes still closed when there was a rap on the door.

"Dad?"

"No, it's me, Freddo. Can I come in? Are you decent?"

"Freddo? What are you doing here at this ghastly hour? And who told you I'm here?" Sable shot up, wildly grabbing around her on the bedclothes to locate her dressing gown she'd spread out over her for warmth. Inwardly, rejoicing at hearing her friend's voice.

"Ghastly hour, Sab, it's eleven o'clock. Have you been partying again?"

"No, I haven't." Stuffing the cushions behind her back, she rubbed the long black locks from her sleepy eyes. "You may come in."

The first thing she saw was his back, as he kicked open the door with his shoe, then he turned around, grinning widely as he displayed the breakfast tray he was carrying.

"Hello, Sunshine!"

His smile, the slick black hair, the glance in the blue eyes under smooth brows. As always when she saw Freddie after a while, it struck Sable how familiar he looked, the odd resemblance between them, almost like a twin brother.

Sable frowned, deciding to look disturbed by his unannounced appearance.

"What *are* you doing here?"

But Freddie was undisturbed, placing the tray on the table with the same broad smile and coming towards her, slopping down on her bed as if it was the most normal situation in the world to find his childhood friend asleep in the middle of the morning in one of the dampest and most uninhabitable places of Alnor Castle.

"Does it matter? I'm here! I'm here for you. Coffee, tea, a freshly baked bun?"

His good humor and infectious laugh worked to perk her up. The shimmer of a smile lingered on her lips.

"Alright, Freddo, maybe I am a little pleased to see another human who isn't around just to rip out my soul. Make it a coffee, to wake up."

"That bad, huh?" The blue gaze rested on her, serious for a moment, but Freddie slipped off the bed and darted to the table.

"You must tell me, Sab, why on earth you're hankering down in this backwater of the barony. You're getting way too eccentric before even hitting twenty."

Sable watched the slim back, the almost graceful movements as he raised the silver coffeepot and poured the black liquid into the gold-rimmed cup, then buttered a bun for her with his little pinky raised. Too graceful for a man. The gossip about his Oxford student time, more revolving around fellow students than girls, had reached her ears. Could it be true? Did she need to marry Freddie Frinton-Smith, not just to redeem herself but also to save him from himself?

As if he'd guessed her musings, Freddie said in a low voice. "You think you're in a pickle, Sable Montgomery, well here's another example of terrible trouble in perfect paradise."

Forgetting her own misery, she immediately blurted out. "What's wrong, Freddo? You know you can tell me anything. You're the only one who knows about my dire doldrums." Making up alliterations had been a fun game since Sable was in pinafores and Freddie - three years older– in plus fours.

Handing her the cup and saucer and placing the buttered bun in her lap, he sat down, staring at the sleet-covered windows with the look of a punished dog. He seemed to search for words, suppressing deep-seated emotions. Sable wasn't sure as she studied his profile, as if trying to find the answer there. Should they...?

With a sudden spasm, Freddie raised himself from the pit of his obvious despair to face Sable.

"Is horrible Henkell still here?"

Sable frowned, unable to follow this new train of thought, while she was preparing herself to hear what was troubling her friend. Her white teeth bit into the bun bad-temperedly and with her mouth full, she spat out. "How should I know? I've set up camp here immediately after returning from the clinic. Haven't seen a soul. And what does it matter? Or do you want to kill him for me?" A sarcastic smile flashed in his direction.

Freddie certainly wasn't himself today as he now took time mincing over her proposition as if it was a real possibility. After a while, he said in a clipped voice. "I would, Sab, if that would solve the problem. I'm hating Germans more by the day and this specific specimen is even more loath worthy than the rest. I'd just hoped Von Henkell would've shown the decency to return to his ambassador post in London. I think his Benz was on the drive, though. Can't even keep his dirty paws off your Ma."

"Don't worry about Mother," Sable snapped, "she won't let anyone's paws, dirty or clean, touch her unless she wants to." And with a sigh, she added. "Alas, not a skill I seem to have inherited from her."

Freddie ignored her last remark. "I don't know what's wrong with these Germans. Never cared much for the Krauts anyway, but since Hitler is whipping them into a frenzy, all hell has broken loose. I was in Frankfurt with David only last week and..." He stopped abruptly, rubbed a weary hand over his forehead, then added in an overly chirpy voice. "More coffee, perhaps?"

"For Pete's sake, Freddo, what's bothering you? You hop from one topic to the other like a restless robin."

Uncertain eyes scanned her face and Sable saw how raw he felt. He looked exactly like the little lost boy he'd been at age ten when his new fishing tackle, a birthday present from his beloved grandfather, was swallowed by the wild current of River Clyde and he stood watching it swirling downstream. That look, lost and guilt-ridden at the same time. 'A soul a tad too sensitive for this world', her father would say.

"Alright." Freddie surrendered. "I truly came here for you, motored up all the way from Oxford in that draughty two-seater of mine to see how you were doing, Sab, but I am not entirely altruistic. Not doing well myself." A new silence, a sigh. "Dad's found out about David and me." A quick glance in Sable's direction, pleading understanding. "Thus far, it's all been just for fun, a bit of old-boys-together play, but with David...it's different. Serious. Real."

Sable listened intently, her heart swelling with pride that he finally confided in her, though she'd no idea what he was talking about. How could two men be serious about each other? In what way? It sounded like something from a novel.

"Dad's furious. Fumes he'll disinherit me unless I get engaged to a suitable debutante or any marriageable girl. This year. Or it's game over." Hurt blue eyes sought her help and Sable felt her stomach squeeze tight, a wave of wooziness. *He was asking her without saying so much. He was.*

Was she destined to marry Freddie, after all?

"But... but," she stammered, "we don't love each other in that way, Freddo. We're buddies, odd creatures that don't fit in with the rest."

"I know." The voice was almost inaudible. "But you're in a dead spot as well, so maybe we can help each other out."

"It's not that it hasn't been on my mind, Freddo. I just think it wouldn't be fair on either of us."

"Well, we are odd creatures as you said yourself. We don't need to live like husband and wife. I'd never claim you or tell you what to do or not to do."

"Like a marriage of convenience?"

"Yes, something like that, though I'd totally understand if you wouldn't want to be associated with a man who prefers his own sex."

Sable thought about this for a moment, had to admit the idea of a male couple didn't really appeal to her, but Freddo was Freddo. If this David made him happy, who was she to stand in his way?

She shrugged. "It's all rather sudden. I was thinking of going abroad myself. Just cut out the past year and start somewhere afresh. Only haven't got an inkling where to go to, or what I want to do."

"We could go to Italy, Sab? Live there for a while, though I'm itching to join the RAF and become a pilot. I'd like to throw some bombs on Hitler's Eagle's Nest near Berchtesgaden."

This last remark made Sable burst out in laughter, a high tingling sound that gurgled up from her throat. "You, a fighter pilot? I still remember you saying the best human action is lying on the soft sofa, listening to Duke Ellington, while snuggling the round bottom of a Johnnie Walker Black Label whisky glass in your hand."

Freddie jumped up from her bed and started pacing the room on his long, slender legs, a deep line furrowing the black eyebrows.

"For once, I'm serious, Sab. Frankfurt and that mess you landed in with that gory German ambassador have changed me. If we go through with this wedding thing, I'll see you're looked after in a place where you want to be, but after that I will join my university air squadron at RAF Abingdon in Oxfordshire."

"Okay, okay. Don't bite off my head. But what does David say about your flying craze?"

"We'll go together. He wants what I want. Now get up, Sab, I've got a plan and I think we could pull it off."

"Tell me first." Sable felt wonderfully re-energized by their conversation, seeing a way out of the cold and uninhabitable library where she had barricaded herself, but the plans for their unorthodox wedding were still completely shady to her.

"How about we go to Glasgow to escape the parish priests and have our runaway wedding today?"

"Glasgow?" Sable looked shocked. The idea of an 'irregular marriage' without her parents was an end-of-the-line scheme even to her freethinking mind.

"Why not? We can do it today if we want. Glasgow's about one hundred miles from here. If you get your lazy bum out of bed now and we hop into my two-seater, we'll arrive before 2 o'clock. Plenty of time to tie the knot."

Sable looked doubtful. "And then, what do we do then?"

"Hang around, get drunk." Freddie's laughter lacked cheer.

"I haven't got a dress."

"Don't be silly, Sab. You've got at least one hundred dresses in your upstairs cupboard."

"I'm not leaving the library." She sounded obstinate.

"Then ring the bell and ask that weasel of a maid of yours to bring your stuff here. We don't have to tell her what for."

Sable liked the idea Freddie was taking charge, and her mind worked fast. Nellie could pack her a suitcase. She'd tell her she was going to stay with the Frinton-Smiths for a week. There would be no red flags about that. And they could slip out the back door and avoid the main entrance. But then additional problems popped up.

"What if my father comes back for me? I haven't got a dime on me."

"We'll phone your dad as soon as we're married. Don't worry. I still have my allowance. We can live on that for at least a couple of weeks. Until our families get used to the idea, we're a decent married cople." Another cheerless laugh. "Now, is it a yes or a no, my dear? I thought you'd jump at a new Freddo-Sab flimflam like a greedy girl."

Sable was aware of the seriousness underneath the banter, and it was ultimately the agonized merriness - her own exact feeling - that made her cry out. "Alright, make me Mrs Frinton-Smith if you must. I'm quite done with being a Montgomery.

∾

Half an hour later they were racing down Alnor Avenue in Freddie's Green Morris 8, the beige soft-top rattling, the wind howling, and her white-leather suitcase strapped on top of the trunk with a piece of rope. Cold and warm in the same breath, Sable felt terrified and exhilarated; too ruffled to utter a single word, but hoping she was finally taking her life into her own hands.

One last glance at the Gothic towers of Alnor Castle, gray, grim and stony-hearted; the hated black Mercedes in the drive, gleaming in the late morning sun. She could still smell the warm leather of the back seat. It made her retch.

Letting herself sway by the moves of the Morris on the curvy highland roads, Sable was sure as her present pain, she'd never set eyes on the place again.

∾

The Highland Raven is coming 27 September 2022. Find out more by signing up for Hannah Byron's Newsletter

∾

AUTHOR'S NOTE

The Norwegian Assassin is a book of fiction based on a period in history, the Second World War, about which thousands of non-fiction books have been written by historians. It's their job to explain to us what *actually* happened.

Alas, the majority of WW2 historians were/are men, who are often eager to point out the heroism of their gender and not sufficiently interested or uncomfortable when the same bravery was shown by women. There are exceptions, as always, but we must be aware that our perception of history is colored by what historians tell us, which isn't always accurate.

As a historical *fiction* author, I serve a different purpose than a historian and can take the few stories we have of exceptional heroines and magnify those.

I do that in every *Resistance Girl Novel* I write but the disclaimer on the title page is imperative to me. I take the liberty to digress from the historical truth to serve the purpose of my story. I counterbalance the 'old boys' code' with my flamboyant and sometimes reckless women.

The Norwegian Assassin is my contribution to shed a light on the brave women(!) *and* men who fought in the Norwegian Resistance movement of World War 2.

This book is in no way an actual account of living persons and has sprouted in its entirety from my imagination. Both the military and civilian actions may lack in accuracy, or are total fantasy. I'm not a historian and I only incorporate actual events when they serve my story. At the risk of being considered disrespectful, I use the world wars as the canvas for my heroines. But let there be no doubt! I have immense respect for the real people who stood up against the tyranny of Nazi Germany. The *Resistance Girl Series* is my way of paying tribute to the generation of my grandmothers and - fathers.

What I *have* tried to portray as accurately as possible is how these women and men must have felt, what they saw, what happened to them, how it changed them. War is a beast, but people are not. I've dived deep under the skin of my main characters to bring out the universal emotions of devastation, pain, courage, doubt, fear and LOVE that trying times evoke.

My respect for the Norwegian hero(in)es of their time is reflected in the names of all the characters that play a part. At the end of this Note you'll find how I changed the fictive names to the real heroes with a link to their resistance work in WW2. The bad guys are similarly woven into the story.

In the scope of *The Norwegian Assassin*, I would like to point out the following liberties I've taken.

Jewish People in Norway during WW2

I have found no direct evidence that Austrian Jews considered Norway as a safe place after Hitler's Anschluss of their country in March 1938. We know, of course, that Jewish families – like the Hoffmans in The Norwegian Assassin - fled to other European Countries, such as France and Holland, where they sadly weren't safe after all. Thus, was the fate Norwegian Jews shared.

In my book Esther's family is deported to Auschwitz in June 1941 but this is historically incorrect. All the Jews living in Norway were rounded up and deported at the end of 1942. I changed this date so I could have Esther join the Resistance movement earlier on in the war.

Many Norwegians tried to help their Jewish countrymen and women when both the SS and its Norwegian counterpart Hird, drove the Jews from their homes. Some actions were successful, where they created escape routes to Sweden. Sweden remained neutral throughout the war and wasn't invaded.

However, of the roughly 2,000 Jews living in Norway, at least 800 were arrested, detained, deported, and murdered. Only a handful survived their imprisonment. Around 900 were smuggled out of the country by the Resistance Movement. This is a remarkably high percentage, and it was partly based on the strength of the movement and partly on Norway's vastness and sparse population, which made hiding and escaping easier.

I realize that these are small numbers of Jewish victims compared to those in other countries, but it's still a story worth telling.

No female assassins

No matter how hard I tried, I haven't been able to find registered evidence that women took up the arms in the Norwegian Resistance. Until the very last, when this book was already edited and ready to go out: Eva Jørgensen (see the background book for her story). The lack of female fighters has surprised me, as the Scandinavian countries are renowned for their gender equality – at least today. In many European countries such as France, Holland, Poland, Russia female militia was an accepted feat during WW2.

I've come to the following conclusions for this lack of female "assassins", though it's not based on real evidence.

1. Norway's male population had not suffered the losses that other countries had during WW1, as it remained neutral and didn't take part in combat. Hence, there

wasn't the shortage of men like in other European
countries, France in particular.

2. The account of the happenings in Norway during WW2
   may be well documented, but have not been translated
   into English and are therefore not readily available
   outside Norway. There might have been more women in
   arms, I just couldn't find them.

One thing is sure: there were no female *commandos* taking place
in the raids described in *The Norwegian Assassin*. There were no
women taking part in the landings on Normandy (D-Day) either. In
most armies around the world female commandos were only
admitted in the last decade of the 20th century and up till today
their numbers are slim. The requirements for passing the physical
tests prove too hard for many women. Alas. Even more admiration
for those who can!

The most well-known woman in the Norwegian Resistance was
Anne-Sofie Østvedt, who was one of the leaders of the Norwegian
intelligence organisation XU, but even information on her is sparse.

The Raids described in The Norwegian Assassin

Two sabotage raids described in the book are based on real
events but have been modified and changed to fit in with my story.
Operation Archery (the killing of Captain Linge) and Operation
Grouse (heavy water plant sabotage). Concerning this last raid, I
absolutely recommend watching the YouTube series called The
Real Heroes of Telemark by Ray Mears. Interviews with the real
commandos (now all passed away) and a reconstruction of how
they did it with a team of British and Norwegian contemporary
soldiers.

The destruction of the cards from the Labor Service, to prevent
young Norwegians from being called up to fight on the German
side (as described in chapter 35) is also loosely based on actual

happenings in Oslo in 1944 but have been given the Hannah Byron twist. Alas, our heroine, Esther Weiss, wasn't really there.

As said before, I did my research on the Norwegian situation in WW2, but this is not an actual reconstruction. For more background information see the Glossary of Terms, or the free booklet Introduction to The Norwegian Resistance, which is a freebie with The Norwegian Assassin.

Explanation of names

All the important Norwegian names in the book lead back to either heroes from the Norwegian Resistance, or traitors. I've changed first and last names. In the eBook you can click on the real name to be taken to the Wikipedia page and find out who this person was.

First the heroes:

Fictional name Real name

Tore Helberg Claus Helberg
    Frerik Gjelsvik Tore Gjelsvik
    Claus Nielsen Roy Nielsen
    Magnus Linge Martin Linge
    Arne Rønneberg Joachim Rønneberg
    Arne Kjelstrup
    Anton Tronstad Leif Tronstad
    Sigrid Gannes Sigrid Steinnes (only in Norwegian)
    Sonja Wigert as herself (only mentioned)
    Skipper Helmik Helmik Knutsen Wallem (no site)
    I only found Eva Kløvstad-Jørgensen at the end of my research and have been unable to incorporate her in my story.

The Villains

Harald Rinnan Henry Rinnan
    Jonas Hagelin Albert Viljam Hagelin
    Jonas Lie
    Vidkun Quisling (as himself, see glossary of terms)
    Josef Terboven (as himself, see glossary of terms)

GLOSSARY OF TERMS

Glossary of Terms (alphabetic)

Anschluss
   "Union", political union of Austria with Germany, achieved through annexation by Adolf Hitler on 12 March 1938. More info: https://en.wikipedia.org/wiki/Anschluss

Auschwitz concentration camp
   Also called Auschwitz-Birkenau was a complex of over 40 concentration and extermination camps operated by Nazi Germany in occupied Poland during World War II and the Holocaust. Over 1.1 million men, women and children lost their lives here, mostly Jewish, but also Roma, homosexuals, politic prisoners and handicapped people. More info: http://auschwitz.org/en/

Chancellor Schuschnigg's referendum
   Kurt Schuschnigg, the chancellor of Austria, announced a referendum in 1938 whereby the Austrian people would decide for themselves if they wished to join Hitler and Germany. If the

Austrians voted against joining Germany Hitler's plan for invasion would be ruined.

Later Hitler told his generals to prepare for the invasion of Austria, Hitler then ordered Schuschnigg to call off the referendum. Hitler knew he wouldn't receive help from Italy, and that France and Britain would not interfere in Hitler's plans, so Schuschnigg conceded. He called off the referendum and resigned from power.

Germany invaded Austria without a problem because no one stood in their way anymore. After taking control Hitler rigged the referendum and the result was that the people "joined" Hitler and Germany.

Edward VIII and Wallis Simpson

Edward was the British king from 20 Jan-11 Dec 1936. He abdicated to be able to marry the twice divorced American socialite Wallis Simpson. After his abdication, Edward was created Duke of Windsor. They married in France on 3 June 1937, after her second divorce became final. Later that year, the couple toured Nazi Germany. Rumors of strong and friendly ties to Hitler remain persistent to this day. Hitler was in favor of getting Edward back on the throne once he'd conquered Britain. That, luckily, never happened. After the war, the couple spent the rest of his life in France. More info: https://en.wikipedia.org/wiki/Edward_VIII

German Occupation of Norway

The occupation of *Norway* by Nazi Germany during the Second World War began on 9 April 1940 after Operation Weserübung. Conventional armed resistance to the German invasion ended on 10 June 1940 and Nazi Germany controlled Norway until the capitulation of German forces in Europe on 8/9 May 1945. Throughout this period, Norway was continuously occupied by the *Wehrmacht*. Civil rule was effectively assumed by the *Reichskommissariat Norwegen* (Reich Commissariat of Norway), which acted in collaboration with a pro-German puppet government, the Quisling regime, while the Norwegian king Haakon VII and the prewar government escaped to London, where they formed a government in exile. This period of military occupation is, in Norway, referred to as the "war years", "occupation period" or simply "the war". More info: https://en.wikipedia.org/wiki/German_occupation_of_Norway

Gestapo

Is the abbreviation of Geheime Staatspolizei (German: "Secret State Police"), the political police of Nazi Germany. The Gestapo ruthlessly eliminated opposition to the Nazis within Germany and its occupied territories and, in partnership with the Sicherheitsdienst (SD; "Security Service"), was responsible for the roundup of Jews throughout Europe for deportation to extermination camps. More info: https://en.wikipedia.org/wiki/Gestapo

Grini detention Camp

This prison camp (Norwegian: *Grini fangeleir*, German: *Polizei-häftlingslager Grini*) was a Nazi concentration camp in Bærum, Norway, which operated between 1941 and May 1945. Altogether, 19,247 prisoners passed through Grini. The total number killed at Grini is unknown. It was mainly used as torture prison by the Gestapo and the police. More info: https://en.wikipedia.org/wiki/Grini_detention_camp

Heavy Water Sabotage

The Norwegian heavy water sabotage was a series of Allied-led efforts to halt German heavy water production via hydroelectric plants in Nazi Germany-occupied Norway during World War II, involving both Norwegian commandos and Allied bombing raids. During the war, the Allies sought to inhibit the German development of nuclear weapons with the removal of heavy water and the destruction of heavy-water production plants. The Norwegian heavy water sabotage was aimed at the 60 MW Vemork power station at the Rjukan waterfall in Telemark.

The three successive raids were Operation Grouse (partly

described in The Norwegian Assassin), Operation Freshman, and Operation Gunnerside. More info: https://en.wikipedia.org/wiki/ Norwegian_heavy_water_sabotage

Herschel Grynspan

(28 March 1921–presumed dead 8 May 1945, declared dead 1960) was a German-born Jew of Polish heritage. The Nazis used his assassination of the German diplomat Ernst vom Rath on 7 November 1938 in Paris as a pretext to launch *Kristallnacht*, the anti-semitic pogrom of 9–10 November 1938. Grynszpan was seized by the Gestapo after the Fall of France and brought to Germany; his fate remains unknown. It is generally assumed that he did not survive World War II, and he was declared dead in 1960.

Hird

The Hird (Norwegian: Hirden) was a uniformed paramilitary organisation during the occupation of Norway by Nazi Germany, modelled the same way as the German Sturmabteilungen and organized by Vidkun Quisling's fascist party Nasjonal Samling (See other entries) More info: https://en.wikipedia.org/wiki/Hirden

Josef Terboven (23 May 1898-8 May 1945)

was a Nazi Party official and politician who was the long-serving *Gauleiter* of Gau Essen and the *Reichskommissar* for Norway during the German occupation. With the announcement of Germany's surrender, Terboven committed suicide on 8 May 1945 by detonating 50 kg of dynamite in a bunker on the Skaugum compound. He died alongside the body of *Obergruppenführer* Wilhelm Rediess, who had shot himself earlier. More info: https:// en.wikipedia.org/wiki/Josef_Terboven

Kristallnacht

A Nazi pogrom throughout Germany and Austria on the night of November 9–10, 1938, during which Jews were killed and their property destroyed. It was triggered by Ernst von Rath's murder. See Herschel Grynspan More info on the "Night of Broken Glass": https://en.wikipedia.org/wiki/Kristallnacht

Linge Company (official name Norwegian Independent Company 1)

was a British Special Operations Executive (SOE) group formed in March 1941 originally for the purpose of performing commando raids during the occupation of Norway by Nazi Germany. Organized under the leadership of Captain Martin Linge, it soon became a pool of talent for a variety of special operations in Norway.

The original English-language administrative title did not have much resonance in Norwegian and they soon became better known as Kompani Linge (*Linge's Company*). Martin Linge's death early in the war came to enhance the title, which became formalised as Lingekompaniet in his honour.

The members of the unit were trained at various locations in the United Kingdom, including at the SOE establishment at Drumintoul Lodge in the Cairngorms, Scotland.

Their initial raids in 1941 were to Lofoten (Operation Claymore) and Måløy (Operation Archery), where Martin Linge was killed. Their best known raids were probably the Norwegian heavy water sabotage. See all info in other entries. More info: https://en.wiki pedia.org/wiki/Norwegian_Independent_Company_1

Nasjonal Samling

was a Norwegian far-right political party active from 1933 to 1945. It was the only legal party of Norway from 1942 to 1945. It was founded by former minister of defence Vidkun Quisling and a group of supporters who also led the party's paramilitary wing (*Hirden*). More info: https://en.wikipedia.org/wiki/ Nasjonal_Samling

Norwegian Resistance Movement (in Norwegian: *Motstandsbevegelsen)*

Was the resistance of the Norwegian population to the occupation of their country by Nazi Germany, which began after Operation Weserübung in 1940 and ended in 1945. Resistance in Norway took place through a variety of actions, military organization, disinformation and propaganda, guerilla attacks and outright warfare. More info: https://en.wikipedia.org/wiki/ Norwegian_resistance_movement

Philipp Etter (21 December 1891, in Menzingen – 23 December 1977)

was a Swiss politician. During World War II, he took a decidedly conservative, adaptable friendly policy toward Nazi Germany and a particularly considerate attitude towards Italy. More info on Switzerland's neutrality during WW2: https://en.wikipedia.org/ wiki/Swiss_neutrality

Ravensbrück concentration camp

was a German concentration camp exclusively for women from 1939 to 1945, located in northern Germany, 56 mi north of Berlin at a site near the village of Ravensbrück. More than 80 percent were political prisoners. Of some 130,000 female prisoners who passed through the Ravensbrück camp, about 50,000 perished; some 2,200 were killed in the gas chambers. More info: https://en.wikipedia. org/wiki/Ravensbr%C3%BCck_concentration_camp

SA

Is the abbreviation of Sturmabteilung (German: "Assault Division"), byname Storm Troopers or Brownshirts, German Sturmtruppen or Braunhemden, in the German Nazi Party, a paramilitary organization whose methods of violent intimidation played a key role in Adolf Hitler's rise to power. More info: https:// en.wikipedia.org/wiki/Sturmabteilung

SD

Is the abbreviation of Sicherheitsdienst (German: "Security Service"). It was the intelligence agency of the SS (see below) and the Nazi Party in Nazi Germany. Originating in 1931, the organization was the first Nazi intelligence organization to be established and was considered a sister organization with the Gestapo (formed in 1933) through integration of SS members and operational procedures. The SD was administered as an independent SS office between 1933 and 1939. That year, the SD was transferred over to the Reich Security Main Office (Reichssicherheitshauptamt), as one of its seven departments. Its first director, Reinhard Heydrich, intended for the SD to bring every single individual within the Third Reich's reach under "continuous supervision". More info: https://en.wikipedia.org/wiki/Sicherheitsdienst

Shetland Bus

was the nickname of a clandestine special operations group that made a permanent link between Mainland Shetland in Scotland and German-occupied Norway from 1941 until the surrender of Nazi Germany on 8 May 1945. More info: https://en.wikipedia.org/wiki/Shetland_bus

SOE

The Special Operations Executive (SOE)was a secret British World War II organisation. It was officially formed on 22 July 1940 under Minister of Economic Warfare Hugh Dalton, from the amalgamation of three existing secret organisations. More info: https://en.wikipedia.org/wiki/Special_Operations_Executive

SS

Is the abbreviation of Schutzstaffel (German: "Protective Echelon"), the black-uniformed elite corps and self-described "political soldiers" of the Nazi Party. Founded by Adolf Hitler in April 1925 as a small personal bodyguard, the SS grew with the success of the Nazi movement and, gathering immense police and military powers, became virtually a state within a state. Its ruthless leader of

Heinrich Himmler. More info: https://en.wikipedia.org/wiki/
Schutzstaffel

Vidkun Quisling (8 July 1887 – 24 October 1945)

was a Norwegian military officer, politician and Nazi collabo-
rator who nominally headed the government of Norway during the
country's occupation by Nazi Germany during World War II. By the
way, in some languages the word "quisling" became a synonym for
traitor after WW2. More info: https://en.wikipedia.org/wiki/
Vidkun_Quisling

Vienna Opera Ball

The Vienna Opera Ball (German: *Wiener Opernball*) is an annual
Austrian society event which takes place in the building of the
Vienna State Opera in Vienna, Austria on the Thursday preceding
Ash Wednesday (a religious holiday).

The tradition of the ball goes back to 1814 during the time when
the crowned heads of Europe and the aristocracy searched for
entertainment after the Napoleonic wars. The first ball in the opera
house took place in 1877 as a *soirée*. The following balls were *redoute*,
a French term for masquerade balls or costume parties, where the
ladies wore their masks until midnight.

The first ball to be named "Opera Ball" was held in 1935 under
the honorary patronage of the Federal Chancellor, but was
suspended during World War II. It was revived after the war; it has
been held annually ever since, with the exception of 1991, when it
was cancelled due to the Persian Gulf War. To this day, the Vienna
Opera Ball is the highlight of the season, with heads of state, political and industrial elite and members of the high society attending.

In February 2020 the first same-sex couple were presented as
debutante and escort at the ball. The two debutantes, Iris Klopfer
and Sophie Grau, were from Germany. Klopfer wore the traditional
white dress, long white gloves, and tiara typical for female debutantes while Grau, who is non-binary, wore the traditional black
suit and tailcoats typical for male escorts.

Wehrmacht

The Wehrmacht was the unified armed forces of Nazi Germany from 1935 to 1945. It consisted of the Heer, the Kriegsmarine and the Luftwaffe. More info: https://en.wikipedia.org/wiki/Wehrmacht

Get the free book on The Norwegian Resistance here.

ABOUT THE AUTHOR

"Ever since I could hold a pen, I've written poems and stories, and I'll write till my dying day."

Hannah Byron is the pen name of Hannah Ferguson. Born in Paris (France) in 1956, Hannah is of British/Irish/Dutch descent. She lives in The Netherlands.

Byron became a published author in 2012 and published seven books under her own name. After a forced break from writing because of family issues, she made her comeback in the fall of 2020 as a Historical Fiction author, focusing on the World Wars.

What started out as a general interest in the biggest war humanity ever endured became a passion and a drive. Byron herself is an indirect consequence of D-Day. Her uncle Tom landed on the beaches of Normandy and helped to liberate Holland. In 1949, her British mother traveled to south-west Holland, where she met Byron's Dutch father.

Studying WW 2 documents and listening to stories of (children) of active participants in the war, Byron made it her fictional duty to give a voice to those heroes and heroines who stood up against Nazism. After the war, these 'ordinary people' resumed their lives and never spoke of their heroic acts. Let future generations hear their stories and understand the devastating impact of war.

Resistance women are at the core of Byron's books. She pays tribute to a generation of women who kindled the women's lib movement, got dirty in overalls, flew planes, and did intelligence work. Today's strong women stand on the shoulders of their (great-)grandmothers. Byron's heroines fight for freedom, equality and... love.

The Resistance Girl Series comprises one book on WWI *In Picardy's Fields*, and – so far - six books on WWII: *The Diamond Courier* (2020), *The Parisian Spy* (2021), *The Norwegian Assassin* (2022), *The Highland Raven* (27 Sept 2022), *The London Agent* (winter 2023) and *The Crystal Butterfly (Summer 2023).*